THE HERMIT
OF
SANT ALBERTO

THE CONFESSIONS OF EDWARD II

+

PETER MOWBRAY

Grosvenor House
Publishing Limited

This book is published by
Grosvenor House Publishing Ltd
Link House
140 The Broadway, Tolworth, Surrey, KT6 7HT.
www.grosvenorhousepublishing.co.uk

This book is a work of fiction. Any resemblance to
people or events, past or present, is purely coincidental.

A CIP record for this book
is available from the British Library

ISBN 978-1-80381-870-2
eBook ISBN 978-1-80381-871-9

ALSO BY PETER MOWBRAY

The Serpent of the Valois
The Second Jezebel

+

For Adam

PROLOGUE

BERKELEY CASTLE, ENGLAND 1327

It was impossible to open the door of the dimly-lit chamber without a sound being detected. Thus, the noise was discernable enough to offer the warning of intruders to a male figure lying in a bed, the head of which rested beneath a rich tapestry. The material rippled from the draught of each gust of wind that circled this imposing fortress at Berkeley. The ominous castle rose up above the small township, its thick dark walls covered with invasive ivy loomed dramatically against the foreboding sky.

One small candle on a table beside the bed had almost burnt out, flickering from the draught. Whilst offering only the merest of light, it bore testament nevertheless to the comfort of this well-proportioned prison cell; for whilst it was a chamber not unlike others throughout the castle, the occupant of this chamber was most certainly a prisoner.

Against a wall that separated two of the windows of the chamber, stood a large oak table littered with letters, books, writing materials and parchment. A goblet and flagon suggested that the occupier was indeed afforded some degree of luxury by comparison to most captives. A garderobe in the corner lay behind a wooden screen; a large wooden chest stood at the end of the bed.

There was a warm brazier in an opposite corner, its embers glowing despite the stiff breeze.

On this wet and foulest of nights, the heavy rain that had poured down most of the day had at last abated. Nevertheless, thunder continued to growl over the old grey castle, the windows of this chamber above the gatehouse were tightly secured, and a heavy drape helped to keep out both the draught and any outside noise. Despite this, the occupant of the cell had heard raised voices only a short time before, but it was not unusual for the guards to shout to one another, especially when the watch was changed, and he thought no more of it. Now, whether by fate or coincidence, the violent thunder ceased to roar for a few seconds as the thick oak door of the cell slowly opened.

With little enough sound, one man crept stealthily and nervously towards the bed, with heart beating fast, and breath held. The prone figure, blessed with acute hearing, had indeed detected the arrival of the nocturnal visitor. Within seconds he felt his heart racing, suddenly fearful, adrenaline taking a cold grip on his stomach. His servants had been dismissed earlier and would have no reason to return. He turned over quickly; eyes at once alert as a looming shadow was bearing down upon him, he had little chance to react.

A coarse-skinned hand clamped over his mouth. In the faint light of the chamber, the prisoner saw only two fierce eyes glaring down at him.

"Do not make a sound, my lord," the man hissed at him. "It is I, Will. Forgive me, my lord, but you must do as I say. You are to be free this night. You must hurry and dress."

The prisoner now recognised the man as he rubbed his eyes, trying to focus on him in the faint light.

Will Shene, his most trusted valet, had left him only a few hours ago, and yet here he was, presenting him with clothes that he had quickly taken from the large chest at the end of the bed.

"What is this, Will?" he asked in a low, calm voice. "What is happening?"

At that moment, more shouts were heard, and the unmistakable sound of clashing steel. Another man had now entered the cell; the prisoner instinctively wary as the man approached the bed and dropped to one knee.

"My lord," he said in hurried, whispered tones, "it is I, Stephen Dunheved. I pray to God you remember me. I am loyal to you and wish you no harm, but mean to take you from this place to one of safety."

"I recognise you, Stephen, but how...?"

"We must act quickly, my lord, questions can be answered later once we are clear of this place. Can you stand? I have men here battling to aid your escape, but we must proceed with all speed lest we are trapped."

The prisoner now took in the danger of this enterprise, and the risk that this man, his followers, and indeed he himself were taking.

"I can stand. Help me, Will."

Within a minute he was dressed, and his valet was helping him into his boots. He paused only briefly to retrieve a worn leather satchel from beneath his mattress and clutched it to his chest. A woollen cloak was wrapped around him, the hood pulled over his head. Its coarseness rubbed at his skin; even as a captive he had been used to finer robes, but at this moment, it mattered little to him. Another man joined them outside the doorway, and the small group then made their way from the chamber, past a look-out who beckoned them on.

The prisoner glanced down at two soldiers that lay outside the cell door - one face down on the cold grey stone floor, his tunic blood-soaked; another slumped against the wall, a circle of blood around his neck. The captive's breath was quickening in nervous anticipation now; he was no coward and yet his life over the past few years had taught him that death was never far away. He was putting his life in the hands of these men - was he too easily duped? Perhaps, but he had always been so. God knows, that was why he was in this place.

The thunder had ceased now, but the rain was again pouring down relentlessly. The scene outside was one of mayhem and violence. A battle was taking place - shouting, cries of agony, the whistle of arrows shooting through the air, some of them swept away by the wind and battering rain. A melee of soldiers and other fighting men, more crudely armed yet battling with fierce intent now hacked at each other, dying bodies littering the ground. A small party of men surrounded the prisoner, forming a protective wall from harm as they made their way, staying close to the thick walls.

They progressed as far as one of the postern gates, mercifully unharmed; the night affording them some welcome cover. The thunder began to roll again, building from a low rumble to a furious roar.

Within minutes, the small escaping group reached the outside of the castle where they hurried towards waiting horses. Stephen announced to them that they must continue with all speed while they could still make use of the hours of darkness that remained. They needed to reach the security of their base before a new day broke.

The prisoner was helped to climb up onto Stephen's horse, glad that he was able to steady himself, confident that he could not have ridden alone. Three other men were already turning away from the outer wall, one pulling the prisoner's servant Will up to sit behind him.

Suddenly, there was a gasp as one of the group took an arrow in his neck, pitching forward and falling to the ground. The prisoner shouted in alarm, but Stephen was already kicking his horse into a gallop, knowing his comrade was beyond help.

The noise from the battle grew fainter as the group headed for the outer causeway towards the forest. The rain and wind bit into their faces, the puddles splattering mud and rainwater up onto their horses' flanks.

The former prisoner, his heart beating furiously, held close to Stephen as he cast a final backward glance at the imposing castle of Berkeley.

Freedom at last.

+++

THE MONASTERY OF SANT ALBERTO DI BUTRIO, ITALY 1334

Dawn was beginning to spread its morning veil of sunshine over the small monastery of Sant Alberto di Butrio. It promised to be another stifling day, with breathless humidity and a heat that would scorch the unprotected. The monastery lay nestled in the region between Genoa and Pavia in the vast tranquillity of Lombardy, sheltered at the top of a steep cypress valley that descended westwards to the episcopal diocese of Tortona.

From his vantage point at the top of the monastery's bell tower, the youthful, gangly figure of Brother Francis finally had sight of an expected cavalcade approaching up the long, rough path to the old building.

The tower, the building of which had only finally been completed three years since, was the brother's favourite place in the whole of this simple tranquil house of God.

With the advantage of a high lookout, Francis could fully enjoy the vast landscape surrounding the sandstone buildings that encompassed the monastery, their warm colour of burnt umber distinct against the walls of rich green fir trees that protected the buildings on two sides. The novitiate's young face held a drooping open mouth, large brown eyes and a permanent expression of awe. He all but hung out of the open archways surrounding the large bell that summoned the community to their daily regular devotions.

His gaze had now become fixed on a small party of horsemen, at least six, which accompanied a richly decorated carriage that rumbled slowly along the rough track. Brother Francis knew only too well that the path through the surrounding countryside could be almost impassable to those unfamiliar with its rough terrain. He, however, had travelled it many times, often to help the hermit, William, gather some of the plants and flowers for the monastery's infirmarian - Brother Alphage.

Though only a thin wiry figure, the young novice was strong and lithe, his almost white skin was covered in the youthful spots of acne from his straight nose down his narrow throat, where his prominent Adam's apple moved rapidly. Long, pale, hairless legs now carelessly exposed above his knee; his wide feet and overlong toes wore ill-fitting leather sandals, presenting an almost comical figure.

Brother Francis watched for a few minutes longer, his young sharp eyes drawn to the small cavalcade, for there were indeed few visitors to this outback community. His observance was interrupted by the impatient voice of Brother Nicolo, the monastery steward, from the bottom of the steps that led up to the bell tower.

"Brother Francis," he called sharply, "do you see anything yet, or are you merely using your task as an excuse to be idle?"

"I see them, brother." Francis tore his gaze from the beautiful scenery that stretched out further than his eyes could see - excellent though his vision was. The youth quickly descended the narrow, dusty steps of the tower, and stepped out of the building into the sunlight, the heat of which was already stifling and oppressive. He screwed up his eyes, blinking against the sudden brilliant light.

Below him, the monastery was, even at this early hour, bustling with life and activity. Many of the brothers were already out in the land surrounding the abbey, large rimmed hats of straw protecting their bald pates from the sun's punishing heat. At the abbey itself, the laundry was underway, garments hung from thin ropes at the rear of the small building that served as a wash house, the heat of the day drying them with convenient speed.

The scriptorium, small though it was, nevertheless held some rare works, and studious brothers bent over their desks carefully transcribing texts and books with glorious elaborate lettering and colours of blue, gold and red.

In the warm, airless weather, the delightful cooking smells from the kitchens mixed with the pungent intoxicating aromas from the workshop of the apothecary blending in an almost heady concoction. Against this calm organised flow of activity, Brother Francis stood facing the frowning monk.

"There are horsemen and a carriage," he announced proudly. "The carriage is red and adorned with gilt decoration, from what I could observe."

Brother Nicolo, a small round figure with a large fleshy face, pursed his lips in annoyance. His sharp dark eyes, almost lost in his full chubby cheeks, missed very little of what occurred within the abbey. A proud and rather arrogant individual, he was, however, a most practical man who successfully ensured the business of the abbey ran smoothly, and yet whilst he lived within the community peacefully enough, he nonetheless gave the impression that he did not particularly enjoy doing so.

Regardless, he tolerated his fellow brethren as best he could, whilst admonishing those who transgressed. It was, he believed, far better that the brothers of the small community be censured by him than ask the Lord's forgiveness for the error of their ways.

Brother Nicolo, despite being a most devout brother of the abbey, was considered to suffer those grave sins of intolerance and impatience; and if there was one individual to whom he liberally directed his considerable ire, it was the novice who now stood awkwardly looking down upon him. The steward tapped a sandaled foot in growing irritation, and closed his small, beady eyes briefly, as though seeking divine patience with the boy.

"As steward of this most holy community, I and indeed the Abbot himself, needed to know when exactly the party of our expected guests had been sighted, not told they were almost upon us, and how the carriage was adorned. How far away, do you think? Minutes? An hour?"

Without waiting for an answer, he sniffed sharply in annoyance and turned away, setting off in the direction of the abbot's chamber. In his haste, he almost collided with another of the brothers and, after mutual apologies, the steward lightly took hold of the sleeve of the other monk's habit, gently pulling him closer conspiratorially.

"I am told, Brother John, that our important visitor is almost upon us, and yet still I am unaware of his identity - it really is most odd."

Brother John made to comment, but the steward continued, barely drawing breath.

"We had the horseman that arrived here last week, eager to see the abbot, and informing him that we were to expect a guest, and now he arrives, neither on horseback or donkey but in an ornate carriage! With a group of horsemen! That is, of course, if our young dolt of a novice is to believed!"

Nicolo cast a look of annoyance at the younger man, who was now rubbing at the side of his habit in an attempt to rid it of a dark orange dust that he had collected from his observation point in the bell tower.

Brother John once again opened his mouth to speak, but the steward again appeared to anticipate the question before it was uttered.

"No brother," he stated, as though talking to a child. "I have no idea who this most eminent visitor is nor why he should wish to visit our community. There is a mystery here indeed, one which we shall no doubt uncover in time."

It was well known throughout the brethren that the steward enjoyed nothing as much as gossip, be it from those who lived within the monastery walls or the few inhabitants whose dwellings were scattered around the locality. It was not for his own interest of course; how many times had he scolded his fellow brothers that they must guard against such trivia? The role of steward, however, permitted him to descend from so lofty a position from time to time if it was in the interests of the monastery.

From the corner of his eye, Nicolo noticed the tall figure of the abbot approaching. The steward turned to leave, advising Brother John that he should not ask so many questions. "Goodness, how you all pester me for details! Now, carry on brother, important guest or not, we have our duties to perform." So saying saying, he turned away, and after instructing the young Brother Francis to again take up his position in the bell tower, he scuttled off in the direction of his superior.

+++

The party of horsemen and the elegant carriage that were the subject of the young novice's interest were making slow progress towards the small monastery. They had journeyed uneventfully along the narrow road that wound its way through a dark forest. Their path now led them through woodland that was less dense, and offered a glimpse of the surrounding countryside, with its rugged gorge and plants that peppered the thoroughfare leading to their destination.

An eerie silence was broken only by the noise of horses' hooves and the rumble of the small carriage. The coolness of the woodland had been a welcome respite from the heat of the sun that beat down relentlessly from a cloudless sky. The passable throughway they had been afforded in the forest was now harder to discern; the dirt path, strewn with mountain rocks and stones, and the dust generated from the horses at the front of the procession, hung heavily in the still air so those at the rear could only try not to breathe in great gasps, as they finally had sight of the monastery.

It had been hoped that, with such an early dawn start, they would have drawn nearer to their destination before the relentless heat would make the journey almost unbearable. The horsemen had at least been given permission to abandon their heavier tunics in favour of a lighter ones. Consent had been granted, albeit begrudgingly, by the older of the two travellers in the decorated carriage, for he was most observant of protocol, even in these stifling conditions.

Whilst ceremony and appearance were of the utmost importance to him, he had nonetheless agreed with the captain of the horsemen that attack from any credible source would be unlikely especially here in this remote spot that surrounded them. It had been prudent, nonetheless, to arrange an escort; it was certainly not unheard of for travellers to be waylaid by bandits or local gangs. Miscreants operated mercilessly even in these most beautiful of surroundings.

A local guide, an elderly man as wizened and brown as a berry, had, despite his advancing years, kept up a steady enough pace on his old donkey, and had guided the carriage and horses as far as the forest, explaining that the way ahead was a simple enough journey, if not the most comfortable. The horsemen had heeded the guide's words to take particular care through the tangle of tree roots that broke through the ground beneath. A horse could easily trip on the uncertain terrain. Various sizes of stones suggested that the formation of a sensible path had at some point been attempted, but, such as it was, it served merely to make the occupants of the small carriage feel rather nauseous as it was jolted from one side to the other. Nevertheless, horses, riders and carriage picked their way through the narrow low mountain paths; copses that grew either side of the path flourished even in the heat. Patches of abundant grass taunted the horsemen with their seductive colour and softness; how dearly they would have welcomed the chance to lie among such lushness, cooling themselves with water from a small brook that traversed along one side of their path. In several places, the path narrowed dangerously, and it was only the skill of the driver of the carriage, steering his horses through gaps in the mountain range where there were often only inches to spare on either side, that had averted disaster.

Suddenly, however, having negotiated a particularly challenging incline, there came a violent cracking sound, and the carriage pitched dangerously to one side, causing the small cavalcade to come to a juddering halt. After several moments, one of the occupants of the carriage, a young man, drew one of the curtained panels to one side, and leaned out, addressing one of the riders.

"My master wishes to know why it had been necessary to stop, and in such a brutal fashion."

A horseman from the front of the party had already approached, anticipating the enquiry. "The carriage has veered into a ditch, and a wheel has been dislodged. Forgive me, but it will be necessary for you and his eminence to step out so repairs can be made."

The young man to whom this had been addressed nodded his head and turned back into the carriage to relay this news to a fellow passenger. After a moment, the main side panel, a rich velvet cloth with gold thread, was drawn aside and the young man jumped down. He was a wiry adolescent, a handsome face framed with a blonde curls and a short chin dusted with the faint shadow of hair and the welcome beginnings of a beard. He was dressed in a plain blue tunic, undone at the neck - a privilege only afforded him in view of the oppressive heat. Once on firm ground, he reached inside the carriage, retrieving a set of small velvet-covered steps which he placed carefully on the stony, dusty ground.

After a moment, a middle-aged man grasped the offered hand, and carefully stepped down to the rough uneven ground. Manuel Fieschi, a notary of Pope John himself, was an imposing figure. The Fieschi dynasty were renowned diplomats and clerics, held in the highest esteem by Italian nobility and the papacy, and indeed throughout the great courts of Europe. The family held vast estates throughout the country, although none as remote as this.

He was tall, at over six feet, and dressed in a fine red robe which he smoothed down with a hand decorated with several rings of varying colour and wealth. He had a noble bearing, with handsome features, a rather large nose and small, dark blue gimlet eyes. His rather pinched mouth twitched intermittently at one corner. Pale skin that both the journey and the heat of the day had tinged with a slight red hue, his noble chin bore only the slight shade of facial hair at its tip. He smiled and nodded in a gesture of aloof gratitude to the men who now set about the task of fixing the carriage.

He removed his wide-brimmed hat for a moment, passing it to his servant before dabbing at his prematurely balding head with a fine handkerchief taken from his robe. Then, with a sigh, he screwed up his face and replaced his hat before looking up in the distance towards the small, quaint sandstone buildings of the Monastery of Sant Alberto.

Now that he had alighted from the carriage, he was better able to focus his attention on the small retreat, and with eyesight almost as acute as the young brother from the monastery, he cast a critical gaze at his destination.

The modest building was in no way comparable to the ornate beauty and opulence of the many monasteries throughout Italy that he knew so well, but it had a charm that not all could boast – a simplistic beauty in both its crude building, bathed in the sun and topped by tiles of terracotta - and one had to marvel at its setting, here in this beautiful but unforgiving land and, likewise, the devotion of the community that lived, worked and worshipped within it.

Like any worthy envoy, Fieschi had taken time to acquaint himself with some of the monastery's history. It had, he was informed, been founded only two hundred years ago, by a hermit named Albert who had been drawn to the isolation and beauty of the area. After some time, a small community had grown and a local nobleman had commissioned the building firstly of a small Romanesque sandstone church, a small tower, a cloister and a handful of small outbuildings, all surrounded by a protective wall. Here, a small but dedicated brethren had grown to celebrate their faith in peace and cultivate the surrounding land.

An olive tree nearby offered some shade, and Manuel stood beneath it, looking up at the branches hat were heavy with the bitter fruit. The delay would allow him the joy of observing the many creatures that surrounded the area, for he was a man of many interests; the fauna of all places on earth held a fascination for him. A small lizard darted out across the ground, rapid movement and then completely still. He watched for a while as it quickly darted in first one direction then another. A cat snake unwound itself from a nearby branch, where it had no doubt been carefully watching the the smaller reptile. He instinctively stepped away, although he knew that the creature was harmless and could inflict nothing more than a sharp bite.

The flapping wings of a large eagle, rising majestically from the trees, made him start as it broke his train of thought; a rose starling took up a vantage point on one of the branches of the olive tree. Manuel smiled at the almost comical raucous noise from the young bird. Here was nature and abundant life even in so remote a spot.

Surveying the land around him, his sharp eyes picked out a lone wolf standing on a rocky mound up ahead. He had heard from the guide that had led them through the forest, that there were certainly several packs of these creatures that roamed the woodland and up on the craggy areas of sandstone that made up the terrain. The guide had also informed them that it was not unusual to see wild bears even. Manuel was unsure whether their guide wasn't merely having some amusement at the soldier's expense; even so, it paid to be cautious.

"Forgive me, your eminence," the young servant held out a small silver tray holding a goblet of cool water. Manuel smiled at him despite the disturbance of his musings before taking the refreshment and swallowing it hastily. Having drained the goblet, he held it out to his manservant, before taking up the offered napkin and dabbing his thin lips.

With the servant dismissed, the envoy looked down to the ground pensively as he pressed his slim hands together as though in prayer, and gently tapped the steepled fingers against his chin. It was a habit that his servants and associates knew well and from which they determined that he was deep in thought on a particular concern. And indeed there was, in the mind of Manuel Fieschi, a great deal of concern.

The still air and burning sun was really quite uncomfortable, and he felt a bead of sweat run down between his shoulder blades. He ran his fingers around the inside of his collar, feeling its damp, oppressive stiffness. The chirping sound of a thousand or more crickets was broken only by the men heaving at the carriage, keeping up a steady pull on strong ropes as they sought to right the damage.

His thoughts ran, as they had done for most of the long journey to this small isolated place, resplendent in its rustic beauty. By now, several monks were running down from the monastery to assist with the repairs. Manuel watched them as they reached the party, panting from the exertion on such a hot day. He smiled at them all, almost bumping into one another as they beheld such an imposing figure as this most important of visitors.

He again recalled all that the task had asked of him. It was he, Manuel, this most loyal of papal servants and confidante of European monarchs, who was surely the final player in the most amazing of human dramas. Indeed, he smiled as he considered that this was surely a tale that even the most celebrated of bards would find too fascinating to be celebrated in song.

With the exception of his master in this matter, only Manuel and as few as possible must know of the discussions to follow. It would be necessary for the head of this small community to be advised to a certain extent; he had heard only favourable reports regarding this abbot, and he felt that some basic details could be confidently discussed. There were, however, some details of his mission that were not to be disclosed, and his face hardened as he considered all that was surely to follow.

The envoy's thoughts were interrupted by chorus of raised voices announcing that the hard toil of the escorts had been successful, and at last the journey could be continued. The group of startled monks bowed their heads in deference to the tall resplendent figure, staring in wonderment at the decorated carriage; such gilded transport was unheard of in these primitive surroundings.

Manuel nodded to the servant as he took the youth's guiding hand and, glancing again at the sandy coloured building ahead, stepped back up into the coolness of the carriage.

+++

CHAPTER ONE

At the far side of the small Monastery of Sant Alberto lay the cloisters, its arched stone gallery barely visible through the dense greenery that wound around the pillars. Beside here was the small, pungent workshop of the monastery's infirmarian. Although not the eldest incumbent, it was generally believed by the resident brothers that Brother Alphage was at least sixty-five years of age, and the good physician took advantage of the fact by actually being five years older. Only he and the Almighty could correct this misconception, and, as the Lord was keeping quiet on the matter, the good brother saw no reason to go confusing his fellow monks with such trivial information.

This quiet, gentle soul was the most skilful infirmarian as well as a knowledgeable herbalist. He sought to administer what he could to repair both body and mind, and was greatly revered in the small community. His warm, comfortable outbuilding had a beguiling aroma of herbs; bunches of rosemary, lavender and mint hung from the low ceiling. Various bottles and jars lined the many shelves, mortars and pestles lay on the heavy oak table that stood in the centre of the room. A wooden tray containing a variety of tools and implements sat on a smaller table to one side of the room, complete with a stack of rolled parchment and quills and heavy books of varying sizes. A much-melted beeswax candle rested in a iron spiral shaped holder, and despite the heat of the day, a small stove flickered in the stone hearth. To one side of the room was another workbench under a small window that looked out onto a neat herb garden, some of which was covered by a rickety straw awning to offer some protection from the hot sun. Presently basking under this cool covering was Timo, the monastery cat; a creature of the purest white coat whose languid, graceful gait belied a speed that kept the monastery food stores free of any impudent rodents.

Alphage had a pleasant, heavily lined face that was fitting for his years, with jowls that were now starting to lend a fleshier complexion. His deep-set eyes sparkled with amusement, as though he constantly recalled a humorous story and was about to burst into laughter. He was no taller than five feet five inches, but carried himself with the dignity of a nobleman. His gentle demeanour and soothing tone of voice put all at ease. He had not been known to display any sign of a disagreeable temperament, and was affable to all who either sought his wise ministration, or visited him for any ailment.

A few wispy strands of white hair were still evident on his otherwise bald pate. Far more hair stuck straight out of both his ears, making him the object of many novice's sniggers. Alphage had long since decided that if they could draw some amusement from such a thing, then he was happy to make them smile. His nose, although large, was nowhere near as big as Brother Dominic's and he, who ran the small but studious scriptorium, saw little amusement in what God had given him. Although, as Alphage had to admit, despite his diligence in carrying out his duties, Brother Dominic saw little amusement in anything.

The monk was of course aware that a visitor of some importance was due at the small monastery, but as he was certain that it was not – as Brother Francis had suggested - the Pope himself, so he felt under no obligation to deviate from his schedule of duties and obligations. He therefore left his workshop and traversed around to the rear of the monastery buildings, continuing carefully down some shallow steps and out through a side gate onto a narrow, dusty track. The route was barely used by the other monks or servants other than to lead out to forest, thick with pine, lush moss and all manner of plants and fungi that Alphage found invaluable for the many poultices and ointments to aid his medical ministrations.

The path led also to the abode of a most private member of the small community of Sant Alberto. The occupant lived as a hermit, preferring to live out his life in solitude, in a home little more than a shack, with only his dog for company. He was known for his reticence to discuss anything that alluded in the slightest to himself or his past. Only Alphage had been permitted to know scant details, and even then with only vaguest account. He could not be questioned, however tactfully, on what had brought him to this remote monastery and, after some time, the monks had ceased to be intrigued by his mystery and accepted him as one who would help the brothers in manual work one day and then retreat to his hovel for weeks after.

The elderly brother considered again this most mysterious man, of whom he had grown so fond since he had arrived four winters past. He had journeyed far, and had arrived exhausted and with a fever. The brothers had taken him in, and nursed him back to health.

The fever was to blight the stranger at intervals since, an almost fatal affliction. A most peculiar incident had taken place later the same day of his arrival when two horsemen had been seen not long after the monks had assisted the stranger into the abbey.

The riders just seemed to be waiting for something or, Brother Nicolo suggested, someone. Making no contact at the abbey or any of the lay brothers working in the close vicinity, they remained for quite some time before simply turning around, and riding off down into the valley. That had created a mystery that had quite vexed Brother Nicolo, and indeed all of the brothers – including Alphage himself.

When rested and with his fever under control, the tall stranger simply introduced himself as William.

It was clear to one of Alphage's experience, that William was something of a 'broken' man. His body was strong enough, muscular and lean, and whilst he was weak from fever, he recovered well enough, much aided by Alphage's continual care. William, although well mannered, was introverted and said very little. The infirmarian sensed a great sadness in him. His constant companion was his dog, and together they existed almost apart from the other brethren, although the dog was affectionate with anyone he met.

Alphage had long taken an interest in the troubles of the mind, and here was a man who seemed to have been worn down by life's woes. What horrors could this soul have endured to have sapped the love of life from him?

Upon complete recovery, William had been only too willing to assist the brethren wherever he could, and indeed had been surprisingly adept in helping dig the new trenches that had become necessary, as well as thatching the small barns which housed sheep as well as chickens, several cows and a goat. He would tend to the gardens with the other brothers as well as using proficient carpentry skills.

The brethren of Sant Alberto had in time grown used to the stranger, accepting him as member of their community despite his lack of religious order, and the mystery of his arrival and the two horsemen had eventually ceased to be of interest. William had said very little of his time before his journey to the monastery, only that he had been a merchant, but had fallen on hardship, and decided that he wanted to retire to a hermit's existence and abandon his wandering days. His story was certainly a familiar one; many came late to God, either by ill health, poverty or more often both. William indeed spent a great deal of his day in solitude and prayer, and he appeared, over time, to have settled into some measure of security and peace.

Brother Alphage had nevertheless felt certain that there was more to the story than just a wish to be settled in one place. Here was a man who yearned to hide himself away from the world. Something had drawn this traveller to this most remote of places so that he might at last find peace in his life.

William had taken an interest in the tending of the herb garden that Alphage had great need of to make the many remedies and salves used in his treatment of patients. It was however William's bodily strength that had proved most beneficial for the community. He was more than happy to undertake some of the more vigorous tasks such as thatching, digging, chopping up the endless supply of wood, and he had been instrumental in rebuilding parts of the church structure that had begun to fall into some disrepair.

The infirmarian also recalled another detail that had added to the mystery of the man. During a hot summer, William had worked tirelessly, but happily, in repairs to the terracotta roof of the church He had paused to take a drink, the sun was at it's height and sweat poured down his muscular torso until his skin glistened in the sunlight. His strong frame exposed as he worked bare-chested, Alphage had heard that one of the brothers had innocently commented on a scar that William had on his arm, was it from battle he was asked? Perhaps a mark since birth, but some lines linked together, letters perhaps.

The inquisitive monk had even reached out to touch it, but William had at once snatched his arm away as though a touch would scald him. He had walked off, only returning to his labours later in the day, but with the scar now hidden under a coarse bandage. No further reference was made to it, but Alphage sensed more mystery.

Recently, William's recurring fever caused him to take to his bed. For days he had been delirious, exhausted by a feverish temperature that even the ministrations of the masterly Alphage had found hard to bring under control.

The black death and all manner of plagues and diseases still stalked the land as they had done for many years in one form or another. Indeed, Italy had been most violently ravaged by the scourge of plague, and Alphage thanked the almighty that Sant Alberto had remained relatively unscathed, isolated from the main trade routes where rats and fleas carried all manner of pestilence from one city to another, one village to the next.

Following a heightened temperature, it had been necessary for Alphage and his assistant to remove the cotton shirt that William wore during the warm nights of his first summer at the monastery, and it was then that Alphage had seen in greater detail the scars on William's forearm - a definite scar that, although an old wound, was still easy to make out – two initials intertwined. Alphage had made a mental note of the scar; his patient was too delirious to be aware of this discovery.

He had raised his curiosity to his superior once, the Abbot himself had reminded the infirmarian that God had his reasons for William to be there with them, and the past mattered little. Nonetheless, Alphage - whilst agreeing with the Abbot's reasoning - had to admit to the sin of curiosity. Maybe it was best to remain in ignorance.

He ambled happily on his short journey until, further along the track from the main monastery buildings, the pathway became barely discernable. Trees had grown more closely together, thus providing a dense canopy; spruce trees that seemed to reach up to the clouds, wiry vines of ivy bushed out from the branches and clung to the rocks and stones that bordered the trickling water.

Alphage walked on for a short distance, until he left the path through to a clearing in the woodland. The small stream that trickled alongside him made its way through a cluster of stones beside what could well have once been a wooden shack. Parts of the original building still stood, but these had clearly been repaired with some skill. A chimney had been reformed, and the roof, though small, was nevertheless well thatched.

Even in this shade, the day was stiflingly hot. Brother Alphage smiled as his eyes came to rest on a small brown mongrel dog playing with a rag doll which he tossed in the air and proceeded to chew once caught. The dog's ears pricked up when the figure approached.

Brother Alphage however, was no stranger, and after a short obligatory growl, the ears folded back and a small tail began to wag furiously, oblivious to the dust that it scattered. The monk leant down, ruffling the short hair, and assuring him that all was well. He looked up at the same moment as a figure appeared in the doorway of the shelter, ducking under the low threshold.

The inhabitant of the small dwelling stood there and a smile spread across his handsome features. He was tall and broad-shouldered, with sand-coloured hair, cropped short to match his small, neat beard. His face, though well set, was lined, adding some age onto what was probably no more than two score years and ten. Hardly youthful, but old enough in these times of uncertain life expectancy.

The brightness of his blue eyes was offset by the tone of his skin, coloured a deep brown suggesting much time spent outdoors. The arms that stretched out to greet Alphage were strong and powerful, and the warm embrace he gave the elder was robust. His large hands were calloused, the nails cut short. His features might well be described as striking. His nose was straight and neither large nor small, but perfectly formed above thin lips that widened into a smile displaying strong white teeth. He was dressed in a homespun robe, much like the habits of the brothers he lived around, although he was not in holy orders. He had always been welcome to eat with the brothers, frugal though their diet was. Should he wish to, he could pray with them, and even follow the routine of their day, governed as it was by religious observance.

Yet he lived humbly with only his faithful dog, Perrot, for company. The hound was a beautifully-tempered animal of indeterminable breed, with large eyes, a rough coat and a devotion to his master, whom he followed everywhere, with the exception of the small church.

This recent exclusion had come about after he had chased one of Brother Anthony's pigs through the church's open door, creating all manner of chaos as he pursued the squealing creature, winding his way through the brethren gathered there for prayer and contemplation.

Thereafter, if his master decided to join the monks in their service, Perrot was instructed to lie and wait outside, which he did, pressing his body up close to the heavy closed door, a slight wagging of his feathery tail whenever he could determine his master's voice above the others with the uncanny ability that canine creatures have to identify one particular sound amongst many others.

The monk sat on one of two large logs that served well enough as furniture. Alphage gladly accepted the offer of some water collected from the small stream by the side of the shack, and he watched the tall figure stride over to the rocky pool, scooping the clear, cool liquid into an earthenware goblet.

His musings were suddenly interrupted by William's dog that bounded up to him, his master following just behind. The tall man passed him the cup of cooling stream water, and sat himself down on the ground opposite the older monk.

William's eyes glittered; his good health was returning, and he felt invigorated by the warm weather and bright sun that determined a way through the dense foliage above. The air, though warm, was nevertheless pleasant and all the surrounding life, be it fauna or flora, basked in its soothing qualities.

Alphage smiled, gently brushing his soft hand against Perrot's ear as the dog sat at his feet, having dropped his favourite toy at the elderly brother's feet. One of the monks had made the hound a doll figure from old sackcloth and, such was its importance, that the dog shared his own bed with it.

William smiled. "He loves all the brothers, but it's you who is his favourite, Alphage."

The elder monk smiled at the dog. "He is a most loyal companion, William."

Perrot at that moment had appeared almost in ecstasy from the attention to his ear and slumped down onto his side, and with a resigned sigh, closed his eyes and settled into a light snooze.

"You are growing stronger, my friend," Alphage said, his quick eyes scanning the hermit for signs of spots on the skin or the bloodshot eyes that had accompanied William's recent malaise.

"Indeed, brother, I believe I am much recovered, but trying to rest as you insisted I must. Perrot and I have not set foot out of this place. The inactivity is hard to bear when I am feeling so much better. Maybe later, I shall attend the chapel. I feel a sense of peace there. I hope also to beg a ration of food, for the fever has left me unaccountably hungry."

Alphage smiled and nodded. "You keep yourself exercised, and that has no doubt stood you well. Yet, a little weight has been lost; a weakened body cannot fight a fever when its constitution is compromised. Still, you must take care even now that you are recovering. I will tell Brother Tomas in the kitchen to give you some broth. Warm though the weather is, it is a most nourishing meal."

They talked on for some time, both at ease with one another's company. William had often wondered what would have become of him had he been been the son of one such as this most benevolent of men. Yet thoughts such as those were ridiculous. Alphage could not have been more different from his own father. A dove against a lion, the light against the dark, such were the comparisons that came readily to him.

The discussion had moved on to William's fever and how he had flung himself almost from his bed as he battled its torment. William had smiled at how that must have looked - ever willing to imagine what a sight he must have been. It was all too rare that he felt lighter of mood, but it was difficult to keep from smiling in the elder monk's company.

Alphage however had now, in relating the tale, touched upon a particular period of rambling, most common of course in fevers such as this, but an interesting insight into one's thoughts.

"Somewhere called Blacklock or Blacklow Hill, I think. You did not forget your devoted pet either. "Perrot!", you called out several times, causing the poor creature to whine all the more for you. The name Hugh was mentioned also, and much else which I could barely understand! A veritable cast of characters." Alphage chuckled.

None other than the astute elderly monk would have noticed William's body stiffen as these revelations were announced. For some moments he stared ahead of him as though in a trance. Alphage was almost certain that his patient had a tear in his eyes, which he blinked away before he rose quickly. The physician, with his keen sense of perception, felt he should go no further with these disclosures, as his patient was obviously affected by his words. Clearly, enough had been said.

The two men sat in silence; the elder man hoping that the younger would confide in him. Alphage had always known that whatever William's life had been before he arrived at Sant Alberto, he was deeply affected by it. Such was the life of this hermit at the monastery; his thoughts kept secret, emotions hidden and memories buried away where few could reach. The infirmarian inwardly scolded himself for his lack of tact; William had worn a pleasant smile on his arrival, and yet the mention of names uttered in a delirious state had clearly dulled the sparkling eyes from only moments before.

Alphage talked for a while about daily procedure at the abbey, Brother Tomas had dropped a heavy cauldron on his foot – empty, thanks be to God -and it had been necessary for Alphage to bandage his big toe, which of course protruded from his sandal, and was the subject of much mirth with the novices. Brother Nicolo was outraged to see that, in climbing over the fence of the pig pen, Brother Anton had got his habit caught on a rogue nail and had torn a terribly large hole that unfortunately exposed his bare bottom. Once again the younger members of the community had been treated to a most amusing incident. This caused even more heated discourse later between Brother Nicolo and old Brother Michael as to whether the lord Jesus himself had possessed a sense of humour.

William nodded and smiled whilst being regaled with this news, but he now seemed suddenly distant, lost in his own thoughts. The monk quietly cursed his bad judgement and lack of discretion. He must atone for that when he prayed next. Words have consequences, he must learn.

At length, Alphage rose to leave, and briefly considered if he should ask whether William was aware that a guest of great importance was due at the monastery this day, the reason for his visit was unknown to the brethren, and yet the monastery was so insignificant as to be unknown to many that lived beyond the dense woodland and high ragged mountains that ensured it was virtually hidden from the outside world. However, something held him back, it was neither his business, nor his place to tell the hermit what he had learned through whispered gossip.

Moreover, he may have already said too much, he could not dispel the feeling that he had inadvertently touched upon names that clearly shocked and upset his friend. Maybe, in time, William would let him into that former life of his, that clearly still had the power to move him to distress or sadness - it was hard for the old man to tell which.

He therefore bade farewell to William and, after patting the now awoken Perrot, shuffled out of the enclosure and along the path back towards the monastery.

When the kindly monk had gone, William sat again, brushing the dust and twigs from Perrot's coat where he had lain. The hound shook himself vigorously, picked up his toy and pushed his cold nose at his master's hand, his strong jaws tightening around his rag doll, as he emitted a low playful growl. The hermit smiled, but he was uneasy. He felt shock at the story of his delirious ramblings, names that he hadn't uttered out loud for as long as he could remember. He thought about such things almost every day - how could he not? - but only in his mind, as part of his private thoughts that should never break free. He felt an almost overwhelming sadness and despair and noticed that he was shaking.

Hugh- what had he said in the ramblings of his fever?

He thought of Hugh every day, perhaps he was not even aware of it. And of course Perrot...William leant down to his dog, cupping the animal's head in his large, calloused hands, and kissed him gently on the top of his head. "Ah yes," he whispered, "always together."

Try as he might to feel otherwise, his mood darkened. Physically he had grown stronger each day, even though Alphage recommended caution in doing too much so soon after his recent fever, and yet with the return of his robustness, the fears came upon him again such as he had not felt for some time. Tonight he would dream, and yet was unsure if he wanted to. He cast his eyes to the sky that peeped through the dense woodland, and he breathed in deeply, repeating the exercise several times, as Alphage had suggested, as a means of inducing calm when anxiety came upon him.

At length, he got to his feet and entered the hovel that had become his home since reaching the monastery. Inside the shack, there were few trappings; a small table with a cup, plate and jug where he would eat. A small fireplace, the ashes cold now as he seldom used it since he had been persuaded to take his meals with the brothers of the monastery, or at least take what they offered and consume it beneath the fragile roof of his home.

A ragged curtain sectioned off his small straw pallet bed, and another small table next to it, upon which lay a prayer book and a small crucifix - the only evidence of the religious environment within which he lived. An old cloak, given to him by the good brothers, hung on a small nail that acted as a hook in the wall. He let out a deep sigh, and then dropped to his knees beside the pallet bed, seeking something from under the straw mattress. Having found what he had reached for, he drew out an old weathered brown leather satchel which he then placed before him on the bed. As he moved to release the binding of a much-used velvet tie, he hesitated. A moment or two of indecision, and then, in a change of mind, he returned the unopened satchel to the depths of the straw bed. How many times he had sat in sad melancholy intending to examine those precious possessions that lay within the soft ageing case, only to replace it unopened as he had just done.

There were occasions, Alphage had instructed him, certain times when one should examine one's past, and yet with a malady of the mind, such as he had diagnosed in this most emotional of men, the time had to be when mental stamina could best cope with it.

A very dilapidated wicker basket on the dirt floor by the hermit's bed was where Perrot generally retreated to, even though he would initially step one paw daintily in the small cot and sniff at his old blanket with distaste and suspicion until he was assured that only he had last occupied it. Yet, once he heard his master's low snore, he invariably jumped nimbly up onto his bed and, as carefully as possible, snuggle down with a contented sigh.

William stretched his taut body and stripped off his homespun robe which he replaced with a pair of light wool hose. No shirt would be needed, for no-one would visit him further today. Alphage was generally the only visitor to his shack, and he encouraged no others. Such had been his chosen solitude. In the early days of his nomadic life, he had shunned others in a desire to be unnoticed; his very survival had depended on his anonymity, and thereafter, he had lived this solitary life by choice.

After some moments musing in thought, he walked outside and glanced at the large logs he had intended chopping up for the monastery, and so, taking up his nearby axe, he selected a piece of the felled wood. His strong muscular arms held the tool aloft, bringing it down with a resounding crack.

+++

Manuel Fieschi sipped at the cool watered wine and sighed. He was grateful to at last be sitting in some measure of comfort, after the less than satisfactory journey that seemed to have taken an inordinate amount of time. Here now, in the abbot's office, he could enjoy some measure of comfort and - more importantly – some cool air. His manservant had been dismissed into the care of one of the brothers. Trustworthy though young Alonso was, he could not be privy to this first meeting with the abbot.

He stood now at one of the two arched windows and, small though they were, they had the benefit of being on the north side of the monastery. Thus, they afforded the abbot with a mercifully cool chamber on this most stifling of days. Nevertheless, crude but necessary wooden shutters had been closed across the second window, suggesting to Fieschi that the shutters would just as efficiently keep out the worst of the winter weather, such as it was.

The room was generously proportioned, though sparsely decorated, with bare walls that were whitewashed and plain; the only decorations being a large wooden cross that hung behind the abbot's chair, and a small mural depicting the crucifixion of Christ and his ascent into heaven; quite coarse handiwork, Fieschi thought, but it had a certain quaintness. Exposed wooden beams across the ceiling showed one or two areas of flaking plasterwork. Two wooden shelves were laden with several books and numerous scrolls of parchment, whilst a large richly-covered book lay open at one side of the abbot's desk where the community's leader now sat, his hands placed palm down on the wooden table.

At this moment, the abbot was trying to take in the full extent of what the pope's representative had told him, and his normal calmness had given way to a mixture of emotions, such was the enormity of the revelation. The sealed letter that Fieschi handed to him was from none other than the pope himself, and he could not conceal both surprise and wonderment. While he sat, absorbed in the missive, the papal envoy took a moment to study the leader of this quaint community.

Abbot Ridolfo was a tall figure, almost as tall as Fieschi himself; he had a long, gaunt face with eyes that appeared dull and humourless, although Fieschi believed him to be of a very amenable character. The abbot's angular features belied a very soft, calming voice; his mouth was wide and fleshy, with a smile that was frequent and displayed teeth that were grey and irregular. He had long fingers that appeared soft, his nails kept short. Patches of rough, hardened skin on his knuckles suggested hands that had not always been clerical, but had seen manual labour in the past. Fieschi's instinct suggested a leader of dedication and diplomacy.

As he read and reread the letter before him, the abbot recalled the messenger that had arrived at the abbey several days before had told him to expect his esteemed visitor, but could give no details of his purpose. Now, as he carefully considered the contents of the papal instructions, it was obvious that this was no chance visit. Indeed, the letter itself commended Manuel Fieschi to the abbot, and that he should use all means to ensure that the envoy was granted complete freedom and access regarding a delicate matter that Fieschi would explain. The letter stressed in strong terms that the matter was not under any circumstances to be spoken of to anyone. Any exceptions would be in Fieschi's sound judgement.

Thus, having absorbed the contents of the letter, he re-folded it and placed it to one side. Thereafter, he answered as best he could the questions that Fieschi put to him, and it soon became obvious that there was much he did not know of the hermit that had become part of this quiet community. His eminent guest had at least solved a mystery that he admitted had vexed himself and indeed the rest of the brethren.

"So, the horsemen were only meant to accompany our hermit as far as this place?"

Fieschi turned and nodded as the abbot continued, "We were curious, of course, and yet there was nothing to suggest the riders had any association with the poor soul that turned up here begging for sustenance and somewhere to rest. Indeed, we were concerned that these men might even wish harm to the poor wretch."

Fieschi made a steeple with his hands and tapped the fingers against his chin. "Forgive me, Father Abbot.

The deception was necessary. The two riders knew nothing of the man they carefully tracked, only that he was to be followed until arriving safely here. Our obedience in all of this matter was guided by instruction from the highest authorities; as you can see, his holiness has a personal interest in this matter."

The abbott nodded sagely as he considered his response. "Of course, we accepted the hermit as one of our own. We have embraced him here and, with God's help, we have sought to mend a body and mind that were sorely abused by the time he reached us. Obviously, you will wish to see him as soon as possible, but I would suggest that he might have the company of our infirmarian; the two have become close, and Brother Alphage is a sensible, kindly man, who is alone in finding favour with the stranger. Our hermit trusts the brother implicitly. I should of course point out to your eminence that, whilst he lives within our community, he is not of our order and brotherhood, and as such, I cannot demand that he speak to you."

Fieschi smiled at the kindly face of the abbot. "I understand, Father Abbot, I hope that he will talk freely with me, of his own accord. I have no intention of causing him any more distress, but merely wish to find some answers that will help those who love him to know that he is at peace. I will, of course, use every discretion. I am guided by your sound suggestion that William, as he is here named, have with him someone he can trust. I approve your suggestion."

The abbot smiled, deciding not to ask any further questions for the envoy to evade and, after nodding in affirmation, he picked up and rang the small bell that rested on the desk. Almost at once, the door opened and an inquisitive Brother Nicolo almost fell into the room. He cast a nervous glance at the visitor, quickly presenting himself with some measure of dignity before slipping both bands into the wide sleeves of his habit.

"Brother Nicolo," the abbot said calmly, "how instinctive you are. Can you fetch Brother Alphage to me here? Ask him to leave whatever he is doing and come at once."

The brother stood for a moment, as though he would enquire further, then nodded in deference and left the chamber.

A short while later, there was a light tap on the abbot's door.

"Come in, brother," the soft voice of the abbot spoke, and Alphage had been invited to sit before he was aware of the tall man in red who stood at the chamber window, his slender fingers resting on the clay mantel. The infirmarian immediately stood up, bowing his head to the fascinating nobleman before him.

Fieschi smiled at him and motioned for him to sit; an approving glance from the abbot, and Alphage sat, his fingers entwined and resting in his lap. Brother Nicolo, having delivered his charge, stood somewhat awkwardly by the door awaiting a similar instruction, but was somewhat irked to be dismissed with a smile from his superior.

"Thank you, brother," the abbot said. "I will not keep you from your many duties." After this dismissal, Abbot Ridolfo waited several seconds as he listened for the slapping tread of the steward's footsteps to grow fainter, and then made the necessary introductions before settling back in his seat.

Without further prevarication, the emissary began his explanation.

"Brother Alphage, what I am about to impart to you must remain in the strictest confidence. I have your abbot's assurance that your discretion in private matters is well known, as is your wisdom and good sense."

Alphage could feel himself redden and inclined his head in affirmation of the compliment. "How can I be of any service to your eminence?"

Fieschi cast a glance at the abbot, before continuing. "What I have to tell you, brother, will come as a shock, and I will, in the days ahead, rely on your sound judgement in a matter that must remain between we three and the one known to you as the hermit you have named William. Tell me what, if anything, you know of him."

The monk was alert at once. He had imagined all manner of requests, but this had taken him by complete surprise. He made every effort to be respectful and obedient as his abbot would expect of him.

"I am, of course, at your disposal your eminence, yet I am unsure how William can be of interest to you. He is a quiet, most private man. I can offer little by way of introduction to him. His past is generally unknown, and certainly I have not been privy to any disclosure about his story, only the merest mention of past times, and then with scant details."

Fieschi nodded as the brother spoke of one or two instances when William had felt happy to talk of past experiences, once or twice glancing at the abbot, who appeared to be deep in thought.

As Alphage paused to remember more than the few instances when William had seemed relaxed enough to discuss anything resembling a past history, Fieschi smiled benevolently at the monk. The recollections of which William had spoken were trivial and relatively unimportant, much as he suspected they would be. The emissary waited politely until Alphage had finished relating past conversations with the hermit. He then sat himself in another chair by the abbot's desk, which he turned so that he then faced the monk, leaning slightly forward to ask a question as obscure as it was unexpected.

"Do you happen to have noticed a scar on the hermit's forearm? A curious question, I am aware, but with my own personal recollection and the little information, I have, this may well be the only means I have of identifying him as the man I have travelled to speak with."

Alphage again looked to his superior and then to the emissary, with slight hesitancy. "He has a scar, yes, on the inside of his forearm. I have seen it once or twice during my ministration to a recent fever he has suffered. The scar has, I believe, much significance - though when I did ask him once about it, he snapped that the former injury was of little importance. He did not offer to elaborate."

The tall nobleman nodded sagely, a slight smile crossed his thin lips as though a confirmation of sorts had been made.

Alphage felt a deep sense of unease. When he spoke again, it was firmly. "What has he done, your eminence, that you should seek him out like this? He is my friend, he trusts me and…"

Fieschi blinked at the directness of the question, but held up a hand to stop the abbot from cautioning the monk for speaking to one of such high office in so forthright a manner.

"Forgive me, brother," Fieschi said. "Your loyalty to this man does you credit. My purpose is most delicate, but be assured I intend no harm. Indeed, it may interest you - and yourself, Father Abbot - that I am actually a distant kinsman of your hermit." After some moments' thought, he smiled. "If I am to have your help in this, brother, it is only fair that you and the good abbot here are assured I have no evil intent. I would, therefore, know one further detail about this scar I have spoken of and then I fear I must reveal to you that this hermit is not the simple wanderer who you think he is. Let me explain further, and I will reveal to you the true identity of William the hermit."

+++

It was unusual for Perrot to bark and, being so unused to hearing it, William had taken a moment to identify that it was indeed his own hound that was making the warning noise. He rose from the side of the stream where he had been washing, cooling his body after the exertion of splitting long lengths of pine wood that now formed a large pile at one side of the shack. Dressed only in his rather ragged hose, he presented a muscular and strong physique with broad shoulders and powerful chest, the hairs of which, though once blond, were now grey and wiry.

Having shaken off the stream water, he walked cautiously around the side of the shack to where a tall man in a sumptuous red robe now crouched, petting the hound that had only a minute before threatened him so viciously. Perrot, it seemed, could be easily bribed and the visitor had had the good sense to come armed - with cheese!

Manuel Fieschi had noticed the movement from the side of the shack, and rose as William stepped forward. For a moment the two men locked eyes, each searching for the recognition of the other. Manuel had been quite young at their last meeting, and there was a chance that he may never have been seen at all by the other.

For his part, William felt a sudden wave of anxiety; no-one ever came here apart from Alphage.

The tall figure in red made a tentative move in William's direction, but said nothing. The hermit allowed the stranger to approach him until he was within touching distance.

"Who are you?" William questioned the man, in a voice that he knew betrayed the anxiety and sudden panic that was building within him. "The monastery is further up the track...."

Fieschi lifted a hand slightly as he spoke, his eyes quickly searching the man's exposed bare arms he looked up again at the hermit. "No - it is you, my lord, to whom I would speak."

William's face turned visibly white, his heart beating faster, and he stepped back, eyes darting from one side to the other like a trapped animal eager to make a fast escape.

The envoy then bowed his head in deference. "My name is Manuel Fieschi - you know of my family, my lord, and I am here at the bequest of his holiness, the pope."

William narrowed his eyes, his voice tremulous, his heart almost exploding with his rising anxiety. "Why on earth would the holy father send someone to seek out a hermit? I am nothing to the pope, or indeed to you. The man whom you seek is not me. I am, as I said and as you see, a simple hermit. I know nothing of the pope or your family. I believe some mistake has been made. You must go now, leave me alone and go - please."

"My lord," Fieschi again addressed him, "I have travelled far to find you. Believe me, I mean you no harm. I know..."

"You know nothing!" William interrupted, sternly now, yet shaking and feeling a sudden nausea. He turned his back abruptly on the visitor and began to walk away, praying his legs did not give way as they felt they would, calling over his shoulder, "I know you not, and would be left in peace please, I would have you respect...."

"Lord Edward!"

The effect of those words on the hermit was instant, and though he had faced away from the visitor, Fieschi was aware of the sudden air of tension. William stopped dead in his tracks, staying so still for a moment that the envoy wondered if he had been dumbstruck with shock.

For what seemed like an eternity, neither man moved. The hermit stood and closed his eyes, a desperate wish to shut out the past few moments. A voice screamed within him, a raging howl that tore through his head until he felt he would faint. He turned around, swallowing nervously. The voice that then addressed Fieschi was a quiet one, filled with both defiance and emotion.

"So, you have traced a hermit to a remote abbey, and assume that it is Lord Edward you have found. You are wasting your time, I know nothing of you, the holy father or indeed this Lord Edward. I beg you to leave me alone." He turned from the emissary again.

Manuel Fieschi played the only advantage left to him as he stared at the retreating man, he called out, "You bear the mark of Gaveston do you not?"

Had the envoy seen the hermit's face at that moment, he would have witnessed a man in total shock; blood pounded through the hermit's head as he closed his eyes. He had not heard anyone other than himself say that name for so long, and it sounded strange now. An emotion built up within him and, looking down, his sad eyes rested on his forearm and the two initials cut into his skin so many years before, and yet still visible. The visitor had of course noticed, the intertwined letters EP. The years had turned his skin brown and yet the scars were visibly pink, although faded by the years. He passed a gentle hand over the old scar, only the slightest touch, and smiled bitterly as a tear splashed onto his skin.

He looked up to the sky, and drew in a deep breath; desperate to remain calm, though the moment threatened to herald a wave of raw emotion. Eventually though, the hermit turned to face the visitor again, his voice quiet and resigned.

Fieschi at this point bowed his head in respectful deference.

The air felt suddenly cold, and yet from distant memory he appeared to summon up some long forgotten dignity, and it was with a noble bearing that he turned and smiled sadly before speaking.

"Well, it would seem your search is at an end, that you have found me at last. Indeed, I stand before you - Lord Edward of Caernarfon, formerly King Edward of England!"

+++

For some moments, neither man said anything, as though the revelation had been a complete shock to both. Fieschi now, for the first time, seemed uncertain of his next move.

The hermit broke the air of silence with a glance at his faithful canine companion, and smiled sadly. "Perrot will eat all of your cheese if you are not careful," he said. "Like his namesake, he is not able to enjoy anything other than to excess."

As the supplies from the stranger had appeared to be at an end, the hound was by now paying great attention to the small bowl in which had been carried this most delicious of bribes from the monastery kitchen, and wondering how to discreetly angle his head sideways into the earthenware dish whilst not upsetting it.

Fieschi smiled as he picked up the small bowl and tipped its scant remains onto the ground, where the dog proceeded to lap it up, seemingly untroubled by the inclusion of pine needles that were scattered liberally from the surrounding trees.

"'Perrot', after Gaveston, of course?" Fieschi said gently.

Edward smiled at the memory. "Always together. One will not be seen without the other."

The look the envoy gave him was one of pity. "I was told by your good friend, the infirmarian, that the hound enjoys this particular treat; I had him fetch me some before I came to find you."

Edward looked over to the clearing where Brother Alphage now stood, although he was unaware of how long he had been there. The hermit smiled at his friend who, for once wore an expression of concern and sadness.

"Who knows?" Edward asked, as Fieschi turned to see the older monk before he spoke.

"The good brother here, and Father Abbot, no other."

The awkwardness that followed seemed like an eternity to all three men. Edward continued to run a light hand over the scar as though entranced by it. Alphage was pretending to fuss over Perrot, concerned for his friend, and yet still in shock about his true identity.

The tall prelate now studied the man before him. Here then was the King of which he had heard so much. A man who had become synonymous with foolery and profligacy. One who allegedly took male lovers to his bed, married the daughter of the famed King of France and yet spurned her and their children; a man who had endured so much and who had lost everything - a wife, a family, his own liberty, a crown and a kingdom, and - more than that – his pride and self esteem.

The enormity of this revelation was, it seemed, only now becoming apparent to the envoy. He must be respectful in the matter. Lord Edward seemed nervous in manner, and would be overly suspicious of new acquaintances. Therefore, it was essential to be circumspect and proceed with tact, and Fieschi was well known for his diplomacy. He had indeed expected alarm and temperament, evasiveness, even fury perhaps. What he did not expect to find was a humble, simple man, so so very different from the image he had created in his own mind during the arduous journey to this place.

The two of them stood silently, each considering the other and the revelation that had been made. It was Edward that eventually drew in a deep breath and spoke quietly, although with a tone of solemnity.

"What have you come for, Manuel? Sant Alberto is in your cousin's diocese I believe; indeed, that was a concern to me when circumstances dictated that I seek shelter and safety here. Yet there was little choice. I know that you and your family have close dealings with the pope, but the holy father himself heard my sorry tale at Avignon, and has no doubt related it to you. There can also be little left to be said that has not been ruminated through the taverns and bawdy houses of Europe, let alone the royal courts. Moreover, who could possibly care whether I am alive or dead? If it is his holiness, then you may tell him..."

"There is one other who remembers you," Fieschi interrupted.

Realisation came to Edward and he stared at the prelate, but said nothing, only hanging his head as though in shame.

Alphage now moved restlessly, not knowing whether he should slip quietly away, or stay and support his friend. The revelation from Fieschi had shocked the older monk, but it also answered many questions that he had asked himself during his time with the hermit.

Edward cast a look of dismay at Fieschi; sadness and bewilderment cast a shadow across his tear-stained face. All he could then do was turn to the entrance to the hovel he called home, and followed closely by Perrot, go inside. He sat down on the cot bed and buried his head in his hands. A gamut of varying emotions exploded within his confused mind, and he could no longer hold back the tears; mainly, rage against this kinsman who was cruelly exposing the deception that he had lived with, whilst here in this desolate house of God; and yet there was also some relief that he need pretend no more.

His mind conjured up the image of the *'One other who remembers you'* - surely he was a grown man himself; little news of such things ever reached this remote outpost, and yet he had learned of some details, usually gossip from some of the well-travelled merchants who plied their trade with the monks from time to time.

Of course he had feigned little interest if told, and yet each word was yet another morsel to be enjoyed in the privacy of this tumbling shack. He shed a further tear that he would never smile proudly at this person of whom Fieschi spoke, never embrace, never feel the elation of pride, never encourage to be gracious, charming, affable and kind. That time had been denied him, and whilst he could blame many, such a list of culprits must surely be headed by himself.

He could do little else now, but maybe unburden himself of the weight of guilt and misery that was becoming almost too heavy as he aged. Memories that whirled like ghostly phantoms in his dreams, plagued his thoughts with questions that had few answers. He who had been born so high and yet had fallen so low.

He rose and looked down at his faithful companion who had followed him inside. They were both orphans of the world, fiercely loyal to one another. He wiped away a single pine needle that had stuck to the dog's tail. He sunk to the floor suddenly and clasped the animal to him, comforted by the creature's warmth. Perrot whined softly, gently licking his master's ear, whilst keeping a watchful eye on a beetle that scuttled across the dirt floor.

Still sitting on the ground, his back leaning against the pallet bed, it was some time before he was aware of shadows cast across the solitary opening that served as a window in his shack. He rose, not without the discomfort of having sat on such a hard surface for for what must have been some time. Something had changed, and he struggled to identify it. There was a change in his thoughts a sudden need to be done with bad memories. He had not confessed to anyone for many years – ironic, when salvation was so close at hand.

Could this at last be some liberation? It had only been fear that had held him back; initially a strong desire to survive, to become lost in the crowds, to become merely one of the many insignificant people of the world. Surely it mattered little now. He breathed deeply, as Alphage had told him, as a means of calming and clearing his mind when the nightmares came upon him. Maybe this was the time to finally let go - William must now give way to Edward.

Outside the shack, it had indeed grown darker and yet Fieschi and Alphage were waiting. The nobleman had found a quiet spot, his face upturned to the sky as the heat left the day. His eyes were closed, and he seemed to be almost sleeping. Brother Alphage was nearby, reading the small prayer book that he carried always. The monk looked up at the tall hermit and smiled.

Perrot had decided that Fieschi should be roused, and it was with a start that he awoke as the dog poked a cold nose into his jewelled hand. He stood quickly, glancing over to Alphage but saying nothing. The two of them had realised that some time was needed to leave the hermit to his thoughts and they to theirs. They had waited patiently for what had seemed some time, each with his own views on what had transpired here.

Edward turned to smile at Fieschi and his manner seemed different somehow; a timbre that added a tone of nobility as he spoke, apologising for keeping the noble emissary waiting in such an uncomfortable spot in a heat that was only now starting to give way to a cooler air. Alphage looked sad and cast his gaze down, unsure what to say.

Edward seemed to sense the infirmarian's disquiet, and reassured him with a smile. "Do not be troubled for me my friend. Maybe it is time, time for me to unburden myself of all I have carried with me for so long. How many times have you invited me to share with you the events that brought me to Sant Alberto? Maybe now I should do so."

He walked away to the edge of the shack that was his home, and sat down on the small bench where he would often sit to break his fast, or just to lose himself in thought. He rubbed both his coarse hands over his short-cropped hair, once soft and golden, now coarse and almost grey.

Both the prelate and the good infirmarian wondered if he was sleeping or once more deep in his thoughts, and it was some moments before the hermit addressed Fieschi. "You have much to ask me, I am sure, but I would be alone now if you please. Allow me some time."

Fieschi marvelled at how dignified this man was. Nobility was indeed instinctive, and he felt he would have been able to identify this former king by his bearing and manner if nothing else. What irony and sadness that a man who had once lived only for lively company, frivolity and excess now lived in a beggar's shack in seclusion and anonymity. He bowed his head in deference to the hermit and, with a brief nod as he passed the older monk, he picked his way through the foliage and proceeded back along the dirt track to the monastery.

When Fieschi had left, Alphage alone stood for some moments lest the hermit should need him, but he had again buried his face in his hands. The monk turned away as he heard the the former king begin to sob.

The following day began as humid and oppressive as had most days in the stifling month of July and, even as the cock crowed loudly to herald a new morning, the monastery was already becoming a hive of activity. *Lauds* had already finished, and there was much to do before the next observance of *prime*. Monks scurried around attending to their various tasks, the morning meal would soon be served, and the community would gather together in the abbey refectory.

In the darkness of his hovel in the woodland, the hermit of Sant Alberto had slept only fitfully. At one point in the early hours he had seriously considered collecting his meagre possessions and moving swiftly on. Leaving the one place he had finally felt safe. Yet, something stopped him. The dark memories did not get left behind, they only travelled with you, grew accustomed to your situation, and when at your most vulnerable, they reasserted themselves.

He lay awake, tormented by memories and images of the past. Characters loomed into view every time he closed his eyes, voices called to him until he abandoned all hope of rest. Maybe now was the time to let go of the past, face the demons that plagued him mercilessly. He looked up at the ceiling of this ramshackle home of his; he had felt more for this hovel than almost anywhere. A king, with many castles, manor houses, estates. The log he sat on outside was so much more than a throne.

What, then, of the individual that Fieschi alluded to as '*one other who remembers you*'? He believed in his heart that it was the one person left who could possibly still care. Maybe it was not only he that yearned to be at peace.

+++

It had been agreed that there was a need for privacy for the hermit to speak further to Fieschi, and the small but secluded herb garden was chosen for the purpose. The woodland track that ran close to the hermit shack, though seldom a busy thoroughfare, was still used by some of the brothers to access the makeshift road that led further up into the surrounding hillside, and thereafter to the small hamlet that nestled within the Sant Alberto community.

The fragrant area was quiet and benefitted from being partly in shade, and yet its wattle walls afforded it some degree of privacy. The abbot had made the suggestion, being one of those that had often found the place conducive to meditation and thought. The hermit himself had tended all the various plants from lemon balm to mint, the heady aroma of rosemary and delicacy of lavender; indeed, it was one of his favourite places.

Alphage had commented that there would be no guarantee that members of the brethren simply going about their business, would not be drawn to, and intrigued by, the eminent visitor, the infirmarian and the hermit meeting together. It would be most unsatisfactory to be seated inside the shack, which barely held the few sticks of furniture within its makeshift walls - there was very little on which to sit.

Having reached the small stream that ran behind his hovel, Edward stripped off his clothes and, taking up the bowl he kept there, scooped up the cold water, tipping it over his head and letting it cascade down his body as he shivered. The wash invigorated him, and after rubbing himself dry with a homespun cloth, he pulled on a simple robe and sat for some moments watching the dawn of the new day, while trying to regulate his breathing as Alphage had taught him. More than ever, he would need to be calm if he was to relive events that had not been considered for so long. Moreover, it would be necessary to speak of misdeeds: greed, hate, forbidden love, death – he had surely encompassed all the sins, and maybe the abbot would feel he could no longer allow such an individual to have any connection to the monastery. As most of the surrounding land had been gifted to the community of Sant Alberto, he would need to travel on again.

Nevertheless, he would speak with Fieschi; it was surely time to confront the ghosts that had clawed at his conscience, relive happy memories as well perhaps - and there had indeed been happy ones, although they had been fleeting, and had always eventually turned sour and regretful.

A low but audible growl from Perrot caused the hermit to turn to the clearing, and there in the advancing dawn stood Brother Alphage, his arms open in welcoming to the excited dog. He smiled and nodded briefly as he took the hermit's hands in his. "Come, Lord Edward," he began, but the hermit shook his head.

"My friend, Edward is my birth name, but I am no longer lord. There be no formality between you and I."

Alphage smiled with some relief; how strange that a title immediately robbed Alphage of intimacy the two friends had enjoyed. "Come then, Edward," he said quietly. "His eminence will wait for us after we have broken our fast, and maybe we can find a little cheese for a faithful companion." And so saying, he smiled and led the way up the track towards the monastery.

They broke their fast in the intimacy of Alphage's workshop rather than amongst the brothers of the community. Brother Nicolo had indeed been almost giddy with curiosity since Alphage's summons to the abbot's chamber, and would surely try to elicit some explanation from the kindly infirmarian.

It was, therefore, after a frugal meal of some bread, cheese and apples washed down with cold water, that Edward and Alphage made their way to the herb garden.

Already the former king felt sick with nerves and, instinctively, Alphage drew him to a small wooden bench that looked out over the colourful landscape and they sat for a moment; Perrot slumped down at his master's feet.

The elderly monk took one of the hermit's hands and patted it comfortingly. "I know this will be hard for you, my friend," he spoke softly. "We all have a past, we all guard a secret. God has none in his flock that have not stumbled and fallen somewhere in their lives. You live with the memories, my dear friend, no-one can take them from you. You will recall poor Brother Paul who was taken from us last winter, his wits were quite gone and few listened to his ramblings; and yet, if one did take in what he said, he spoke of his long life. The poor soul could not remember what meal he had just consumed a minute after he had risen from the table where he had just eaten it, and yet he remembered many things that had gone before - a childhood, his parents, his first entry as a young novice to the house of God. By the end, everything that kept him alive was taken, but he still remembered something of his journey in life. I say this, Edward, to let you know that you too will always recall what has happened in your life; what you choose to say now may unburden you, for I know it is a weight you have carried for many years."

Edward smiled at the kindly face before him. "Alphage," he said quietly, "my tale will not be an easy one to hear. God knows my sins are many. I am no longer proud or ashamed, yet a gentle soul like you must first be warned, that my revelations may well shock and alarm you."

"And yet, here you are. God has not struck you down. You live simply and quietly here at Sant Alberto helping where you can, giving your time to assist others. Life has maybe been cruel to you at times, and as I watch you grow older, as we all do, I sense that past times do indeed weigh heavily upon you. What you choose to say to the emissary from the holy father and yes, myself, if you are comfortable to include me, will help you. The emissary speaks of another who would dearly love to know what became of you. God has carried you when you have had no strength to walk, he has seen everything, when you have been too blind. What you tell us is already known to the almighty, there is no higher authority."

Edward rubbed his tired eyes, and he breathed in deeply. All of what his dear friend was saying gave him a strange kind of inner strength. Alphage was correct - as he always was. If his story could serve as little else, it could answer many questions for the one who now carried the weight of great responsibility that he had been unable to bear.

He smiled down at the hairy chin that now rested on his knee, large sparkling eyes that switched from one man to the other. His master stroked the dog's head gently before he stood up and held out a hand to his older companion.

"Shall we begin, my friend?"

+++

The fragrance of the monastery herb garden was beguiling and almost heady. Neat rows of sage, basil, fennel and thyme lined the boxed beds, with various labels identifying each plant. The mass of overpowering oregano enjoyed its own bed, given its propensity to overtake everything planted next to it. Variously-sized pots lined up along one of the garden's walls which enjoyed some welcoming shade under a wooden awning. The pots would later be used to transfer those herbs still growing by the time the weather became more inclement and there was a need to shelter them from the frosts that covered the vast land around the monastery. Sweet-smelling lavender grew not only in a fragrant abundance all around the outer surrounds of the garden, but hung in bunches from the wooden awning to dry. A small wooden door in the corner of the garden led out to the small monastery kitchen.

Manuel Fieschi had himself suffered a restless night. The relative ease with which he had been able to successfully approach the hermit had surprised him. He had no wish to see into other man's soul, and yet he was fascinated by his very existence. He had decided that it was prudent nevertheless to be cautious, and indeed respectful; when all was said and done, the hermit was a former king, the son of a king and the father of another. If he had learnt anything from working with the pope himself or his immediate advisers, it was to exercise patience. A lifetime of obedience and political statecraft urged him to address the man as Lord Edward at least; and yet wisdom urged him to consider how best to gain the trust of the hermit. His instructions had been clear, and he would execute the task as responsibly as he could.

Manuel rose as he heard the familiar sound of sandals slapping against the ground. His mouth felt dry in anticipation. He would try to banish from his mind all the information he had been given about this recluse. He had been afforded so much time during his journey to plan what he would say, how he would formulate their discussion. The words of the holy father uppermost in his mind, delicacy and tact were to be used.

Edward and Alphage approached, the hermit looked pensive and nervous as he bent his head to duck underneath the low archway that led into the fragrant garden where he had whiled away many hours, toiling with great satisfaction and solitude. Alphage wore an expression of calmness and smiled as he bowed his head to greet the emissary.

Meanwhile the hound, Perrot, had immediately begun investigating the unfamiliar scents that hung in the air, unceremoniously declaring the garden his territory, if only for a short time, by cocking a leg against a wooden barrel.

Fieschi had chosen a cool corner of the garden where they could - at least for some time - avoid the relentless heat that was promised by a bright, full sun.

Edward sat on a stone seat opposite the envoy, whilst Alphage sank onto one of the small clay walls that separated the herbs, and proceeded to pick and prune at some of the aromatic plants. Edward noticed that no scribe attended their meeting and questioned the absence of one, although he had been relieved.

"I saw no need," Fieschi explained. "I am blessed with an extremely good memory. My attendant is most trustworthy, but the less written word there is of our discourse the better."

The hermit glanced at Alphage, who in turn nodded encouragingly, and Edward began, not addressing Fieschi directly, but almost to himself.

"Events of the past, of which I must tell you, have haunted me daily. Faces of so many that curse my dreams. As you will hear, I recall every speech, every look and every fault. Those that have shared my triumphs and disasters, have laughed with me, cried with me, and have in turn lived to regret their association with me. This tale is not one that I happily relate, but it is time it was told, and those for whom you visit here will maybe, when told, begin to understand." He looked directly at the papal envoy, and was about to ask questions, but resisted – there would be time to speak later of those for whom Fieschi had made such a long, arduous journey.

+++

My father, the great warrior Edward, terrified me as much as he did the Welsh and the Scots that he relentlessly pursued during his lifetime. I was not expected to ever reach the throne. My brother Alfonso died unexpectedly a mere four months after my birth, and my mother followed him to her grave less than four years later. From what I was told as I grew to manhood, my father's temperament changed once she was gone. Theirs, it appeared, was a union of the heart as well as the political.

A tale of her adoration of her husband was often told. It was said that she had travelled on crusade with him and, one day as he rested, he admitted a messenger who attempted to assassinate him using a dagger, the tip of which had been laced with poison. Before the killer was overpowered, he had managed at least a draw of blood which though seemingly no more that a glancing blow, was in danger of infecting his whole body. Legend has it that my mother came upon this scene and, immediately, realising the danger to her lord husband proceeded to suck the poison from the wound before spitting it out.

As a romantic young boy, I delighted in the tale and almost wept at the devotion one could feel for another, enough to put their own life at risk. If I ever think about the instance now, on reflection, I remain unconvinced by the truth of it. Oh, I have known such adoration; men say they will die for you, will carry out all manner of deeds to prove their devotion. Do they do this for you or for themselves?

Suffice to say, my father took her death badly and, for some time, retired from public life, hiding himself to grieve in private; and in doing so, distanced himself from the children she had left him. As I recall, only six of us outlived her, of the fifteen she had borne.

The role of prince was all I had known, so I can say little of how it compared to that of a squire or a nobleman. Maybe I should have tried to discover, but if truth be told, I was simply uninterested. It mattered little to me. I enjoyed the trappings of wealth and luxury. I was a prince - why should I not have such comforts? Childhood was, for a period at least, happy. I had spent much time with my sisters - five in all. The girls were, of course, expedient. Expected to be subservient and dutiful, we were pawns in the game of royal alliances. You may know, Manuel, what became of them all; I have little memory of them now.

Those developing years seemed to pass quickly enough. I was given into the care of dear Alice. Her surname escapes me now after so many years; I have forgotten so much, but I recall a kind devoted woman, a large fleshy face, a firm but gentle manner. I was to have no other maternal figure until it was announced that my father intended to marry again. A treaty with Philip of France was to contain two particular clauses; my father was to wed Philip's sister Marguerite, and I was to be matched similarly with his daughter – Isabella.

To a young prince, the idea of marriage was purely to make a political alliance, and once having been informed of the clause by my father, it would appear that my personal opinion was of no concern. Therefore, I considered it for a short period and then it simply ceased to be of any interest. I knew from Alice that my father and mother had enjoyed the rarity in a royal union where both individuals loved each other. Theirs was indeed a love match. I never felt that for Isabella, and yet...well, we shall talk of that in time.

My stepmother however, remains a fond memory. She was, at twenty, nearer my own age than that of my sixty-year-old father. She would be welcomed by many, my father's attendants and courtiers alike, if only because of her ability to soothe my father's growing unpredictable temperament.

Day-to-day life for the heir to the throne was as expected - I was given my own household, and within it I sought to surround myself with those who made me happy and any that interested me. Later, I would join my father on one of his obsessive campaigns against Scotland. I gave a good account of myself, and as a result, appeared – for the time being at least - to find favour with him.

What could I tell you about that great warlord, the infamous 'hammer of the Scots', whose aim in life seemed to be consumed by conflict. By that I do not allude only to warfare, of which no doubt even this haven has heard some tales.

I can say only that at the time of my emergence from the shadows of my youth, I despised few others as much as I did my father. I told Piers one day, that duty bade me to love him as my lord and king, but I would never like him. A man should see in his father everything he should aim to be. I was expected to see him as my hero. Instead, I grew to hate him, and the fire of that hatred never abated. His temper, which it is my shame to admit I had inherited, to an extent, was often trained on me; my failings, my folly, my idleness, my frivolous companions. How my mother would be ashamed of what I had become, "God rest her sweet soul." He would turn from me as though overcome with the grief of it all.

His fierceness was legendary. As he aged and considered his own mortality, he would often summon me late at night, usually when he was invariably deep in his cups. We would sit in silence for some time, I would listen to his heavy, laboured breathing, smell his wine soaked breath, waiting for the inevitable rage, the familiar criticism of my conduct which would inevitably pour forth. I studied his grey, lined face. Dull, soulless eyes looked out under heavy lids, one of which drooped lazily. His hair and beard predominately grey and unkempt. A tall man, broad-shouldered and imposing.

As I grew up, I learned the signs, anticipated the moods as they became more frequent. He longed for me to be an image of himself; as a young man, he had embraced the lessons of fighting, swordsmanship, strategy in warfare, combat by any means.

His legacy was poisonous. Of course, I can blame him for much. By the time of his death, the weight of kingship he passed to me was indeed a heavy burden; a country virtually bankrupt. Please believe me when I say I had all intentions of righting the injustice of his incessant heavy taxation. Warfare was expensive, and in my father's eyes victory for the English must be paid by the English; and the poorest felt the burden the most. The English armies were exhausted. Fighting men were worn out from incessant campaigns to quell the Scots or punish the Welsh. How, even after all these years, the execution of William Wallace is still so vivid an image. You may not know of the Scotsman Wallace, but his end was one of the most brutal. A supposed lesson for all rebels to heed, yet it served only to enrage the Scots even more. Long campaigns in all manner of weather, though thankfully the royal camp was more comfortable than those of the common soldiers.

As for me; here was I showing an undignified interest in swimming and rowing. Yes, Manuel, I see you are surprised. I did indeed love to swim in the waters in London or Windsor, as well as the lake at Langley.

These names will of course mean nothing to either of you, so forgive me. In truth their names are almost distant to me. The enjoyment that these activities gave me was one I refused to give up, even though my father's courtiers frowned upon an activity that was surely only to be employed when saving one's life! It was *beneath* one of such exalted birth as myself. Unconventional? Yes, I would agree, but that did not stop me. When did I last swim? I can barely recall now.

Any favour, even to his own son, was conditional. The king took complete control over my household; indeed, I could make appointments, but ultimately, these needed his approval. The make up of the household is unimportant - officers, chancellors and others of whom I shamefully say I took no notice. My household was large, although early on, I took little interest in how it was made up or, indeed financed. Some of those that served me, I would grow to like, even love of course, but others were simply my father's creatures, who would work on his behalf, reporting anything that suggested matters were not as he would wish.

Much of my time then was spent travelling - miles of road, towns that received me with cheers and waves, all manner of welcome and I remember how happy I was to be out in the open; the wind on my face, the sun on my back, the freedom away from a stifling court, all serious faces and dark undertones. My father was irritable and unpredictable, all was oppressive and dull. His sycophantic courtiers learned to judge their sovereign's mood and temperament. When he was not butchering the Scots or the Welsh, he held a frugal and dull court. How my young stepmother must have hated her life enclosed by such dark oppressive shadows!

I, however, took the utmost delight in surrounding myself with singers, minstrels and the like. Travelling troubadours, actors and acrobats were all encouraged. I think often of my beloved Langley, my favourite place in the world, a name I do recall vividly. Here, would I think, was my introduction to a love of buildings and renovation, here I would appreciate and take part in thatching some of the palaces outbuildings and stables. Ditching and hedging gave me much satisfaction. Manuel, how shocked you look! An opinion shared by my father's courtiers. Rustic pursuits were not the life for a prince. One could be prince or commoner – not both!

Over the years, even after becoming king, I retreated often to Langley when in need of solitude and security. The palace had been a gift from my father, who had inherited it after my mother had died, for it had belonged to her. Built around three courtyards, with a moat, I recall the beauty of that enchanted place that she had taken time to develop, establishing the grounds and gardens, planting fruit trees and developing quiet walkways beneath rose arbours, flowers of all varieties, statues depicting animals and suchlike. I breathed in all its scents, much as I like to do here in this garden. What a lifetime has been spent between solitude in that garden to the harmony in this. I felt peace at Langley. It was to there I retreated whenever I wanted to hide from the world.

I was pleased to be the founder of a Dominican priory there and supported their order during my reign. More importantly, Langley Priory was where I would finally entrust the body of my brother, Perrot. I digress again, forgive me.

An important event changed everything for me; I was summoned to my father who tried to explain his next campaign. At the time, the Scots were relatively subservient, and my father then turned his attention to his old enemy – France. We English have hated no other nation more than we have the French. Philip IV, who was to later become my father-in-law, was a wily cautious character of great cunning, a trait - that I can say with less charity than I should – which lived on in his offspring. Under the rule of Philip, we the English lost our last-held territory, Gascony.

I recall so vividly my father's rage. He raged at his councillors, describing the French as – well, I would not desecrate this holy place by repeating the language, but you may imagine it was most colourful! For days, none dared to approach him with news from Scotland that the nobles there were again rebelling. Wars on two fronts now presented themselves, and it was at that time that I began to play a more important role in affairs than hitherto.

The king entrusted to me the responsibility of protecting the realm, should the French decide to use this period when our resources were most severely stretched to plan an invasion. I recall even now, at such an age - twelve or thirteen, I do not recall exactly - lying in my bed at night waiting to hear that the enemy had landed and an invasion was underway.

It was not until much later, that my father determined that he would use all influence and alliances with the other powers in Europe and quell the threat from France once and for all. I was to formerly accept the sworn fealty of all the nobles in the land. Earls, churchmen, all bent the knee to me, although it must be said, some more reluctantly than others.

Of course, the role I played was symbolic, little more. Yet, I was trusted. Not that I could have used any royal authority, had it been necessary - the nobles would have seen to that. Nevertheless, it was recognition from my father. As I have mentioned, I was to enjoy some military responsibility when we made further incursions into Scotland.

Some time later, my father gifted to me his lands in Wales. You will not know of it I suspect, Alphage; by your nod of recognition, Manuel, you do. Suffice to say, it is a kingdom within that of England, under rule of the English crown, a hard-fought rule. How many men have died for the love of their homeland and those who would take it from them? I hold strong feelings for Wales even now, its people offered me support during my great troubles, of which you will hear more.

I had promised to escape the formality of court and take Piers there many times, I promised we would ride into the rugged mountains, fish in the lakes and sleep under the open sky.

+++

Edward was silent and had stood up as though propelled by some vision. Perrot instinctively sat up from where he had been dozing at his master's feet. Manuel and Alphage looked to one another. Fieschi made to reach out and touch the hermit's arm, but Alphage stood up himself, motioning Manuel to hold back.

"Edward, he quietly asked, "do you wish to continue?"

When Edward spoke, it was with emotion. "So many memories, I had not thought of these times for so long."

Alphage smiled thinly and, reaching out, laid a comforting hand on his friend's arm. He glanced behind to Fieschi, who looked troubled, raising an eyebrow in enquiry.

"Perhaps that is enough for now?" he suggested. "There are still our devotions to observe. Perhaps..."

Edward glanced at his friend and then up to the sky as if seeking some divine intervention. "No," he stated with a heavy resigned sigh, "I must continue."

Alphage had been assured by the abbot that, if necessary, he could be excused from the devotions of the day during this time, so the old man nodded sagely, and the hermit sat again. Fieschi nodded to the infirmarian, and proceeded to fiddle awkwardly with one of the jewelled rings on his hand while he and Alphage waited for Edward to resume his story.

"So," Edward said with a sad smile, "it is time I spoke of Piers."

In truth, my father had become acquainted with Piers Gaveston before I did myself. His father had served with mine and indeed, my own tutor, Guy Ferre – a Gascon himself – had, I think, suggested to my father that I might enjoy his company, and that he could possibly inspire me to enter the jousts that were the very lifeblood of the English nobility, but in which I had not taken the slightest interest. By all accounts, my father found Gaveston a most amusing fellow and was struck by the sensible and pragmatic young man. I believe above all, my father liked the fact that, although knowing his place, Piers was not overawed by the old king. Where so many would find themselves stammering if questioned or opinion, Piers Gaveston belied his years by being both bold and respectful, and answering the old king's questions with confidence.

A banquet held in honour of my step-mother the queen, for what reason escapes me now, necessitated my appearance along with my retinue, as well as those of my father's court, and all others currently in high favour.

This was my first glimpse of Piers Gaveston, and I permitted myself the liberty of carefully scrutinising the Gascon that my father appeared to hold in such high esteem. The sight was – perfection!

I did not know of any other that looked so at ease with himself. He was tall, maybe as tall as myself, with shoulder-length jet black hair. His face was the most handsome I had ever seen. His skin was smooth and unblemished, eyes of green that sparkled with life and humour and a certain devilry. His lips were full, dark pink and sensuous and parted into an easy smile that showed his straight white teeth, and revealed small but distinct dimples. His jawline was firm and square, with only the faintest dusting of facial hair; a small cleft in his chin completed this most beautiful of faces. I, who had myself received many compliments on my own looks, now felt ugly and crude by comparison.

He was broad-shouldered, the cut of his dark green tunic complemented his chest and torso that narrowed to a slim waist. Slim-hipped though he was, his brown hose covered what appeared to be strong legs, with muscles evident through the material. His feet were covered with rich brown suede boots, pointed at the toe in the current fashion.

I smiled to myself; so few men concerned themselves with the fashion of the day here at my father's grey, outdated court, and the Gascon was drawing many glances for that alone; one sensed that many disapproved of such gaudiness, yet I noted that Piers welcomed the attention – negative or otherwise.

I must have been staring overlong without realising it, for I was suddenly aware that he had returned my gaze. He smiled at me, nodding his head in deference. I immediately looked away, finding some pretext to converse with another. When I looked over again, Gaveston was gone. I surprised myself that I was actually disappointed. I scanned the large hall for the sight of that jet black hair, but he had vanished.

I remained strangely unaware of the remainder of the evening, so lost in thought about him. My dearest friend Gilbert de Clare, a handsome, jolly companion, tried to lift my spirits, yet I remained forlorn. I decided to retire early; strange, that I had looked forward to the occasion as one of the few where there were many of my dearest friends to entertain me, to laugh over old pranks and buffoonery and bring some sparkle to the usual drab and austere court events. Now, I was deflated, almost sad.

As I lay in my bed that night, I still questioned my mood during the evening; one moment so light and strangely carefree and the next agitated and forlorn. There was one obvious reason of course, but I drove this immediately from my mind, although the memory itself flooded back, until I was forced to consider it. Some thoughts last forever, and will not be banished to that obscure part of the mind where we hold those instances that we are adamant we want to forget, and yet, whether by command of heart or head, we can never fully suppress. Piers, I decided, had neglected to present himself to me as well as my father, and whilst I was never one to stand on ceremony, especially in those days, I was determined – as far as Piers Gaveston was concerned - to remain censorious. Although he had effectively become one of my companions, I was still intrigued and wary of him. Nor, when we did eventually become friends, were the circumstances certainly propitious.

One particular afternoon, I had announced my intention to ride out for fresh air. I have always been happiest outdoors, but my spirits were already lifted by an unexpected assignation. I had the previous night, enjoyed my first full experience with a woman. The event in question had been arranged by my good friend, Gilbert de Clare, although I was to learn later that my father had let it be known that he did not disapprove of such an antic, and indeed wondered why one of my companions had not yet arranged such a surprise event. Surely it was time I experienced the pleasures that all men enjoy. I will not shame these recollections by divulging more about that, but suffice to say that as I prepared for a horse ride that morning, I was happy that another stage of my - let us say - education had been reached the evening prior.

I recall that I turned to have my riding boots pulled on and was surprised to find, not my manservant, but the Gascon himself. For a moment I was unsure what to say, but Piers, I was to learn, was never tongue-tied.

"My prince," he said, flashing a grin as he got down on one knee and looked up at me expectantly, his glittering deep eyes quickly darting to the stool beside me. I felt a fool for not having the sense to sit down so the boots could go on. I seated myself, and he grinned again as he carefully removed the soft shoe from my foot and deftly arranging the riding boot which he then helped pull on. I remained speechless whilst he worked on the other foot. I watched his hands - delicate looking, but strong.

Did I imagine that he found a delight in playing the squire? Eventually, I found my voice, clearing my throat.

"Gaveston," I said, "you are the last person I expected to carry out such a task. I am grateful of course, but..."

He remained on one knee as he looked at me earnestly. "There should be no task that your highest attendants should not perform. Forgive me sire, I have wondered how best to approach you and speak with you. Yet each time I think you may receive me, you are surrounded by our mutual friends, courtiers and suchlike. This may be the most idiotic of ruses, but you have at least spoken to me, so the sacrifice of my exalted position from unknown companion to mere squire has been worth the indignity."

He then rose and, in a grand gesture, bowed low. I must have looked a dolt just staring at him, but then suddenly I burst out laughing. He grinned again, those perfect white teeth flashing against his light brown of his skin.

"Did I need an excuse to speak to me?" I asked. "You must get up, please." He did so, and I signalled to the seat beside me. I recall even now after so many years, his scent of lavender. I think that is probably why I love this herb garden so much.

Piers continued, "I am troubled for you, my prince," he stated.

I was surprised and said so. "I am well enough," I assured him. "What could ail me that you need to be troubled about?"

"You seem sad," he said softly, although we were quite alone and there was no-one to hear us. "I have taken the liberty of watching you closely, and I detect a sadness, a loneliness about you. I too have lived without a mother's affection and under scrutiny from others. Forgive my boldness, but you seem quite alone. For all of us, your companions, you are a lone figure awaiting a destiny that terrifies you. There, I have said too much!" He rose suddenly. "I have allowed my thoughts to take hold of my tongue; forgive me, my prince, I meant no disrespect."

I looked up at him, unsure of what my response should be. I was certainly not offended by his words, even though to suggest that I was in anyway in fear or trepidation about my duty could be termed as a gross insult. I was never really one to stand on dignity, certainly not in those days, and I took no offence at his words. I realised that what he said was true. I was nervous about the future. The weight of expectation grew heavier with each day. Why should I be offended at some other noticing it? I found myself staring at his retreating figure before I realised that he had interpreted my silence for anger.

"Piers," I called to him just as he reached the chamber door, "please, stay a while, I take no offence. Your company would be most welcome."

He turned back to me, his handsome face seemed to light up and he grinned again. "Do you play dice, my prince?" he asked.

"Not awfully well," I answered truthfully. "I lose heavily to Gilbert quite often."

"Ah, that rogue," Piers laughed. "I shall see if we can maybe even the deficit with de Clare, he's an incorrigible cheat you know."

We laughed again, and my plans to ride out that day were abandoned. We talked of many things; I cannot recall them now, but his manner, his self-confidence and most of all his quick wit and general good humour were a delight.

He briefly mentioned my tryst of the previous night, and if he sensed my embarrassment, he was too discreet to allude to it. "I have noticed the young lady in question, a sweet young woman with a beautiful face and a beguiling smile. I compliment you on your choice, my prince!" he laughed and winked at me conspiratorially. I knew that I blushed at his ribald teasing, but said nothing, and Piers had the good sense to take the teasing no further.

The hours passed quickly, and we talked much, and drank more wine than I should have, but his company was so infectious and easy. No pretence, no formality, just one person getting to know another, laughing, at ease. So much for my intention to remain censorious!

Laughter came easily to him, and I was in turn often overcome with mirth. He made fun at some of the dourer and more pompous members of my father's court, and his gift for mimicry was a revelation. Something of course that would have more serious consequences in time to come.

When he finally bade me goodnight, I lay on my bed, hands behind my head, and smiled. I had made a good friend, I believed. A friendship that would endure despite many obstacles in the years to come.

+++

Walter Langton, Bishop of Coventry enjoyed being a landowner held in high esteem as he was by my father, who had made him treasurer. The vast woodlands in Windsor were effectively his property and were noted for their fine deer that roamed there in large numbers. I never cared for the bishop, not then at least. Yet it was in a mood of devilment and, in hindsight, arrogance that emboldened me to suggest a hunt. Although an indifferent jouster, I enjoyed hunting, and could that morning think of no better sport than that which could be found on the bishop's land. The sky was clear and blue, and although a chill hung in the air, it was bracing, and the cold breeze blew gently in my face as I, accompanied by five companions including Piers, led our small riding party out with a leisurely gait at first, but soon building up to a vigorous gallop.

I look back now and groan when recalling the arrogance of my youth, but it was then most prevalent in my nature, and I saw no reason to not do whatever I wished, especially as I was enjoying some measured harmony with my father.

My plan was to hunt deer – Langton's deer! The bishop was known to have great pride in having introduced a variety of deer to the common herds, some from his friends in Europe, and had indeed banned any from hunting the creatures on his land. Even now I can still recall the look of horror on the faces of my companions at my suggestion that we demand that the bishop allow us the liberty with his herds. It seemed that none but I was eager to hunt; but suddenly Piers drew his horse nearer to my own.

"Might I suggest, my lord, that with such an abundance of fine animals, the bishop need not know that we have even been here? Even you, my prince, may meet with refusal by the bishop."

I heard more than one intake of breath at such a suggestion and uneasy glances were shared among my companions, but like myself, they found Gaveston's enthusiasm hard to resist. Some short time later we had circled the perimeter of the great park, and practically broken through the fencing with our horses. A beautiful stag was sighted and Piers and I led the others and gave immediate chase. We had a first killing and then another, only to suddenly be pulled up short by several keepers who were now also pursuing us on horseback, and who demanded we halt.

It did not appear that I was recognised and was about to dramatically announce my identity when the party men separated, and the bishop himself rode his mare up to the group. After a moment's shock, he turned his piercing dark eyes angrily on me. He had, it transpired, been nearby with his park keepers discussing some areas of trees to be felled when our indiscreet cheers had been heard.

"Lord Edward, what is the meaning of this outrage?" He glared at me with barely-concealed fury, his sharp features growing red with indignity. "These are private lands, *my* lands, and none are allowed to hunt or indeed to ride here unless I give permission. I am...!"

"Bishop!" I snapped, feeling my face flush with the heat of embarrassment, cool though the air was, but in front of my party, there must be no loss of dignity. "You are reminded, my lord bishop, to whom you speak! How dare you address me thus? A pox on your outrage! You own these lands by courtesy of the crown and, as such, you are in no position to refuse me entry here. Kindly remember that. I am minded to speak to my father of your effrontery."

Langton was not in the least cowed by this and rallied without hesitation.

"Indeed, my lord, your father the king will most certainly hear of this, have no fear! You are respectfully asked to leave my lands at once!"

I recall how I had felt, the flush of embarrassment on my face. I was uncertain now, the bold adventure had seemed amusing, but I had not of course reckoned with confronting the bishop himself. I fought inwardly to respond regally and boldly, but I could offer nothing more than a stammered reply,

"The devil may take your foreign deer, my lord bishop." I spat with venom, and turned back in the direction we had come, my companions following all too eagerly behind me. Not before, unfortunately, Piers threw back his head and laughed loudly. Langton could not have failed to hear him; and indeed the last view the bishop had of my Gascon brother was Piers halting long enough to jump from his horse, pick up one of the fallen deer, and sling the animal over his steed, before remounting and galloping up behind the rest of us.

Here, then, was the embryonic devil that was to become the centre of my world. I joined him in that laughter, but the relative seriousness of our companions served as a warning of the retribution to follow.

I saw nothing of Piers over the next month as he and several other of my friends had been banned from attending me. Langton was as good as his word, and had immediately complained to my father in the strongest terms that he dared, that he had been humiliated and verbally rebuked by myself before being both insulted and laughed at by my companions. Plus, he had needed to order extensive, and costly work to repair the damage that had been caused by our japery.

My father was furious, such was his reliance on Langton as a sound adviser and competent treasurer, that not only was I to make a humble apology to the bishop, but I was to be deprived of all funds that came directly from the crown, from which to pay my household. In addition, I was forbidden the company of 'certain persons' that the bishop suggested to my father were becoming 'influential with me'.

Langton was as wily a politician as any of my father's barons. A thin, gaunt man with skin as white as a chaste maiden, he had long bony fingers, the ugliness of which he disguised with jewelled rings; his nails were long and unkempt. He had, Piers once remarked most aptly, the face of a cadaver; sharp, small eyes of the darkest grey, which narrowed in a warning of his displeasure. His high cheekbones and thin, cruel mouth gave him an almost ethereal image.

I considered him to be a villain, yet my father valued him highly, especially as an advisor on administration and matters of finance. I still believe to this day that the bishop, in his annoyance of our deer poaching, conveyed to my father his concern that my household was becoming known for its excesses.

Any who knew the old king were well aware that he was constantly short of money, and therefore any suggestion that his son was wasting his allowance on frivolous trappings would have vexed him greatly. Such was the discord perpetrated by that prelate that put an end to any cordiality that may possibly have existed between us.

Indeed, rumour was rife that Langton had misappropriated funds and had been careless with his administration of the vast amounts that the constant wars drained from the exchequer. Nevertheless, my father valued him highly, and any hope I had of revenge would have to wait. Whilst the old king lived, Langton was safe.

It was sometime before my father's mood softened and I could finally run my household without the need to plead with my friends or indeed my own sister Joan. Nevertheless, my own court kept some distance from my father's – publicly, tensions still existed. As did the exclusion of Gilbert de Clare, and more importantly – my dearest Piers. My Gascon friend had kept up a correspondence with me, so that my general melancholy was relieved somewhat. Letters delivered by Hugo, his most loyal servant, arrived with pleasant frequency. I recall those early days of our friendship, and remember Hugo well. He was short and plump, with a mop of unkempt brown hair, a button nose and a complexion that bordered on scrofulous. I wondered that Piers was attended by this antithesis of his own careful grooming and appearance, yet he trusted Hugo above all others and, in time, I also saw the qualities in the boy who was devoted to his master entirely. He would play a part later in this story.

The fragile peace that had followed my father's brutal execution of the Scottish rebel William Wallace was soon broken, and more war in Scotland seemed imminent. For once, I recall my father with pity. Of the 'old campaigners' of his youth, few remained, and on one sorry occasion I had been called to him. I approached his chambers with reluctance; meetings between us never went well, and by chance I witnessed a side to him that I had never seen before.

The chamber door was slightly ajar, and as I peered through the gap I could see the sobbing old man that was my father, his head buried in the lap of his wife, my stepmother. She was soothing him as best she could but he was moaning softly between sobs. Time was running out for him. Marguerite was scarcely old enough to know how to deal with this most unusual of emotions from her sombre older husband. Yet she rocked him slowly like a baby, stroking the wiry grey hair as she did so. She noticed me, moving her head discreetly to signal me not to enter.

After a moment or two, I turned away and retired to my own chamber, dismissing my attendants.

In spite of all that had happened between us, I wanted to rush to him, fling my arms around him, to tell him I would take some of this great burden from him, tell him that I loved him. What a strange emotion I felt suddenly for this irascible old man who had scorned me, criticised me so often, belittled me in front of his own court. As my tears fell, I forgave him everything. Why had so much time been wasted?

Time would surely not afford us the chance to make amends, to repair the fragile bond that had always existed between us. I imagined that he had always loved me, and yet had been forced by duty to keep his children at arms length – myself especially. I slept uneasily that night; taunted by insecurity and a strange fear of what may be to come.

News reached me sometime later that my father, in a deliberate signal of the passing of the old regime, intended to knight up to three hundred young men whose fathers had also been knights, to attend a special ceremony and pledge their allegiance to the crown – and of course willingly join the army about to do further battle with the endless threat from Scotland.

The ceremony itself was all pomp and chivalry with a vivid pageantry. The sombre court had suddenly exploded in colour and activity, as though we had all been waiting to be delivered from the oppressive clouds of gloom and despair. Great lords and ladies thronged the court, for once casting off their usual drab, grey costumes in favour of brighter gowns of reds and yellows, doublets and surcoats of green velvet and caps of crimson that sported elaborate feathers.

I had not had sight of Piers for many days, and I admonished myself for such foolishness. Yet, in those days so long ago I was looking for love, to know that someone cared for me merely as Edward. Someone to whom I could whisper those secrets and fears that we all have. Someone who would still care even if I were not heir to the throne.

Was I wrong about Gaveston? Surely not. In Piers I saw all of what I wanted that someone to be. We had spent much time together and now it was too late to claim indifference to him; I was already bewitched. Yet he was missing, and I searched the large crowd for sight of him. Surely he did not intend to snub the occasion, that would indeed have been almost treasonable, and I knew that I would not have been able to support him were he to act so ambivalently about such an honour and occasion.

Where was he? Who was enjoying his company since he had been out of my sight? I felt a strange sensation of betrayal, and - I'm ashamed to admit – jealousy, that others had enjoyed his company when he should most assuredly be in attendance to me?

I could, of course, have insisted that he remain in my party wherever I went, remind him that his loyalty to me was paramount, but that would be further evidence of my arrogance. Moreover, if we were to develop the bond I yearned for, it must be based on our mutual feelings, not one that I had needed to command merely to assuage my own insecurities.

Nevertheless, I had a duty to perform as part of this great ceremony to come, and I prepared myself for it. I was to be knighted by my father, and then I in turn would ennoble my faithful companions as well as other sons of the nobility. The day prior to my knighting, the excitement and anticipation helped to distract me. I spent much of the day receiving and enjoying the company of my erstwhile companions including Gilbert de Clare, Humphrey de Bohun and Edmund Fitz Alan. These were at that time my closest companions although, as I grew older, I learned to share my thoughts with others, including men such as Walter Reynolds who I would one day petition the pope to elevate to the archbishopric of Canterbury. Walter was a man I liked immensely; humorous, genial and affable to all. A man who would, in years to come, break my heart and cause me much anguish. That evening I should have been elated and excited, but I felt an emptiness I could not shake off. Eventually, I claimed tiredness and a need to retire, to rest in preparation for the events to come.

The attendants who had helped me to disrobe, finally finished, and I dismissed them all to enjoy some solitude and quiet from the din of the occasion. I watched from my window for some time. A sadness and a sudden lethargy overcame me and I was so lost in thought that I was unaware that someone had entered.

I was awoken from my reverie by a soft, lilting Gascon accent. "I hope I am not too late, my prince. It's taken me two days to decide what to wear! Do you think dark green suits me?"

I turned around quickly and there standing in front of me, with a smile I can still see after all these years, was Piers Gaveston. I don't know what was in my mind, but suddenly I flung myself into his waiting arms, hugging him so tightly he eventually had to laughingly tap me on the shoulder to let him breathe! I could have wept tears of joy! Eventually I held him at arm's length while I studied that beautiful smiling face, and then – I kissed him.

+++

It was some moments before either Alphage or Fieschi considered what had just been said. The air was palpable and still, and neither man knew quite what to say. Alphage had travelled much before arriving at Sant Alberto, and considered that he knew much of the lives of men and their proclivities; his eyes dropped to his lap as much to hide his disquiet as to whisper a prayer of forgiveness for this troubled man. How often had he told the hermit that God knew all and forgave all; it was surely not for the old monk to judge.

Fieschi hid whatever he felt at these last words, behind a veil of indifference; he too had learnt much in his life, and in contrast to the elderly monk, he was aware of much information regarding this king turned hermit. Something told both men that there would be much that they would find difficult to comprehend in the revelations to come.

Edward turned his head briefly - to Alphage in particular - the old man smiled, and the hermit looked up at the blue, cloudless sky and sighed before he continued.

I and those I was to knight were to hold a vigil for the occasion in the abbey at Westminster. To say that it was a vigil of silence would be less than the truth; there was chatter, laughter and boisterous behaviour as excitement grew for the ceremony to come. It was hard to stay still and to observe the solemnity of the occasion, much to the annoyance of the monks whose Benedictine rules were strict with regard to talking, especially whilst in the abbey. I look back now on the irony of the ceremony, as I knighted also on that day Hugh Despenser, the younger, and one Roger Mortimer of Wigmore. Had I known what would befall me from the hands of the latter, I swear I would have used the ceremonial sword to run him through rather than anoint him with such honour.

As for the former? Well, I don't recall that Hugh and I even spoke, much less spent time together. Not then at least. Hugh would be the future. I remembered few of them other than my beloved brother Piers, or Perrot as I had now taken to calling him. As I tried with as much solemnity as possible to carry out his knighting with an air of haughty indifference, as I had the many others that day, I could not help but feel a burst of pride. Like the others I had ennobled, Piers looked downwards as was customary, and yet I could not stop myself reaching down, and with my hand under his chin, tilting his face so he looked up at me as I created a knight of this bewitching son of Gascony. I heard one or two gasps at this break with protocol and etiquette, but they mattered so little to me at the time.

My father held a magnificent banquet to celebrate the occasion. He stood, tall and dominating, commanding the attention of everyone in the great hall, his loud booming voice oath declaring that he would serve a beating to the Scots army that they would never forget. He would, he claimed, avenge the damage done by the Scottish leader, Bruce, and thereafter raise his sword again only in the enterprise of a further crusade to recapture the Holy Land.

Whether the great Edward Longshanks truly meant what he declared, I could not say. Watching him stand and burst forth with a tirade against his enemy the Scots, and the glory of the long ceremonies we had all endured over several days, I saw again the father I grew up fearing. In the near silence of the great hall, he spoke with passion and fervour. His very words seemed to inspire courage and pride into every man that heard him that day. I recall looking to Piers, and found him in the thrall of the great king, and I believe several of the men who had fought beside the old man, wiped away tears as they listened.

When Piers and I spoke later, he appeared to be in complete thrall of my father, much to my annoyance.

"Do you not feel the fire in your guts when you listen to him in full force? Such a man I will gladly follow to Scotland."

"You will be in constant danger," I said, immediately feeling foolish for pointing out the obvious. "You long for it, don't you, Perrot? The fighting, the glory, vanquishing the enemy. My father will drive you hard, you may not survive."

What I had hoped to achieve by this, I am now not sure, but it irked me that Piers would so quickly follow my father into battle, knowing that as a result he and I could well be parted forever.

Piers took my hand in his. "You will also see fighting, Ned." I loved the familiar term he used for my name. "We will be victorious. Both of us, glorious in our brave deeds, revered and worshipped as heroes. Minstrels will sing of our valour; women will swoon at our feet." He laughed while he held my face in his hands; his eyes glittered like stars and his face beamed. He was truly eager to reach Scotland and, while I felt a great pride that this was the man I would call brother, I also felt alarm that he would come to harm. Perhaps at that moment I truly realised how important he was to me.

He would laugh and long for the fight to come, but I knew I would feel a great unease until this campaign was over, and he had survived it. Surely fate would not play such a cruel trick on me; to have found one so important to me, only to loose him tragically. I believe maybe it was my memory of this time that sowed the seeds of doubt I always had about warfare. Be it for French land or to quell the Scots, it mattered little to me then. I was not fearful of battle, yet I saw the futility of it.

To mention as much to my father would bring down all manner of fury, another opportunity to doubt my competence; yet, each time he left to carry on his endless quest to vanquish the Scots into submission, I prayed that it would be the last. I had not been raised to doubt my purpose; my father had devoted the majority of his life to warfare, and in my turn, although less skilled than he, I accepted the purpose of killing one's enemies: slay or be slain.

The campaign in Scotland that followed some time after was brutal, and to my eternal shame, I had more than a hand in the suffering meted out to those who the king deemed traitors. I can close my eyes and see the starving children huddled together, waiting for fathers who lay rotting on the battlefields; peasants and nobility were all classed as enemies, and the punishment was the same for both. Bruce himself had fled the field at Methven, and yet we pursued his family ruthlessly. God help me, forgive me for my hand in all that bloodshed. I gave it no concern at the time.

+++

Edward hung his head. Clearly reliving such carnage, and particularly his role in it, was a burden that he had carried alone. He had never confessed, never considered how scarred he had become as a result, and yet now he seemed almost broken by it. He turned his face upwards to the sky and, breathing in deeply, he shut his eyes for a moment or two before continuing.

From that time onwards, Piers was seldom out of my thoughts, and indeed we were always in each other's company. We would talk endlessly, quite often late into the night. Together we drank, laughed, gambled and roistered with our small band of friends. I do not believe I was ever as happy again as I was during those heady early days of our friendship. As I recall it now, it seems foolish to be that reliant on another's companionship to make you happy, and yet it was true that I hated to be parted from him. I was young, I was foolish and I was headstrong. Why does fate cast us the hardest lessons when we are too young to know how to deal with them? I had no idea, but I truly wanted Perrot with me always.

The confidence that I gained from spending time with Piers made even my dealings with my father almost bearable. My friend cautioned me to act with as much understanding as I could. He was old, and no man could reach the age he had and not feel worried and burdened by the weight of responsibility. I tried always in those discussions that took place between us, to be both considerate and patient.

I arrived for just such a summons one evening. He was seated by a roaring fire, alone but for a few attendants, who I sensed were grateful for my intervention. He had the maudlin, almost bemused look that indicated he had drunk heavily. His speech was slurred, and the blink of his eyes was slow and heavy. No doubt he would be irritable; indeed, he was angry most of the time, and only the elders of his court could recall the lively, fearless, enormous figure that had led them into so many victorious conflicts.

I speak of his legendary anger, and yet I too inherited this Angevin temperament, although mine was rarely long-lived. I forgave easily. He, however, raged at everyone in sight, and thus to be told to be gone from his presence was an order that many were more than happy to obey.

Wine had a large part to play in his moods. I drank often, but always for the pleasure of it, and to prolong a happy mood. My father, by contrast, drank to forget, to lose himself, and ultimately to try and make sense of his growing fear of a life somehow unfulfilled. Many said that the death of my mother had wrought a great change in him, and I knew he missed her keenly. Whilst

I had never doubted his fondness for his younger wife, she was no substitute. Many thought, as I, that his endless campaigns against Scotland had wrought an almost constant compulsion to break their indomitable will.

As I aged, I subsequently had little patience with his wine-fuelled ramblings. The future was important to me, let the past be done with. How ironic that now I too have only the past to dwell on.

He motioned with his hand for me to sit opposite him. "I summoned you some time ago, boy," he growled at me. "I will not be kept waiting."

"I apologise, father, I rode later than I expected and was only just having my bath when your servant arrived."

"A bath?" he shouted at me derisively. "A bath! By Christ's wounds boy, a bloody bath. Women bath, if they must. You would pretty yourself with soaps and scents like some damsel. Who the hell taught you to bath?"

A quick smile threatened to break the serious face I always wore for such occasions with my father. I thanked my good fortune that the dull light in the room afforded me the disguise of my amusement.

He leaned unsteadily forward, framing his slow words with all conviction. "Prince though you are..." he began, nodding blearily, as though to confirm his words, and belching loudly. He raised a finger in preparation to announce some momentous decision. He then smiled at nothing in particular; his train of thought appeared to have run out and he abandoned it. He lazily brought his goblet to his lips many times, pausing, as though to say something, and then deciding otherwise.

"My lady, the queen, believes I am too hard on you, boy, thinks that I should be kinder. Kinder! Yet you know, don't you Edward, that I am raising you to be a king after I am gone, someone who will be feared by those bastards in Scotland, someone to put a boot up the arse of that French whoreson Philip?" He returned to his wine for some moments. I wanted to run from that oppressive room, from his drunken ramblings. I had little tolerance of him sober, and thus this mood was already becoming torturous.

"You will marry that bastard's whelp, what's her name?"

"Isabella, father."

"Yes, that one. Still a child, of course, but do not fear that, she will be ripe for the marriage bed. Old enough to bleed, old enough to butcher, eh boy?"

He disgusted me. Ours was not a relationship where we could exchange bawdy tavern talk. I had little experience of women, and admit that the bleed of which he spoke I was largely ignorant of. I felt nothing but revulsion.

"Some tell me you have a fondness for that Gascon squire you are always with."

I felt a sudden coldness within, although I could feel a heat rising in my cheeks.

"There is talk..." His voice trailed off into his wine goblet, and I prayed that he would take the subject no further. "They say he is a catamite! Is he boy?

Does he lust over you, as I am told, or is it you?" He leaned towards me, one bushy eyebrow raised, his lazy eyes suddenly piercing. "Is it you that invites that pretty boy to your bed?" His drunken stare felt as though it pinned me to my chair.

I thank the lord God that I was able to restrain myself from knocking the goblet from his hand. Rarely had I hated him as much as I did at that moment. I fought desperately to find the words to defend both my own and Piers's honour, but in those few moments my father had sunk back into his seat, and he let out a loud sigh and muttered something about how the love of a good woman would be the making of me and I must ensure that I sired as many whelps of my own as I could.

I made the conscious decision to hold back any retort or explanation now he had started to talk of my mother, "God bless her sweet soul," his voice breaking at the words. It seemed then as though he was barely aware of me. I stared moodily into the fire and the hypnotic draw it always has, almost bewitching, fathomless and cruel.

When I looked up, the old man was snoring gently, the wine goblet resting unsteadily on his knee. I looked at him for a moment; forlorn and pathetic, old and tired. I sighed again and, reaching over, I took the goblet from his hand, placing it on the nearby table. It curiously occurred to me then that I had never held his hand; the coarse, hard skin was alien to me, and I brushed a finger lightly over his now unclenched fist.

I had heard much from my close companions about their fathers, and most seemed to have enjoyed a strict yet compatible bond. Such was the life of a king and his prince - duty prevails.

I gave the sleeping figure one last look, of pity, and I walked from the chamber, closing the door quietly behind me.

CHAPTER TWO

There were, of course, many in my father's court who took time to voice their condemnation of what they saw as the vices of the age – our age! The friendships I made invariably drew interest, most of it fleeting. Piers Gaveston however seemed to warrant more attention than others, and both he and I were not without detractors. Such was the business at court – you will no doubt be aware of it, Manuel – that gossip would always eventually find the ear of the king. And so it was that my father learnt that I was becoming less and less like the son he had intended me to be.

I need look no further than my nemesis Langton to find the instigator of the poisonous words dripped frequently into my father's ear. I feared that the king would again severely restrict my allowance, yet having only some weeks prior granted me the valuable duchy of Aquitaine, my reliance on the exchequer was significantly less than it had been. No, the bishop's dislike of me was to take a far more personal turn.

My father had approved of Piers in those early days. "An able future commander, noble and brave," he stated. He had seldom seen one so young that had the skill at combat that the Gascon had. "Strive to be like this young man, my son and I will be proud." He honoured Piers by this acknowledgement, and it did not go unnoticed by many of the barons. Indeed, my cousin Thomas, now Earl of Lancaster, stared at Piers with a look of envy. I did not think it of any importance at the time; only later was I to realise that this dislike would manifest itself into such tragic circumstances. Hate simmered in my cousin's mind, and there it festered, allowed to grow into a venomous hatred.

Relations with my cousin had not always been cold; he and his brother Henry were sons of my father's brother, Edmund, and both older than I. Thomas was a striking figure, tall and broad shouldered, with a strong jaw, small sparkling eyes. His hair was black, swept back off his face and tied in a queue that rested on the nape of his neck. Thomas and I had enjoyed each other's company and often hunted together. He had at one time been determined to instruct me to the sport of jousting. I had ridden a horse for as long as I can recall, but the joust was something I could never fully enjoy.

We had been friends then; now age and responsibility had altered our once close relationship, until I felt our familial connection awkward and his presence overbearing. When in each other's company, I was aware of his general animosity and contempt towards Piers.

Thomas would enjoy one turn of events however that rather besmirched Piers's reputation with the old king. Following victory over the Scots, I announced my intention to leave that cold, harsh land and head towards Canterbury. I had written to Piers that my intention would be to finally meet my two baby half-brothers, Thomas and Edmund. Indeed, I was certain that these new additions to his brood had invigorated the king enough to enter into more warfare in Scotland. I welcomed the chance to spend some time with my stepmother, and Piers's company would be a welcome addition.

I was slightly confused to be told that the messenger I had sent with my letter to Piers had returned and needed to speak with me. I recall the sudden coldness that gripped at my stomach, and I felt physically sick. Surely he was safe. Please God, he had not been killed or badly injured even. Surely I would have been told. I would not have been surprised had my cousin brought such happy tidings himself; how he would relish the opportunity. So many thoughts, each more violent and tragic that the one before, assailed me as I prepared to react as nobly as possible to the impending tragic news.

The man entered, falling to one knee and handing me a letter – with my seal upon it!

"Is this some jest?" I questioned him. "You have returned with the same letter I entrusted you to deliver into the hands of Sir Piers Gaveston." I bade the man rise as he explained fully.

"I could not deliver the letter, my lord, as Sir Piers had already left for France."

"For France? Why?" I was unaware there were dealings for which my father would send Sir Piers to France.

The messenger, however, continued, "Forgive me, sire, but it seems that Sir Piers - along with my lord Hereford, Sir Roger Mortimer and others - left to take part in a tournament. They are, as a result, in bad favour with your father, the king."

After questioning him on some irrelevant details, I tossed the man a coin and dismissed him. To leave for a tournament – abroad especially, and without the permission of the king - was folly indeed. My father would be furious.

I was hardly less furious myself! Not a word to me of his intent, I had wanted us to visit Northampton together, I had not seen him since he had departed for Scotland, and yet...

I felt suddenly stupid. Why should he not go? We were not bound to one another beyond our close friendship. He had, on more than one occasion, reminded me he need explain himself to none but his king! It was true, I could not argue with the logic of it, but I was sorry he had not even thought to send me word of his intentions.

The following weeks were torturous, the long train of my retinue barely stayed long on any stop we made; and I gave very little attention to the missives from my father, some demanding whether I was aware that my friends had decided to leave the country without his permission. I gave his anger no heed.

I longed to see Piers again, longed to hold him close and bind him to me. It was then I realised that maybe that was what I should do. He was more my brother than the two new half-brothers, closer than my sisters certainly. I would create our own brotherhood! Make him as much my brother as if he had been borne by my own mother. I felt elated at the ingenuity of my idea. All that was now needed would be to persuade the king to pardon the folly of these rogues.

In this regard, my own step-mother was to prove my friend again, and it was through her intervention that the old king begrudgingly issued a pardon, with a furious caution that his benevolence would not be granted a second time for such an offence. It was thus, suitably chastened and grateful, that Piers would return to me. I would discuss my idea of our committal to one another soon, but firstly I wanted to bestow upon him a gift that would at last make him an equal if not greater than those who made up my innermost circle of companions.

Meanwhile, I was relieved of the burden of warfare. I was pleased to hear that my father was proud of my conduct in the recent conflict with Scotland, but I had little stomach for the destruction of men who are sent to an early grave by their commanders. I had seen too many lifeless bodies, and was sorely afflicted by the futility of it all, but such was the way of life – and death. I did what I could for the family of any of my closer comrades who had been slain in battle, but I was not a born fighter.

I returned to Langley and, with a rare sense of freedom, threw myself into the physical, exhausting work on this most beautiful estate. The workers had long become used to me stripping to the waist and toiling with the loggers, thatchers and blacksmiths. This work was my joy, and although my working amongst them had become a familiar sight, they were never completely at their ease. I would invariably encourage them to swim with me in the lake, or compete with me in a test of strength, yet they did not experience the joy of it as I did. After all, they could swim at any time, and with their own kind. I felt their discomfort but, try as I might, I was unable to put them at their ease. I was happy to be with those that my cousin Thomas treated with such derision – the commoners. Perhaps I envied their simplistic lifestyle.

I had one morning risen early and headed down to the lower fields to help, as I had promised, in the digging of some new ditches. The picture must have been an amusing one; my manservant helped me strip and exchanged my formal tunic for woollen hose and thick, tough boots. It was a sight that the workers and servants on the estate were used to. As a boy, I had been fascinated by skill and hard work that went into maintaining these vast lands.

Once appropriately attired, I threw myself into the work. The air was cold that morning, a frost had settled on the ground making the soil beneath hard and unyielding, but I had soon built up a healthy sweat.

So immersed in my task was I that I did not hear or see a group of horsemen cantering along the road leading up to the palace itself. Nor was I aware that one of their number had broken off from the rest, and was headed down to the field where I and my fellow workers toiled. I had not even noticed the hush that had descended as the lone horseman approached.

"So, my prince," said a familiar voice, "no sooner are you denied my steadying influence than you fall back into disreputable behaviour! Can I not trust you to...?"

I jumped up and flung myself at Piers Gaveston, almost weeping with joy.

"Sire, please!" he implored, pushing me away with affected irritation. "My new doublet, ruined from that dirt on your chest."

I punched him playfully. "You shall have a hundred just like it, my brother," I countered, and yet I censured him even at this moment of our reunion. "You impenitent bastard! How could you just abandon me here alone and bereft of your counsel, such as it is? Not a word of your intent. For once my father and I are agreed that your behaviour is…."

Piers had fallen to his knees in front of me. "Forgive me, my prince," he hung his head in shame. It was all I could do not to stroke my hand over his black wavy hair. "I am undone," he continued. "Alas, I have no answer other than the selfish desire to enrich myself. I will go, it was foolish of me to come here and expect you to welcome me back into your service after such deception."

I took hold of his collar, raising him up to look into those deep, fathomless eyes. "Piers," I said, "enough!" I could feel the displeasure drain from my face and I hugged him to me again, almost with a fierce grip. How could I ever be angry at him? One look at his sweet expression and it was I who was undone.

We both laughed, suddenly, our delight breaking the tension that threatened to ruin our reconciliation. I was aware that the work party, with whom I had up until then been happily toiling, were now silent and embarrassed at the scene before them. I left them to the remainder of the task, sent the manservant on ahead with the horse and, with my arm around Piers's shoulder, walked joyfully on towards the castle, my happiness complete.

Daylight streamed through the windows of my chamber; something about the sun and its warmth made the spring and summer so welcome to me. To watch the deer, hear the birds. I had a fascination with nature, and enjoyed questioning the gamekeepers and gardeners about types of flower and deer, so often to be found around the perimeters of the castle grounds. I would spend time with my grooms, too. Having learned to ride from an early age, of course, I was comfortable around them; and I had now learned the art of shoeing the horses myself, much to the surprise of the farrier. It felt good to be free of the shackles of duty.

Later that day, Piers lay on the bed in my chamber, picking at some strands of silk from the covering, while my valets bathed me and proceeded to dress me in clothes more befitting of a prince. I watched him now and noted a slight sadness in him. He looked lost in thought, almost troubled. I knew he hated inactivity, as much as I did myself, yet I had the arduous physical work which I enjoyed so much. Such work was not for this Gascon, he would complain about the heat, the dust, his ruined tunic, and he had been aghast at the state of the peasant's clothes that I wore while carrying out the task of which even he could not explain. At one point, he had picked up my discarded hose with a look of complete distaste, pinching the material as he held it at arm's length before dropping it as though it bore the contagion of leprosy. I smiled at him, he returned the smile with a grin, a look of completely misplaced innocence. How I loved him.

"I don't think I could have borne one further day without you," I said.

"I felt as though I would perish away when I heard of my father's fury with you having left to travel to France for a tournament. What were you thinking?"

"Alas, my prince, I was never one given to thinking. The need to be in the cut and thrust of the fighting and maiming was a struggle to which I easily succumbed."

"As apposed to single-armed combat, at which you were just as likely to be injured or killed," I countered.

"Well, if you insist on seeing the morbid side of things, then I cannot argue. Yet, I am here now, all in one piece, and with some significant victories in the jousts. You would have been proud of me."

"I am always proud of you, Perrot, yet your recklessness alarms me."

Piers laughed, rolling onto his back and sighing. He kicked his legs up in an attempt to reach the canopy above the bed, and I wondered – not for the first time – what kind of a child he had been! He loved Langley, easily as much as I, and I felt here we could be alone, away from prying eyes and suspicious courtiers. Here we could just be ourselves. It was not easy of course. By virtue of who I was, I would rarely be without various courtiers, servants and such, and I began to ensure that, when I wanted to be left alone, none would gainsay me. I adopted this same fashion with some success when I later became king. Much harder though it was when the king must be ever-accessible.

"Now I am back in favour with your father," he stated, "I am expected to return to his court. We shall have but a few days to enjoy ourselves."

I sighed in resignation. It was true that I would be expected to join my father soon, and yet this seemed cruel to speak of such things when he had only just arrived. I dismissed my attendants with a wave of my hand, and as soon as the last man closed the chamber door, I assumed a more serious approach.

"I've missed you, my brother," I said solemnly. "My days are darker than the night without you. We must never be apart again."

"Ned," he began, but I talked over him.

"I mean it, Perrot, I am lost without you, the sunshine means nothing for I am cold within. The dark nights are long and tortuous. You ask why I work tirelessly at such activity that no prince should indulge in, but the energy tires me so that I may lapse into exhausted sleep rather than sit before a roaring fire and stare into the flames, lost in the thought of you."

There followed a long silence. Had I said more than I should have? No, I meant every word. I wanted him to know how I felt. Of course we had on many occasions declared our affection for one another, but this was different. Life was less exciting without him, the idyllic days at Langley meant nothing to me if he was not with me to enjoy them. I had other companions of course, but they were not like Piers Gaveston, not like my brother.

He swung his legs off the bed and walked over to me, almost petulantly, like a scolded child, but as he knelt before me, I could see his cheeks were wet with tears.

"Perrot, what ails you? Forgive me if I have said aught that…" This time it was he who broke in.

"My dearest, darling Ned. I missed you more than I can say. You maybe mistake my frivolous behaviour as disinterest, yet it is not that I do not wish us to be together." He seemed to be desperate to find the right way of expressing his feelings, but he continued, "Yet, don't you see, my beloved prince, that you call me brother, but you know – no, let me finish, I beg you. You know I am nothing but a squire. Your father accepted me to be knighted by you, one of the proudest, happiest days of my life, but that does not make me your equal, of course. Neither am I anything at his court other than a Gascon soldier who has found favour with the prince. I am a drifter, Ned, and ever shall be. In time, our love will sour and I will disappoint you. I am nothing."

"No!" I said crossly. "You will never disappoint me. I will raise you so high that you will outrank all others; you shall have titles, land, anything I can give and share with you shall be yours."

Piers smiled sadly, and raised those beautiful green eyes to meet mine. "Ned," he said softly, "let me stay with you tonight. Let us drink wine and sing and laugh, and collapse with satisfied exhaustion when we are done. Let there be no talk of war, no Scotland, no court, no rules, and most importantly – no woollen hose that smell like a pig's pen, and do absolutely nothing to show off your fine calves!"

We both laughed loudly. It was impossible not to be infected with this enthusiasm. He suddenly clutched me to him, and together we danced, knocking carelessly into tables, upsetting wine goblets, until we were too overcome with mirth and collapsed onto my bed. He rose suddenly and from his cloak that he had flung to one side when we had returned to my chambers, he took out an object covered in rich velvet cloth, pinned with a small metal clasp. He climbed back onto the bed beside me, and handed the package to me.

"For you, my prince," he stated with as much solemnity as he could manage.

I looked first at him and then to the package. "Ah, what trickery is this, Perrot?" I said with caution. My Gascon brother was known for his practical jokes, I had been on the receiving end of several myself.

For just a brief moment, though, Piers seemed almost offended.

"Forgive me, Perrot, but I -" My voice broke off as I opened the package to reveal a small dagger sheathed in soft rich leather. I drew out the weapon and gasped at the beauty of its blade, which was engraved with patterns so intricate I would not be able to describe them, but the beauty of the piece was surely its hilt. Made from ivory, it was shaped as a dragon, the serpent's trunk and tail coiled around the tip in exquisite scales and claws, and breathing the metal blade as its fire.

I have held jewels, diamonds – all manner of precious stones. I had fought with swords forged in Castile with pommels of pearl, yet I swear I had seen nothing so perfect in all my life.

For some moments I said nothing, until Piers could bear the silence no longer.

"Are you displeased with it, my prince? I had hoped you would find it to your liking."

I hugged him suddenly, and felt that I would cry from the emotion welling inside me. "Perrot, it is the most exquisite thing I have ever seen, it is truly beautiful. Surely the expense of it though…"

"Indeed," he assured me proudly with great satisfaction, "I had it made to my own design. Forged in France, so you see I was not just enjoying the tournaments, I was making enough money to bring my prince the finest gift. So, you will think of me every time you have cause to stab or slash someone with it!"

We laughed together again, this time it was my tears that were shed in joy.

Later that evening, we drank together and Perrot proceeded to mimic some of the older members of my father's court: Despenser - sticking out his belly and walking with a lazy gait, licking his lips. It had never occurred to me that he did so until that moment that Piers aped him; Langton - his pursed lips and his birdlike walk. I delighted in his creation.

"You are truly wasted, Perrot!" I managed to say between guffaws of delight. "You should be a mummer!"

We sat on the floor of my chamber and played dice, at which he won a rather large amount from me. He told me of the conquests in France, and the fear that my father would banish him from the kingdom for his involvement in the group that had left for Scotland without their king's permission.

"I would have come and found you," I said, and I believe even now, that I would have done so.

As we drifted into a companionable silence, I again took up the dagger -and had a bold idea, but one that I was suddenly sure would bond us together for eternity.

"Let us exchange a blood bond, Perrot. Let us be truly brothers in every sense. It is what I desperately wish for. Let the first blood on this beautiful blade be yours and mine."

He looked at me without saying a word, his eyes glittering from the candlelight. I suddenly feared he would refuse but, while still fixing me with his bewitching gaze, he rolled up the sleeve of his shirt, exposing the skin of his tanned arm, strong and darkened with black hair. I did the same, my skin paler than his, but my arm thicker with muscle and dusted with my fairer hair.

Almost in a trance, I removed the blade from its sheath, and we both looked down as I took hold of his arm and placed the blade in position. It was with a surprisingly steady hand that I carefully carved out our initials *E P* entwining the letters, a symbolic decoration of our brotherhood. He winced only slightly as the blood coursed down to his elbow before dripping onto his leg. I then took the blade and deftly carved the same initials into my own forearm.

He whispered suddenly, "Do not press too hard, Ned, too deep a cut there can be fatal!"

I then lowered my head, and gently kissed the wound I had made on his arm. The hair from my beard must have stung against the bloody flesh as he jolted slightly. When I looked up it was to find him staring at me as though lost in thought, the intensity on his face was a look I had never seen from him before.

With his blood on my lips, I then turned to my bed, and taking the now soiled blade, I cut from the bed covering a long strip of the velvet cloth. Piers took it from me, pre-empting my intention. We then placed our forearms together so the stinging wounds met, and he then gently laid the strip of material over our arms and wound it around our limbs, until they were loosely bound together as one.

We continued to look into each others eyes as I spoke softly to this man with whom I had entered into such a solemn pact - "Nunc et usque in aeternum."

Perrot's eyes filled with tears as he spoke in affirmation of my oath. "Yes, my prince - my brother, 'Now and forever.'"

+++

"God's death! Get you from my sight!" My father bellowed at me. I thanked the almighty that there were few in attendance on the king that afternoon to witness my humiliation. Those that were in my father's chamber that day discreetly made for an exit. Even that odious sycophant Langton, whilst no doubt revelling in my shame, slunk back into the shadows. He had himself been on the receiving end of my father's rage on occasion, and those that had, rarely forgot the experience.

The old man's eyes flashed threateningly, and I watched his large hands clenching together as his grey, whiskered face trembled in fury. It was I who evoked such anger in him that day, and whilst I had prepared what I would say, I felt my resolve ebbing away. I had decided to speak to my father about some lands for Piers. Some endowment that would elevate his status at court, whilst assuring him of income. I had suggested that we could bestow on him the title of Earl of Cornwall, and all the land associated with it. A low, sinister chuckle came from the shadows where Langton lurked, like a sinister black spider.

I had entered the room with as much of a confident air as I could manage. Even at times when we were in accord, my father and I had a volatile relationship, the famous Angevin temperament present in both of us.

He had been in conversation with Langton, who deigned to offer a quick bow of his head in respectful recognition. My father had seemed in an irritable mood, and I had started to speak before I realised that I should have chosen a better occasion.

Having heard me out, and issued his warning to leave, he was not best pleased that I had persisted with my request. His grey, tired eyes became transfixed on me. His oaths were nothing new but, having told me to get out of his sight, he had glared at me for some moments before he stood and, within two strides, had hold of me by my collar, which he bunched up into his gnarled fist. When he spoke, it was with a cold fury.

"And what makes you think that I would agree to allow you to bestow such an honour upon this Gascon squire? Why would I entitle such to one who is not of this Royal family? The Earldom of Cornwall will be bestowed upon your younger brother, it is not there just to be given away to someone who, although we think well of him, has none of the heritage of the noble barons in this land! Never, boy, do you hear me? Never!"

He pushed me away and I corrected my shirt, but I was not finished.

"He shall have Ponthieu, then!" I declared with as much bravado as I could muster. "Ponthieu is in my ownership, it came to me through my mother and it is therefore mine to give as I see fit. Yes, I shall...!"

Suddenly, I was staggering backwards after a shove from my father. I landed on the floor unhurt, but he rounded on me again, kicking out, and I doubled over in pain, winded. He then reached down and had hold of me by my hair. He brought his face within inches of my own, I could hear the evidence of a congested chest, feeling the spray of saliva that collected in the corners of his gnarled lips.

"You, who have neither the good sense or ability to win by stealth or battle, any lands for yourself, will not gift those you have been given to one of your squires!" He glared at me through almost demonic eyes. He coughed wheezily from the exertion as he pushed me away for a second time, and returned to his chair.

By now, I was hurt, both in pride and body, but whilst on every other occasion when he had lost his temper with me I had made a hasty exit, my own temper was rising as I got angrily to my feet, snarling at him, "When you are dead, I shall give Piers Gaveston everything but a crown. While you rot in your grave, I will dance with joy!"

I turned and stalked from the chamber, ignoring the roar that followed me. I was now in as much of a fury as my father, a fury that could not be sated; I reached my chambers and when one of my pages approached me, I grabbed him by the neck and flung him at the door. He hit it with a gasp of shock as well as pain. He then got to his feet and scampered out in fear for his life. I recall hurling furniture around, smashing anything that would break, sweeping to the floor books, flagons, goblets, anything I could lay hands on. Eventually, I was exhausted and sank to my knees, covering my face.

I was aware that someone had entered the chamber, and I looked up to see Piers standing staring at me, and around the room in disbelief.

"My prince, your servants really should tidy up better, just look at the mess they have left!"

I glanced up at him through tears of fury. His face did not alter, but when he spoke, it was calmly and quietly.

"I assume that I am not to be addressed in future as the Earl of Cornwall?"

I buried my face in my hands and groaned, relating to him the story of the war with my father.

Piers continued as though the matter was of no significance "How silly!" he stated. "We can't even sit and drown our sorrows, as – well...!" He motioned a hand around the desolation in the chamber. "We had better dine in my chamber this evening, at least there are chairs and tables which are thankfully all fixed together. Shall we extend an invitation to your father, do you think? No, perhaps not." He extended his hand to me, and helped me to my feet. His eyes sparkled and he winked, his mouth twitched slightly as though a grin would break from them. His humour at times was devilish, even now when he surely knew our cause was a lost one. Yet in a way he almost revelled in the chaos that the mere mention of his name created; if he was hated at least it proved he was not to be ignored.

I had, of course, to abandon the idea of bestowing such a generous endowment to my beloved brother. The king had refused to see me, and I was for once without my usual peacemaker – my stepmother, Marguerite. As long as the intention was to hand the Earldom of Cornwall to either one of her sons, she was never going to champion my cause.

Worse was to come however and, with the passing of several days, just when I had begun to think that my father's fury had burnt itself out – as my own did – both Piers and I were horrified by the king's next move.

I was informed by my father's lackey Langton, that Piers was to be exiled from the court indefinitely. I could feel emotion well within me as the poisonous bishop explained, to his great joy, my father's wishes were irreversible.

"Of course, sire," he said with that whining, almost lisping voice of his, "I naturally sought to suggest an accord could possibly be reached with yourself and the king regarding the Gasc...- forgive me – Sir Piers! - some way surely that would please all concerned and put right this most disagreeable situation."

"How good of you, bishop," I almost spat the words.

He rung his long-fingered, bony hands together, much like a great cat that would then jump and scratch at your face. He inclined his head. "I wish only to mend those bridges that have become broken. My dearest wish is that there should be peace between all."

The impulse to smack the supercilious smile from his face was almost more than I could control, yet I sighed and sunk deeper into my chair. "Just tell me, bishop, if you please."

Langton smiled again. He indicated a seat. "May I sit?"

I cast him a withering look. "Only when I decide if you are staying," I stated, waiting a few seconds before I testily waved assent.

"Your father, the king, has this day met again with the magnates of the realm and they are – fearful that you would, as a result of your close friendship with Sir Piers, despoil the realm. It has been agreed, therefore, that your friend shall henceforth be exiled to Gascony until such time as his majesty deems fit to recall him."

My eyes must have flashed dangerously, because Langton appeared uncomfortable, and in fact flinched when I rose to reach for some wine to steady my growing desperation.

"'Despoil the realm'?" I was incredulous at the absurd over reaction. "I will go to my father..." I began, but Langton raised a hand in caution.

"Think wisely, sire," he intoned. "Having decided on this action, your father will not be dissuaded."

"He despises someone who has grown close to me, he regards all my companions with disdain - Piers especially so," I countered.

The bishop arched a bushy eyebrow and smiled again, if one could call it a smile.

"If I may, Lord Edward, your father has concerns - not just for your...personal favouritism of Sir Piers. In truth, I believe his concern is not the affection that you hold for the Gascon, but that you would lavish on him lands, estates of your own, titles even that would create division among the magnates."

How Langton enjoyed every malicious word that dripped from that evil tongue. I sank back further into my chair, furious at the indignity of it all.

"The Gascon..."

"Sir Piers!" I interrupted, pointedly reminding him.

The bishop gave a pained expression of his folly and inclined his head.

"Quite so, my lord. Sir Piers will have his expenses paid from the exchequer, and in addition the king has agreed to grant him sufficient funds while he awaits recall. Might I suggest that discussing this again with him may well cause him to rethink his generosity? Furthermore, I am bid to tell you that, in addition to this, you personally are to swear oath that you will not receive Sir Piers under any circumstances, unless he is recalled by the king alone."

I could have howled at the injustice of it all, but I could think only of was my distress at Piers being gone from me. At the time, I am ashamed to recall, I gave very little thought to my beloved brother's feelings. I was appalled that the magnates had helped to decide my darling Perrot's fate. I would live to become accustomed to such an arrangement.

Langton had been watching me for some time as I became lost in my own thoughts. When I again glanced at him, he grinned, his thin bloodless lips parted to reveal small, greying teeth.

"Of course, sire, I have done what I can to minimise the distress I know you are feeling, but alas…" He shrugged his bony shoulders and spread his hands in desperation, "…his majesty would not relent. Forgive me, sire, I did all that I could."

At that moment I was unsure by whom, given such a wide array of choice, I was most disgusted. Yet it interested me that, while enjoying my discomfort, the bishop considered it important to have me believe that he worked on my behalf. Was he, then, the first rat to desert a ship that was slowly sinking? Was there reason to suggest that he would not always work for the same master? A foot in both camps perhaps? Langton was as much a diplomat as he was a rogue; I longed for the day when I could deal with him as I wished. Yet at the time I could not have cared less about his machinations.

"On the twenty-sixth of this month of February, you are summoned to meet with the king and others here at this Priory at Lanercost, to swear upon the Holy Sacrament that you abide by your father's instruction," the bishop announced with barely concealed glee. He studied me carefully, and I could have readily stood up and boxed his ears.

There was, of course, very little I could say, other than dismiss my father's crony. Once he had gone I beat my clenched fist on the arm of my chair, feeling the sting of tears that began to well, and yet these were not only tears of despair and sadness, but anger too. A page entered, bringing wine, and made the error of overfilling the goblet. As the liquid spilled over, I glared at the fool and immediately lashed out, knocking him to the ground where, before he could get up, I kicked at him in a fury I could barely suppress.

I must have railed and inflicted blows upon him, ignoring his cries. In an effort to escape from the room, he had tripped, and yet I dragged him up again, and continued to thrash him. My manservant, Will, entered the room upon hearing the commotion. He was the only servant who would have dared get in my way, but this he did, and probably saved the boy from serious harm by telling him to run! I raised a fist as though to strike, and though Will has himself been on the receiving end of my anger before now, he was so often the voice of reason.

"My lord!" he exclaimed.

I stopped, my arm in mid air, and glared at him. We locked eyes for a moment. I was panting from the exertion, but did not strike. After a moment more, I felt my knees weaken, and I fell to the floor exhausted. Will put an arm around me, helping me to a couch, where I lay, as miserable as I could ever recall being.

My family's notorious Angevin temper had cost many a servant a brutal beating, but invariably I felt utter horror later, when my temper had cooled. I too had been on the end of my father's fury. I was therefore horrified when seeing the servant boy some days later sporting bruises, a swollen mouth and a blackened eye. I summoned him and gladly paid him a year's wages by way of apology. I did not have to do so, of course, but as a rule I looked after those who looked after me. Moreover, money - I believe - should be spent when appropriate; a good deed done, an acrobat's performance, an actor's recital, the glorious sound from a chorus of gifted singers. My relationship with money was ever a troubled one.

It would not, however, improve my current situation. Piers and I were to be parted and, no matter how much I raged at the injustice of it all, there would be no changing my father's mind. My only hope, therefore, was that the enforced separation would not be for long. It seemed that the more I dreaded each day being one nearer to his exile, the faster they seemed to pass.

I was able to delay the inevitable to some degree, and I begrudgingly respected my father for not insisting on Piers's immediate departure. How much of this was due to him or my stepmother, I would never know. Yet, the Queen had changed slightly in her attitude to me since I had wanted to bestow on my dearest friend the title that I knew had been promised to my half brother. We never seemed to recover the closeness we had once enjoyed, which - as with so much else - I regretted.

Those last days with Piers, before this enforced parting, were painful for both of us, made only bearable by the hope that the day would soon come when we could be together once again. God forgive me, but I longed for the day when I would inherit the throne, not for the want of power and control, but to be able to make decisions and choices without heeding others. I ached for those days to come before Piers forgot all about me.

Little did I know then, as I prayed for the day when power would be mine, that what I longed for was, in truth, a doomed inheritance.

+++

I thanked God that my dignity remained intact as I proceeded to swear on oath during that dismal ceremony at Lanercost that I would not, under any circumstances, advise my beloved brother to return to England until such time as the king, my father, permitted it. Piers spoke nobly and with conviction and in complete deference to the king, and my father was satisfied.

I hated the old man so much on that day as he drew all his gruff energy into the proclamation and nodded in satisfaction that his actions had indeed broken his son's heart. It was not lost on me either, that my father did not treat my Gascon brother with any contempt or anger; it was obvious to me that this was less about a favoured companion, and more about his exasperation with me.

Already he was preparing for another assault on Scotland. "I need you with me my son," was his pathetic reasoning. "We must have no other distractions."

During those all-too-swift days before we were to be parted, Piers and I kept very much to our own company. I assured him often that the exile would not be for long, that when he returned to England we would begin to enjoy all that life had to offer. Piers's imminent departure was made more bearable for him by the prospect of competing in a tournament; and whilst I had no love of the joust and suchlike, it made me happy that he had, at least in the short term, something to look forward to.

By the time of his departure, I had showered all manner of gifts upon Piers and indeed Hugo, his manservant, as well as others in his service who would also leave with him. It was as though in doing so I could feel I had given him enough to make this enforced separation easier for him to bear, to give him some of the comforts he had become used to.

Of course I was aware that Piers's exile would not leave him a total pariah; my father had forced us to part, but I was aware that there was certainly no inference that his banishment of Piers in any way suggested that he had offended the king. He would not necessarily be welcomed in any of the royal courts of Europe, but neither would he be refused their hospitality.

We were a sombre party that rode out of London and headed to Dover and the departure that I feared would break my heart. Spring was in the air, and I cursed the season for its bright skies and cool evenings - times when my brother and I would have enjoyed hunting through the days and long evenings by the fireside, talking of our future plans and the happiness we could enjoy. Now all this seemed so far away as though it were but a distant dream. How on earth could I ever bear to live life without him, even for what I prayed would be a short period? I raged often at the despair of it all, yet Piers, to my great annoyance, seemed to accept the situation with his usual carefree attitude. Only once did he give into his frustration of the banishment, and yet his ire was directed at me rather than my father.

We had dismissed all attendants one evening, and I had paced the room, more anxious now that we had reached Kent and were nearer to his ultimate departure at Dover. Piers sat on the floor before the fireplace, losing himself as he studied the hypnotic flames. When I rose, he reached for the wine jug, draining the last of the sweet liquid into his goblet. He sighed at the lack of refreshment, annoyed both at that, as well as my constant restlessness.

"For the love of God, Ned, do sit! I swear that my head aches at your constant pacing. Here, have some...on no, there is none! I shall call for some more wine."

I swung round at him. "Is it easier, Perrot, if one is drunk? Easier to deal with this living nightmare if you can barely remember what it is?"

He hiccupped, grinned at the surprise spasm and drained his goblet.

"You seem so adjusted to this impending doom, I wish I could find it as easy to bear. Yet you say nothing. Hardly have you said a word in anger about this banishment, not at my father, Langton, the magnates of the court who will all take such comfort from this."

"What more could your father do?" he answered, suddenly abrupt and serious, slurring his words slightly, his eyes fighting the need to close and sleep.

I was incredulous at his remark. "What worse could he have done? You seem ever eager to excuse his behaviour as though you accept this as a necessary step."

"Is it not so, Ned? I am banished from the kingdom, from where I have always been in relatively high favour.

Your father disapproves of the friendship that you and I share, of your affection - an affection that may ultimately lead you to raise up this Gascon knight to where he has no place to be."

"So," I countered, "you would accept this banishment rather than go against his will?"

"What would you have me do?" He had risen now and I could, even in the dim light, see the flashing in his green eyes, sense the temper building within him. I had never known him to be really angry, as he had seen me on many occasions. And whilst I felt disconcerted, I was almost pleased that he would at last stop pretending that this did not hurt him as much as it did me. He moved closer to me until I could reach out and touch him. The over indulgence of wine had loosened his tongue.

"You pout and huff, Ned, you kick, you curse your father for this indignity and indeed my acceptance of his command. So what would you have me do? I can do nothing but obey, or did you imagine that I could refuse to leave? I am banished, Ned. I arrived at the English court with high hopes, despite being nothing but a squire, and having no gift other than a dangerous ability to unhorse an opponent at the tilt, a brave spirit, and a sharp wit. Yet what do I have to show for it? Tell me what, damn you!"

I went to move past him; his verbal onslaught had taken me unaware, but he caught me by the sleeve and roughly pulled me back.

"So!" I screamed back. "This is my doing, is it? This is my folly that has brought us to this..."

"It has brought you to nothing - nothing has changed other than a favourite playmate has been cast aside for you before you can make any grievous mistakes.

You still have the titles, the luxury, you remain the prince who will one day inherit all, and on that day you will give no thought to the Gascon who your father wisely put out of reach. Perhaps I should accept this as a blessing, that at least I will no longer have to endure the snarls and looks of disdain that I currently do. Yet, I tolerate them all - your father, Langton. All this I endure. It is not surrender, it is expediency. The need to survive!"

I tore his hand from my sleeve, and in doing so revealed the vivid wound from our pact. He looked down, noticing it as I did.

"And yet, you tolerated this, Perrot. Was it all a deceit? You could have left at any time. Why stay and endure this torture of which you speak? You have all the world to conquer, you could make your fortune in France, anywhere in Europe would willingly -"

"Because I love you!"

The words, shouted with emotion and fury, silenced all else; for a moment all seemed to be still. He had hung his head, and when he looked up at me again, tears were coursing down his hot cheeks. He then cupped my face in his hands, and stared intently into my eyes as he repeated himself.

"Because I love you, Ned."

We leaned into each other and he kissed me suddenly, with an urgency that I had never experienced before, and I held him close to me as he began to weep, softly at first and then with heart breaking sobs that threatened to burst from him in a torrent. He ran his fingers across the scar of our intertwined initials.

"This scar is only symbolic, my prince. If my heart is ever cut open, the same insignia will be found there, too, etched into my very soul."

We must have stood like this for some time. Piers swayed slightly, as much from his emotional outpouring as the wine, and I helped him to my bed where he lay, spent of all energy. I lay down beside him, cradling him in my arms, and realised that he was frightened, as indeed was I. Racked with emotion, he soon slipped into an exhausted sleep. As he snored gently, I wiped the hair from his forehead and whispered to him that I would welcome him back into my arms soon and we would never be parted again.

+++

Dover was a busy town, and not one for which I felt any particular affection. Our retinue had settled in the great castle, the final stage of a journey that I could forestall no longer. It was no doubt considered appropriate as a place of departure for my beloved brother by being the closest port to mainland Europe. Dear God, they could not wait to be rid of him! The dreaded day of Piers's departure came upon us all too quickly, and I felt almost physically sick as the tragic scene that I had tried to put off played out before me.

Cliffs of white chalk dominated the coast as far as the naked eye could see. The port was thronged with all manner of men, traders, fishermen, all shouting, laughing and going about their daily lives as usual. Administrators thronged the crowds with soldiers keeping order amongst the vast numbers that seemed to come from every direction. The stench of fish and other livestock was oppressive and nauseating. Beggars seemed to be everywhere, only slipping quietly away when their presence was noticed by the guards.

Crowds had of course been restricted for our purpose, kept behind barriers while our cavalcade took up position. Most of the crowd were silently in awe of the grand procession of our small but nonetheless elaborate party. I nodded and smiled, and many waved their hands. I believe they were bewitched by the sight of Piers, with his dark, brooding good looks, and his ever-ready smile. His rich red cloak with its fur-lined trim matched by the splendid red and gold saddlecloth of his horse. To many he must have looked more princely than I, and I was proud of the dignity of his bearing and his gracious manner to all who cheered as we passed by. Under any other circumstances, I would have been happy to venture out with some of the local fishermen, to walk around the prosperous markets. This was, however, no time for such frivolity.

Since the evening when he had shown himself to be as heartbroken as I at this departure, Perrot and I had mutually assured one another that this parting would not be forever. Moreover, his own personal safety was a concern to him. He was a most reluctant seaman, detesting any travel on water, be it a rowing boat on a castle lake in the countryside or the precarious and unpredictable English Channel. I held no such concern, I had mentioned several times on our journey, that the clement weather suggested the crossing would be an easy one.

As we tried to keep each other optimistic about our separation, he was careful to keep his own counsel about what circumstances would precipitate his return to England. It was not believed that the king would change his mind any time soon, and therefore only his death would allow Piers to return safely, but such treasonous talk would have the direst consequences.

It had occurred to me that my father, or indeed Bishop Langton, would have spies amongst our party, and anything in the least sacrilegious would find a ready ear at my father's court. One instruction that would surely have cost me much had it been discovered was my suggestion to Piers that he travel, not to Gascony as intended, but to Crécy in Ponthieu, and there await the news that he could return to England. Dismounting from our horses I embraced him, holding him closely as the time grew nearer to his departure, not wanting to release him for fear I would break down. I breathed in that unique, beautiful fragrance of lavender until I was almost heady from it. I had promised him that I would make this as easy for him as I could. We broke apart and I walked with him to where loading of all his possessions and luggage of his household were now complete. The ship teemed with all manner of chests, boxes and costly tapestries. Large cages of live swans and even herons. A special ornate wooden cage containing two doves – one for each of us, I had declared. All manner of personnel ranging from a chamberlain to run his affairs, yeomen, squires and various servants plus the knights that I prayed to God would protect him in exile – I lived in fear that assassins would follow him and finally ensure he would never return to me. A brief nod from Piers to his faithful Hugo, indicated that he was ready now.

We hugged closely again, and I whispered to him, "This will not be for long. I love you Perrot, always know that."

He returned my embrace, his eyes betraying the strong resolve he had made to remain positive in this most desperate hour of our separation.

"Remember me, my prince," he whispered in my ear. "When the nights seem so long and the days seem dull, I am with you always."

He released his hold on me, turned away and almost bolted up onto the ship, racing up to the prow and leaning over, flashing one more smile as he drew up the sleeve of his tunic and kissed the wound where our initials were scarred. I truly felt my heart would break. I stayed and watched until I could barely see his figure, and then with a heavy heart, I again mounted my horse, riding up to the chalk cliffs to watch as the ship and my broken heart drew slowly apart.

+++

Where could I go after such an ordeal? Langley, of course, where Piers and I had spent so many happy days. I was barely aware of the journey there. Urgent dispatches from my father caught up with me, directing me to rejoin him at Carlisle, where he was assembling the army for another campaign in Scotland.

I felt in no hurry, and ignored the entreaties to a degree. Perhaps I believed that, in doing so, I was making a stand about how I had been virtually forced to agree to Piers's banishment. Perhaps, in hindsight, I should have headed north to meet the king and his army. Instead, I threw myself into the pursuits I loved so much; I swam, worked for a time with many of the farmers, helping them to fence their lands, thatch their cottages. The forge I had built at Langley was a delight, and I instructed the blacksmith to teach me his craft, and I worked sometimes until dusk, arriving back to the palace covered in dirt, my chest and back coursed with sweat. It is there I believe

I have been happiest in my life, almost a world away from the formality, the pressure of duty. In those first few days without Piers, it was my sanctuary. I left eventually and travelled to Lambeth in order to begin the inevitable task of preparing for further war.

I had received letters from Piers – through an intermediary, for fear of our correspondence being misappropriated – and I eagerly broke the seal of a newly arrived missive. I could almost hear his voice say the words. I pictured him as the genial host to the local dignitaries, and felt the pain when he talked of his loneliness in the small hours, when he would wake cold and uncertain and realise again that, at present, he had no home.

I pondered on this as I stood at the hearth in my chamber and, leaning down, committed the parchment to the flames as I usually did, not wishing to trust our written words would not be discovered and retold to my father or Langton. My mind was lost in the flickering fire as the chamber door was flung open.

Two plainly-clothed men entered, both dropping to their knees before me. I was taken aback and glanced up at my principal valet, Will Shene, who had followed the two arrivals into the room.

"What is this?" I began, but one of the men now stepped closer and again dropped to his knee as he held out a letter to me, which I took hesitantly. The seal on the parchment was that of the Earl of Warwick. At that moment, the bearer looked up nervously but spoke calmly and clearly.

"My Lord - the king, your father, is dead."

+++

Brother Alphage sketched a cross at Edward's final words announcing the death of his father before looking up as the monastery bell announced the hour of sext. He had listened with great reverence to all that the hermit had said, finally offering a quiet prayer for the long since dead king of England. The events of which Edward had spoken, had at times been difficult, even uncomfortable to hear, and yet he had nodded with encouragement when his friend's tone had expressed difficulty and supressed any censure he may have felt. It was difficult to imagine this troubled man as almost wishing for his father's demise, that he may at last be rid of the shackles that bound him.

Fieschi had kept his eyes focussed on the former king, looking down only when the hound Perrot rose, shook himself and resettled, with an exhalation of boredom. He had heard some of this story from members of his family that had been nearer to the scene of events that Edward related. Very little had appeared to surprise him, and anything that did was concealed by his inscrutable self control. Unlike the elderly monk, he felt no shock at Edward's words that condemned his father as a tyrant and a bully. Kings seldom enjoyed a close bond with their fathers; the elder taught the young how to fend for themselves, lead their armies into battle and learn the politics of power. Seldom had a prince not thereafter eagerly sought their own father's demise, that they may yet enjoy real power rather than watch from the outside. How many fathers had resented the rise of a son who henceforth would become a thorn in their side, a volatile and over-confident youth?

As for Edward himself, the tale of his former life appeared almost cathartic. He had begun hesitantly, almost frightened to recount the often painful narrative of an existence that seemed a lifetime ago. Yet, as he progressed, he seemed to almost relive the events again, one moment smiling at a particular incident, and the next a quiet reflection of some of the most personal and painful events.

A sallow looking youth from the monastery kitchens had arrived with some bread, cheese, fruit and pitcher of cool water with goblets. Alphage cleared a small nearby table of half-potted plants, and the youth laid out the provisions and left.

Edward broke up a piece of the freshly baked bread, and tossed some of the cheese to Perrot. Alphage mumbled a prayer for this offering, while Fieschi took up a small knife and began to peel one of the shiny red apples.

Edward wore a look of quiet contemplation, and there was a silence broken only by a low growl as Perrot noticed the intrusion into the garden of a small rosy starling that pecked at some of the bare earth in an unseeded corner of one of the beds. The dog watched the bird for several seconds until considering that a chase would be futile, he licked his lips from the nugget of cheese and, after assuring himself that no sad expression would lead to any further generosity of food, settled down again into a lazy doze.

The three men picked at the remains of their meal in silence, until Edward sighed and continued.

+++

The days following the death of my father were, I am ashamed to say, ones of satisfaction, during which

I contemplated all that would now change. I travelled with all speed to Carlisle and from there to Burgh-by-Sands to view my father's body. I dismissed the knights that held the traditional watch over the corpse, and there I stood, alone, staring at the man who had been the most dominant force in my life up until then. Now he lay, silent. It was such a surreal experience not to find him barking orders or admonishing me over some issue. I declare that I expected him, even now, to open his eyes and berate me. So much of my life had been spent in torment from this powerful figure who seemed so much smaller in death. His rugged, lined face, framed by the wiry-haired beard and long curling hair, once rich and abundant but now grizzled and grey. I lifted one of his heavy, coarse hands; its fingers hard like leather, the nails short and cleaned since his death. I drew the hand up to my lips and gently kissed it as a tear unexpectedly dropped on his sleeve. I wiped the tear away, curious at my emotion. I cared nothing for him, I admonished myself. I let the hand go and turned away.

It was done.

+++

I had rarely felt as elated as I did upon the return of my beloved companion Perrot. Upon my urgent summons to Ponthieu, Piers had immediately set out for England. Once informed of his recall, the prime barons of the realm reacted with varying states of fury - only one or two appeared indifferent about it, but the real shock was yet to be announced.

Whilst I awaited his return, I instigated the first charter of my new reign, and I sat whilst the great earls studied it. My clerk, Thomas de Newhay, had drawn up the proclamation, and it was his finest work, beautifully set out and richly decorated. I smiled with great satisfaction as he set the document down in front of those first lords of the realm. I took a moment to reappraise these magnates that had – unwillingly, I was certain, bent the knee and sworn homage and fealty to me as their new king. I had informed them officially of my plans to elevate Piers, but they had no idea how high I intended to raise my darling brother. Grave and serious faces now looked upon the document that had been presented. I exalted in the power that was now mine to wield. Indeed, Perrot himself would only learn of it when he finally returned to me.

Here they sat, each in turn scrutinising the great document before them with varying degrees of surprise and disappointment, outrage even:

The Earl of Lincoln - blond haired, and portly with few discerning features on his wide fat face.

My cousin Lancaster - as handsome as Lincoln was ugly. Black haired, his moustache and beard closely trimmed; tall and noble with sharp cheekbones and a small mouth. Strikingly-featured though he certainly was, his inscrutable look was enough to cause unease.

Surrey was of a much stockier build; pale, almost white skin that featured a large, lazy mouth and small dark eyes.

My musing was interrupted by a noise at one end of the table.

The Earl of Pembroke, tall and thin with jet-black hair and a large pointed nose had uttered a curse of some kind and now looked at me with an insolent air.

"My liege, this document confers upon Piers Gaveston the Earldom of Cornwall."

I grinned, amused to see him for once completely bemused. "Indeed it does my lord," I replied. "I have read it."

The Earl reddened slightly, but continued. "The title of Cornwall has surely always been bestowed upon one of royal blood. Moreover, your late father had intended to grant the title and estates to one of your grace's half brothers."

I recall the annoyance I felt in having a voice of dissent to this first declaration of my reign. "My lords," I stated, ignoring Pembroke entirely, "you have the charter before you. I would have you witness it before me now." I stared down at them from my great seat at the head of the large oak table.

One by one they signed, yet not one of them appeared to be happy with doing so.

Only my brother in law, Humphrey de Bohun, Earl of Hereford had the decency to remain silent, casting his shrewd brown eyes to his feet whilst the others murmured a rumbling of dissent. Edmund Fitz Alan, the Earl of Arundel, smaller than the other lords present, and with almost boyish features, seemed to hold back until certain of the intentions of the other lords.

I noticed then that one of the barons was absent. "My lord of Warwick is not present, why is that?"

One or two of those present looked down to their feet or at each other with obvious embarrassment. It was Lancaster that spoke up.

"He is unable to attend, your grace, feeling as he does that the grant is contrary to the wishes of the late king."

I could gladly have struck him for his insolence. "Yes, my late father had apparently declared with his last breath, that Piers should not be entitled in any way, and you all swore to ensure that this would not be done. Indeed, I heard of it!" I declared hotly. "Yet thus far, I have heard no conclusive declaration from one who was there when he said as much. The reign of my father has ended, and any oaths made to him ended with his final breath – except your vow of obedience to me. Need I remind you of it?"

I felt at once empowered; I was the king and none would gainsay me now that I had the crown.

Sheepishly, and with reluctance, all the assembled earls bowed their heads and, taking the quill from one another, affixed their names. Recalling the event now, all I was interested in was the honour and pride my beloved brother would feel once this title was bestowed upon him. This would be the first of many clashes with these nobles. In hindsight, I see now that at the end of my father's reign, many of them rightly enough expected to enjoy the rewards of their fealty to him. Further lands and titles should have been bestowed upon those that had served faithfully. Such titles and lands that I could give would have done much to bind these lords to me, yet I acted rashly, seeing no reason to honour them all further. Another of the many acts I should have reconsidered.

"I realise, my lords," I stated, "that there is unease between my new Lord of Cornwall and some of you, but you will have done with any petty jealousies and trivial grievances or risk my displeasure."

All those gathered registered surprise and indeed annoyance. Pembroke wore a cynical expression, whilst

Surrey's eyes narrowed with an almost evil glare. My cousin Lancaster wore a look of clear amusement; his eyes fixed on me.

Did I read the early signs of the defiance I was to suffer at his hands in the future? As I met his gaze, I felt merely the joy of the power I now held, yet it was I who eventually looked away first.

The subsequent meeting with the gathered lords began to bore me, and I admit I could barely conceal my agitation to be done with it, such was my eagerness to continue with the arrangements I had made for my dearest Perrot's return. I longed to have him with me again; my circle of friends meant nothing without him among them, although he had long been the only company I was content with. I nodded to my secretary, who carefully removed the charter from the table and handed it to me. I glanced down at those seals, barely able to conceal the satisfaction I felt.

Thomas now drew back one of the chairs and sat, leaning on the table. "Your grace, cousin," he began, "there are now matters we, your loyal nobles, would discuss with you."

"Such as?" I replied, not without some annoyance. "I personally have a great deal to do cousin. I must see to arrangements for Piers's return to us."

"Your grace," began Pembroke, "there is much to be done regarding your coronation, and there is your own marriage…"

I waved a dismissive hand at him with impatience. "Well… we can talk of my marriage later – tomorrow, maybe," I said testily. "As for my coronation, arrangements will only begin once my lord of Cornwall is returned to us, for he will most certainly oversee the event."

Lancaster arched one of his perfectly-shaped eyebrows and, with what I was certain was the slight upturn of the corner of his mouth, broke the silence my declaration had caused. "Your grace. The coronation of the king of England cannot be left in the hands of one who is – shall we say - "unfamiliar" with the customs surrounding such an event. There are the bishops to convene, lords of the realm to assemble...."

"Of which Piers Gaveston is one," I retorted, "Or at least will be as soon as he is returned to us."

Lancaster stared at me. Again I felt the discomfort at his scrutiny, unnerved by his intensity. Pembroke now added his voice to the growing unrest in the chamber. "Your grace, your coronation must not be treated as mere theatre. There is too much importance for that, the majesty and solemnity, protocols must be observed."

"As I am sure they will be, my lord," I retorted. "I have no doubt that my brother Perrot can rely on your full support, my lords – no, Sussex! I will hear no more dissent on the matter. Once my lord of Cornwall is rested and re-established here at home with us, preparations will begin in earnest."

The chorus of outrage was building and I at once sought to distance myself from it, as I would make a habit of doing in the future.

"But, your grace!" Surrey spluttered.

"Enough, my lord – later, I have said!" I stood up swiftly and swept from the chamber to utter silence. The gathered barons bent the knee to me, but I did not need to be told that the faces behind me would certainly have registered fury.

So much could have been different had I been able to listen rather than ignore what I did not want to hear.

My father would have silenced such dissent with fury, and this early skirmish with these powerful men should have served as a warning of the tragic difficulties to come. Of course, my naivety precluded such a foresight, and I would suffer for it later. All I could think of, however, was the return of Piers and how idyllic life would be when he returned. Reflecting on these events, so clear to me still after all these years, there is much I would have done differently. Yet I could not be other than I was – not then, at least.

On a perfect August day, bright and warm, Piers and I were finally reunited at Dumfries, he having travelled from Walter Reynolds home in London where I had already sent letters to him. Our joy at being together again was emotional as well as heartfelt.

He had lost none of his exuberance, and his face was as fair and perfect as I had remembered it, having pictured it in my mind from the time I rose in the morning to when I closed my eyes at night. I hugged him to me so tightly that he had to tap me on the back to release him for fear of my hurting him.

"My king, I had forgotten your strength, I declare I am almost crushed!" We laughed again, as I had felt I never would do after his exile.

Later, when we were alone, I promised we would never be parted again. He declared himself humbled by my intention to ennoble him. Yet pretended to be almost indifferent to the plan. I wonder, on reflection, whether he, like the other barons, foresaw the error in bestowing such a gift. All I could think of at the time was the pleasure it gave me to elevate this most beloved of men with this high honour.

We held a lavish feast in honour of Piers's return, attended by many of those lords that had so reluctantly agreed to my beloved brother's elevation to the Earldom of Cornwall. As we made merry that night, dancing and drinking, I took no notice of the group of barons who stood sullenly on the fringes of the celebrations. Piers goaded them playfully - so I thought. Trying to involve them in the celebrations, his entreaties were either ignored or met with a frown of dismissal. Only my cousin Lancaster seemed to make an effort to join in, and I wondered briefly whether I had been hasty in considering him to be against my beloved Perrot. I watched my brother that evening and wondered at my good fortune. All would be well. Piers was already drunk on both the free-flowing wine and the happiness he felt, and I could not supress my delight at him.

It was soon after his return that I ceremoniously vested Piers with the ermine cloak of earldom as my chamberlain announced to the gathering court his new title and all the landed details of his elevation. He knelt before me, and as I fastened the heavy cloak that hung so proudly on those wide shoulders, I believed my happiness to be complete.

One evening, as we relaxed, exhausted from another day of hunting and merriment and the careless abandonment that seemed to fill our days, Piers brought to my attention one whose position must be considered now that I was king.

"Why must we talk of Bishop Langton?" I asked. I had put the man out of my mind as much as possible. As soon as my servant had removed my boots, I dismissed him and stretched out my legs and raised my arms as though reaching up to the ceiling of the chamber.

"He has a great deal to answer for, Ned, you know as much," he replied in a serious, unfamiliar tone.

"Well, yes, we must consider him, but not now, not while we are enjoying this freedom which we have craved for so long."

Piers seemed pensive and said little over the next hour, until I realised that something troubled him about my late father's loyal servant who, of course, had shown both of us his enmity.

I stifled a yawn and rubbed my tired eyes. The last thing I wanted was to be reminded of serious matters. "Very well, what would you have me do?"

Piers looked at me for a moment as though considering his words carefully and, rising from his seat by the window, he drew up a chair opposite mine and rested his elbows on his knees, staring into my eyes with those dazzling, clear blue ones of his own. "You know, my king, that your late father left you not just a crown but the most colossal debts as well."

I looked at him, perplexed for a moment. "Well yes, of course, I know that," I answered, "I am not a complete dolt!"

Piers grinned at me, that flashing devilish smile. "Of course, Ned. Nevertheless, the treasury is all but exhausted. You said yourself to Lancaster that it may not be possible to continue the campaign in Scotland now he has appraised you of the financial burden of continuing the expedition that your late father insisted on year after year."

"And?" I enquired.

"The finances of the nation were in the hands of Langton, and I have word – from a most trusted source, that there are whispers of corruption. I think if we were to look for a scapegoat for all this, Langton is the first name that comes to mind. Consider this, my king: we have an opportunity to enact vengeance finally on that wily snake who would have parted you and I forever had fate not intervened."

I mused over his words, spoken with a venom unusual for Piers. He was right, of course, Langton was no friend of ours. How strange, I thought, that I seemed to consider the effect of my decisions on "us" rather than myself or England. "It shall be done, brother," I assured him solemnly. "Any man that would work to tear us apart will be cast down as assuredly as I will raise you up."

Piers smiled at my words and leaned towards me, cupping my face within his soft hands. "Together, my king. Now and forever."

+++

I was true to my word about Langton. I had him stripped of all titles, benefices and properties. I had let the charge of corruption take root in the minds of the lords of the realm. I had to admit that I was surprised that none of these upright men, so loyal to my father, seemed unhappy to allow the reputation of one of his former most trusted servants to be besmirched without dissent. I had Langton taken to the Tower of London and, after appointing the Earl of Lincoln to build a plausible case against him, I felt justified that for Piers and myself, a score had indeed been settled.

My joy was complete when Piers suggested a suitable replacement for the vacancy should be filled with our own partner in adversity – Walter Reynolds.

Following my father's funeral and interment next to my mother in Westminster, we moved on to Berkhamsted and I announced to my beloved brother a further surprise, and my greatest joy. I informed Piers that I had arranged his marriage. Not only that, but the bride would be my own dear niece, Margaret de Clare. I would most willingly have married one of my own sisters to Piers, but alas, two were already married and a third had betrothed herself to God and had become a nun. Margaret de Clare was as near to immediate family as I could wish for, being one of the daughters of my sister Joan. A most dutiful girl, for whom I had always had a great affection.

The joy of this was not only that she was both a sweet-natured young woman and sister to Gilbert, a companion that had been part of my household, and who was well-known and liked by both Piers and myself. The true joy for me was that my darling Perrot was now, indeed, part of the royal family itself. I delighted in the shock that crossed his handsome face as he took in the enormity and symbolism of the arrangement.

"I told you, my dearest brother," I reminded him, "that I would raise you so high that men in this kingdom would treat you as they do me."

He hugged me tightly, with tears in his eyes at the honour I was so happily bestowing.

I had said little to Margaret, assuring her that I felt her to be so close that only she would be good enough for him. I don't recall that I said much more to her; it mattered little in any case. She could not fail to find joy in the match, and was merely doing her duty to both her family and her king.

Thus my heart was filled with pride and love as I watched my beloved brother and his new bride. Together, he and I planned the ceremonies without a care for the expense. Nothing would be too costly; all would be just as he wanted. The wedding feast was fantastically-designed. Piers looked every inch the gallant, his rich suit was white velvet, trimmed with gold thread. Costly jewels adorned his hands, a pearl brooch at his throat. He looked as dazzling and handsome as I had ever seen him. The outfit was one of several that he changed throughout the day, each one costlier than the last. Yellow, powder blue as the afternoon wore on, now dark green with shimmering jewels as the long day eased into the evening. As befitted his new role, he basked in the admiring looks from the courtiers and behaved throughout both the ceremony itself and the subsequent banquet as the loving, attentive new husband.

Occasionally I would catch his eye and he would wink at me; a gesture I was sure implied that nothing would come between he and myself – certainly not a wife! I could not in all honesty claim that I did not harbour any jealousy towards my niece, but I remained satisfied that, whatever ceremonies blessed their union, I alone held Piers's love.

Of course, there were those within the court that disapproved of the marriage, purely on the grounds that elevating Piers to the royal family was inconceivable. I cared little for the opinions of the barons, they had little or no idea about the love Piers and I shared, and I did not expect them to adore my brother as I did. Their disapproval did nothing to alter my wishes. I was the king, and as such I could do as I wished, and what

I wished was to further secure the bond with my brother. The lords could stand in corners, whispering to one another, childishly sneering and bemoaning that the Earl of Cornwall had been once again favoured by the king. Word would usually be related back to me. Robert, my fool, was an expert eavesdropper, and generally ignored by the more serious of the barons, who would unsuccessfully kick out at him whilst he performed magic tricks before them.

Thus I believe was the beginning of my irritation with these great lords of the realm, and their devious, spiteful ways. An irritation that would soon give way to hatred. It was also becoming clearer that whenever they spent any time with Piers, he in return wreaked havoc with his devilish humour where they were concerned.

He was well aware that he was not liked by most of them, and was fighting back by being the cause of embarrassment to them, either by name-calling – often within their hearing - or imitating their mannerisms. I guiltily admit that I found these episodes very amusing; a king with greater wisdom than I would have checked Gaveston's arrogance and at least sought to pacify these victims of his cutting humour.

My father would doubtless have beaten Piers with his own hands and cast him from court in ignominious disgrace; a salve to cool the tempers of these detestable men. Unfortunately, I was no such ruler; Piers felt quite safe in the knowledge that he could snap his elegant fingers at these lords and they were – at least for now - unable to do very much about it.

Was I really so naive about the dangerous game both Piers and I played in those early years of my reign? In time of course, fate was to prove that I did indeed understand very little. Such is the folly of youth, and Piers and I drank heavily from the well of careless abandonment. Looking back from a life of lessons learned the hard way, there is much I would do differently, and yet my life at that time was so inextricably linked with my Gascon brother. During those early years of my reign, caution and prudence were indeed minor considerations.

I would have you know, my dear friend Alphage, and you also Manuel that, contrary to accepted opinion, I did not entirely ignore my duties as king, and there were many occasions when I would literally refuse Piers's entreaties to ride, hunt or generally enjoy the trappings of king rather than the responsibility of one, and I would meet with my council to attend to the serious issues at hand. Heaven knows I was not always minded to consider state matters, but issues pressed and I knew that I could only ignore them for so long.

My wedding was a prime consideration now that I had Piers back, and he begged to be allowed to take principal charge of arrangements. I could deny him nothing as he rained kisses on me and became almost childlike in his torrent of ideas and suggestions for both my impending wedding and indeed my coronation also. Nevertheless, other issues were more immediate, yet even in my absence he was never without arrangements of his own.

A grand tournament was arranged by Piers to take place in his estate at Wallingford, and as usual he threw himself into its planning. He delighted in telling me later that, although chilled by the December winds, the castle ramparts were lined with brightly coloured heralds, and he had gone so far as to fashion a large banner which combined both my own insignia and his. The attending barons were, of course, horrified - as I should have been. In time, I could scarcely believe that I had not seen the outrage of such a well intentioned idea.

To suggest our arms were one and the same was bound to court condemnation, and yet I could only feel even more love for him in designing something that would represent our union as brothers. In the evenings, the tastefully decorated castle glowed in the warmth of candles and roaring braziers, but it was the hastiludes that would add further kindling to an already smoking fire.

In those heady days, Piers had few rivals to match his prowess in the tiltyard. Even Surrey had been heard to admit that Piers was almost unmatched in his skills. I must confess to a total indifference towards competing in such tournaments as this. I did, however, delight in hearing of my beloved brother's success, and he was invariably the victor in the contest. Many knights would generally compete, but it was the most powerful of magnates that would draw the most interest. As expected, the outcome was a victory for Perrot's side; many young knights had flocked to his banner, eager to impress the Earl of Cornwall, and the day was won.

I avoided meeting with the council as much as possible. Those things bored me so much. Not only that, but I resented the intrusion. What was the point of being king if I could not enjoy some levity? There more than enough able men to deal with the day-to-day running of things. I generally passed over official documents with little more than a cursory glance at what I was signing.

The fury that the barons would have felt at this indignity should, again, have served as a warning to me. Nonetheless, I could feel only pride that Piers had been so handsomely valiant. He truly was everything I aspired to be, and whilst I held my breath each time he competed, lest he be unhorsed or badly injured, I delighted in his prowess.

As for the powerful lords, I could see no reason why they should still hate Piers so much. Such was my folly, that I could not yet see the approaching storm.

+++

"Gaveston, regent? You jest, surely, man!" I could hear Warwick's booming voice even as I neared the council chamber. Piers and I looked at one another and grinned. I had made the decision to entrust my brother with control of the realm during my absence in France, much as I would have preferred to take him with me. Who else could I trust to act in my best interests? It was necessary to travel to France to marry the young Princess Isabella, and the sooner it was done the better.

The two of us giggled at the joy of causing the council such a stir, but I was by then thoroughly enjoying being king. The powerful barons would be reined in and realise that, as their sovereign, I had the power to do exactly as I wished and they would just have to live with my command. I had seen my father often enough in complete control, daring any to question his decisions.

I put a hand to my mouth lest my laughter be heard, and we entered the chamber where those gathered rose to their feet. "My lords, I smiled as I sat at the table.

"God's death, Warwick, you look like you have sat in the sun for too long, what ails you?"

At that moment, Piers, standing at my shoulder, leant down whispering in my ear. "Maybe the black dog of Arden has scented a bitch in heat – how fascinating!"

I laughed and Piers grinned, nodding his head towards a fuming Warwick, who was now redder than ever. Piers took his seat looking smug and satisfied that he had goaded Warwick so early in the meeting.

"Well, my lords," I began.

"Forgive me, your grace," Pembroke cut in, "the Earl of Lincoln is not here, we must wait."

I looked at him with a questioning gaze. "If he is not yet here then he is excluded, it is not for the king to wait upon his council. Still we are in the majority, everyone that matters is here..."

"And, indeed, some that don't matter!" Piers cut in waspishly. Within seconds Warwick had reached across the table and lunged at him, his chair falling to the floor behind him.

Piers made no attempt to evade him, confident in any case that Warwick's reach was not close enough. He merely laughed loudly and took up the goblet of wine he had brought with him, draining its contents.

Warwick's face now looked close to erupting. "Do you further seek to insult me, Gaveston?" he growled.

I was finding this play before me far more amusing than I should have, and tried valiantly to remain composed. My fury at Warwick for his behaviour was heartfelt, however.

"The Earl of Cornwall," I spoke angrily, emphasising Piers's title, "made no gesture of insult to you, Warwick. Now, you will be seated lest you anger me further!"

My cousin Lancaster allowed a look of controlled amusement to cross his handsome features before he spoke, ignoring the episode that had just taken place.

"My cousin," he began, "your decision to leave the running of the realm to this - my lord of Cornwall - has taken us, your council, by surprise. I am unsure why, as premier of your council as well as your dearest cousin and friend, I myself have not been bestowed this honour."

"My order, as your king, is to make the Earl of Cornwall regent in my absence, I see no problem about the fact; Piers is more than capable of making any decisions that may need to be made." I reached to my side where Piers sat, and patted his arm. "Who better than my dearest brother to be keeper of the realm while I am in France? Indeed, is he not also a member of our royal family, now he is married to our niece? You forget this, my lords, when you plot to undermine him at every opportunity – aye, I know of it! Do you think me such a fool that I am unaware of your failed machinations and hatred towards him?" I realised that as my voice raised, I was getting irritated. Even Piers was looking at me in embarrassed silence.

"Sire, the Earl of Pembroke began, "We, your council..."

"Of which my lord of Cornwall is a member."

"We, the remaining members would suggest that the burden of this high office may be too heavy to place upon the shoulders of one so inexperienced in the ways of government," Pembroke continued as tactfully as possible.

"We will note your concern, my lord. We will also formally agree the extent of such powers that we entrust to the Earl of Cornwall. He will act on my behalf, knowing my mind so much better than the rest of my council; then those of you who do not travel to France will, I'm sure, offer the Earl every assistance in undertaking this role."

Warwick ran a hand through his hair in exasperation, muttering as he did so. I could not catch his words, but there was no doubt they were offensive.

Lancaster wore his look of controlled amusement with his eyes fixed on me. It often occurred to me that he enjoyed this sparring as much as Piers did. Yet something told me that I could not trust him. He might well enjoy such a spectacle, but he was a danger I knew I must never underestimate.

"Perrot, I am bored with this," I yawned – with no pretence - I found such meetings both tiresome and overlong. "We shall take a brisk ride now, I think!

Is that new mount I gave you really as fast as mine? We shall race....no! Pembroke, you may not suggest. I am done with this! You have my instructions."

Pembroke, whom Piers delighted in calling "Joseph the Jew", looked even more sombre than usual. The other sea of faces merely looked forlorn and I stood, no longer wishing to tolerate their moaning. The assembly stood and I marched from the room. I did not need to be told that behind me Piers shot them all a look of triumph as he performed a mock bow before following me out.

+++

Negotiations for my marriage had been undertaken for some time, and whilst I thought the whole process dull and uninteresting, I was aware enough of my obligations as king, to realise that I had a duty to perform.

Whilst the formalities bored me, I was not against the institution and the need to provide heirs. Since Piers's own marriage, I had seen that having a wife did not mean the end of what had been enjoyed before betrothal. Isabella, my bride to be, was described to me as beautiful – although, at only twelve years of age, such claims were merely words as she was too young to have developed any beauty. Yet, I was assured that she was a most dutiful girl, and I hoped that we could together make an agreeable match. Moreover, there were political and financial considerations that made the match important. I had listened to my father's lectures enough to have retained an understanding of what a royal match with France was worth.

My belief that my bride would bring not only herself but also a handsome dowry that would help replenish an ever-depleted treasury was dealt a severe blow. The duchy of Aquitaine was to formally pass to the English as a more formal ownership than had previously been the case. However, my prospective father in law, the French king Philip, declared that the duchy was a generous enough dowry as it was and he saw no reason to provide more.

I raged impotently at the council about it, but there was really little I could do. I had been warned to be wary of the cunning French monarch and his sons, and I would do well to be so. Other than that, details would soon be finalised and I was delighted that Piers excitedly took control of arranging the necessary celebrations once myself and my young bride returned.

Even so, I sensed in Piers a mood of sadness from time to time when I talked of Isabella. I had ordered some improvements to the Palace of Westminster in preparation for the new bride and yet, when I excitedly tried to discuss them with him, I was aware that my beloved brother was troubled.

We had managed to enjoy some measure of privacy at Langley, and as we lay together in my bedchamber, my hand gently stroking his head as he lay against my shoulder, I felt again the sense that he was troubled.

"What ails you, Perrot? You have been melancholy these last few days. Does the idea of being regent in my absence trouble you? We can change our plans if you would rather relinquish the responsibility."

"No, Ned," he answered, "the burden you give me I gladly undertake. I just…" He broke off and wiped his face with the back of his other hand. He was upset and I could not bear that.

"What is it?" I insisted gently. "Tell me."

"Ned, will you?"

"What?"

"Will you still care for me when you are married? As we do now I mean. I fear that, once duty and responsibility commit you to this marriage, you will need me less."

I sat upright quickly to look down on him He looked so sad, and yet his concerned expression almost made his beauty more ethereal. "I could never love another as I do you, here and now," I stated, almost choking over my rising emotions. "There will never be another that will take your place. What I do now in marrying I do for expediency, for duty, for nothing else. I love you Piers. I love you. Sometimes my heart aches from loving you as I do. I am nothing without you. Until the day I die, my heart will belong only to you."

I leant down to him and kissed him, longingly, with a passion that almost frightened me. He cupped my face in his hands and held me there as he looked at me with those beautiful blue eyes of his that I will remember for the remainder of my life.

"I love you, Ned." He drew me to him, holding me tightly as if he would never let me go. There was so much I wanted to say to him, but didn't know how or even what exactly, although I did know that this man would be forever engraved on my heart and that nothing would ever come between us.

As we lay together that afternoon, our passion spent, and tears shed with such emotion that we could not supress them, I felt a fear that I knew I could never live my life without him. I dreaded our time apart, be it a few hours even. This love scared me. It was so strong that I had no control over it. What must one do when you felt this strongly for one other person so much that you were blinded to all else?

I watched him, sleeping now, and silent with only a shallow contented breath. His perfect lips slightly parted, an occasional twitch at the corner of one eye. I took in all of that perfection and felt a hot tear of my own. I loved this man so much. If I could be marrying him instead of the French princess I would be truly happy, but we had long since made our own pact and that would survive long after Isabella's wedding corsage had dried and crumbled.

Even now, as I relate the tale of our behaviour - high on the list of mortal sins - I would have more gladly risked purgatory than forego the love that I felt.

Yes, I would marry, as he had, but nothing would break our love and our bond. He would be my one love, and I his, for as long as we lived.

+++

Manuel Fieschi signed the letter he had spent some time composing, and after sprinkling the page with some pounce, he folded and sealed it before removing one of the rings on his long fingers, using it to imprint the wax with his personal seal. The missive would be taken by one of the party of horsemen who had accompanied his train, and begin its journey to the Papal court at Avignon. He sighed in contemplation before handing it to his manservant who was standing at a respectful distance. Once alone, he reached for a leather bound journal that lay on the desk, and taking it up, he then spent some time in detailing all he had heard thus far from the hermit king.

Abbot Ridolfo had insisted that the envoy use both his personal sleeping quarters as well as his office during his stay at the monastery. Whilst the sleeping accommodation was far more provincial than he was used to, he was grateful to have some small comforts that the abbot's chamber afforded him. The cell – for it was little more - was plain, with whitewashed walls, peeling in places, and a tall dresser upon which stood a plain wooden cross. A desk, creaking slightly with any pressure, a plain bed laid with crisp white sheets and a small table next to it on which stood a new candle. Manuel smiled at the threadbare rug that lay on the stone floor; no doubt a hastily procured comfort, a nod to some semblance of luxury for a man of his importance.

The long meeting with Edward in the herb garden had, at times, been uncomfortable to listen to, and the events discussed weighed heavily, now the envoy had chance to consider the former king's discourse.

As a slight shadow had begun to cast over the garden, it was a surprise to all three men, that the hour had grown so late, and it had been agreed between them that rest and contemplation should be observed for the remainder of the day. Edward had seemed almost absent-minded about the decision, so lost had he seemingly become in relating the events from so long ago.

Manuel stifled a yawn and stretched his long legs out under the table. How strange that merely listening could be so exhausting. He had known much of what the former king related to him and Brother Alphage - superficially at least. The more intimate aspects of the revelations had been listened to without comment or censure. Certainly, Edward did not seem concerned about any discomfiture his words may have caused, so seemingly lost was he in a deep well of thoughts and emotions. Indeed, he appeared at times as though he talked only to himself.

The bell announcing the evening meal suddenly rang out, startling him from his musing. The envoy's meal would be served to him here in the abbot's room. There was much to contemplate, and the solitude of the quiet monastery was most welcome. Manuel felt no need to disturb the smooth running of Sant Alberto any more than he had already, and discretion at all times was therefore of the utmost importance. He rose, crossing to the window and resting his hands on the stone sill. He looked out across the landscape, revelling in its simple beauty. He smiled as he understood what had kept England's one and only deposed king here. Surely there was a simplicity in life here that he must have yearned for in the past.

He must rest well tonight and prepare to hear and consider the continuing story of this most troubled former monarch. What, or indeed, whose hand had guided this enigmatic prince to the follies that would label him as the most foolish man in Christendom? Further revelations would no doubt help make sense of it all, but Manuel was under no illusions - what had thus far been somewhat uncomfortable to hear would no doubt continue to shock, even horrify.

Certainly, he had been most surprised that the good brother Alphage had not found the tale too shocking. There was a sensitivity in most religious orders that would have been breached by what Edward had began to tell them. Manuel must certainly commend the noble abbot for his wisdom in choosing the infirmarian as a witness to the sorry tale that had to be related.

His reverie was interrupted suddenly by a gentle knock at the chamber door; the evening meal had arrived.

Brother Alphage had prayed for sometime after he, Manuel and Edward had separated. He had gone firstly to pray, and as expected had been the focus of much interest from the other brethren. Even as he had left the small chapel, he could hear Brother Nicolo admonishing the other monks for their inquisitive glances.

"It is none of our affair," he had stated as he shooed them away to their duties. Yet, he himself had glided over to the infirmarian, laying a comforting hand on his arm. "Brother, how have your discussions been going?"

A smile danced upon Alphage's mouth; it was impossible, of course, to have held a small meeting without the steward finding out where it had taken place. The infirmarian charitably decided that it was surely in the abbey's best interests to have such a curious steward. No sooner had Alphage started to form a response that he intended to be both polite and vague, than the calming deep tone of Abbot Ridolfo could be heard.

"Ah, Brother Nicolo, there you are." The statement was not elaborated upon; clearly this required his physical attendance. Reluctantly, the inquisitive brother patted Alphage on the arm as though in understanding, despite not having actually been told anything.

The nod that the abbot gave the infirmarian was accompanied with an understanding smile, and Alphage once again blessed God for having given a calling to the wise and benevolent man that led the community at Sant Alberto.

Having thus escaped a potentially uncomfortable interrogation, the elderly brother made his way to his workshop. The door had been left open by the infirmarian to dispel the warm within as much as confirming hi belief in the value and advantage of fresh natural air.

The elderly monk drew his wooden stool to the open door and sat whilst he pondered on the day's events. He sighed as he took up some dried poppy heads and a bowl, coaxing the small black seeds into the wooden dish. The brittle heads crackled as his industrious fingers crushed them. Such work helped Alphage to concentrate, and he had much to consider. The story he and the papal envoy had heard from the hermit had been hard to take in. To have been asked to listen to the story of a man whom he had formerly treated as a forlorn figure with a troubled past, who he now had to identify as a deposed king had been quite a leap of faith, and yet he doubted that he could entirely comprehend this most troubled of souls.

Father Abbot had talked with Alphage, not doubting the charity and benevolence of the monk, but preparing him for the burden of what he was to learn. This was, the abbot advised, no ordinary story; and judging by what Fieschi had told him of the hermit, Alphage must prepare himself for revelations that he would find hard to hear.

The infirmarian had not lived a sheltered life by any means, and the ways of men – even those judged to be men of power - were not unknown to him. He was satisfied that he was a sound judge of people, and none more so than the hermit he had grown to know during his time at the monastery. Yet here was a tortured soul, one that had clearly known a comfortable life despite its early trials. The humbling of such a man would have come at a great cost. The hermit's story had only just begun.

Alphage muttered a prayer for guidance; he was certainly not one to censure; all men, whatever their story would be judged by a much higher authority than his. He looked up at the sky and surmised that the bell announcing the evening meal would be ringing soon. After which he must pray again; never had he felt the need for God's guidance as much as he did now, yet he felt sure that the Almighty would be more than a little preoccupied in guiding the tortured hermit who surely baring his very soul.

+++

Long before the chorus of birdsong that announced the dawn of a new day, the former king of England rose from his cot bed, its blankets cast to the floor. Calming rest had eluded him for almost the whole night. When he was able to sleep, his dreams were full of so many faces, the past almost playing out before him. Having, like his master, abandoned his bed, Perrot lay on the dirt floor and rested his chin on one paw, yet still keeping a close eye on every pacing step, and raising his head only when Edward deemed the hovel too small to pace around and walked outside to sit in the coolness of the early hour.

The hound chose one of his familiar spots to lie out on, and whined softly as he watched his master cover his face with his hands before rubbing the palms over his shorn hair. This would be, of course, the coolest part of the day and was the time that usually Edward felt most at peace, at one with nature, the flora and fauna that in this hidden paradise made all troubles seem worthless.

Yet Edward was troubled; the previous day had torn from him thoughts and memories that had lain long-buried and, in resurrecting them, he had felt both redeemed and traumatised. So strange, he thought, that he could recall almost every word spoken, though could not recall any of his sisters without serious concentration. He could almost feel himself reliving those moments with Piers, the anger of the royal court, his own resentment at his father. He had woken from an all too brief sleep, certain that he could again smell the lavender scent that Piers always wore. It served to remind him anew that he was alone. He would never stop loving Piers and missing him sorely. His love for Hugh had been different – but Hugh was for later.

He collected some of the cold stream water which he drank while he broke his fast with some berries and an apple. Strange how he enjoyed the simplicity of this frugal meal when once he had regularly dined on roasted swan, lampreys and deer, the finest delicacies. How far he had travelled in all respects.

The coolness of the early dawn began to give way to an increasing warmth, and he was uncertain how long he had sat there, with Perrot's chin resting on his foot, patiently waiting for some activity. Edward heard the monastery bell announcing the hour of lauds. He stood and breathed deeply, closing his eyes as he silently prayed for strength and forgiveness for the further revelations that were to come. How much simpler it could be to just slip quietly away from Sant Alberto with Perrot and travel on to somewhere else where he could be just another stranger in the crowd. Yet, having started this journey of redemption, he knew he must see it through. He surely owed it to the "one other who remembers you" - perhaps he, more than anyone, deserved the truth.

By the time Edward arrived at the herb garden, both Fieschi and Alphage were deeply involved in discussing the medicinal properties of many of the herbs that Sant Alberto cultivated, and it was some moments before they were alerted by the joyous and excited Perrot, who was transfixed by a dish he was certain contained something that demanded to be eaten. Alphage happily set down a wooden bowl of raw meat, patting the hound fondly. The two men greeted Edward and, after the observance of a prayer to give them all strength and wisdom in the tales to come, the three of them sat as they had the previous day, and Edward drew in a deep breath.

+++

By the time I was preparing to leave England for France, Piers and I had become closer than I would have believed possible. I trusted him like no other; my love for him knew no bounds and yet my joy was spoilt because of the baron's growing resentment of him. Piers had become powerful. The ear of the king is a much treasured possession, plus my brother and I began to issue decisions as one, and upon much reflection I realise that, in raising him up and allowing him more license than any other, I was exposing him to new insults - Piers was not one to forget a slight, and consequently his sarcasm and vicious wit were used on an ever-increasing list of victims.

Of course, I knew the barons despised him. Yet I could not discourage him, I enjoyed his wit towards them; all of life was a game to him at that time, and I was at last enjoying the freedom of discarding the shackles that had held me in check for so long. I was free, I had Piers, and more importantly – I was the king.

Lancaster had the impertinence to question the bond that Piers and I shared on many occasions. One such day, he had ridden out with myself, Piers and a number of our closest circle as we hunted. The day was warm and lazy, and, whilst there had been business of state to be dealt with, I saw no reason that my council, and lords - who never ceased to tell me they were mine to command - could not deal with the dreary day to day running of things. The arrangement suited Piers and I, allowing us more time to enjoy the pleasures in life.

I watched as my dearest Perrot loosed an arrow at a fleeting stag, and after a wild cheer, he had galloped off to claim the prize. He turned to look at me, his face glowing with excitement and pride. How I loved that boyish grin that I can almost see now after all these years. I shut my eyes and yet... Well, no matter!

Anyway, my cousin Thomas was on hand to spoil the day. "He shoots a straight arrow," he remarked begrudgingly.

I nodded agreement, assuming the compliment to be genuine. "Is he not perfect at everything?" I said, brimming with pride. "And yet you despise him, cousin, you and my other lords snipe at him continually. You belittle him, talking over him when he has something to say. He unseats you at the tourney, and yet, rather than commend him for his superior jousting ability, you glare at him with murderous intent. Sometimes when I look at your visible hatred of him I fear for his safety. Believe me, cousin, were anything to befall my brother, I would hunt down the perpetrator and slay him like a dog!" I was almost shocked at my own vehemence, yet I meant every word.

Lancaster arched an eyebrow as he heeded my words. "You speak with much threat, Edward. Gaveston is certainly unpopular, it is true. But surely you see why, surely you see that as long as you raise him higher and higher, you bring shame on yourself?"

"What shame is there in wanting my brother with me? And the favour is mine to give, Thomas. Why would you take him from me?"

"Because he will be your undoing, can you not see that? For God's sake, Ned, he is not your brother! I can be silent no longer. He has no royal blood, even the nobility he has is questionable. This is pure fantasy that you fawn over him as you do as though he is your equal. He is only equal to your Earls because you have raised him high, and would have us treat him so. You shower him with land and great wealth. No one can speak with you unless Gaveston is present, and indeed all requests to share your company are only permitted by him. You leave members of your council to kick their heels while they wait for you to be done with hunting and play acting. Your plan is to have him act as regent while you are in France. A man who, not so long ago, was banished from the kingdom by your father. You have gifted him a wife that further binds him to the house of Plantagenet, and brings him great wealth. Do you not see the damage this does? Our enemies laugh at us. Your father spent most of his life fighting the Scots, and yet you ignore the problem. The French king, soon to be your own father-in-law, claims to be concerned about the rise of one who is of no discernable dynasty, and that he is shocked at the gossip that reaches him."

"Ha!" I retorted, "he should have a care over who he listens to and what he hears from those who would think evil of us. As for the Scots, my father wasted a fortune and many lives in his maniacal pursuit of taming that race. Forgive me if I turn away from the slaughter of women and children..."

"In God's name, Edward!"

"Enough, Thomas!" I was beginning to anger. "You have said enough, and your words border on insolence. If it be my wish, I will raise Piers Gaveston as high as I might, and none of you will stop me lest you want to find yourselves dismissed from my court."

Thomas looked at me with gimlet eyes that held my own. In them I saw hatred and disgust. At that time, I did not care about either. He then turned his mount and rode away, dispensing with the formality of even a cursory nod of deference to his king.

As I watched him go, I breathed a sigh. Why did he and the others make so much out of the favour I bestowed on Piers? If they could only see him as I did, get to know his kindness, his wit, his love for his king. I knew that would never happen. The bigots still lived the way they had with my father. I wanted to live and laugh and enjoy being king, not let it be a burden that I would resent carrying all my life.

I watched Lancaster ride off into the distance. He would have to learn to serve his king, not just take for granted that his familial ties permitted him to question his sovereign. I turned away to watch as Piers and Gilbert de Clare could be heard laughing as they rode up to me. If only we could all stay like this, always laughing, always happy. Yet a strange feeling had taken up home in my thoughts, one that I could not explain. I cast it away and prepared to congratulate the hunters.

I don't recall how soon after this episode my life took a further turn, and I was faced with another step on the road to maturity and responsibility that most men must follow – marriage. So, then, to Isabella.

+++

My royal entourage travelled to Dover for the impending journey to Boulogne. I missed Piers already, having left him in London as regent during my absence. This had, of course, enraged the barons that were not to accompany my party to France. I had insisted that the realm could not have been left in safer hands. Who better than the man I called 'brother' to hold the reins of power? Piers, I knew even as I rode out of the capital towards Kent, would enjoy keeping the nobles in line, and there was no doubt that the situation would only further enflame the hot-blooded temperament of the barons.

Whilst his powers were limited more to a ceremonial role than exclusive power, he would command the nobility pay subservience to him, and I grinned to think of the mischief he could get up to while I was away. It was nonsense to suggest that Perrot would be incompetent in the role; a signature here and there, the formalities of domestic issues and minor functions were all that was needed. I felt heartened when he stared at me, momentarily dumbfounded by the honour I did him. I was, of course, elated to witness his joy. In those early years of my reign I seemed to be making a reasonable success of being king. Much of the day to day running of realm fell to others, although at my command, and I was content to delegate much in the way of responsibilities, thus allowing Perrot and I the chance to enjoy the trappings of kingship.

I had been left in no doubt, by my council, that the treasury was all but empty, but this surely did not prevent me from spending where I saw fit. Loans had been necessary, the details of which were of no interest to me.

So, here then, I set off for France. The journey was primarily to meet and wed Isabella of course, but her father Philip, King of France, would also have me swear fealty to him, as was customary - and indeed, unpleasant, and not without humiliation! Nonetheless, the duty had to be observed, but the marriage must be completed first.

The crossing to France was particularly ferocious, and the stormy sea during November was not for the weak-stomached. Piers would have been clutching at me from the first spray of seawater!

For myself, I found the experience invigorating, and spent a great deal of time learning the craft of being a sailor aboard such a large vessel; the crew, when they were not fully engaged in their duties, were puzzled by my questions, and yet seemed content enough to share their knowledge. I smiled at the faces of one or two of the lords that had accompanied me in the journey, almost disgusted that I would fraternise with those of such a low and common occupation.

As Isabella and I met for the first time at the door of Notre Dame in Boulogne, the bells that had rung across the city for the whole morning now at last fell silent. I only glanced at her superficially; she was undoubtedly pretty, a clear complexion, long fair hair and a small button nose, this particularly at odds with the men in her family. The over long, bulbous-tipped nose of her father's ruined his otherwise perfectly handsome face. Her most dazzling feature was, however, her large blue eyes. Certainly, she possessed attractive looks as did many of her family; her father was known as being "the fair" and she could certainly lay claim to that title herself, even though so young. That glance apart, I now look back with some shame that I took no more notice than that. I had no desire to bed a young girl of twelve, and yet of course both of us knew our respective duties. A consummation was as necessary as a binding contract, and yet I am glad to say that I put duty second on our initial night together.

My experience with women had been limited and, with the exception of my early escapade planned by Gilbert de Clare and a few other brief but enjoyable romps, I remained largely ignorant of the pleasures of a regular mistress. Forgive me, Alphage, when I tell you that both Piers and I enjoyed the ribald behaviour of rather base women. The novelty of which soon wore off for both of us!

Nevertheless, I observed the formality of our union, although we did nothing more than embrace and kiss. Even then I recall how innocent and uncertain Isabella looked on that first night together, I could have whispered reassurances that in time she would not feel so nervous, but alas, to my eternal shame I did not.

Her charm was not completely lost on me, and I believed then that were she to accept my dear Perrot as my close brother, that we could enjoy a most agreeable union. Her appearance was certainly fair, and thus would meet with Perrot's approval. He detested anything ugly, especially women, declaring once that Warwick's wife should be kept indoors for fear of frightening children with her over-long nose and pinched mouth!

I recall few details of those days in France - I saw little of my new wife, and was content enough with that. We had to appear together at the never-ending feasts and receptions, a continuous throng of European dignitaries and nobility, and when there was any respite from them, King Philip lectured me about Gascony and other issues that I can no longer recall; indeed, I had forgotten them by the time he had finished telling me. There was no doubt that he wanted to display his generous spirit for all to see, and in that I had to admit, he was most benevolent. Isabella came with no dowry, as estates and lands, notably Aquitaine, would be returned to the English crown, from whence they had been forfeited years ago by my father.

The magnanimous gesture was not lost on me; Philip made clear that the gift was given so that he would one day hope to see a grandchild command them. He did, nevertheless, bestow many great jewels on me as well as some magnificent warhorses.

I began to make plans for our return to England as soon as protocol would allow, and I had already arranged for the jewels Philip had given me to be sent ahead of us, complete with instructions to Perrot to store them safely. I had begun to feel impatient to be away from the stifling French court; for all the ceremony and the obsequious attention. I was keen to return to London – and Piers.

It was to my new bride's credit that she stoically endured a Channel crossing as turbulent as the one that had brought me to France. Indeed, it was only as we neared the Dover port that our ship seemed to settle and I could make out the crowds that gathered, and could hear their shouts and cheers. In the midst of all the throng I searched for one face, and when I saw it I felt a surge of joy – Piers!

No sooner had my barge glided into its berth than my brother and I strode over to each other with beaming smiles, we stood inches apart for a momentary stare and warmly embraced. I held his face in my hands and kissed him fully, breathing in that familiar lavender scent. "I felt I would die if I had to endure one more day apart from you, Perrot."

"And I you, my king," he replied. "Just as I was getting the hang of being in charge. I have upset one of the bishops – I forget which - by saying he was overweight! Oh, and apparently I was indiscreet to the Dowager Countess of Norfolk. You will see her with your sisters over there. I don't recall now what it was that upset her, but I am "shameless" apparently!"

I laughed aloud. "Then very little has changed," I said, embracing him again.

I was aware suddenly that several bows and curtsies were being made, and turned to see my new bride being escorted from her barge that had followed my own from the ship. I stepped back and gallantly reached out to take her small cold fingers in my hand as I proudly introduced Isabella, the new Queen of England. I recall a slight trepidation as I did so; I had not realised how necessary it was that Piers approved of my new wife. I need not have worried, as Piers displayed the utmost courtesy in a sweeping bow, before touching his lips against the hand that Isabella now offered.

"My Lord of Cornwall, I am happy to meet you." Despite her obvious nervousness at this first greeting in this new country, it was a gracious attempt. I wondered how much she knew of my brother beforehand that she recognised him before any introduction was forthcoming.

"Your grace pays me too much honour," Piers replied nobly. "I am your servant." I beamed at his exquisite manner, and could not resist a glance at some of the nobles gathered. They would surely have hoped for a coldness between my bride and my darling at this first meeting. If Isabella had seen my familiarity with Piers she gave no sign of it. None could observe this scene and deny that Perrot had behaved gallantly.

I looked at him with tears of pride welling in my eyes. All would be well I was certain of it. I had done my duty and married as expected, and I was with Perrot again.

As we walked from the dock, Piers walked at one side of Isabella, and I the other. I was so unaware of all else then that I paid not the slightest attention to the barons and dignitaries out in all their splendour and, apart from the briefest of formalities, I ceased to notice them – such was the hold Piers had over me.

Throughout the journey back, Piers kept up a narrative about the court and his adopted country, never once treating her like a child, despite the fact that she still was one. I heard her laugh at him once or twice. It was a joy to hear that he who had so completely won my heart might also do the same with my new bride.

The road to the capital was thronged with crowds, all cheering and eager to catch sight of the the new queen, although I was alarmed to hear several voices shouting to Piers. I caught only snatches of words, but that was enough to disquiet me. Certainly this was a different reception than he had enjoyed the last time we were in Dover, when he had been cheered ahead of his banishment from England. I had been warned by my cousin Thomas on a previous occasion that there was unease about Piers and his companionship with me. The very lowest tavern in the stews of Southwark to the lords and their ladies at court laughed at him, and his mannerisms were mocked. I had at the time passed this off as Thomas sowing seeds of discontent where none existed. It mattered little to me, in any case - I did not intend to live my life worrying about bawdy house gossip.

Later, when I was alone with Perrot, he had voiced his own concern about how rumours were being spread about his dominance of me and that he had appropriated money from the exchequer. "As if there were enough money to do that!" he exclaimed. "You do realise, of course, Ned, that the treasury is all but empty?"

I laughed suddenly. "Yes, I know, you helped to empty it!"

Piers would not be so easily mollified. "Be that as it may, to suggest that I have furtively bled the coffers dry is an insult. I don't do anything furtively."

I walked over to him, standing by the hearth in front of a roaring log fire, and I hugged him to me. "My own sweet Perrot, let them hang for their insolence, I will not let it spoil this homecoming. Besides, I have been thinking, I will shortly gift Isabella some land and estates and, of course, you shall have similar gifts. I will not have you treated less favourably just because I have become a married man!"

He smiled at me and we embraced again. Afterwards, we talked of the lands I had in mind to give him. I always enjoyed gifting anything to Piers, such was his excitement and his constant thanks. I was generally happier being the giver of such things rather than receiving them. Such is the way of kings and princes; born to affluence and riches, they in time become mere baubles. The barons would no doubt feel aggrieved, but they did not concern me. I was their king and had spent so long being repressed and dominated by my overbearing father that I would not countenance being told what to do.

Our evenings were spent in merrymaking and I sat and viewed my company. Gilbert de Clare, who was always a great comfort to me. We had grown older together, and had enjoyed many riotous times. My dear French cousins Henry Beaumont, his sister, Isabella, Lady Vesci. Isabella had been held in high esteem by my father and I enjoyed her dry wit and amusing anecdotes. I vaguely recall Hugh Despenser, the younger of that name. Strange that I was almost unaware of him then. My mind of course, was inevitably preoccupied with Piers.

He and I stayed together that night and, as we lay next to one another, he told me of his plans for the upcoming coronation. I delighted him by stating the whole event was to be organised by him alone.

"For you to do as you will. Moreover, Perrot, you shall carry my crown, I insist upon it. No, no, I will not be persuaded otherwise."

He looked at me with general disbelief. The ceremony traditionally followed precedence, and even he knew enough to be aware that my plans flew in the face of what was expected.

"What care we for tradition, Perrot?" I asked him. "I am the king and who better to take pride of place after myself than one whom I love with all my heart?"

"Your queen, possibly" Perrot stated, tapping his chin as though in deep thought.

I laughed at his foolery. "Ha! She is but a girl and, as my wife, she must understand that, as her lord and husband, I am not to be questioned. By the same token, the great barons will be expected to afford you every courtesy and aid."

Piers stuck out his stomach. "I cannot see "Burst Belly" or "Joseph the Jew" being satisfied with that! Nevertheless, it would be the most fun, I agree!" He linked his hands behind his head as his eyes sparkled with mirth and delight. He really was so adorably enthusiastic when faced with planning events. "We shall have matching costumes do you think? Indeed, I shall use only the finest cloths, and you, my king, will look resplendent. Not too much of course, or I shall be unnoticed by pale comparison and that would never do!"

We laughed again and talked long into the night. As my eyes began to grow heavier, Piers seemed to be growing in energy and by the time I could no longer stay awake, he was sitting up in bed with a small writing desk on his lap - plans were certainly underway.

The following morning, I was woken with a request from my council to meet with me to discuss important issues. They had dogged me for days to discuss issues following my marriage, the upcoming coronation and all manner of dull proceedings that I was too wearisome to contemplate. I instructed my steward to convey my apologies to the council, and that we would certainly meet at a later time. Having done that, I willingly answered Piers's entreaties to cast away the servants and attendants that seemed to be ever with me and go hunting, just us two. We hunted for stag and rode for hours that day, the fresh cold air blowing away the dullness of the late evening we had shared.

When we at last returned, I believe we were staying at Eltham at the time, we were exhausted from the day's merriment. I was piqued to say the least when, no sooner had I dusted the dust from my boots, I was informed that several of the barons demanded council with me. I groaned at the suggestion. Piers, however, told the bearer of this tiresome news that the council should be informed that the king was tired and they could wait upon his pleasure! I looked to the messenger and smiled as I nodded in agreement.

All I really wanted to do was to bathe away the aches of a day's riding and then sleep. It was in my chamber and after a welcome meal that I languished in a hot bath. Piers had taken over from the servant that had been attending me, and dismissed him. Now, as he squeezed the fragrant water from the bath cloth down my back, I felt blissful and relaxed - until suddenly the chamber door opened and in marched the Earl of Warwick, closely followed by Will, my personal attendant who was offering loud remonstrations that he could not just enter the chamber of the king in such a manner.

Startled as I was by the intrusion, Piers voiced his condemnation before I could speak. "Goodness, the black dog has slipped his leash! What do you say my king? Shall we toss him some of the scraps from our feast earlier? There must surely be a bone we can tempt him to fetch, out in the palace gardens perhaps!"

I laughed aloud, yet Warwick's face looked like thunder.

"You idiot!" he snarled at Piers. A dog really was a most fitting comparison. "I come to speak with the king, not his pet monkey."

"A king who, as you can see, is enjoying the relaxation of his bath, yet you burst in unannounced..."

"Furthermore, you offend the Lord of Cornwall!" I countered, before Piers could speak. "Say what you must and be gone, my lord, before you risk offending me also. God's death, my father would have had your head by now for such insolence!"

"We, your council, have waited all day for your return; there are matters to discuss of the utmost urgency, while you and this catamite play commoner and king!"

"Ha! Commoner, catamite!" exclaimed Piers. "Your insults are nothing new to me. Indeed, you'll be pleased to know I've been called worse. If you ever do have an idea of your own, my lord Warwick, be sure to let us know first, I would hate to die from shock!"

Warwick spluttered in his fury.

I attempted to be rational yet regal and I kept my voice as steady as I could. "The council will await my consent it will not be dictated by you. Now, leave me."

Warwick did not move, and in that moment all that could be heard was the noise of a growling dog, the noise coming from Piers broke the palpable tension in the room, and I could feel my sudden anger abate and a grin began to spread across my face. Warwick's eyes were like fire and his hand went to his side where normally a knife would hang, but there was nothing there, as was the custom in the vicinity of the king.

"Leave me!" My words now spoken with barely concealed anger. The look that Warwick gave Piers was one of cold hatred.

"One day, Gaveston," he again snarled. "One day." With that, he strode from the chamber, my shocked servant Will followed – with, I noted, a slight grin!

For a brief few seconds, there was complete silence until, almost in unison, we both burst out laughing. Even as I recall our mirth, something troubled me, but

I gave it no further consideration. That night we drank and laughed and talked of the coming coronation, which Piers was to arrange. Our plans must be relayed to the barons. Piers was certain they would be overwhelmed with joy at the news.

+++

It was late one night soon after that, that Will entered my chamber to announce that my cousin Thomas was impatient to see me with a matter of the utmost urgency. I felt restless, and though my habit was to go to bed very late and consequently rise late the following morning, I was fatigued and had announced my intention to retire early. That being the case, I was in no mood to suffer more chastisement from my arrogant cousin, but if the issue was urgent, I had best be advised. Yet, with Piers away from court visiting his estate in Wallingford, I assumed that my cousin's visit concerned him – it usually did.

Thomas entered the chamber, without the courtesy of an apology for the late intrusion and, after a cursory glance around the chamber, he came straight to the point. "Cousin, I come from a meeting of your lords and council, my discussion could not wait."

"So it would seem," I answered, as Will wrapped my fur cloak around me, and slid my feet into leather slippers.

Thomas looked at him, nodding briskly, "Leave us!" The instruction was most irregular, and I was momentarily shocked by his lack of protocol.

Will ignored him and glanced at me, awaiting – quite rightly - my order of dismissal.

I gave a long, tired sigh and nodded to my manservant to leave the room. Thomas waited until the door had closed before he walked to a nearby table and poured himself wine, which he gulped down thirstily.

"Do help yourself, cousin," I said, with annoyance that was starting to build in my tired head.

He seemed to realise his impudence and looked away with some embarrassment. "Cousin, I have been tasked by your barons to bring you their grievances…"

"Which could not possibly have waited until morning? Very well, I'll wager it concerns my brother, the Earl…"

Thomas slammed his goblet down onto the table, making me jump. "Enough, Edward!" He almost screamed at me. "He is not your damned brother; why must you persist in calling him so? He is only an Earl because he has bewitched you into making him so! This cannot continue, you must surely see that, or has Gaveston so entranced you that you do not see what is happening before your very eyes? He shares your every waking hour, he shares your bed, dammit, and the young queen's chamber only feet away! I - we - the council, can tolerate this no more!"

I had rarely seen Lancaster so angry, his dark eyes flashed moodily, his jaw clenched in fury. I stood and attempted to draw myself up into a dignified posture, but he continued mercilessly.

"For God's sake, Edward, the man has seduced you and yet you do not see it. Is his pretty arse really so beguiling that you would make yourself a laughing stock just to kiss it?"

I swallowed nervously at his cruelty, yet I was not completely without a response. "Have a care, cousin,"

I warned him. "You go too far and your words offend me. I am still the king and you a subject, be you an Earl, cousin or otherwise."

He made to start his remonstrance again but I cut in.

"You dare to speak thus of one who has been more loyal to me than any of my family or court…"

"Your father banished him!" His voice rose again.

"Well, I am not my father!" I retorted, my temper now simmering.

"More is the pity!" came his response.

We stood for a moment, him and I. Both of us needed to win this battle of wills, but I saw now why it was so important to wake me rather than discuss the matter in council. Truth be told, I had failed to appear at so many council meetings, where it may well have been the intention of the barons to argue their case.

Thomas sighed, running his hands through his black hair. He bowed his head and reached for a nearby seat, glancing at me expectantly. Eventually I nodded towards the chair, where he then slumped, letting out out a further dramatic sigh.

"It is not my wish to hurt you, Ned. I would see you happy and content, more so now that you have your young queen at your side, but it must be she that is there. It must be to the queen, not Gaveston, that you whisper your innermost thoughts, your plans for the future. Did I not advise you once that, if you wished to keep Gaveston with you, at least keep his presence and influence discreet?"

I did indeed recall his words. We were closer then, of course, and yet I did not regret that I consciously paid his warning no heed. I continued to stare at his bowed head, uncertain what to do, yet I had a suspicion of what was to come next, and when his words were uttered, I felt myself almost stagger at the brutality of them.

"He cannot stay in England, Edward, you must see that?"

I looked straight into his burning eyes and shook my head as I spoke. "No, I will not cast him away, you and the other lords are traitors to demand it of me. He is part of myself, I feel wounded when he is away, and I cannot live happily without him here - without Piers there is nothing!"

Thomas seemed to find my words risible, and scoffed in derision as he rose. "Then there must be a reckoning, Edward. I am charged by your council to inform you that, once the coronation - that you have let this fool organise - is done with, we shall seek his exile. The many titles and estates that you have lavished upon him will be rescinded and we will seek to banish him from the kingdom."

I stared, horrified by his words. What gave me as much concern as the hatred they clearly had for Piers, was the obvious risk that Thomas was taking in summoning me at such an hour to berate me and inform me of what was to happen – in my name - to one whom I held in higher esteem than any other. It struck me that there was no fear in my cousin. He would not dare to have spoken thus to my father, but he obviously saw me as much weaker, and he purposely struck at something that was so sacred to me that I would know that I should heed his words. Was I, a king not yet crowned, a puppet that would dance to the tune of the barons? I stood motionless for some moments, and Thomas went to speak further, but I raised a hand to still him.

"No, no more; you will leave me, Thomas."

"Edward, let me -"

"Enough! Leave me, before I have the guard outside come in and force you out." I sat and buried my head in my hands and, when I looked up again, he was gone.

I kept the details of my conversation with Lancaster from Piers. He had returned to court with a multitude of ideas for my impending enthronement, and seemed almost giddy with excitement, a countenance greatly at odds with my own. I had not spoken with any of my lords on the subject of Piers's exile, casting it from my mind and assuring myself that if I ignored the problem it would cease to be an issue. Nevertheless, I was angered by the impudence of the council attempting to impose their wishes upon me, and I became even more determined to ensure that all would know of the great esteem in which I held my darling Perrot.

Nevertheless, I knew enough of etiquette to recognise my obligations, and made a conscious effort to make friendly overtures to Isabella's uncles that had travelled with us from France, along with her brother, Charles. Louis, the Count of Everaux, was a pompous ass with a long, bland face and dull, lifeless eyes. The Count of Valois differed only by virtue of having an even duller countenance, a sallow complexion and the most appalling stench to his breath. Apart from the French delegation, the distinguished attendees included my sisters, Margaret and Mary, the former with her husband John, the Duke of Brabant, my young half-brothers Thomas and Edmund, as well as the Count of Savoy and Henry of Luxembourg. Many others of course, but after so many years, I forget them now.

The morning of my coronation was a cold one and as I walked along a trail of flowers strewn over the walkway. I took in the spectacle of the event. Crowds had gathered throughout the morning. So much so that Isabella and I had been forced to be led into Westminster Abbey by a side door. I was horrified to learn later that some of the temporary seating actually collapsed, causing great injury.

Whilst I had given my beloved Piers charge of the main event, there was, of course, an accepted cavalcade; the pomp and ceremony that accompanied such an occasion was a tradition that could not be ignored. Isabella, looking nervous and expectant, walked beside me under a canopy of royal purple silk carried by the Cinque Port barons. The other major barons, dressed splendidly in cloth-of-gold, preceded us along with the prelates and dignitaries that held the sceptre with the cross and golden royal rod. My good treasurer and friend Walter Reynolds, now Bishop of Worcester, carried the paten of the chalice of Edward the Confessor, followed by my chancellor.

The congregation appeared suddenly to cease their excited chatter and wonder at all the pageantry when Piers Gaveston came into full view, carrying before him the crown, nestled on a purple velvet cushion. In all my many days with Piers, I had never seen him look more noble and handsome. He was dressed resplendently in royal purple silk, studded with pearls that reached to his throat. His long fingers glittered with precious stones of all colours. I could have wept at the sight of this brilliantly-attired man who was so vital to my life. Yet I could see faces that showed disgust as well as awe. Piers looked straight ahead, dazzling yet conscious of his role which, by his own design, was a superior one to all others.

As for myself, after being lifted onto the royal throne as was the tradition, I allowed my brother Piers to carry out the important job of putting on my right spur, this being a significant task that I had requested him to carry out. Such was its importance that few could fail to see the favour I bore him above all others. Other tasks, that should have been shared with the great nobles of the land, I had ascribed to my darling Perrot - so much so that there were audible gasps and mutterings, which in turn grew to shouts of disgust!

I did not care, I was enjoying the grand spectacle and buoyed by this pricking of the nobles' vanity and sense of importance. How little it mattered then. In time, of course, I would rue those mistakes, but then, only Piers and I mattered. Isabella seemed generally bemused by the whole event and I naturally put this down to inexperience of such an occasion, and her youth. Apart from that, I paid her little heed.

With the ceremony at last at an end, we proceeded to Westminster Hall for the coronation feast, once again arranged and organised by the despised Earl of Cornwall. The vast hall had been bedecked with flowers, garlands and bright candles in gold and silver lamps, casting splendour from the vaulted ceiling that presented an almost ethereal vision. Colourful standards flapped slightly, their dazzling colours of blues, yellows, and reds. Along the tables were silver flagons of red and white wines and dishes holding all manner of delights.

I was further delighted to see the look of horror on so many faces when it was noticed that, as I had instructed Piers, there were tapestries bearing my own royal arms next to those of Piers's own eaglets. The statement was, I hoped, not lost on those barons who may well have believed that his role had been merely to organise the wedding feast. Furthermore, I sat Isabella naturally by my side, but placed Piers on my other side. I searched out the face of my cousin Lancaster, whom I found looking at me also, wearing an almost cat-like smirk. I wondered at the time whether, just for that second, he had admired my boldness. I admit to being more unnerved by that look when I had expected a face of barely controlled rage.

Throughout the feast, I paid attention to none but Piers, we drank and joked as though a pair of reckless youths. I playfully fed him grapes, he dabbed at my mouth when I neglected to clear the crumbs from my beard. I was not completely unaware of the scowls from Isabella's uncles and the others of the French party. So many illustrious guests, and I had made it known to all of them that my beloved was going nowhere. I did turn to see that Isabella was content, and although a smile passed between us, I paid her little heed – as usual!

I would fiercely deny the later accusation that I ignored her for the whole of the banquet, and indeed most of the day, but she was little more than a child, and I was not a nursemaid! Wedded though we were, we could certainly not converse and laugh as Piers and I did. Besides which, I felt sure she would soon tire and leave the festivities. It was hardly my fault that she chose to remain until her eyes became heavy from the exertions of the day.

+++

The parliament that opened only several days after the coronation was a ghastly affair and one that sought to finally destroy my brother Piers. The coronation was seen as proof positive that Gaveston had sought to undermine the other nobles by his arrogance and his control over me. Seldom have I witnessed hatred of someone as much as in that gathering. The barons and earls were almost in full agreement that Piers must be exiled, and indeed, they voiced their intentions to make it their sole purpose until he was banished. He had, they declared, sought to humiliate and denigrate them, and their loyalty to the crown forced them to be rid of him – for my own wellbeing!

They accused him of behaving like a second king, and being unworthy of the vast estates and titles that had been heaped upon him by an erring liege lord.

I, of course, railed against their will being imposed upon me; I was their king and their petty grievances would not force me to banish the man that I truly loved above all others. I would never let him go - never!

Two men amongst those detestable magnates did, however, speak in my favour, and whilst one was to remain loyal to me for the remainder of my reign, the other was a surprise so great that I spent time attempting to fully comprehend why he should now appear to be of support.

Thomas of Lancaster was a most unlikely ally, yet he attempted to reason that, although he was shocked at the boldness of the Earl of Cornwall, especially at the coronation that had just taken place - and it was true that Gaveston had caused a great deal of anger by his impudence and boldness with the king -perhaps a compromise could be reached.

The other that joined Thomas in support was Hugh Despenser – called "the elder" to distinguish him from his son that bore the same name. I will talk more of the younger Hugh later in this long tale of woe. The elder of that name was a giant of a man, with a jolly countenance and an affable nature, who greatly respected by many, and whose loyalty to me I had never doubted. Thomas, I could not understand. He had berated me so fiercely before about the helplessness of my situation, and left me in no doubt as to his disgust for Piers, and - by association – myself. I would endeavour to be wary however, as Lancaster was a sly fox and I sensed an ulterior motive.

At our next meeting, he feigned indifference to Gaveston and merely declared that, as one of royal blood himself, he must baulk against any criticism or threat to the crown. I knew Piers and I must keep our own counsel. To Thomas, I stated again that I intended to keep Piers with me regardless.

It must not, however, be supposed that the threatened uprising from the barons lay entirely at my feet. At the end of my father's reign, he had been in a constant battle with them and their desire for more land and titles, as well as a greater control of events. It was to my father's credit that he had kept some control over them. Only now was I beginning to realise that his words to me during one of our late night meetings - to "be wary of those bastards or they will bleed you dry" - had been sound advice. It was clear that the threat to Piers and myself was all too real, and we both avoided the subject in the vain hope that we were safe as long as we did not discuss our fears.

We would discuss it, however, late one day after a solemn evening's entertainment. Piers had arranged a display by a group of fools, acrobats and singers to lighten our mood. The performance, whilst highly amusing normally, did little to lift our spirits. I had a lot of time for the company of mummers, jugglers and the like; I enjoyed their abilities and their acts never normally failed to cheer me. Piers glanced at me and one look was enough to prompt him to throw the troupe leader a bag of coins and thank them for their performance. They bowed low at me and I managed a weak smile of gratitude before my servant, Will, ushered them out of the chamber.

I rose from my seat and leant down at the hearth to throw another large log onto the crackling fire, leaning against the mantle and staring into the dancing flames. Piers had dismissed his manservant, Hugo, and we were alone.

"You have to let me go, Ned," Piers said softly, knowing exactly what was causing my misery.

"Never!" I stated with heartfelt determination. "I will not be dictated to, forced against my will to do the barons' bidding. It is against my rights as their liege lord, I am the king and I will not be shackled in such a way!" I beat a fist against the wall, then bit at my knuckles.

I felt Perrot's hands, then, taking my bloodied ones and gently holding them to his lips. "Forgive me, Ned, that your love for me has brought us to this. I never meant for such disharmony between you and the barons. Well, alright, maybe just a little!"

I laughed at him, incorrigible as always, but at least he had brought a smile to my lips. I took that beautiful troubled face in my hands, and he leant towards me, our foreheads touching. We remained like that for several moments, silenced by the weight of our current predicament.

"You realise there will be civil war if you keep me with you?" Piers said eventually.

"I know that, Perrot, but I dread that less than I do you being taken from me."

He stepped away from me with a deep sigh. Pouring us both some wine, he brought mine to me. "You have much to think about, Ned. Do not let me be the reason this country is torn apart."

"I will not let that happen, Perrot, but nor will I let you go merely because I am told to."

He looked at me with sadness in his green fathomless eyes. "Is it for me you would fight, or to ensure the barons know that you will not be ruled by their wishes?"

"For you, always!" I declared. "How could you think otherwise? I would surrender my crown tomorrow if it guaranteed we could live together without sanctions."

Piers smiled impishly at me. "Ah, but then, my king, you may cease to be so valuable to me. Who could I turn to when my king has no power, money or influence? What about the pope? Do you think he would find a use for a handsome Gascon knight with a firm, shapely arse?"

I looked at him and laughed aloud. How could I ever live without him? I had asked myself the same question day after day with no answer. "The idea of you with the pope does conjure up an appalling image," I said, trying to continue with some levity.

"I am in danger, aren't I?" he suddenly stated seriously.

It is to my eternal shame that I realised that I had never really considered that he may well be fearful of his life. I didn't believe Piers would be frightened of anything, and yet it must be considered that his own life could be in peril.

"I will not let anyone hurt you, my brother…"

"Do you not consider that they laugh at me because I have your protection? With you taking the blows for me, do you not think that makes me feel less of a man? Let one of them meet me in joust or one-on-one combat, that I can do gladly, but this way I am seen as a coward who hides behind his king!"

"Why do you care?" I asked. "Does it matter what they think?"

"It matters to me, Ned!"

We both looked at one another, startled by our words. I had not thought of him as hiding behind me, the notion was ridiculous. It was now he who paced around the chamber, draining his goblet of wine and refilling it, thirstily gulping it down.

"We cannot be parted, Perrot; I would die without you."

Piers let out a drunken chuckle. "We may yet both be slain, in any case."

Suddenly, I rushed to him, pulling him close. "Don't let them force us apart, Perrot. My life is nothing without you!"

"Ah, my sweet, gentle Ned," he responded, holding me tightly. "Remember our solemn vows?"

I stared tearfully into his eyes as he pulled at the sleeve of his shirt, exposing our entwined initials and gently kissing the skin, all the while staring, unblinking and intense. I felt a tear run from my eye and course down my cheek. "Nunc et usque in aeternum."

It was late when I awoke, still fully clothed, the fire now burnt out, with only a few defiant embers remaining. The room was cold, and Piers had gone. He had sat on the floor at my feet leaning his head against my knee. He must have waited for me to fall asleep and then left. Life for me would be as cold as the chamber, yet I had woken with the same resolve – I would never let him go.

+++

CHAPTER THREE

Edward drew in a breath and drained the earthenware cup of the cool water. He stood and stretched out his arms, eager to move around after what, for him, was a long period of inactivity. He had always been a restless man; ever ready to throw himself into the rugged and vigorous pursuits that had helped him build such an impressive physique. Whilst age and his privations had speckled his shortly-cropped hair with grey and added weight to his once slender stomach, he was still a strongly built man.

"Forgive me, my friends, for my accurate recollections of Piers's words and actions. He was rarely subtle. Indeed, whilst for him every disrespect was intended where those for whom he did not care were concerned, that is not my intent as I relay his often careless speech."

Alphage held his rosary between his soft, aged fingers as though drawing comfort from them, whilst Fieschi's features were placid and rarely showed any emotion. Rapt, he drank in the ex-king's every word. He was keen to ask questions, and used the break in Edward's tale to do so.

"So, the longer your relationship with Gaveston continued, the more perilous the situation became," Manuel stated.

"Indeed, my friend. The barons hated him most violently. It was to my shame that I did not notice, or perhaps did not want to notice, what storm was brewing. At that time, I trusted no-one more than Piers. Both of us were inexperienced in government and giving little heed to the consequences of our actions. As time went on, I showered him with all manner of gifts; lands and estates, jewels and all manner of costly items. The treasury was empty, but I paid no heed to that. I was the king."

"And the queen?"

"Ah, yes, Alphage, the queen." Edward refilled his cup with water and re seated himself. "I took so little notice of Isabella. I curse myself for my folly. She was so young, and yet whilst she physically failed to interest me, she was old enough, and astute enough – even at her young age - to assess the situation. Moreover, there was no shortage of enemies within my court who were only too glad to explain what she did not fully understand. I could have been more attentive. There she was, caught up in the mistrust and turbulence that my ongoing determination to protect Piers was causing. Have no fear, my friends, Isabella was to prove far more resilient, as my tale will relate. Suffice to say, those early years of our marriage were not harmonious, yet I certainly bore no ill will towards her, any more than Piers did. She was merely another player in the intrigue that seemed to surround us. She told me many years later that... no matter, we shall speak of that in time."

Edward looked up towards the blue sky and after allowing the still radiant sun to warm his face, he continued.

I roared with laughter at the mummers' act. These vividly coloured characters danced, leapt and play-acted and I felt for the first time in ages as though I were free and happy. My darling Perrot had engaged this troupe and even written and instructed the performance they were now giving.

Glancing around, I was surprised to see several of the barons enjoying the spectacle, for once leaving animosity aside to laugh and make merry. Thomas of Lancaster, Surrey, Pembroke and even Warwick – whether seated or standing, appeared to take some pleasure from watching the players.

That was until the main act of the performance turned ugly. An actor wearing a headpiece that resembled a large hound was led onto the stage wearing a rope as a lead around his neck. He was followed by a character dancing whilst playing a small fiddle. He in turn preceded an overlarge man with an extended stomach that burst out of its restricting shirt. Last of this horrific ensemble was a tall individual with an enormous hooked nose. These individuals proceeded to dance along in a line; the great hound stopping to relieve itself on the stage, and the large-bellied man to spill even more of his guts.

I, like the rest of the audience, was stunned into silence for a moment, but then proceeded to laugh. I cannot recall when I had last seen or heard anything to make me laugh as much. Tears rolled down my cheeks and I feared my heart would give way. Beside me, Isabella smiled, but I think did not comprehend who the characters represented. Suddenly there was uproar. Warwick, his face incandescent with rage, pushed courtiers out of his way as he tore towards the front of the audience where Piers sat beside me.

He managed to grab my brother by his tunic, ripping the collar. Had not Hugh Despenser and a household knight held him back, he would most certainly have struck him. Lancaster, too, had reached the scene and was grasping at Piers's sleeve.

Piers seemed to find the reaction of the audience as much fun as he had the performance itself. "Why, my lord Warwick," he stated, "what strong hands you have! If you intend to rip off my clothing, at least wait until we are alone!" Despenser had almost to physically hug the earl in order to save my favourite from Warwick's hands.

Piers then turned his attention to Lancaster, himself being prevented from dragging him from his guardians. "Thomas," Piers continued ruthlessly, "is it true what is said about men with large noses? Do they also…?"

I stood up immediately, trying to quell the pandemonium. Suddenly, in the mayhem, a voice called out: "Sire - the queen!"

All eyes turned suddenly to Isabella, who appeared to have fainted. Attendants rushed to her side, and for a few moments all was quiet. I pushed the ladies in waiting away, swooped Isabella up in my arms and carried her out of the room. I instructed the guards in attendance to restore order as I laid the queen down on a couch in the antechamber.

I heard shouting still and a brief clash of steel. I suddenly thought of Piers, and for a moment considered leaving the child's side to ensure he was safe. Then, suddenly, the chamber door opened and Piers slipped inside, his face a display of concern.

Isabella opened her eyes and, I recall, I wiped away a wisp of her hair that had rebelliously escaped her headdress. She smiled and made to sit up. She appeared to be quite well, and I sat back on my heels and glanced to Piers, who showed on his face a look of uncertainty which matched my own.

"You must take greater care, lord of Cornwall," the queen said as she patted at her gown.

I was unsure of what to do or say next. "But, my love, you..."

Isabella smiled with satisfaction. "How else to stop those great lords from tearing Piers apart with their bare hands? Some water please, my lord Cornwall."

Gaveston found his manners quickly and poured water into a goblet which she took with a smile of thanks.

"My dear," I said, "you show a maturity beyond your years." I kissed her hand.

"But you must take care, husband. I do not fully understand the significance of what we just watched, but I know enough from the idle chatter of my ladies that many of the lords hate you, Lord Gaveston - you too must have a care."

"Was it not one of the funniest displays you have ever seen?" I stated, rising and embracing Piers. We both roared with laughter. "Did you see the look on Burst-Belly's face? And the black dog, I swear I thought he would erupt into flames, such was his fury!"

"And the player whom you cast as my cousin Thomas, it was as if I were seeing his twin, even down to the sneer!"

As we enjoyed again the hilarity of the act, I glanced back at Isabella who watched us with a troubled look on her face.

"You must rest, my dear. I will send your ladies to you, you have been distressed enough." So saying, Piers and I giggled as we left the chamber, without a backward glance.

In the weeks that followed, tensions continued to grow between the great barons, myself, and Piers. Several times I thought Piers had gone too far in his hatred of the magnates. His imitation of them was merciless, and on more than one occasion they had threatened violence against him. It was reported to me, by spies at the French court, that even king Philip joined the barons in their hatred of Piers.

That much was not surprising; any tumult at the English court was met with pleasure by Isabella's father and, had he been a puppet-master, he could not have orchestrated things better. Whether my young queen had gossiped to him I was uncertain, but I had already heard that what he perceived as "distressing revelations" regarding our wedding feast. I was unsure what could possibly have been said, as I felt the occasion a great success. Who else but my dear Perrot could have arranged such an event?

Relations between the barons and Piers intensified. They demanded on many occasions that I agree to exile him. The hatred that now existed between them was threatening to get out of hand, and many of the allies I still had advised me that, so great was the animosity, the country was surely heading for civil war.

The barons in particular objected that anyone wishing to have audience with me must initially apply to Piers for what he called "a vetting procedure".

This, of course, was intolerable to many, yet I could see no harm in it. How to tame the resentment that all seemed to feel towards my beloved friend was a question I asked myself often. Yet it was something as simple as a nightmare that ultimately convinced me that I must make the decision to part with Piers, albeit temporarily.

In the vivid dream, I was running – where, I know not. I was being chased through woods and even across a stream. I stopped suddenly and a body fell from the trees just in front of me. I stooped down to turn the body over but there was no face there. I cried out and then suddenly the body was no longer there but had been replaced by the head of my beloved brother Piers stuck on a pike, blood dripping steadily from the severed neck...

I lay awake, frightened that I would relive that horrendous scene if I attempted to return to sleep; all I could think of was that nightmare and Piers's severed head. Added to which, those barons that were still loyal to me attempted to reason with me that every day Piers remained in England was a dangerous one. Roger Mortimer was one of the many voices that urged caution and good sense and to exile Piers – at least for now.

"It will not be for long," I promised Perrot. "If I let you stay longer, I fear that Warwick, Lancaster or any of those bastards will find a way to hurt or even kill you!"

Piers looked at me with reservation in his eyes. "I understand, Ned. You must dwell on it no longer. Just promise me it will not be forever."

I could feel my emotions beginning to build, and I hugged him to me, the tears stinging in my eyes. "I promise you Perrot," I tried to state with conviction. "I am sending you to Ireland as my lieutenant. That way, there will be no dishonour."

The look on his face was one of sorrow, but I detected slight glint in those beautiful eyes. Like myself, he hated inactivity. Moreover, he would be determined to make the role a success. I knew that I would long for him, but I also knew I had very little choice. I left Piers to make his own arrangements; his young wife, my niece, would go with him, even though I had promised she could continue to live comfortably in England.

It was shortly thereafter that Robert Winchelsey, the archbishop of Canterbury, added further fuel to this emotional fire and threatened to have Piers excommunicated if he did not leave the country by the middle of June of that year thirteen hundred and eight.

I travelled to Bristol to see the couple sail to Ireland, Perrot complaining that he had only just recently recovered from the last trip by sea. "You see, my king," he told me on the journey to Bristol port, "the Irish are a strange lot, I am told. The first thing I shall do is smarten them up, as apparently they are positively barbarian in their dress!"

Keeping up this stream of amusing declarations seemed to be an attempt to retain some levity and trivialise the occasion.

He would, I told him, retain his title of Earl of Cornwall but, alas, all other titles and the land I had lavished upon him would revert to the crown. This went some way, I hoped, of reassuring my niece - Perrot's young wife Margaret - that they were certainly not destitute.

Our goodbyes seemed almost familiar somehow, and we said very little as the time to set sail arrived. I took him in my arms, and promised again that this would not be forever. He smiled that beautiful smile of his and he laid his hand on my face, wiping away a tear from my cheek. I closed my eyes, and when I opened them again he was standing looking at me.

"God bless you, Ned," he whispered hoarsely.

I knew that in replying I would break down, so I left him and walked to my horse. It was too cruel to stay; I could not do it. I reined my horse and gave one final look back. "Until we meet again, Perrot," I almost whispered, to myself as much as to him. Then I rode away. My heart was broken again.

+++

Edward had covered his face with his hands, and some time elapsed before he looked up again.

"So," Manuel ventured softly, "you returned to your duties once Gaveston had left the country?"

"If you mean did I seek the comfort of my wife, the queen, then yes I did. How easy to look back and see that I had done untold damage to myself, my country, Isabella and, of course, to Piers. I had allowed my infatuation and the love I bore him to blind me to all else. Yet even then, I do not know if I would have acted differently if I had known what devastation was wrought through our deep friendship. The barons were another matter. Now I would see whether it had really been their hatred of Gaveston or their hatred of me that had forced them to threaten civil war. Some were still loyal to me, although they were in the minority, and yet I kept them close by. I was by no means done yet, however, and I had no sooner ridden away from Bristol, tears streaming down my face, than I was plotting."

Edward rose again and walked to the edge of one of the fragrant bushes of lavender, where he grabbed at a handful of the aromatic stems, rubbing the light purple flowers into his hands and then covering his nose and breathing in the scent as though taking strength from it. The fact that the smell of the shrub was a favourite of Piers Gaveston's was not lost on either Alphage or Fieschi, yet neither commented on the fact. Edward crouched now to stroke the dozing Perrot, who, like his master earlier, stretched out his limbs in delicious contentment.

"I realised that I had to start by trying to explain to my father-in-law and the pope himself that court gossip had forced me to exile my friend, and yet assure them that the stories they had heard presented a false picture of events.

Isabella's uncles would have given Philip a first-hand report of the wedding feast, about which they had apparently been so furious. I told them that Gaveston had not once asked for favour from me, and that the earldom of Cornwall was my decision. I realised that my step-mother, Marguerite, who was also Philip's half sister, would have felt aggrieved at the title of Cornwall not being bestowed on one of my half-brothers. I could therefore not hope for any help from her and, in truth, she had featured even less in my life than before my father died.

I insisted that the barons had risen up in anger because I had shown favour to one who had been most loyal to me. I thought I might possibly receive a favourable hearing from Philip who, above all kings before him, believed in the right of kingship and might be appalled that one's subjects could revolt against their liege lord and king.

Whatever Philip may have thought, I considered my situation and how best to get Piers's return. I simply began to adopt a charm offensive.

You seem surprised, Manuel, do you only take me for a fool? Forgive me, I do not censure you, I know it must seem as though I had not acted particularly charmingly towards the likes of Lancaster, Warwick and the others. Nevertheless, if I was to win them around, I would have to play at being their friend as well as their king. Plus, they had demanded the exile of Gaveston as the price I must pay for their loyalty, and now that he was gone there was surely little they could force me to do that I had not already carried out. Their further opposition would seem puerile at best."

"So, you won them over?" Alphage asked.

"Some of them at least. Many of them were greedy, and that gave me a perfect opportunity for largesse. Especially as so many of Piers's titles and lands had reverted to the crown upon his banishment. Meanwhile, relations with Isabella began to thaw. Since the mummer's performance when she had amazingly duped the lords and prevented outright bloodshed, our relationship had not been warm. I understood later, as I did about so much, that I had acted without concern or appreciation for her help. It was certainly the case that, with Piers gone, I frequented my young wife's company more than I had before. I began to see her less as a little girl; she had already proved in that violent episode at Eltham, that she was far more astute than I gave her credit for."

I spent Christmas of that year I had lost Perrot at Windsor, but then reverted to my favourite castle of Langley. During those long days and nights, I sat brooding, restless and anxious. Some days were made easier by the company of Isabella, who I had to admit was proving a welcome distraction. I envied her youth; although I was only twelve years older, I felt a burden that should only have come with advancing years.

I recall we walked together one day that spring at the Tower of London, a beautiful, bright sky, and warm enough to be outside which I always preferred to the fog of winter fires and heavy cloaks. I talked to her about my love of nature and she of her interest in birds. There was much I didn't know about this princess from France - yet how would I know?

Isabella declared she had been told of my love of "rustic" pursuits; she had never heard of thatched roofs and was amazed to learn that I swam and even fished! "But, my lord, surely you have your servants for such things as fishing?"

I laughed at her look of horror that I knew well how to dig a trench, work with a blacksmith and sail a boat! There we walked down from the Tower to the banks of the great Thames. The river was busy, small crafts crossed from one side to the other, ferrying passengers, while other crafts held produce to sell. Up and along the bank, a moving mass of people: tinkers, prostitutes, old men herding sheep through the throng; children, barefoot, danced and dug into the marshy banks, ever watchful for food or dropped trinkets.

"Do you not swim in France?" I asked, knowing that she would be aghast at the very thought of such a thing. I laughed again, and then, even though two of her ladies in waiting accompanied us at a distance, I peeled off my hose, pulled my shirt over my head and, to her look of horror and her ladies' blushes, I dived naked into the river. I trod water as I called out to her. She exchanged her shocked demeanour for one of delight and clapped her small hands in glee.

I swam quickly to the edge of the bank and hauled myself out, shaking the water from my hair. I certainly could have chosen a better place to display my prowess than the grey, ugly water that ran past the impregnable fortress and through the city. I laughed at her innocent delight, and she glanced at her waiting ladies, who, after risking a brief glimpse of my nakedness, feigned an interest in something growing in the hedgerow. I grinned, but dressed myself quickly before bowing extravagantly in apology.

I have recalled that day often since. The contentment I felt in Isabella's company seemed strange somehow, and yet I did not find it unpleasant. We walked a little further; though wet, I felt no discomfort.

"My lord?" she asked, at which point I stopped her.

"You must feel happy to call me Edward; we are married, are we not? Let there be no formality." I was at once reminded I had said the same to Piers.

"I shall call you 'Ned', shall I?"

"No – never that! Only Lord Gaveston calls me that!" I had not intended the words to sound so harsh, and one look at her face was enough to tell me she was close to tears.

"Forgive me, Isabella, I spoke harshly but meant no harm." We walked on, now in silence. The mention of Piers had somehow clouded the day and I felt his absence acutely in the minutes after.

"You miss him, do you not?" Isabella eventually said, softly.

"Every hour of every day," I stated, almost to myself, "but it shall not be long before I will have him back with me. Though I know your father thinks ill of him, all he has heard is false, vicious lies from those who wish Perrot harm."

She coloured at my words, and I wondered how complicit she had been in relaying to her father all the scandals about Piers. I could not bring myself to demand she not discuss such things with her father. I supposed that discretion would come as she learned to be loyal only to me. We walked silently for some moments before she spoke again.

"I am sorry you are lonely, Edward."

I stopped and looked down at her. "Once he is back with me, I will never be lonely again."

"Am I not enough for you?" The question took me by surprise, and I scoffed at her cruelly.

"You are still a child my dear, I have no mind to consummate our marriage whilst you are so young, and there are things you could not hope to understand."

"Then tell me."

"There is much you have to learn about the ways of men. Not all is as simple as it seems."

"I do not understand," she spoke earnestly.

I carried on walking for a few paces, unaware that she had stopped. I had caught the slight tremor in her voice, and I looked up at the sky. "We must return to indoors, clouds are gathering now, there may well be rain."

If the truth be known, I was at a loss for an answer. She seemed petulant, suddenly a child again. What could I tell her that would not seem any more heartless? Few understood the bond that existed between myself and Perrot, and I was sure that a young innocent like Isabella would find it impossible.

"I want to know."

"Piers is precious to me, I would gladly die for him, happily surrender all my worldly goods if I had to. And you, as my wife, will treat him well," I stated firmly. "Perrot is my brother, and none – even you - will cause him any harm. Do you understand?"

Isabella's blue dazzling eyes filled with tears. I had no experience of young girls who cried. I looked beseechingly at her two ladies in waiting who quickly approached.

"Your queen is tired. Escort her back to the Tower, I will follow shortly." My dismissal of Isabella seems brusque as I retell our words that day. I watched her being escorted away and felt some pity for her. I could be a bully at times! How strange that we see our faults when it's too late?

I was still unsure whether our conversations were relayed back to her father in France. What had for me started brightly and in surprisingly good humour, too, had ended in cruel words, but I had to remind myself she was only a child.

Whilst I was enjoying some success with bringing some of the barons over to my side, Thomas began to distance himself from me. Ironically, on reflection, he had been less intolerant of myself and Piers. Oh, he was still an ass about it, and readily spoke cruel words, and now he seemed to have become a figurehead for those magnates who criticised me and were deeply opposed to Gaveston's return. I felt emboldened, however, to send a delegation to Avignon, primarily to seek an annulment of the excommunication that had been placed on Piers.

If I at least managed to secure that, it would surely be difficult for my councillors to still oppose his return.

I faced an uphill battle to have Piers recalled and reinstated but, foolish though I often was, I knew that the barons and I played a dangerous game; whilst they had got their way with Gaveston's banishment, they could not deny he was by all accounts making a fine success in his role in Ireland. I could bribe and promise all manner of inducements, yet I knew that the price I would pay for any help would be settling their other grievances.

I ached to be with Piers. I imagined his delight in proving to be so successful in his role of lieutenant in Ireland. How he would be holding feasts and tournaments, revelling in his triumphs. No doubt also flirting outrageously with his captains' wives – as well as the captains themselves!

Piers thirsted for adulation, desperate for new converts to fall at his feet, to hang on his every word. Shy maiden or young impressionable soldier it mattered not; all must pay due homage to this most demanding of idols. What folly and humiliation we endure for those we love!

Love certainly had no part to play in my cousin Thomas's plans. Some slight disagreement - I forget what, such was its triviality - infuriated him and he left court. The remaining magnates were now without their spokesman, yet they wasted no time in voicing their grievances and demands. Moreover, their intent that Gaveston's recall would come at a price; that being agreement to reforms.

How it all bored me! I wanted nothing as much as to retire to Langley with Piers and live a contented and satisfied life without the burden of kingship. Yet, it was my birthright and there was, I believed, no reason why I could not have my own way!

I would run my court as I deemed fit; yet the great barons of the realm continued to accuse me of spending to excess, allowing the lowest-born to inhabit the court - a reference, no doubt, to the singers, jesters and the like that I paid to entertain me. God knows that these good people, poor though they may be, were nevertheless a delight to me. It was said that I distributed large sums of money on these entertainers for the most trivial of service and yet it gave me such joy to do so. I had little experience with money; I spent liberally, but I believed that, as king, it was entirely my choice how I spent it.

Of course, the country's finances were in a ruinous state – when were they not? My own father had bled the country dry with his incessant wars in Scotland, and I was all but a pauper king when I inherited the throne. I had spent liberally on Piers, and that was their real concern, but why should I not? He was my dearest brother, and such gifts were necessary to appease and comfort him when the barons continually urged me to exile him and mistreated him like they did.

As usual however, I did not realise that this was a deep grievance with the magnates, and there was much more. I was, they told me, "ill-advised by others". I allowed those of my inner circle to flaunt their wealth, and indeed, I had turned a blind eye while these "villains" extorted money from the poorest in my realm. Not only these grievances, but criticism that I had all but lost Scotland! No mention made that my father had carried on an almost life long obsession with conquering that barren, cold land, and had little to show for it. With the scant experience I had in battle-craft, I sincerely doubted if Scotland could ever be truly conquered, and I had no great desire to try and do so.

Events seemed to move so swiftly that I was barely aware of the tension that now existed between myself and the lords of the realm. A demand by these men that I should address these concerns angered me, and I raged at any who would listen. I screamed at my servants, giving poor Will Shene a beating when, on one occasion I had seen him bowing in deference to Warwick. I admonished him for doing so, knowing as he did the bad grace that existed between us. I withheld money that was rightly due to Will for his services to me, with the rejoinder that his loyalty was to me was absolute. In future he should answer to no other but me. Spiteful perhaps, but justified.

Of course, I hated myself for this behaviour, and my dear Will made no attempt to defend himself against my verbal onslaught, or the blows that rained down on him.

Isabella was unhappy when she learnt of the episode, yet I let her know in no uncertain terms that her role was not to question me. It seemed I faced dissent from all sides - the earls also had plenty to say about my use of the royal exchequer. I thought very little then about how my spending affected the poorest of my realm.

People must pay taxes and their overlords should live well; there was a structure to society and – as I pointed out in no uncertain terms to my council – a prince was to be marvelled at, held in awe! Piers had said to me many times that the status of the king must be paid for. It mattered little to me then that I did not necessarily care where the wealth came from, as long as it came from somewhere. Moreover, did I not exercise considerable largesse to all who pleased me? Actors, jugglers, singers, I paid them all handsomely. I must surely not be censured. The poor were taxed too much and, indeed, I was accused of misusing the power of purveyance and my very actions were threatening to make me increasingly unpopular.

Matters were reaching an uncomfortable stage when, during one of the many meeting that the barons forced me into, the veiled threat was issued that I should take heed of their words to me lest I find that they would renounce the fealty to me that they had sworn and - more alarmingly - that they might denounce me as their king and liege lord!

I watched their faces as these demands and threats were made to me. Warwick, of course, enjoyed every warning he uttered. Arundel and the others stood and stared at me. Warwick's gaze, as usual, was most unsettling. The others seemed tense and yet determined. How I wished Piers had been with me. He would have stared these arrogant men down, unsettling them each in turn with his customary wit. However, I was alone and, try as I might, I was almost forced to listen to their demands. I must be advised by them and certainly not by Piers Gaveston! Yet who had been more faithful than he?

I had rarely felt so alone, and yet Isabella was becoming an unexpected ally; her soft words and sensible advice seemed odd coming from one so young and inexperienced – though, of course, I must never forget she was her father's daughter. The Capetian blood that ran through his veins ran through hers also, and she may have been receiving regular advice from her wily French father.

As far as Philip was concerned, I had finally agreed to the suppression of the Templar knights as he had been hounding me to since I had become king.

I did not see their order in quite the same way as the French king. Philip had accused these honourable men of grave sins: witchcraft, sorcery, sodomy, anything that blackened their name and reputation. Philip's greed for the great wealth that the they possessed was insatiable.

I had, thus far, managed to avoid making a decision about the members of the order that currently resided in England. It will be to my own shame that, desperate for any help my father in law could give me with regards to Piers's recall from exile, this would come at the cost of banishing the Templars from my realm.

With the meddlesome barons I had no other choice than to agree to the formation of a group of lords to be named Ordainers who would henceforth undertake to review and reform the royal household and make such changes as were necessary. In all other matters, I was urged most strongly to consider my role as king and realise that mistakes had been made, which I was to redress. I thought long and hard about all of this, and deciding that my wisest course would be to at least be seen to consider addressing the many concerns the Ordainers had.

It must not be thought that I was entirely without allies. I had considerable support especially from Hugh Despenser. Hugh was a giant of a man, immensely strong and ever faithful. A robust fellow with rosy cheeks, blue eyes and a mop of spiky brown hair that amused me daily. He could generally be relied on for support, pitting him against his fellow earls when defending my honour. His son - also Hugh, and called "the younger" to avoid confusion - was a companion from my earlier years, although I had not paid him a great deal of attention in the past. He seemed to quietly take everything in and his passive features belied an intelligence that I longed for.

Not built as his father, he was nonetheless attractive with sharper features than him. While not as fair faced as Piers, he was not unattractive with high cheekbones, a small nose and vivid green eyes that missed nothing. When he spoke, it was quietly, with a slight lisp. He had been knighted when I and my companions had been, years before. I felt I could trust him; he, too, was vocal in his support, although he was generally ignored. Something that he never forgot, as my story will later tell.

Now, for one of the very few times, I considered what my father's response to these troublesome lords would have been. I rarely considered the old man in any respect, yet it made me smile to think of the look on his face were he to have been presented with a list of grievances. Yet, I was aware that he had experienced discord with the nobles himself. Certainly, on one or two occasions at least he had simply bribed them! Given them lands, a manor house, import licences, all these men had their price, and it may be, for now at least, that I should be seen to pay. Whatever was necessary, I would do it.

After the indignity of these matters, I retired to my beloved Langley, and took to my bed, where I stayed for several days, refusing admittance to anyone except Will.

God knows, I had never missed Perrot so much as I did then. One could never be alone for long; the court travelled and, of course, there were demands on my time that could not be avoided, much as I tried.

When time permitted, I loved the release that physical work gave me, and here at Langley I felt free to lose myself in the exhaustion of the manual labour that so disgusted the court. Indeed, even Piers raised an eyebrow when I helped to thatch a roof on one of the Langley estate worker's cottages. His looks of abhorrence made me laugh, as so much about him did – dear God how I longed for his return.

+++

Walter Reynolds beamed at me as he handed over the document from Avignon, sealed with the personal insignia of the pope. I stared at him for a few moments, before taking the document and after reading the contents, I let out a loud cheer. Piers's threatened excommunication had been overturned! Finally, a turn in my fortunes! I leapt from my chair and lifted poor Walter off his feet, twirling around with him so many times I felt giddy.

"Now, my dear Walter," I said excitedly as I set him down, "we have the tide with us, surely this will mean Perrot's return."

Walter, straightening his tunic from my rough celebrations, attempted to present a statesmanlike posture. "My lord, this is a victory of course, but it must be tempered with..."

"With what, Walter? What can possibly spoil my joy?"

Hugh Despenser stepped forward. "I think what my lord bishop is saying, your grace, is that that without the other barons' consent, there can be no hope of recalling my lord Gaveston yet."

"Why ever not? To hell with the lot of them!" I held the scroll from Avignon as though it were the Ark of the Covenant, and to me it was just as valuable.

Both Walter and Despenser continued to advise against acting rashly in view of this papal document; whilst I heard them, I took little notice of what either of them said, excited beyond words that my ordeal of loneliness might soon be at an end.

+++

I could almost hear a collective groan as I opened that June parliament of thirteen hundred and nine. I was exultant! Piers stood proudly by my side, and I felt that all of my concerns were at an end. I had won over most, if not all, of the high lords, and obtained a revoke of Piers's excommunication.

I was delighted to see that there were no voices raised over my dearest brother's estates of Cornwall being restored to him. It was, therefore, a rather pathetic, weakened delegation that had the temerity to remind me of the promises I had made in order to secure his return. Naturally, I dismissed the issues for the present; nothing would prevent me from the enjoyment of having Piers back with me. Even Isabella, who had up until now behaved with reservation as far as my darling Perrot was concerned, seemed happy to see him and his wife Margaret, of whom she also seemed fond.

I held the first of many grand banquets to celebrate Piers's return to England. Jugglers, acrobats and jesters entertained us daily, well into the small hours, and I was liberal in my praise as well as financially to these entertainers that I loved so much. It was nonetheless apparent – to all but me, it seemed – that, whilst there were few raised voices at Piers's reinstatement at my side, he was far more bitter to them than I had expected.

A hunt had been arranged as part of my darling's homecoming celebrations and, no sooner had all the party set off, I was witness to some idea of the discord Piers felt towards the lords that had made his life so tiresome. The day had begun coldly, yet the sun shone and the sky was clear. The party was a large one, and all were eager for the sport as we set off at a pace. I adored riding, and had done from a very early age.

Piers and I, along with a few of the noble lords, had stopped under a large oak tree, where a velvet awning had been erected. Chairs and small tables added to the comfort and servants served us with wine and sweetmeats.

Several of the stags we had killed were being loaded onto a cart, which we watched with appreciation. I had taken down two myself and Perrot and others present had praised my prowess.

"I declare you are the finest horseman in the country, my king," Piers claimed, squeezing my shoulder affectionately after we dismounted. I looked at his glowing features with pride.

"I swear the Irish must have fallen to their knees in your very presence," I replied.

He looked as though he was considering the idea, "Yes, I think you are right, my king, although they are a brutal lot with some strange customs. The furnishings were quite appalling and there seemed little in the way of any fashion. Of course, I soon changed that, and indeed we introduced some much needed taste and refinement to what is essentially a peat bog!"

I laughed at the very thought of what his face must have looked like upon such a sorry place.

The tall, imposing figure of lord Warwick stepped closer. "You appear to have suffered much, my lord," he sneered, "yet how well you have borne all discomfort with your customary ease. Indeed, the Irish must have been so grateful that you alone have led them out of darkness into the light."

Several of the party chuckled and Warwick beamed as he stuffed several sweetmeats into his large mouth.

Piers, as always, was up to the challenge from Warwick's barbs. "Indeed, that is so, my lord; I truly believe that they saw me as their king."

There were audible gasps at this outrageous effrontery, and yet I laughed aloud. "You are king above all men, my dearest Perrot."

We laughed together, but the Earl of Lincoln took a threatening step towards Piers, so closely that he was inches away from his face.

"Have a care, my lord of Cornwall," he hissed, "lest your treasonous talk get the better of you."

Piers merely raised an eyebrow and curled his lips with distaste, as he stepped back. "Pray, speak from further away Lincoln, your breath positively reeks of onions! Eat less of them, my lord "Burst Belly", they will only give you a bilious attack. Dear, oh dear, the stench! You need only breathe heavily in the direction of the stage and the poor creatures will fall, we have no need for arrows!"

I began to laugh, but before I realised what was happening, Lincoln drew his dagger and held it to Piers's throat. Suddenly there was pandemonium.

Piers knocked the dagger away, and I saw on his face a look of hatred and resentment.

"Enough of this!" I cried, but no-one seemed to hear me.

Piers had the look of a madman and grasped Lincoln by his tunic. With a cold fury I had never witnessed in him before, he snarled in hatred, "Threaten me with your weapon again, my lord, and I will tear your head from your shoulders and force it up your arse!"

I jumped up quickly and, to my relief, Despenser pushed his way forward and managed to place his burly form between the men - Lincoln now looking pale and Piers wearing a face of fury.

"Enough I say!" I rose, and others that had seemed to close in on the warring couple stepped back as I did.

"My lord of Lincoln, you will offer the Earl of Cornwall an apology. No weapons will be raised here in my presence; do you hear?"

Lincoln's eyes darted to me and back to Piers, before he shrugged off Piers's grip on his tunic and, without another word, marched swiftly away to where a groom held his horse; mounting quickly, he turned and galloped away.

I sighed with some relief, yet Piers stood where he was, almost transfixed by the episode. The whole party seemed to break up. One or two of the other lords, who had no doubt enjoyed the spectacle, took their leave until there were only a few courtiers and Piers remaining, whom I went to embrace.

Without hesitation, he stepped away from me. "You should not have let him go without the apology to me!" he exclaimed bitterly. "The rest of those dogs would have cut me to pieces given half a chance, and yet you let him go." He was now red with fury and almost on the verge of an explosion of emotion.

"The man is an idiot!" I said, dismissing the incident.

He snapped his fingers at a servant carrying a jug of wine, and poured a goblet full, which he drank down thirstily. He refilled it, waving a dismissive hand at the servant.

"How can you let me suffer the indignity of it? Now all will say that I had to be protected by the king, that I could not have dealt with that ugly bastard on my own!"

I was truly amazed at him. I had rarely seen him so upset, and yet I did not understand. He had turned his back to me, and I placed my hands on his broad shoulders, laying my forehead on the base of his neck. I closed my eyes, breathing in his lavender scent that I adored so much.

"Forgive me, Perrot," I whispered. "No one shall stand against you. I shall dismiss Lincoln from court, I shall find some pretext to send him abroad. What would you have me do?"

He said nothing, but I felt his shoulders sagging with resignation as he spoke, his tremulous voice on the verge of emotion, yet with a powerful resonance. "What good would that serve?" he asked. "I wish to God I had not returned. For all that was wrong with Ireland, I enjoyed respect there - I was treated as lord, someone to be highly regarded. What have I here? I am tolerated because I am your shadow; whilst I am close to you I am safe from an assassin's blade in my back. Make no mistake, Ned, they will cut me down, and there will be nothing you can do to stop them."

I blinked at the onslaught of his words. I was unsure what to say as he released himself from my grip on his shoulders. "Perrot..." I began, but he had already marched to his horse.

"I beg your leave, my king," he announced brusquely as he swung himself onto the saddle and, with barely a glance back at me, rode away.

+++

Piers's mood fluctuated greatly at times. We would have furious disagreements, as well as bickering about the most trivial things that he claimed were an insult to him. Yet I knew him better than any, and these desperate moods were often followed by elation; his mood would lift and he would again become the dazzling spectacle he played so well. Nonetheless, there were matters that we could not easily ignore.

Life under what had essentially become the Ordainers' council was difficult, and yet both Piers and I did little to make matters any easier. The meetings bored me a great deal; I delayed and obfuscated. I had never been comfortable with the complexity of being a king; I had always been content to be advised and, in most regards, accepted the council's advice.

War in Scotland had become a much discussed topic in such meetings, and so it was that Warwick and Lancaster set out the current position. Nobody liked the sound of their own voice quite as much as Warwick, and so it was that he appeared to be admonishing me for my lack of determination to continue a campaign that my father had never fully completed.

Piers naturally found the whole topic tedious, and would yawn with great extravagance whenever Warwick drew breath to continue his diatribe.

"We have a duty, sire, to the memory of your late father, to march into Scotland and finish the task he began and, indeed, spent his life fighting to achieve."

I sighed deeply, as did Piers – with much more emphasis. "My lords, I have questioned many times the need to pursue a further campaign. My father had become obsessed by the mission, and I have no heart for the fight. You tell me constantly about the poor state of the nation's finances, and yet some of you are impelling me commit to another venture in to Scotland at a ruinous cost. What say you, my lord of Cornwall?"

Piers rarely sat at the council table during these meetings, preferring to languish at a seat by the window. "Forgive me, my king, I have not been listening closely; the noise seems to go on and on and I admit to feeling unaccountably tired. Now, what did you ask?"

I grinned broadly, but was aware of a hissing noise coming from Warwick, whether this was as a result of the implication that his voice had driven Piers to a dream-like state or the breach of etiquette by asking the king to repeat the question.

I made a conscious effort to look regal and sombre. "My dearest, the question of a further campaign in Scotland."

Piers stood up from his seat and stretched out his arms above him. "What a tiresome subject, can we not discuss something more interesting?"

"What would you suggest, my lord?" Lancaster enquired with a sneer.

Piers assumed a thoughtful pose, as though seriously considering the question. "Well, I was going to suggest a tournament, my dear Thomas. I have long promised our young queen that she would enjoy the spectacle of our gallant lords engaged in our famous jousts. And yet maybe our great lords here would prefer to contest in a less perilous exhibition, as I am, of course, often the victorious in the joust?"

I knew Piers was not generally one to boast unless it was to rile others, and this statement was as much to goad the lords as anything else. It was certainly the case that Piers was usually the victor in the joust, a fact that they found dangerously frustrating. The mood in the chamber thus became cold and dark looks were exchanged.

The portly Earl of Lincoln shifted uneasily in his seat. "I think, your grace, that we should return to the matter in hand; that being a proposed new offensive against Bruce and the Scots. Perhaps, my lord of Cornwall, you might have an opinion that does not centre on frivolity? These are urgent matters that require serious discussion."

Piers threw back his head and laughed. "You do me a disservice, my lord. I take the matter of the Scot, Bruce, most seriously!" He turned to me and winked. "A dangerous man, and they say he is merciless with his women! Can you imagine?"

"For the love of God!" the sombre Pembroke exclaimed in an exasperation that was clearly felt by the rest of the assembled lords.

Warwick wore a face of seething annoyance. "Can you not contribute to a single issue discussion without debasing its importance with your immature comments and observations?"

"You too misjudge me, my lord," Piers stated contritely. "I merely pointed out a personality flaw, although how he is merciless, I have yet to discover!"

I could not help but grin; how easy these men fell into Piers's trap.

Warwick, with a growing irritation, addressed me directly. "Your grace knows that even the Queen's father recognises Bruce as King of Scotland, and has indeed sent envoys to attend his parliament!"

I frowned at the reminder. "I have written to the King of France in the strongest terms about his recognition of Bruce's position. The queen has assured me that she will also write to her father regarding our displeasure"

Piers could see that the reminder from Warwick had struck a nerve with me. "Perhaps this distasteful subject should be discussed at another time when his grace is not so tired. You look exhausted, my king." He rubbed my shoulder affectionately. "I fear we rode for too long this morning." He turned to the other lords. "His grace will return to this matter in due course; for now I suggest some respite from this tedious talk. Maybe some music, a tableau that I know your grace's players have perfected for your pleasure."

My face lit up. "Oh yes, let us enjoy some music! As usual Perrot, you read my mind."

The members of the council began to express their displeasure at this. "Let us leave this my lords. For now."

A grumbling undercurrent of voices met my decision, disgusted looks were thrown at Piers, who looked very happy at having enraged the nobles once again.

Only Lancaster stood silently, leaning against the wall as I left. He wore an almost sinister smirk on his dark features. Not clearly outraged, but all the more menacing for not seeming so. Why was it that only he had the ability to make me feel so uneasy? Had I had just made another serious error?

Once outside, we laughed together. Piers linked his arm through mine and we hastened to my chamber where we gave vent to our mirth.

"I thought Warwick would burst into flames with fury at you!" I managed to say between gales of laughter.

Piers immediately blew out his cheeks like a bellows, then proceeded to undo his tunic as though he was bursting from it. "'Burst Belly' was certain to have ruptured something, I fear!" he said.

I summoned a servant to bring us wine, and we spent the rest of the day in glorious laziness. Drinking, eating and laughing. I gathered all my dearest companions and called for my musicians, the flautist that I loved so much and the jugglers and acrobats that made us roar in approval at their antics.

The exhaustion that Piers had me feign, to rid ourselves of the barons' odious company, was eventually real enough, and it was quite late in the evening when, much the worse for all the wine I had drunk, I was aware of Will helping me to disrobe. I had barely reached the bed before I fell into a deep sleep.

Life for Piers and I was a game. I was the king, and yet I was to be subjected to conditions. Restrictions from meddlesome barons who were determined that I should suffer for the effrontery of having a close bond with one I called my brother. A man that asked for nothing other than to enjoy his life to its fullest, and whose crime lay only in exposing the villainy and greed of power-seeking men.

I should have stopped Piers, of course, yet I chose to feast on his bold humour which laid raw the base humanity of those who saw themselves as God's anointed, even higher than their king! I was Perrot's hero, and he mine, and together we discarded old friendships and made few new ones – what need did we have of them when we had one another? Together we believed ourselves invincible, a mighty flame that the Ordainers would not extinguish, at least until the bond I had with my brother Perrot was crushed beneath their gilded spurs.

Yet, I was too drawn to Perrot to fear such men. With him, I too could be bold, act with impunity and speak with a reckless tongue. I too could goad Warwick and Lancaster and laugh at them when their backs were turned - and sometimes when they weren't!

The effrontery they felt would have been assuaged had Piers not continually bested them in the combat and jousts that he always won. The earldom would have mattered less to them had my brother not considered himself as their equal. They who could trace their lineage back to the Conqueror could not accept that this Gascon upstart considered himself nobility.

I could make men rich and powerful or I could cast them to the gutter. We played out our days like the actors in a court drama, and Piers played his role to the utmost. Did I encourage his excesses? Maybe so. I do know that I did nothing to curb his foolishness. I half-heartedly admonished him when it was clear that he played a dangerous game taunting the barons as he did, yet I laughed as he gave each of them a nickname. Pricking the egos of men like Warwick and my cousin Lancaster gave me a great deal of personal pleasure.

Yet there were times when even I considered it prudent to listen and take heed of the newly formed Ordainers. Their confidence grew, as did a general tension both within and outside of the court. I had my own sources of information, as did Piers - and, when word reached me that there were ugly rumours and disquiet within the city of London, I was enraged. I stormed at anyone who dared to be in my company about the injustice of being king and of having to sacrifice my pleasures in order to rule a country that I began to see as ungrateful and unkind.

Of course, I look back now with a different mindset. I did not forgo my pleasures for the sake of the national good. Indeed, I made certain that I indulged in all the vices I enjoyed, and why should I not?

Yet, I forced myself to think logically about my position; ergo, I finally gave consent to a further campaign in Scotland. This would at least buy me some time and, when I had enjoyed some success, I would be better able to answer the audacious Ordainers who claimed that my folly had all but lost the gains that my father had won. I imagined the old man now, that grimace of disapproval, those rheumy eyes that had struck fear into me so many times.

I journeyed north with Piers, along with Isabella and the lords Gloucester and Surrey. The remaining Ordainers were left to kick their heels and plot as they might, and again I raged at the very treachery, but there was little I could do. Of course, they were duty bound to provide me with resources with which to mount a suitable offence, yet they supplied a bare minimum of soldiers. Success in Scotland was therefore essential.

Yet, the campaign was not the triumph I had hoped for; the dire lack of finance to mount a successful campaign was evident and I had sense enough to realize that, although I had attempted to make a reasonable and forceful entry into Scotland, it was serving me only as a pretext to avoid the Ordainers.

I settled, therefore, to stay at Berwick on the Scottish side of the border.

It irked me considerably that the Ordainers considered their time better spent in considering how to reform the royal household.

Isabella seemed happy enough, and it was often that she alone was able to soothe my anger and frustration. She charmed all that met her and, although troubled by our circumstances, rarely displayed annoyance or frustration. I had sent Piers and Gloucester to parley with the earl of Carrick – I refused to refer to Bruce as king – and thus Isabella's company was a great comfort to me.

We dined alone one evening, and I was grateful to dismiss the servants and just shut out the endless traffic of courtiers, a deputation from the Archbishop of Canterbury, scribes, servants, ladies in waiting – the tumult of people was endless, and my head ached from the noise of it all. Eventually I had dismissed them all, and after stalking the room like one of the caged lions in the royal menagerie, I allowed Isabella to pour me some wine and lead me to a seat by the fireplace where large logs hissed and spat, throwing out large flickering flames. The chamber was warm enough that

I wore only a cambric shirt with the riding britches I had not changed since my daily ride earlier.

I was content and surprised when she stood behind my chair and proceeded to gently caress my rigid neck. I felt the delight as the tension began to give way under her supple caress. I closed my eyes and exhaled a satisfied sigh. Her small hands seemed tiny next to my muscular shoulders, and yet her fingers, now divested of their usual jewelled rings, were surprisingly strong.

Although my manservant Will and even Piers had massaged my aching limbs on many occasions, theirs had been almost rough, almost brutal by comparison. I felt more relaxed than I had for weeks, and felt a mounting pleasure as Isabella's palms slipped casually down to my chest, smoothing the finely woven cloth. I felt myself harden at the caress, and I instinctively took one of her hands, kissing the palm before I directed it inside my shirt. Neither of us said a word, and as I drew her from behind me to stand at my front, she looked fearful, as though uncertain of her desires. I looked at her then, not as a child but as a young woman, her face flushed, her lips full, parted slightly. I stood then, towering over her. I leant down and kissed her gently, once, twice and then with greater fervour. I felt almost a feverish urge for her that I had not experienced before. In one swoop, I lifted her into my arms, carrying her from the outer room where we had been, kicking open the door through to the bed chamber.

I began to tear at the gown, as eager as she was to divest herself of it. I breathed in her scent, heady and intoxicating. I pulled at her under gown until her small, exquisite breasts were exposed. I kissed them, gently at first and then with an urgency and passion. She drew in a sudden breath as I pinched her nipples and allowed my tongue to flick over them. She held the back of my head, pulling me to her while I deftly ran my hand down her side and then across her leg to her inner thigh, before I inched closer and closer to the warmth between her legs. Her back arched in ecstasy and her moans grew more fervent. I tore off my hose and all but ripped the shirt from my back.

Isabella stared at my now erect member and a look of fear crossed her face. I had to remind myself that this was a new experience for her, and we had not been so intimate with the exception of the occasional immature fumbling that I felt duty bound to perform. I lay next to her and sensed her hesitancy. I drew her hand to the head of my prick and pressed her fingers around it while I continued to kiss her neck and breasts.

Within moments I parted her soft thighs and, kissing her fiercely, entered her - gently at first, inching until I felt the rush of her maiden blood. I looked at her then and she had begun to cry. A small whimper, but she held me so tightly I felt I would suffocate! I had no desire to butcher her, and momentarily began to think I had been too rough in my desire, but she held me tightly still as I felt myself grow to a climax. I thrust into her a bit further, and felt my seed fire from me in what felt like a never ending explosion. I let out a satisfied roar, and after drawing out of her, I all but collapsed beside her, panting from the unfamiliar exertion.

The room was silent, and for some while I lay listening to her own heavy breaths. Neither of us said a word, and I felt a sudden guilt at having rushed the episode. Then gently I felt a hand reaching for mine, and then she was close to me, snuggling up against me, caressing my chest and softly playing with the hairs that covered it. I leant down to her and kissed her tenderly, and then we slept.

+++

"So, Edward, after you sent Gaveston to parley with Bruce?"

The hermit had been silent for some moments, reliving that first passionate evening with Isabella, which he had done – but to himself. There were some memories that could not - and indeed should not be spoken of outside of the marriage bed. Whatever he might have felt towards Isabella, there intimacies would not be spoken of.

"Forgive me, my friends," he eventually said, "I became lost in my thoughts. Where was I? Ah, yes, Scotland. We settled at Berwick upon Tweed. The place was cold and inhospitable, dank and dreary, despite the luxuries of the royal court that travelled with us.

Suffice to say that, despite my optimism, the campaign was a futile one."

Edward leant down to stroke Perrot, who had settled down by his feet. The hound made a half-hearted attempt at enthusiasm, but decided that the day was still far too warm to engage in anything other than a warm lick on his master's hand, and flopped down again.

"And the Ordainers?" questioned Fieschi. "They imposed these reforms?"

"Indeed they did, Manuel. God alone knows what my father would have done in my place, even though he had faced similar insolence in his reign, but never to a degree such as this. His fury would have been heard here in this garden of tranquillity!

No, my indignity was to be complete, I was king in all but name. Piers continued to be a thorn in the Ordainers' sides, yet still I did nothing to rein in his folly; alas, I merely encouraged it. Yet all that I had done was follow my heart rather than my head. I encouraged him when I should have cautioned him.

I wallowed in Piers's adulation, refusing to realize that, unchecked, his company was poison to me. Yet, he will remain the love of my life, and if I had my time over again, I would still give my kingdom for a night in his arms. Ah, Manuel, this unsettles you, but love has caused me so much anguish. It is the catalyst of everything that has befallen me.

No matter, let me continue...

My hopes for a brighter future were dealt two significant blows at this time. Firstly, the death of the Earl of Lincoln, Henry de Lacy. One of the hateful Ordainers, it was true, but one to whom I could bear to listen. His moderating views were not always mine, but he had a great deal of experience and I had the notion that he may well have been the only voice of reason that Warwick and Lancaster might pay heed. He had been regent during my absence in Scotland. Further animosity was created when I entrusted the honour of replacing him as regent to my dear comrade and nephew, Gilbert de Clare, Earl of Gloucester.

What made this new situation particularly uncomfortable was that, with Lincoln's death, my cousin Thomas now inherited – through his wife who was Lincoln's sister – Leicester, Salisbury, Derby and Lincoln. Thus, together with the vast estates he already owned, Thomas had become the most powerful and certainly the richest earl in England.

How I seethed to imagine my cousin rubbing his hands in glee at the good fortune that had been bestowed upon him by de Lacy's death. More than his burgeoning wealth, however, was Lancaster's growing arrogance. I was delighted to learn from Piers's spies that some of his fellow Ordainers were whispering about Thomas's overbearing attitude, and how he felt himself the overall decision-maker and even dismissed their views, suggesting his own should be all that mattered. I prayed to God that he and Warwick would clash heads and one destroy the other.

I recall an instance when Isabella and my beloved Perrot were as one about my dignity in the face of my cousin's growing effrontery. I endured an act of blatant disregard from my cousin towards me, his sovereign lord. I burst in upon Isabella's chamber, brandishing a refusal from Lancaster to pay homage to me, as was expected, for the vast lands he now controlled.

I felt, somehow, a new chapter had begun in my marriage to Isabella. She was maturing as a woman and I was certainly beginning to trust her sound judgment as her confidence as queen began to grow. I found I enjoyed her company, and was at times grateful for the calm voice of reasoning. I had been of course most fortunate that, whilst she may have felt ill of Piers, she hadn't shown it. Was I fooling myself in thinking that the three of us could live in harmony? Only time would tell.

Piers was perhaps indifferent to Isabella rather than rude; I don't believe he considered her as anything more than my wife. He was certainly civil and respectful of her position as his queen. Yet Isabella was still unsure of where she figured as my wife. Perhaps it is to her great credit that she was uncertain enough of the strength of my relationship with her, and would not show any animosity she may have felt for my beloved Perrot, lest it undo the bond she was trying to make with me.

Now, as I pushed one of her pages aside in my temper, I merely felt a blind fury that would inevitably leave me enraged and exhausted. "Do you believe what that arrogant devil has now done? Let me tell you!"

Isabella put her needlework to one side, quietly dismissing her maids and attendants with a wave of her hand.

I was barely aware of them leaving. "Churl is the perfect name for him, Piers chose the most perfect title for the blaggard!"

"You speak of the Earl of Lancaster, my dear?" she said quietly.

I brutally kicked at the logs beside the fire grate, sending them scattering across the floor.

"Who else? Who else could cause me such insult? He advises me that, despite my summons that he pay homage to me for his new lands, he will not as he refuses to cross so close into Scotland to do so! God's teeth!" I felt my very blood boil, and I seem to recall I actually ripped Lancaster's letter with my teeth and spat it out before I picked up a nearby stool and hurled it across the chamber where it smashed against the window, breaking both!

I turned eyes of fury towards Isabella, as though seeking an answer, but found her looking petrified. I had seldom raised my voice in her company before now. I held out my hands to her, and she rose and warmly embraced me. I had no need to scare her, and certainly did not intend to. I held her close, her favourite scent lingered around me.

Even as I recall these events from so long ago, I can almost conjure the perfume, although it's origin is lost to me now. Strange how a smell can conjure up an individual in one's mind. Perhaps, dear Alphage, this will in some way explain why I can often be found here in this garden where the lavender grows; I am reminded of Gaveston every time I rub its flowers, breathing in the exquisite aroma.

I held her tightly to me, and sought to find some words to temper the horror of my visit. I kissed her on tip of her small nose, which made her giggle. Our embrace was cut short suddenly, as Will burst in to the chamber. I was alarmed and opened my mouth to demand why an invasion so like my own was necessary. Will, however, would not do so without good reason, and the very alarm on his face suggested bad news.

"My lord! Your grace!" He could hardly get the words out.

"Will, what is this?"

"Your grace, it is the Earl of Cornwall. An attempt has been made on his life!"

I all but pushed Isabella away - in that moment I did not realize she was even there. I felt as though my blood turned to ice, and felt suddenly light–headed, as though I would swoon. "Oh God, no! Is he alive? Please God, tell me he is safe! Who brings this news?"

"His manservant, Hugo, has ridden here with all speed; his master is sorely wounded and is therefore travelling here closely guarded."

I followed Will out to the antechamber where Hugo fell to his knees before me.

"Good, Hugo, get up, tell me at once what has occurred!" I felt truly nauseous.

Hugo would never have abandoned Piers had he not been commanded. Hugo pulled the cap from his head, his scrofulous features now redder than usual. His wet hair clung wildly across his windswept face.

"Your Grace, we were ambushed as we left our camp. My master said he would dine and then set out to return here, but as we rode out through woodland, we were assailed by a group of horsemen. Two men in particular singled out the earl deliberately. He was caught unaware by a blow to his head that knocked him from his horse. One of the men jumped down from his own mount and drew his sword, but my master was quicker, and after they clashed and fought, my master ran the attacker through. The other men were either slain by the earl's guards or escaped back to the woods from whence they came."

I reached for Will, who quickly moved a stool for me to sit down lest I fall. "And the identity of these vagrants, were they local bandits?"

"No!" came a voice from the doorway.

I threw myself at Piers and began to weep. After a moment of just holding him, I pressed his face between my tremulous hands, before my fingers ran down his cheeks as though reassuring myself he was truly alive. He looked dishevelled, and I then noticed the bandage around his arm, its red-stained cloth suggesting a serious wound.

"Call my physician!" I demanded, and a valet who had followed Piers into the chamber turned and ran. I led Piers to a chair.

Will poured some wine into a goblet, which the wounded man drank down in hasty gulps.

"Who has done this?" I demanded coldly.

Piers's voice was shaky. "Ned, I beg your forgiveness."

"My forgiveness for what?" I asked.

"I have killed a man this day. A man I recognise."

"Well, who?" I asked impatiently.

"Thomas de Walkyngham - believe me, Ned, I acted in self-defence."

"Thomas...? I don't know who..."

Piers took in a deep breath and suddenly winced in pain. "Walkyngham is one of Warwick's retainers."

"One of Warw..." I started, then I realized suddenly that this had been a serious attempt on Piers's life and, not surprisingly, coming from one of Warwick's henchmen.

"I'll have Warwick's head for this!" I felt my anger rising again.

Suddenly, a small hand rested on my shoulder. I looked up to find Isabella at my side. I wondered later, how long she might have stood there after I had brushed her aside in my eagerness to talk with Hugo.

"You have no proof, my lord," she spoke, somewhat coldly. "If you charge Warwick with having a hand in this, you will only add to the gulf that exists already between you."

"But this is an outrage!" I cried. "Piers must be avenged!"

"He has been avenged already," she countered. "His henchman, as you call him, lies dead, having come off worst in the attack."

I looked at her and back at Piers, who had now shut his eyes. The physician, a small, curly haired chap with a jolly face not in keeping with his serious profession, had arrived, bowing low to me and Isabella before he knelt at Piers's feet. He deftly cut free the blood-soaked bandage. Hugo assisted with removing his master's clothes and Piers was helped to his feet when the physician suggested he should lie down while he attended to the wound.

"Take the earl to my private chamber," I announced, rising to my feet and following them. I turned back at the door, just in time to see Isabella turn and walk away.

+++

By the time the physician had finished treating and dressing Piers's wound, it was late in the evening. I lay on the bed beside him. He was sleeping now, after being given a foul-smelling liquid that would apparently help with both the pain and aiding a restful night. The sword cut had fortunately not appeared to be life-threatening, and the still smiling physician assured me all would be well after dressing the wound each day and resting. I took a small bag from my belt and, without counting the coins inside, I handed this to the grateful servant and he backed away, closing the door behind him.

I just lay watching Perrot, and feeling suddenly so bereft and useless. This time, he had been lucky. Yet, now it became clear that men like Warwick were prepared to go to any lengths to rid them of this most beautiful of men.

Now we both knew that he could never be entirely safe from his enemies. Piers could goad, mimic and make fun of these great lords, but their mission in life was to see him removed altogether, once and for all. For a long time, I lay awake listening to his breathing, shallow and peaceful now in his drugged sleep.

The bond that held him and I together felt suddenly fragile. I dreaded a life without him. This time it was a sword wound to his arm; what next? A dagger to his throat? A bolt from a crossbow? A draft of hemlock into his wine?

My head began to teem with all manner of devices that could be used to destroy this man that I would never be able to live without. I shook my head at such thoughts and then Piers sleepily opened his eyes. I propped myself up on my elbow. I don't know if he was even aware that it was me beside him. He raised his hand and gently touched my cheek, before allowing his arm to flop down beside him again. I leaned across and blew out the candle beside him.

"Goodnight, sweet prince," I said softly as I moved closer to him, before sleep eventually took me.

+++

The Earl of Warwick, as expected, disclaimed any knowledge of the assassination attempt on Piers, stating with horror that he was shocked that anyone in his patronage should attempt to carry out such a heinous crime.

His protestations of innocence were enough to convince me that he had been fully aware of Thomas de Walkyngham's actions.

There was, nevertheless, further uproar when I announced that I had absolved Piers of all blame in the man's death, and pardoned not only him, but others in his retinue that had injured anyone in the attack. I had no reservations about doing so; any attack on Piers was an attack on me.

Piers himself seemed much troubled by the event. Not necessarily about the attack itself, and his part in it. His courage was certainly not in doubt and I was satisfied that I had diffused what threatened to be an explosive situation. It was his taciturn mood that troubled me more. He had clearly expected me to declare him guiltless, and yet behaved almost truculently once I had done so.

"You pardon me, Ned, and I am seeming to hide behind you, allowing you to offer me your protection. The barons think me weak, cowardly even. Could I not have threatened to meet Warwick on the field, a combat to restore my honour?"

I was surprised at his ingratitude, and said as much. "What would be achieved by that?" I countered. "We should have even more tension than we already have. Besides, I could never risk your life that is so precious to me."

I moved to embrace him, but he turned away.

"Do you doubt my ability to defeat the dog, Warwick?" he shouted.

"Piers, what is this? I know only too well that you would clearly best Warwick in combat, but harming him would set upon us, like a hornet's nest, danger from all sides. Surely you see that?"

He continued to look at me angrily, his beautiful face distorted with rage. He paced over to the window of the chamber, leaning his head against the stone wall. We were silent for some time, before I grew impatient at his truculence and walked to my desk, picking up a sheet of velum and reading its contents. He turned, curious at my silence.

I then called out for Will to bring me a quill and ink. Once this had been brought, I signed the sheet and affixed my seal to the bottom of it. I nodded to Will to leave, and held the document out to Piers, who walked over and tentatively took it from me.

"What is this?" he asked - not without some measure of suspicion, I was disappointed to note.

"It would appear that your would-be assassin held some manors and land in Yorkshire, they are now yours. A settlement that his family and Warwick will agree is just compensation for the attack on you."

He looked at me and a broad smile transformed his truculent manner to the softer face that I loved so much. He fell to his knees and kissed my hand.

I leant down and, in return, kissed the top of his head. "I would do anything for you, my brother, Perrot. To me you are a hero, a gallant, and that is not in doubt by anyone. I shall protect you always, and I will not apologise for that."

When he looked up again, it was with emotion in his eyes. "We will never be safe, Ned; you do know that?"

I smiled. "I won't let them defeat us. Even now, while they strive to cut me down and limit my power as king, we are stronger. Together we are invincible - Nunc et usque in aeternum!" I brushed his hair from his check and cupped his face in my hand. "I love you, my brother. Your brush with death has shaken me; we must take care."

He made a noise of dismissal, as though the threat was too negligible to consider – but reluctantly, I considered it. I was happy now. He loved the gifts I bestowed on him, and I so enjoyed the pleasure it gave me to give him things such as this. What wealth I had, I was happy to share with him. Of course there were grumbling voices that would have me curb my expenses, but I refused to be a pauper king; moreover, it was within my power to bestow on Piers anything that I wished, and I would continue to do so.

+++

I was pleased to be heading south again; we had been in the north for at least eleven months and I was heartily sick of it. The cold weather, which seemed the only type on the borders of Scotland, left me feeling miserable.

My fury at Lancaster for making me - his king - travel to accept his homage at Haggerston on the English side of the river, was an indignity that infuriated me, yet there was nothing I could do but agree. Thomas and I exchanged a kiss of peace – whilst both considering how best to destroy the other – but he totally ignored Piers, offering him neither a greeting nor any recognition at all.

Piers was infuriated, and raged at the insult, as did I. Yet, there was little to be done other than add this offence to the ever growing list of abuses by my cousin.

One good omen was that my dear Gilbert de Clare, Earl of Gloucester, and Thomas of Lancaster seemed to be at each other's throats more frequently and I was encouraged to think that this would cause enough disharmony amongst the Ordainers that there would be opportunities to make the most of the unrest and fracture the alliance of the barons to my advantage. I knew that most of the barons regarded Gilbert as young and inexperienced, and tended to patronize him. Added to that, of course, he had been a close companion of mine since boyhood, and was married to my niece and - more damning – he was Piers's brother-in-law!

Despite my protestations at not letting him out of my sight, Piers was to remain at the stronghold of Bamburgh in the north. I had made him promise to write to me daily. Concern for his safety since the attempt on his life occupied me greatly. Yet, I had bowed to the inevitable and agreed to summon parliament. The Ordainers must have their day!

I raged anew at the Ordinances. These detailed over forty clauses covering a range of grievances that I would resist with all my conviction. I took up the documents laid before me scanning them superficially at first, looking for the inevitable name and finding it soon enough. I sighed deeply as I took in the words, shaking my head in despair. No! I would not agree to exile Piers, not again.

He was, they declared, 'evil counsel' who was drawing to himself royal power and royal dignity. It branded him an enemy of the king and his people; Gaveston was to be completely exiled, never to return, and this no later than the first of November. If he had not quit the kingdom by then, he was to be treated as one who was an enemy of the state.

I surrendered to the tears that always came readily to me when faced with issues so close to my heart. Yet, they were as much tears of hopelessness, of anger, despair and indignity. Whilst this was the worst imaginable of demands, there were others.

Naturally, my immediate close circle of friends was to be disbanded; I was to agree to dismiss some of them that were deemed 'unsuitable' and accused of giving me false counsel.

Given my recent failure to engage in battle with Bruce, I could no longer announce an intention to wage war in Scotland or anywhere else without the agreement of the barons. Gifts of land and other grants were to be approved beforehand. Moreover, any I had made already - which I had - were to be revoked until my debts were settled! All manner of financial restrictions were to be imposed, thereby effectively handing control of the exchequer to the Ordainers!

The seizure of foodstuff and other victuals was to cease henceforth. The Ordainers claimed this must be implemented in order to quell the resentment felt, and which might in turn lead to open revolt. A ridiculous stipulation! The populace had always been expected to supply their king with whatever was necessary. In effect, the kingdom was mine to take what I would from it; this had always been the case. I could only imagine my father's fury were such an idea put to him. Indeed, as I called my father to mind, I imagined him, wherever he was, sighing in great disappointment at how I had come to this.

I truth, I was in a weak position and it was therefore with a heavy heart that I granted Piers a safe conduct to London. Arrangements were to be made for his exile to Europe, and I did all I could to keep him comfortable regarding his household. It had been decided that his wife, Margaret, would not accompany him into exile, she being heavy with their second child. I would insist that she receive financial assistance as well as retaining Piers's castle at Wallingford.

As much as I feared his loss, I was also greatly troubled that he would not reach London alive. How simple it would be for a hidden assassin to waylay him during the journey to London. Was his household secure? Was he assured of the loyalty of all who served him?

It felt as though I existed as a ghost during those torturous days while I waited for him. Isabella showed herself to be truly loyal and understanding to me and sympathized with the anguish I was enduring. Without Piers, I began to rely on her support, which she gave without reservation. Indeed, she had been heard to voice her displeasure to Thomas of Lancaster at the vindictive treatment being meted out to my beloved brother. She had written to her father, assuring him that she found no fault in the Earl of Cornwall's behaviour towards her.

Finally, I had decided that I could not bear to say goodbye to him personally, my grief was too acute. What could I possibly say to him that could make this wretched situation any more bearable? I wrote to him, of course, begging him to believe me that I would bring him home again, whatever the cost and declaring over and over my love for him, and the the tears I wept when I thought of him.

Piers and I planned for him to travel to Flanders, and Isabella, I later learned, arranged for her own contribution to ease any financial burden he might suffer despite the arrangements I had put in place. She reasoned that, with the Ordainers now in control of the exchequer, it would be far harder for me to send money to Piers than she.

When I was advised that Piers had set out for his journey to the capital, I doubted I could bear the hopelessness of it all if I had to look into those beautiful eyes and say goodbye for who knew how long. It was the only way if we were to be parted again. I knew I could not again hold him close to me and watch as he disappeared for an unknown future, so I would save us both the anguish and heartbreak. I assured him that we could exchange letters through a secret means that I had arranged and, having done all I could, Isabella and I departed for Windsor.

During those long empty nights of solitude, Piers was often my only thought; I would recall one of our first nights together, torturing myself until hot tears began to sting my eyes and I could only sit up, drawing my knees up under my chin and rocking to and fro. I watched the solitary candle, momentarily fixated on the beeswax following its course from the flame as the hot liquid spilled over and trickled down the sconce as it cooled.

I longed for Piers's company again. To feel the safety of his strong arms that held me close to his warm, fragrant body. I tried to consider the worst – life without Piers. Would we ever enjoy such nights again? How could I ever live without him? If he was truly lost to me, I knew I could never love the same way again.

As angry as I felt towards treacherous men like Lancaster, Warwick and the rest, Piers had done little to endear himself to them. Why had I not pleaded with him to resist the temptation of goading them to anger? Why was he not content to just live and love as we had, instead of wanting more? The answer, of course, was at the pit of my stomach, and it made he heave, like a sour bile that I swallowed time and again because I could not bear to face the reality that I could have stopped him; I could have reined in that pride, that vicious malice that he felt towards those who would always be his betters, even with all the glory, land and titles I could bestow on him.

Instead, I had done nothing. Whatever and whomever else I could blame, my heart would always hold me responsible.

The Christmas festivities held little interest to me that year of our lord thirteen hundred and eleven. Isabella and I celebrated at Westminster; the palace was bedecked with garlands of winter pines, gold and red banners fluttered throughout the great hall. Sconces of bright warming candles infused with spices and incense threw their magnificent light high up into the vaulted ceiling. Swathes of glossy dark green holly with its vivid red berries, trails of ivy wound around columns and draped from the rafters.

Isabella adored the festive season, but it was difficult for me to find any joy in it whilst my mind was occupied elsewhere. We feasted on all manner of sumptuous meats, fish and pastries. Warm spiced wine, puddings, wafers - I had been able to at least afford to spend some money on assuring we were regally fed and entertained!

I had singers, dancers, acrobats to entertain us and, as usual, I insisted that they were well-remunerated. How Piers and I had laughed and made merry at Christmases past; he had a great love of the spectacle and richness of the season. What a cruel time to be alone.

I had sent Piers many letters and we were able to keep up a regular correspondence. He complained little, but I knew he missed being with me here. He had sent word to Margaret, and even to Isabella, but I knew his heart would be heavy.

Piers's banishment had certainly not corrected all ills with the barons who, I was reliably informed, were arming themselves should disagreements result in open civil war. I raged at the many indignities set upon me, that I was now merely a puppet king, bound to do the bidding of the detestable Ordainers. In truth, if the tensions still existed after Piers had been forced into exile, what had been the point of sending him away at all? My fury turned inevitably to self pity; was ever a king as censured as I? Why should I not have with me those whom I loved most?

Day after day, life became torturous to me, I could find little to rejoice about, much as I tried for Isabella's sake. The festive season only seemed to highlight that my heart grieved for Piers's company. I lay awake one night, as Isabella slept peacefully beside me. I turned to look at her and smiled at the innocence on her young face. Her fair hair lay partly across her brow and I gently rearranged it with the lightest touch lest I awaken her. I was beginning to rely on her good counsel more often of late. She was certainly wise beyond her years; whilst her father's cunning was lost on Isabella's oafish brothers, she had, I believed inherited his sharp, astute intellect. I smiled again at how simple life could have been had I never met Piers Gaveston; would I be as tormented as I now was? Would I have felt the same joy and excitement with anyone else other than he?

I pondered on these and other questions during one unsettled night, when at last I had made a decision on what to do next. Neither Isabella nor I were early risers, so I had time before the small army of valets and attendants would descend upon us, and the chambers become crowded with dozens of chamberlains, visiting bishops, lords and ladies and all manner of human traffic. At once I roused Will and sat informing him of my intentions. Was ever a king or lord more fortunate in the loyalty of their servant than I? Whilst he might well have been able to advise me as to the folly or good sense in my plans, he merely took in my instructions and prepared to carry them out. I sat and wrote two letters; one was to be taken at once to my niece, Margaret, at Wallingford Castle, the other was to be given – only in person - to the Earl of Cornwall.

+++

The long trek north was cold and slow. I had declared my intention to review the modifications I had planned for Knaresborough Castle. I knew that the journey would raise some suspicion, but I felt no need to justify my actions.

The arduous journey was not helped by my niece's apparent discomfort. She was due to give birth to Piers's child soon and, as much as I loved her dearly, I was beginning to find her constant complaints about her discomfort and the cold weather rather irritating. I knew little enough about such things, but reasoned that the process could surely not be so bad, given that many women had more than one child! I was, however, not totally unsympathetic and we broke the journey as often as possible, although I chafed at the delays.

Margaret was otherwise a charming travelling companion, and I did not doubt that she looked forward to reuniting with her husband. She had been the perfect wife for Piers, and he in turn had always been most attentive to her and kept her well. She was not unhappy with the match and had been fiercely loyal to him.

We arrived in York, where Margaret was delivered of a fine girl. I felt an emotion that was strange to me, when I visited the new child. I was taken aback at the noise the infant made, which drew much amusement from the mother and her ladies in attendance.

"She has her father's eyes, do you not think, your grace?" Margaret stated proudly.

I laughed. "She certainly has her father's voice!" I joked.

I took little notice of the baby thereafter, although I recall at the time a pang of jealousy that this small screaming individual could invoke so much love. I don't know if my jealousy was towards this newborn child that made her father's beautiful blue eyes well with tears each time he would hold her, or because I was yet to experience such a unique event. Isabel and I would hopefully be blessed with children ourselves, and maybe I too would feel what many called an unbreakable bond.

Whether my own father had felt such emotion with myself or my siblings was doubtful. He was a man whom one could not imagine being softened by the feel of a newborn baby's soft skin. Strange that after so many years, I could not recall a visit to the nursery by my father - not that it mattered now of course.

+++

I rode through the coarse, rough, cold landscape that often made the north of England so inhospitable. The journey to Knaresborough Castle was uneventful, and

I thanked God for that. I travelled with only Will and two soldiers, leaving the rest of the party at York. When at last we arrived, the daylight was beginning to fade, long shadows cast an ethereal glow from the lanterns on the newly completed keep, and I was grateful to be out of the biting wind that had risen fiercely during the ride.

After our arrival, it was with some urgency that I retired to my chamber. Once there, I nodded to Will and he moved over to one wall and pulled back the large tapestry that hung there to reveal a small door. He hastily inserted a large ornate key into the lock turning it until the soft audible click was heard.

The small candle that Will held out to me would provide enough illumination to guide me safely. Even as I hastened to my task, I allowed a momentary doubt about what I had planned. Supposing my plans had been discovered? Lancaster certainly had his own spies at the court; much as I tried to root them out, it was difficult to know of every stable hand or valet. In my late father's time I had given no thought to having faithful servants working for me whilst they served other masters.

Now, of course, in hindsight – as I seem to consider all my ills - it would be only prudent to be aware of what others were planning. Recalling these former days, I don't believe I enjoyed the love and trust from others that was necessary if one was to enjoy unconditional devotion. When I was a prince and heir to the throne, I don't think it ever occurred to me that it was necessary to court the respect and love of others, I assumed that it was a given that, with majesty, came love, loyalty and all the other impossible attributes expected from adoring and loyal subjects.

Yet I had my own informants, few though they were. I could not, on reflection, be surprised that few men at such a time were willing to become embroiled in what was fast becoming a potentially explosive situation.

At the doorway, the entrance was narrow. I stooped down and crossed the threshold, travelling quickly along the uneven walkway. The air was dusty and stale, the hard grey stone walls as cold as ice. At my feet, something squeaked and scurried away, once or twice I had to fend off an almost invisible cobweb, so fine as to be unnoticed until one became tangled by the delicate silk thread. Surely only rats and spiders would find any comfort in this cold, dank corridor.

After some moments, the pathway dipped slightly and in front of me I came to a further small wooden door. I turned the handle which opened with a small creak and, ducking down again, I stepped into the dimly-lit chamber before me.

I had gone no further than a stride when I was suddenly grabbed from behind. A strong arm held me around the neck whilst the candlelight in the room caught the blade of a knife, its tip a sharp indent on my throat.

Momentarily, I was stunned with panic. That was until I smelt the waft of lavender, and a familiar voice whispered into my ear.

"One should always knock before entering a man's chamber, my king. What if I had been bathing? How embarrassing!"

I grabbed the arm and, after its release, I turned and flung my arms around my beautiful assailant.

+++

The warmth of the room was welcome after the coldness of the passageway. Small though the chamber was, there was every comfort – as I would have expected. On one side a candlelit table held several dishes, meats, wafers, a dish piled high with fruit and a generous silver flagon filled with the very best wine.

In one corner, a curtain masked the obvious garderobe, in another stood a brazier, its glowing embers sprinkled with herbs that created a warm and heady aroma. An ornate wooden chest sat at the end of a generous sized bed draped in costly deep red velvet. Piers Gaveston created luxury in the most inhospitable places.

Small and parochial though it certainly was, I would look back on that night as one of the most private we had ever spent together. For that one night, we were entirely alone, no pages, no valets, no courtiers, bishops, lords, ladies or wives!

One may suspect that as king, solitude and privacy could be commanded. Yet, it was not so. The court was everywhere, living and breathing like a great dragon, constantly watching, laughing, drinking, fighting even! Privacy was impossible, and I thank God that Piers and I were able to enjoy some measure of it at least. Affairs of the heart or intrigues of the powerful were an ever-present situation, and as king I learned to live with it, as did Piers and those after him. The court had a million eyes, and they never closed.

We dined on the veritable banquet – where on earth he had managed to procure it, given the secrecy in which we met, he didn't explain. I sat back into my seat feeling a deliciously warm contentment. Piers swivelled in his seat and swung one of his legs over the arm of his chair as he questioned me about the latest developments, delighted to learn that he and Margaret now had a daughter.

"This was a gamble, Ned," he said with a sudden seriousness. "We don't yet know if it will prove costly."

I looked at him, while he poured us both more wine. "I couldn't lose you Piers, not again."

"We must give thanks that the couriers worked swiftly," he said. "I had barely had my new clothes unpacked when your letters arrived. The one commanding me to return being the one I welcomed most. Yet, a gamble, as I say."

"I chose this castle for your return, confident that none would suspect it of being a hiding place. Were you treated well by my sister and brother-in-law?"

"Well enough. When I received word from you to return, I felt it prudent to stay long enough not to raise suspicion, yet I believe your sister suspected that there was a particular reason for my decision to leave."

I smiled. "Yes, my sister, the Duchess of Brabant, was ever astute, yet I do not doubt her loyalty."

Piers continued, "I was able to secure a passage to England on a small merchant vessel. Then, of course, I couldn't decide whether to travel heavily-disguised as a merchant or maybe try my hand as one of the ship's crew! But as you well know, I am not a good traveller on sea, so that presented a drawback. One would think after so many exiles, I would be accustomed to it."

I laughed at the thought of it.

"So, I arrived safely and rode with all speed, with only Hugo for company and stopping only when necessary. Your letter said to come straight here. I admit I had forgotten about this little secret chamber that we discovered by chance on a visit here once. I must say, it was nonetheless galling to secrete myself here in a castle that is in my hands! Or should I say, was!"

"The castle is yours by right; all your lands will be returned, as will all titles and rights that those bastard Ordainers have taken with such pleasure."

I felt a surge of anger, frustration at the intolerable situation we were now in, but more determined than ever that Piers would return to me. "We will travel to York to visit Margaret and your new daughter, and after that your exile will be officially revoked! Damn the bastard Ordainers for their treachery!" My simmering fury threatened to erupt into the infamous Angevin rage. I reached for a goblet, but at once Piers clamped his own hand over mine.

"Please, my king," he teased, "we have only the two goblets. If you are to smash them I shall be forced to drink straight from the pitcher, which will spill down this extremely expensive doublet."

I laughed then, as he could always make me. To see the humour in things was one of the qualities in him I loved the most.

Later, as we laid side by side, well fed and rather the worse for the wine, of which Piers appeared to have an endless supply, the mood seemed to change. I continued to rant at the impossible situation that the Ordainers had now placed me in. Piers grew more silent. The more wine we drank, the more maudlin he became.

"What you propose in restoring me from exile will bring the might of the barons down on us." He seemed suddenly serious. "You must see that, Ned. Is that really what you want?"

"Do you doubt my love?" I asked hotly.

"Not your love for me, but your sense of duty. You seem hell bent on handing them your crown and kingdom for what? For me?"

"How can you doubt it, Perrot? This has all been for you, it has only ever been for you."

I sprung up and straddled him as he lay beside me. I took hold of the collar of his shirt and shook him whilst I began to scream at him. "For you! This has all been for you! I won't live without you!" I sobbed. "I won't! How can you dare doubt it, doubt me?"

"Ned, I fear you must let me go...no listen to me, listen!" Suddenly I tore at him, I slapped him across the face while he attempted to grasp my hands. My temper was rising and I began to rain down blows as my rage grew to a tempest.

Then, suddenly, he struck me back. A blow so forceful that I was swept off my knees, reeling against the poster at the foot of the bed, banging my head sharply. The silence in the chamber was palpable.

I looked at him, aghast with the horror of what had just happened. He at once sprung off the bed and reached for me. I swear he was as astonished as I was. "Ned, dear God, Ned...Ned forgive me!"

He reached for me but I shrugged him off. With the exception of my father, no-one had ever struck me before; apart from the pain, I was shocked that he, of all men, would strike me. Now he gathered the velvet coverlet from the bed and buried his face in it as he sank to the ground, sobbing great gusts of tears. I had seen him cry before, but this was something different. He wailed with such gut-wrenching anguish that I was taken aback. What had just happened? What had turned the beautiful intimacy of our earlier evening into a veritable storm that had overwhelmed both of us?

The hot tears ran down my face as though they would never cease. Piers's sobs continued for what seemed like an eternity. He sat crouched on the floor, his knees drawn up, and he rocked back and forward still clutching the coverlet in tight fists, the knuckles white and stretched.

At length, I got off the bed and knelt before him. That beautiful face, yes, even in anguish and pain, still beautiful. His eyes beginning to swell from the torrent of his tears. I took the coverlet and dabbed it against his face. He did not look at me, but continued to stare vacantly. "You must let me go Ned, because I'm scared, Ned, I'm scared." He had said as much before and my heart broke for him.

I took his face in my hands, his tears damp against my skin. "You are safe with me, I will always take care of you, you know -"

He interrupted me earnestly, "I fear for my life, Ned - I who have always seemed so dismissive of danger. I don't want to die, Ned, I don't want to die!"

He began to sob again. "Let me go, send me away! Banish me with the same vehemence the Ordainers do! Let me hate you, Ned! At least that would make it easier!"

"Never!" I shouted. "We will never be apart. I love you, Perrot, so much that it hurts. Every day, every night. How can you ask me to let you go, after all that has passed?"

"How long before you begin to regret the price you may well pay for keeping me by your side?" he then asked quietly, "when you are possibly overthrown, exiled yourself. Are we to live off the benevolence of others, wandering across Europe, outcasts from all whom we love and hold dear?"

"I would never regret it - never!" I almost spat the words in my growing frustration.

"Of course you would," he countered, sniffing and attempting to pull himself together. This time he took my face in his hands. "Ah, my king," he smiled sweetly, those gorgeous eyes sparkling from his tears, "how little you know of the minds of men. First there is trust, then regret then death."

I drew his hands from my face and kissed the palms before letting them drop to his lap. I stood up, stumbling unsteadily to the table and the flagon of wine. I threw back a full goblet of the wine, slumped onto one of the seats, resting my head down on the damask tablecloth. My mouth was starting to feel tender where Piers had struck me.

When I looked up again, I could hear Piers snoring gently. Still on the floor, his head now resting back against the nearby wall. I staggered to where he sat and sank down beside him, laying my head gently in his lap.

+++

I awoke wearily on what I assumed was the following morning. Without the benefit of a window in this secret chamber it was impossible to know. I was back on the bed and lifted my heavy, aching head. At the side of the bed, seated in a chair and looking as though he had rested well, Piers sat watching me, he smiled. Only a very slight redness in his eyes betrayed what was otherwise a look of good humour.

When he spoke it was with a cheerful tone. "Ah! My king, so glad you could join me, I hope I didn't wake you. You're lazy, lying in bed; one would think you had not a care in the world. Have a drink to revive you."

I propped myself up on one elbow and took a gulp from the goblet, spitting out in disgust. "God's death, this is no better than piss!"

"I bow to your apparent superior knowledge, my king. It has nonetheless, alerted your senses and, having done so, I suggest we take advantage of you being awake to get away from this place. Oh dear, I think you have the beginning of a bruise about your eye; you really must be more careful and learn to dodge my fists when we fight. I am, however, happy to believe it was all a bad dream – please don't wake me up!"

I groaned at the weight of my thumping head and his constant cheerful chatter and dropped back onto the pillow. All of a sudden I felt the force of some cold water hit my face, a veritable bucket-load in fact - I sat up, aghast.

Piers let out a gale of laughter, setting down the bucket that had contained the offending water. I went to grab him, but he was too quick. I cursed him, but his laughter was infectious, and soon I could see the funny side of the jape. I sat on the edge of the bed and allowed him to pull my soaking shirt over my head.

"Piers, last night -" I began, but he held a finger to my lips.

"We will speak of it no more, Ned; I am done with melancholy. He frowned as he noticed the bruise he had dealt me during the night's drunken argument. He leaned close and kissed it softly. "Forgive me, Ned, I never should have struck you, please forgive me."

"My darling Perrot, I would forgive you anything. Even the dousing, but not last night's curdled wine!" We both laughed then, leaning towards one another, our foreheads touching.

"Come, my king, let us be away from here. We have a long ride to York - and my wife and child. We should be gone. Even though there are but a few retainers in the castle, it is still better that I leave discreetly."

I felt strangely bemused by the events of the previous evening. Wine had a habit of bringing out the worst in Piers; making him morose and vulnerable. The passion we both felt about the situation had sullied our evening. Even as we rode hard for York, I could not rid myself of the image of him so distressed and frightened. He had been my support in our travails. This most recent exile, though brief, had caused him more concern than those previously. He had grown tired of running, weary at the constant danger in which we both found ourselves, and it troubled me that he at times appeared to consider the situation perilous, and feared for his own safety. Nevertheless, I had stated that as soon as we had reached York I would have the news proclaimed that I had revoked his exile and had deemed him both good and loyal, and would have this declared without delay. His lands and titles would be restored in full. I was determined that we must look forward.

"The lords Ordainers will recognise you as befits the honours I have bestowed on you. Do you hear me, Piers? I will have you by my side."

His reunion with Margaret was touching. As usual I found myself strangely affected by resentment at the joy he seemed to derive from being with his wife again. Indeed, Margaret had stated to me on our initial journey, that she missed him, as she knew I did. She was an astute woman, beautiful and kind, and had always been a favourite of mine. I was aware at how ridiculous my jealousy was, and yet I preferred not to be present when they were reunited.

"Is my infant not the most beautiful child, Ned?" he asked when we dined together that first evening.

"She is indeed," I agreed. "I hope Isabella and I are similarly blessed when God sees fit to grant us the same happy event."

We were both skirting round the issue that concerned us the most and eventually I sought to reassure him that all would be well.

"I mean to have you always by my side, Perrot, you do know that?"

He looked at me and smiled, yet his reaction seemed sad. "I love you Ned," he stated. "I would to God that we could be together always, but the Ordainers will have their way; they have banished me on pain of death. It is only my love for you that has caused me to return again. Yet we are always running, always playing this dangerous game of cat and mouse. I have made bad enemies of powerful men. Do not fear that I love you any less for our present misfortune, but I realise I am the cause of this bad blood between you and the nobles of the kingdom."

I strode over to him and took him by the shoulders before embracing him, clutching him tightly. "We will win the day, Perrot, I promise you, or I will die trying."

He smiled impishly at me, that beautiful twinkle in his eyes that had always melted my heart. He then took my arm and rolled up the sleeve of my robe, exposing the initials we had branded on each other so long ago. He leant down and kissed the letters.

Suddenly, he broke away. "Come, my king, we must celebrate our reunion and the birth of my daughter! Let us command minstrels and acrobats! We must have guests, even the dreary ones that followed you to York, God help us. What a pity the wild dog of Arden is absent, he would rejoice at my return. Even Joseph the Jew should be here to welcome me back. We should insist they dance together for our entertainment!"

The image delighted me and we laughed together as we planned the festivities to follow.

For several days we enjoyed a carefree existence, dining and drinking, and I sent word to Isabel to travel north to join us; I had to admit that I missed her. Quite a strange emotion that I could not explain. Was this love? Certainly not the love that Piers and I enjoyed, but a warm enough feeling to satisfy my desire to see her. I admit now, that I was certainly finding her counsel steadfast, and her letters to Piers during his exile had been kind and expressive of genuine concern. He had been greatly touched by them, as was I.

News reached me that the Ordainers had been given word about my revoking Piers's exile and his reinstatement. This troublesome council now met in London to consider their next move. It did not take them long to respond with the declaration that I would be unable to draw any funds from my exchequer. Naturally, it was then necessary to fund our living costs by using any means; as I viewed it, I was King of England therefore who would gainsay me the perfect right to use what I pleased in order to support myself and my companions? There would be many that would gladly give to their royal master, I was certain.

The Ordainers lost little time in insisting that Piers either surrender to them in person or at the very least leave England and never return. Their intransigence left me little choice other than to take precautionary action and ready certain strongholds for the imminent threat of civil war.

We were a rather morose court by the time Isabella arrived after what had been an arduous journey. With her arrival came a breath of fresh air, and we celebrated as though all of England was making merry rather than living with the ever present threat of war between myself and the Ordainers.

Piers presented himself before Isabella and thanked her for her kind letters and promise of funds to aid him while in exile.

"It appears now, my lord, that you have no need of our help now you are recalled by my husband, the king."

I looked at Piers and smiled.

"His gracious majesty has seen fit to recall his humble servant once more to his side," Piers stated as he took Isabella's hand and lifted it to his lips.

"Let us hope," she continued, "that the king's enemies can reconcile with him sooner rather than later. I do not get the impression that they have missed you!"

Piers let out a gusty laugh. "I think we can all safely say that there are no planned festivities to celebrate my homecoming!"

Those few around us laughed politely, but it was feigned, and we all knew that each day could bring the threat of more menace. Sensing a darkening of the mood of the assembled courtiers, I instructed minstrels to play and my finest singer William to entertain us until the early hours. I watched as Piers and some of the other knights played dice, leaving them to their games which would no doubt involve heavy drinking and riotous behaviour.

It was good to see Piers enjoying himself, and especially if he was the centre of attention. He revelled in regaling stories of his prowess and skills in the tourney. How I missed those days when my companions were always laughing and carefree; they seemed so long ago.

Isabella had retired to bed by now and, having no great desire to gamble, I took my leave also. I entered the chamber we shared, quietly lest she be asleep. However, she was sitting having her long fair hair brushed by one of her attendants. I watched the scene for a moment or two until the handmaiden noticed me and dropped into a low curtsey. I bade her continue, but Isabella dismissed her with a wave of her hand.

She seemed pleased to see me. I looked at her and smiled, she was turning into rather a beautiful young woman; she had grown, although still smaller than I. I took her small soft hand and held it to my lips. Suddenly I drew her to me and kissed her mouth with a stronger desire than either she or I expected and...well I will spare you, Alphage, and you, my kinsman, the details; suffice to say that I believed myself contented in our union. I prayed to God it would always be so.

In the weeks that followed, we seemed to be inundated with troubles and ill fortune. The only light of positive joy was Isabella's announcement that she was expecting our first child. My delight at the news surprised me, I had not given much thought to the prospect of fatherhood, although I could see the delight it gave Piers, and all I could hope was that my child would not grow to hate me as much as I had despised my own father! God only knew what further mischief the Ordainers would have caused by the time the child was born.

News came that my cousin Lancaster was himself travelling north with the intention of capturing Piers and consequently I made preparations to leave York and travel further to Newcastle. I had taken the precaution of sending Isabella on to Tynemouth. Trying to allay her concerns about civil unrest from the Ordainers was not easy. She was becoming an astute young woman - she was aware of a great deal and would not be fobbed off with a few words that would pacify most women. Nevertheless, she would travel to Tynemouth, as I instructed, whilst Piers and I considered our next move.

We sat one morning, planning what should now to be done. We needed to rally a force of some sort. I had summoned as many barons, viscounts and loyal men as I could, ordering them to arms for what I now believe would be the start of a civil war. I had heard that Lancaster was holding jousting tournaments as a devious means of assembling armed men to his banner.

There was news from my scouts that Lancaster was but a few hours away from us. I admit that that grave news shocked me.

Piers questioned my informant for some time before dismissing him. "What now Ned?" he asked me.

"Well we can't stay here, can we? The sooner we are away from here the better, and as light handed as possible!"

"You can't be serious?" Piers stated indignantly.

"What choice do we have? We must leave now! To Tynemouth!" I looked in desperation at Piers, but he smiled impishly as he threw an arm round my shoulder.

"I cannot believe you mean me to abandon the Lincoln green silk suit you insisted on me having, I've not yet worn it!" I could not help but laugh.

Even after all the years we had been together, I was still uncertain whether he was jesting with me or not. "Well, it will eventually find its way to 'Burst Belly', no doubt. All that beautiful material ripped to shreds as he attempts to fit his bulk into it!" The image made us both laugh but, though the tension was broken, it was imperative that we make haste.

+++

We reached the relative safety of Tynemouth to find Isabella anxious and fearful. She was in no danger I assured her, especially as the Ordainers saw her as a potential ally in their damnable plots to destroy Piers. Moreover, the lords would know by now that the queen was carrying the heir to the throne. She was, in truth, the safest of the three of us.

I was beside myself with concern, not only for myself, but particularly for Piers. I made preparations to leave Tynemouth without further delay. Isabella accepted without rancour my instructions for her to travel by land back to York.

I had entrusted the young knight Roger Damory with taking a suitable escort and travelling with the queen.

A knight relatively new to the court, I had noticed Damory a couple of times, as had Piers who mentioned that he looked too innocent to be at my court. He was quite tall, broad-shouldered and handsome, with brown eyes and a small scar across the bridge of his straight nose. He wore a neat beard and his brown, wavy hair fell to his shoulders. His ears seemed to stick out slightly, which made me smile. I felt certain that Isabella was in good hands, as I prayed would I be, although I had yet to tell Piers that he and I were to travel to Scarborough – by sea!

Knowing his aversion to sea travel I struggled to consider any other means that would assure us some measure of safety. Scarborough Castle was, I believed, as safe a place as any given the proximity of alternatives. With Lancaster again pursuing us, I prayed for Isabella's safe journey to York, assuring her that all would be well.

Piers looked down at the small boat that would be our means of flight with a look of panic and foreboding. Were he able to walk Scarborough, I am certain he would have chosen that option rather than be at the mercy of the capricious North Sea. I swear he trembled as he stepped unsteadily onto the small craft. We were certainly a ragged crew that set sail on that bright but chilly morning.

With the wind behind us, I could only pray for our safe deliverance. Piers declared, after only a few minutes at sea, that he would on reflection have preferred to travel with Isabella by land! Our boat, thought small, held itself well. The choppy water would, on occasion pitch us one way and then the other, and I knew Piers would be yearning for a calmer pace. We had only a couple of loyal knights and a small crew. In addition, Piers had sworn he would not travel without his faithful Hugo, who took out a small flute and proceeded to regale us with his rather limited repertoire of tunes. Only Piers would insist on his manservant accompanying us. I wish we could have had more fellow travellers with us, but in view of the haste, we had been obliged to leave our household behind. I raged inwardly at the delight Lancaster would enjoy at finding we had left behind so many valuable items.

There was space enough for Piers and I to enjoy some privacy, and when he wasn't vomiting as the craft moved up and down in the volatile sea, he was quiet and pensive. I sought to allay his worst fears, both about our safety on the journey, and what I intended to do once we reached Scarborough.

"You are to hold the castle, Piers, surrendering to no one but me. I will travel on to York as we agreed." I hated the thought of leaving him, but the castle was well fortified and surely safe enough for him. I would need to pray that our pursuers were noble enough not to attempt to lay siege to the place.

"Do you remember our first meeting, Ned?" It was the most animated my beloved brother had been since we set sail two days since. Night was fast approaching; the worst part of the journey for me was the night time. There was nothing bracing or adventurous about travelling at night in a small boat with few comforts and limited provisions.

"I think of it often" I replied. I reached for his hand, and he gripped mine tightly in return.

"I thought you the most perfect creature I had ever met" he stated.

"Because I was the Prince of Wales?"

"No, because you were the most handsome, dashing character. Innocent and curious about life. I often thought to ask you to run away with me, somewhere away from the intrigue and malice of the English court. I fancied we could live in a small forest hut, living off the land. You could fish in a nearby stream, thatch the roof of the hut and chop up firewood, whilst I just sat and watched."

We laughed suddenly and I poked him hard in the ribs. "And what did you think of me, Ned?"

"I believe I have never known anyone like you, Perrot. My life seemed dull and vacant until your presence at court. You looked to me like a god. Your face, your body. That smile! That wicked grin that never fails to bring a lump to my throat. The night we made our vows to one another was the most perfect I could have imagined. I admit I was scared though."

"Scared of what? – Me?"

"No not of you, but what to do with all the love that you suddenly generated in me. I had no idea I was just a human body devoid of any feelings and emotions. When you set fire to my heart, it raged like an uncontrollable inferno. It is my folly that has led us to this day isn't it?" he asked suddenly.

"The folly was in others, Perrot; jealousy and hatred for one man who dared to believe he was good enough to be by my side. Your folly has only been to have loved me as unconditionally as you have. Many think that the decision to have you made Earl of Cornwall or act as regent were forced upon me, as though my love had blinded me and that I was unaware of the spell you had me under. Those wishes were mine, though, and I raised you as high as I might, but I often wonder if I unwittingly condemned you to a life of scorn and misery by accepting all the honours I could give you."

We were silent for a while and then I chuckled.

"What is it?" he asked.

"I was just thinking that, as much as I enjoyed them, that the nicknames were maybe a step too far."

"Ah, my king, but I only know how to go too far!" We laughed again, seemingly without a care in the world, rather than being little more than fugitives. We were silent again for sometime and I felt my eyes getting heavier until the sway of the craft jolted me awake. His hand was still linked with mine and I could hear his light snoring. I turned my head towards him.

"I love you, Perrot, my brother, I love you," I whispered. "Nunc et usque in aeternum."

After a journey of almost five days, we finally reached land. Even for one as happy with sea life as I was, it was a relief to have made it in one piece and to step onto firm ground. We must have looked a sight, but luckily there only a few fishermen who helped us land the boat and, with the exception of some locals who merely stared open mouthed at us, we were mercifully unnoticed.

Our first task was to establish how far away our pursuers were and I groaned; a force was travelling swiftly towards us. If only good news could travel as fast as bad. There was little to be done other than establish Piers as best we could and I would leave for

Knaresborough Castle with all haste and arrange what forces I could. Mean though they were, there was provision enough for Piers to be able to hold out until I could send word to him to either leave Scarborough or for him to welcome me back there with a force to meet the Ordainers. On no account was he to surrender the castle, even if I be brought there as a prisoner myself!

I dared not wait longer, but as I drew Piers into a final embrace, I felt more alone than I ever had. He appeared resolved to the situation, and I certainly did not doubt his courage. Yet as we held one another, I felt him shudder, and when I drew away from him, I saw that he was crying. I kissed one tear that coursed down his cheek and closed my eyes lest I start weeping myself.

We walked to the drawbridge where my horse and one of the knights that had travelled with us waited. We embraced again.

"Ah, my king," he said and smiled. "Ned, don't forget me, please don't forget me."

"Fear not, my brother," I said, "I will return to you soon, it will be too short a time to forget you, Perrot!"

It was only after I had saluted him and cantered off with all speed, that I drew my horse to a standstill. He hadn't meant not to forget where I had left him...I turned quickly, just in time to see the drawbridge raised, and he had gone.

I rode hard for York, with Hugh Audley, one of the two knights we had brought along with us. The other, William Montacute, I had left with Piers, with instructions that he was to act as go-between while Piers and I were apart. Both Hugh and William were household knights, and certainly likeable enough. William was a serious looking character. Small by comparison to most of the other household knights, he was dark skinned and hirsute; I was unsure whether I knew of anyone with such a wiry-haired beard, which was as black as soot. /he had thin lips that were ready enough to smile, for all his brooding seriousness, and his eyes seemed to be watchful of everything, darting from side to side as though seeking danger before being confronted with it.

Hugh Audley was quite different - a lanky frame that stood at least as tall as myself. He had a sharp looking face, sallow cheeks, brown eyes and a large, aquiline nose, a trimmed beard and closely-cropped hair. For all his high cheekbones and thin, almost colourless lips that rarely broke into a smile, he was a very likeable man, witty and clever and apparently a more than competent jouster.

It was good to have young men like these around me. During the periods of time when Piers was in exile, I hungered for good company. I could not help but wonder if they would remain as loyal to me as others had. These musings passed the time, as well as being a distraction from my sadness at leaving Piers. I was determined that, when we were reunited, we would triumph over the Ordainers, one way or another.

Isabella looked tired and sickly, which she informed me was quite usual for one in her condition. We sat and I relayed the awful boat trip that had taken the best part of five days to achieve. I couldn't help but give way to exhaustion, feeling suddenly the tension of such a perilous voyage. My manservant Will and valets of the bedchamber who had travelled with Isabella, helped undress me and it was late the following morning when I awoke.

The following few days were spent desperately trying to raise an army – from anywhere! The task seemed impossible, and I was beginning to feel despair set in.

Further bad news arrived; later on the same day that I had left Piers, traitors had arrived to besiege Scarborough Castle. I raged at the impertinence and treachery. The list of these devils made my blood boil and my heart sink.

The Earls of Surrey and Pembroke, Robert, Lord Clifford and Henry Percy.

"Damn traitors, all!" I raged at Isabella – indeed, at anyone who I came into contact with. All servants slunk away from me, terrified of the inevitable explosion of fury that would angrily erupt. I threw furniture, smashed anything breakable, pulled down tapestries from the walls, after which I sank to the floor gnawing at my knuckles until they bled.

After I had exhausted myself, crying hot tears of frustration and anger of all that had brought me to this impasse, I slumped into a chair and waited for further news, desperate to know if the proposed siege had begun. When word finally came, it was worse than I feared – Piers had surrendered the castle!

William Montacute ran a hand through his wet hair, drenched from the heavy rain that had fallen for most of the day, and handed me a letter from Piers. I took it, but did not open it, instead asking him to tell me what he could. William's eyes darted around the chamber, almost as though he was checking how best to get out. I steadied myself to try and stay calm; no good would come of berating the knight because he brought ill tidings. I made him sit, and he helped himself to the wine I offered. After a long gulp, he ran his wet mouth across his hand.

"My lord of Cornwall had no choice, your grace, their army brought siege engines with them. We held on as long as we could but, fortified though it was, there were insufficient provisions for any siege of intent. There was no other way. The Earl of Surrey left the forces some way back and approached the castle on his horse. He dismounted and stood with his hands on his hips, shouting that he wanted to engage the Earl of Cornwall in direct discussion about his surrender.

"But I insisted that he was on no account to surrender, what was he thinking?" I said bitterly.

It was to Montacute's credit that he was ready to defend Piers's actions "Forgive me your grace, but with the castle in danger of being battered down and all who defended it put to the sword, the Earl of Cornwall made the only decision he could; he was no coward who gave up at the first sign of attack!"

His words stung me, as well they should. I knew Piers would only have surrendered if there was no other choice. Montacute stood, stiffly, and without looking at me. I could see he was angry, and perhaps did not trust himself to say more.

"Have I your leave to depart, your grace? I must return to Scarborough."

I suddenly felt sick with it all. I nodded to him in answer. He had almost gone out the door when I stayed him.

"Montacute, what did the Earl of Cornwall say to Surrey when he approached?"

The knight's serious, pained face suddenly broke into a rare smile, his straight white teeth dazzled against the blackness of his beard. "He said nothing at all your grace. He just ran up to the ramparts, stood on the parapet of the wall, and in full view of his lordship, pulled down the front of his hose and proceeded to piss down to where the Earl of Surrey stood!" With that, an embarrassed Montacute nodded in deference and quickly left.

I considered the response Piers had made, and I began to laugh, merriment that quickly turned to tears as I sank into a chair and sobbed.

+++

I officially sent word to the enemy commanders to cease their besieging of Scarborough, but my messenger did not return, no doubt held captive. I seethed with indignation. I learned that Lancaster had seized the valuable baggage that Piers and I had been forced to leave behind as we fled. Not only that, but my cousin treacherously stationed a considerable force between York and Scarborough to engage anyone who would attempt to relieve the siege.

Montacute relayed to me, several days later, what had occurred when Piers effectively gave up his attempt to hold the castle, which was now considerably damaged by the relentless bombardment from the powerful siege engines. He had few provisions, and had all but given up hope of any army coming to our aid. Eventually, Piers made the only decision he could, and he came out of the castle in order to discuss terms.

Piers would be taken to his own fortress in Wallingford, where he would be held under house arrest until he could be brought before parliament, where his fate would ultimately be decided.

I felt powerless to act, but all was not lost - as I saw it, at least. I wrote in desperation to my father-in-law, the King of France, even offering to grant him custody of Gascony if he would help to keep Piers safe. I asked Isabella to write to her father on Piers's behalf. I even shocked my advisors by claiming I would gladly recognise Bruce as king of Scotland if he would grant my beloved sanctuary in that volatile place. What more could I do?

+++

I slept fitfully most nights. Isabella was constantly ill, and I kept away from her. She kept to her own chamber with her ladies in attendance. It was impossible to know her thoughts on all that was transpiring around us. I never found out whether she corresponded with her father on Gaveston's behalf, but I doubted that she had. I was able to keep a minimal correspondence with Piers, although I was certain that our letters were unsealed and read before they were passed to either of us.

June of that year was hot and uncomfortable and - though I paced the apartments like a caged animal, frustrated at the impossible situation that now presented itself - I felt strangely optimistic. Piers and I had weathered many storms before and I had a mind to now agree in full to the Ordainers' demands with regard to the running of the kingdom. Let the lords have their day. I would send Piers to Ireland again. He had often said that he had forged good relations with a few of the warlords and I could, I believed, furnish him with arms, money and anything else he might need. It may be that he would have to make a decent show of leaving, and

I would just have to endure being parted from him for a longer period of time - just until tempers had cooled or I had regained more control of the Ordainers.

It was on a glorious summer day when a horseman arrived. Something caused me to feel a sudden chill. William Montacute had been bringing me news regularly as well as taking letters between Piers and myself. I had, therefore, expected Montacute to enter, but not Piers's manservant Hugo - and when Will ushered them into the chamber, I feared negotiations were going badly; how I prayed that Piers would keep a civil, respectful tongue. Now was not the time for his usual japes in his dealings with the barons.

Montacute bowed and looked downwards in dejection, but Hugo threw himself at my feet in floods of tears. I nervously looked at the knight, who now stood to attention, taking a deep breath and uttering the words that I would carry with me for the rest of my life.

"Your grace, I regret to tell you – the Earl of Cornwall is dead."

+++

CHAPTER FOUR

Edward, can you continue?" Alphage had put a gentle hand on the hermit's shoulder as Edward wiped away the tears that fell, streaming down his cheeks as though they would never stop. The former king stood immobile as the haunting tale had unfolded. It was as though he was bewitched by some unseen power that rendered him senseless.

Fieschi continued to look down at his feet. Of course he knew something of the story; news reached the pope by all means and all sources. Secretaries, envoys, papal spies' informants dressed as beggars, musicians and actors. Some dangerous assassins could infiltrate the most highly-placed palaces by donning a fool's outfit or playing a flute.

Alphage could almost feel his friend's pain, as the story of the former king's favourite played out to its inevitable conclusion. He who had travelled widely and seen enough misery and heartache in the world could only imagine the grief that Edward must have lived with every day.

Everything had gone quiet. As though created for effect, the sky grew darker as hovering clouds began to shut out what had, moments before, been warm sunshine. Now the air was still, with a palpable hidden menace as though anger would erupt at any given moment.

Both Fieschi and Alphage jumped in alarm at the sudden rumble of thunder. Drops of cool rain began to drift lightly down at first and then the drops grew bigger, falling harder, with greater certainty.

Edward had not answered the infirmarian; he remained as a statue, staring straight ahead as though transfixed.

Fieschi looked up at the threatening sky and drew his tunic tighter around his neck, standing up and speaking to Alphage directly. Edward did not hear either of them, and when he remained immobile as though resisting the gentle urging of the monk to take shelter, both men reluctantly made their way to the shelter at one side of the garden.

Edward still stood silently. The rain, hard and unrelenting now, was beginning to lash down on him, coursing down his face, soaking him from head to toe. Perrot whined softly at his master, but would not leave his side, occasionally shaking himself, sending the offending water in spiral sprays. The thunder clouds had now grown darker. Edward looked up at the sky, and sank to his knees.

Alphage eventually could not watch him any longer and, grabbing a cloak from the herbalist's shed, he hastened as quickly as he could to the kneeling figure, wrapping it over Edward's head and shoulders, and eventually succeeded in drawing the now soaking figure over to the shelter.

The rain continued as the humidity grew and all three men, although wet, were not cold. Edward feeling only the sensation that he could get no wetter than he now was, so the rain mattered little.

Fieschi looked to the hermit and, despite a sniff of derision from Alphage, asked Edward what had transpired once Gaveston had been caught; surely he was accorded some legal representation, the dignity at least of an honourable trial.

Edward breathed in through his nose and his shoulders sagged with a deep sigh as though summoning again the memory of that tragic day when he had lost the man he loved more than anything in his world.

"Piers was taken from Scarborough and left in the custody of the Earl of Pembroke, 'Joseph the Jew', Piers called him." Edward smiled. "Of all the Ordainers, he was the most acceptable. I swear that, although he was riled at the impertinence of the nickname, I always believed he rather enjoyed the effect that Gaveston's name-calling had on the other lords, especially Warwick."

Alphage had found a spare monk's habit behind the door of the potting shed, and now helped Edward undress, reaching up to put the dry clothing over the hermit's head.

Fieschi gave Perrot a look of distaste as the animal gave himself another furious shake that rippled from his ears all the way down to the tip of his tail, the spray covering the nobleman's robe. Were that not enough, the dog proceeded to rub the side of its face against Fieschi's leg until satisfied that the worst of the water had been dispersed.

"Pembroke was to take Piers to his stronghold in Wallingford," Edward continued, staring blankly at the ground. "Deddington is a place near the great city of Oxford, although the names and areas won't mean anything to you, of course. I profess that I was not familiar with Deddington myself, but anyway they rested at a priory there. Pembroke had a manor at a nearby place called Bampton, only some twenty miles away and decided to take the opportunity to visit his wife there, leaving Piers under close guard." Edward again stopped a moment to collect his thoughts. "The Earl of Warwick has a network of spies and informants second only to the King of France, I believe, and, naturally word of where Piers was now being held reached him. How he must have rubbed his grubby, fat hands in glee! A priory, barely-guarded, let alone defended, was an easy target for one as accomplished in stealth and mischief as 'the black dog of Arden', as my beloved brother so aptly named him. He arrived the following morning at dawn, before Pembroke had returned. Having brought a force of men that easily overpowered the guards left by Pembroke, Warwick had his henchmen drag Piers from his bed and, dressed in only hose and a shirt, he had him walk barefoot behind his troupe, wrists tied behind him.

The streets were by now lined with curious onlookers, who, upon realising who the captive was, proceeded to jeer at him, some throwing mud and other debris as they passed by. Having humiliated their prisoner, once the populace had followed them for some time, they sat Piers on an old nag for the ride to Warwick castle. Once there they threw my beloved brother into a dark stinking dungeon and waited for the other barons to arrive, their quarry now manacled in the dark."

"Who related all this to you? Surely not the Earl of Warwick himself?" asked Fieschi.

"No," Edward replied, "Piers's most loyal manservant, Hugo, was taken too. Powerless to save his beloved master, he could only watch as the horror unfolded."

"This then was told to me by faithful Hugo who, on arriving with the ill tidings, virtually collapsed. Let us continue..."

+++

I stood motionless while Hugo sobbed uncontrollably at my feet as he related the ghastly events. He had paused in his telling and I knew the worst was to come.

"Tell me, Hugo," I demanded, determined to punish myself with every last detail, each of which stabbed at me like an arrow.

Hugo began to tremble, whether from the shock, fear of my reaction or because each utterance pained him as it did me. "They seemed completely uninterested in my presence. I could ride and, with my own horse, I followed at as close a distance as I dared. Eventually my lords Lancaster, Arundel and Hereford arrived and they prepared to do their worst. The lord Warwick seems to have lost heart in his vengeance, and declared that he would play no further part in what was to follow. My master was taken then to a nearby place known as Blacklow Hill. I tethered my horse discreetly and I was able to watch from a distance under the cover of the dense hedgerow. Lord Thomas announced that in their charity, they had determined that they would afford my lord a noble death. They had my master kneel on the ground; he spoke only to commend himself to you your grace and declare he died this day your loyal and beloved brother. One of the men-at-arms then ran him through with a sword and, as he lay dead, they.... they...cut off his head!"

With the words eventually uttered, Hugo wept uncontrollably. Eventually he continued, "They left him lying there, not once giving thought to what would happen to his corpse. I stayed with his broken body for the rest of that day, not knowing what to do, in fear that the lords would return to desecrate the body further and do me some harm if they found me there. My lord was a muscular man, and would not be easily lifted onto my horse; even if I could have carried this out on my own, I had no idea where I should take it. A group of common peddlers came along the road, and I begged their help. They agreed to carry the corpse to Warwick's castle. They laid it onto their rough cart and I followed. The Earl of Warwick refused to take ownership of it, however, and the peddlers had no other choice than to return it back to the place of execution, where I sat with it."

Hugo sobbed and pulled at his hair, his grief was heart breaking to witness. Eventually he continued, "Word must have reached Oxford because, as the day passed, a group of Dominican monks arrived and said they would take the body with them back to their house, where they proceeded to embalm it and sew the head back on to the body. It lies there still, your grace. The monks said they would watch over the corpse, but would be unable to bury it, as my master was under excommunication. I left his body with the good brothers, and rode hard to get here - I could think of nowhere else to go." With the shedding of this burden of grief, Hugo again sobbed without control.

I blessed my fortune in having a close and noble servant in Will Sheene, who helped Hugo to his feet.

Montacute stood, his head bowed, quietly sobbing himself, and Will directed them from the chamber with a glance at me, before the door closed behind them.

I opened my mouth to scream, but nothing sounded. My cries were silenced; I stood, dry-eyed, desperate for the howl of pain that grew from my guts to my throat. Then I walked over to my desk, and in one swift, angry movement, I swept everything from it casting them to the floor. I then surveyed everything in the chamber - and proceeded to destroy it.

+++

It was two days later when Isabella gave orders that the door of my chamber was to be broken down. I had locked it and refused entry to anyone.

The queen had everyone dismissed apart from Will, and together they helped me up from the floor and onto a chair, possibly the only item of furniture I had not completely smashed to pieces.

I turned a blank, tear-stained face to Isabella. "Piers is dead! They have butchered him, he is slain!" Isabella blinked quickly, yet I was sure I saw her eyes fill with tears - whether for Perrot or me, I was uncertain.

She smiled, sadly, "I know, dearest, I know."

The days seemed to drift by without my comprehending anything. It is to Isabella's lasting credit that she barely left my side unless it was to officiate, on my behalf, all those monstrously boring tasks that I had shunned so often in the past.

I cruelly subjected myself to the torture of having Piers's manservant Hugo brought to me to relate again and again the details of that awful day. Later, of course, I considered how much this must have pained Hugo personally, but I cared little for that at the time, so intent was I in extracting every last pathetic detail. I took out from an ornate wooden box, the velvet strip of cloth that had bound our wounds together all those years ago, its dark dried stain still visible. I wrapped it gently around the initials on my arm, using it to wipe away my tears.

How does one grieve, I asked myself? I had never lost anyone so close. I had never mourned my father because, God forgive me, I was so glad once he was gone, that I was free of the torment he caused. I had been so young when my mother had died that I could scarcely remember at all now. Nothing seemed to help me make any sense of the tragedy that now surrounded me; there were reminders of Piers everywhere.

Each day I would expect to hear him laugh or sing – he had such a dreadful singing voice! All my plans evolved around him. Where does one start to piece their life together again after such a loss? I could not recall a time without him. He had been the love of my life, and I knew that I would not love Isabella in the same way, and that indeed there would be no other that I could love as much as my darling Perrot.

Isabella begged me to try and carry on, even in the face of such grief. At least in public if nothing else, she had said. She would never truly understand; she who had been the adored princess, the dutiful daughter and apple of her father's eye, the jewel in his crown. Marriage to me had made her a queen. In many ways I thought her cold. She could at times be devoted and understanding, and I even believe she might have missed Piers herself. They had not been close to one another, but I believe she had grown to tolerate him.

Plus, of course, Isabella was always charmed by flattery and no one could flatter with such ease as Piers Gaveston. Charm and wit were his currency, and he spent lavishly.

I recall that, later, I had his chamber at Langley locked and held almost as a shrine to him. In days to come, I would go there alone at night which was when I missed him most. I would run my hand over the rich bed coverings, the finest velvets and silks, all decorated with costly golden thread. I would handle the beautiful jewels, rings for every finger, costly chains, pearls and rubies. And, of course, there were his clothes, a dazzling array of the finest cloths of almost every colour - blues, yellows, greens, there was no colour that did not suit him. I sat at his closet and took up a beautiful ornate bottle of dark red glass set in an intricate metal casing; I removed the glass stopper and held it to my nose, breathing in the lavender scent. I would never be able to smell that most pungent herb without bringing him immediately to mind. I took the bottle with me and swore to wear it every day as he had done.

My temper was short - worse than ever - and Isabella and Will bore the brunt of it. I did not want to be bothered with annoying women or pestering servants! I did not seek Isabella's company at night, preferring to be on my own. I would scream to be left alone, and yet call for Will to sleep on the floor of my chamber on those nights when the solitude was unbearable.

And then, finally, one day I discovered the one thing that gave me a purpose for living – revenge!

+++

Shouting at servants, courtiers and wives was directing my inner fury at the wrong people. They had not butchered Piers Gaveston, but of course I knew who did.

I received word from the Earl of Pembroke who wanted me to know that he had been outraged at the conduct of Warwick and Lancaster and the others in abducting Piers from his charge. His fury was quite genuine; it was an affront to his honour, and whilst he admitted to seeking Gaveston's capture, he never countenanced his execution in such a brutal way, and certainly not without a fair and legal hearing. The fact that the other lords had taken it upon themselves to capture Piers whilst he was effectively under Pembroke's protection was reason enough for him to turn away from the other Ordainers – for the moment at least.

Pembroke had always been both a direct and honest man, and I was glad to have him on my side in this. The Earl of Surrey had also been horrified at Warwick and Lancaster's actions. I was beginning to feel emboldened by their criticism of my cousin and his other cronies.

Yet, in my pathetic grief and sorrow I found an anger against my darling brother. Piers had done little to endear himself to the powerful lords of the land, yet how could I blame him and not myself? Why had I not told him to resist goading them into anger? Why did I allow him to taunt them with the nicknames he gave them? Why was he not just prepared to stay by my side, to just live and love rather than want more? I wrestled with so many unanswered questions, and yet the result was of course obvious. I felt it in the pit of my stomach, it made me heave and I swallowed the truth like a sour bile time and again.

The truth of it was I did not want him to stop, I enjoyed the faces of those power hungry earls when Piers would tease them into a reaction. Piers made each day unpredictable. He sensed that I was probably too weak to face down the barons, and sought to redress the balance in my favour by focussing their attention on him rather than me. It had been I who had raised him up so high, lavished him with all manner of gifts, titles, lands, castles - anything that he wanted I would gladly give him.

I had spoiled him in every way and every sense; spoiled him like a greedy child who wants everything and will sulk or behave with petulance until getting their own way. More tragically, I had spoilt Piers himself. Turned him from a friendly, brave and charismatic knight into a detested sycophant that everyone appeared to hate from the highest bishop to the lowest tinker. I had given him everything but honour. By the end, I had done everything for Perrot except protect him. From the day I learned of his cruel death, I never stopped telling myself that, but for my own arrogance, my beloved brother Perrot would possibly still be alive.

Yet, I clung to my perceived status of divinity. I was the king and, as such, surely answerable to none but God. That was exactly how Piers also believed, and when he felt the balance of power beginning to shift towards the vainglorious barons, he sought to turn things to my favour. Yet, he could never be safe, he had made far too many enemies for that. Those who determined that he would pay a heavy price for his insolence pursued him relentlessly. Apart from their personal grievances, they could never permit any one individual, apart from perhaps the queen, of being too close to the royal ear. How many more years would Perrot have lived if only he had heeded the warnings that were so obvious to all but the two of us?

Dear God, I feel this wound will never heal.

+++

Tensions ran high during the weeks following Piers's murder – I viewed it as nothing less! - and I believe that my hatred of the earls, particularly Warwick and Lancaster, sustained me and emboldened me to begin to fight back.

It was a sombre cavalcade that travelled on towards the capital, and even the warm summer weather did nothing to heal the mood. I had often declared that in summer there was no better place on earth than England, and yet as we travelled through woodlands of endless bluebells and the merry chirping of birds, the sighting of young deer, rabbits, and the delicate fluttering of brightly coloured butterflies, we could as easily be travelling through snow storms. Nothing eased the mood.

I had left Isabella behind at York, feeling it safer than subjecting her to the unpredictable days ahead. I understood that the pregnancy was progressing normally, and I prayed all would be well. Thinking of her condition brought to mind the journey Piers's widow Margaret and I had undertaken. She who was at the time so close to her confinement and would be delivered of a fine girl. How proud Piers had been. I would see that his widow and the child wanted for nothing.

Unexpected news did reach me that there had been something of a disquiet in the north of England against the brutal execution of Gaveston. Many, although not disappointed that Piers had been removed, were horrified by the means that had been used, and were openly questioning its legality. To have the better part of opinion was unusual for me, yet I savoured it, feeling a greater justification for my supressed rage and torment. Pembroke and Surrey were now allies and urged action.

Hugh Despenser the elder and his son Hugh both urged caution, as did Henry de Beaumont, whom the Ordainers had been so adamant about removing from my circle of friends. Was I in a strong enough position to effectively plunge the country into civil war?

The tensions were palpable enough as we neared the gates of the capital, and I summoned the mayor and leading aldermen to a council at Blackfriars. My first concern must be to hold the capital. I spoke to them earnestly and with as much anger as I dared show. Urging them to hold firm and not permit my enemies to enter the city. The delegation retired to consider my words and returned to swear that they would ensure that the capital was protected against my enemies.

I dismissed them with my gratitude, yet even I had enough sense to recognise how capricious the citizens of London could be. Those that bent the knee to me now could just as easily turn on me, and hatred of Perrot was enough of a motive for them. Even now, with his lifeless body barely sewn back together by the Dominicans, Piers Gaveston was still a cause of division. How much can one man be hated?

I could sense that all those around me waited in anticipation for something to happen; for the situation to progress to a bloody conclusion. I would have liked nothing better than to have Lancaster and Warwick at my feet, indeed, the thought was in danger of becoming an obsession.

At last I decided on diplomacy, at least for now. I summoned the Earls to meet me at Westminster, although I had forbidden them to enter the capital armed. After that, I waited.

News was brought to me that, in a flagrant disregard for my command, Lancaster, Warwick and Hereford had indeed arrived in London equipped for battle. I raged at their impertinence, although why should I be surprised at their insolence towards their king?

My dearest nephew and companion from my youth, Gilbert de Clare, as Earl of Gloucester, agreed to be the go-between for myself and the venomous trio of earls. I began by sending him with an instruction to ask why they had entered the city bearing arms when I had expressly forbidden it?

Later, Gilbert stood before me, no doubt wishing he had never offered to be mediator. "In their position your grace," he spoke nervously, "the lords insist this was only done so they could protect themselves for any that would do them harm."

I let out a loud, bitter laugh, completely devoid of any humour. "Ha! Do they think I am like them? It is not my way, my good Gilbert, to avenge myself against an unarmed enemy. Surely it is only cowards who would act so, and I am no coward! Tell them that, my Lord of Gloucester, tell them that!"

Gilbert's shoulders visibly sank, and I looked at him not without pity. I sighed wearily, "Oh, Gilbert, come sit by me here." He moved to my side; he seemed suddenly older; how strange it seemed that Piers's death seemed to have sapped the life out of his companions - myself foremost. "Ah, my friend, what will become of all this? I cannot forgive them, although they will send you here with pretty words and glorified excuses."

Gilbert looked away, and I sensed his despair. "You must see, Ned," he addressed me in the familiar term only used by those dearest to me, "they believe that they merely rid the country of a traitor. They insist they are your friends, your most humble servants, and anything they have done has been for your own good."

"Humble servants? Ha!" the notion amused me greatly. "There is nothing humble about them, they do not recognise humility; they have the blood of one dearest to me on their hands as well as their consciences!" I stood and turned to him, rubbing my hands over my face.

"Gilbert, I am tired, so tired. Forgive me, my friend, we will talk tomorrow, I can think no more tonight." I suddenly felt a wave of exhaustion, and I slumped into my chair set up in the great hall of Westminster, its vast ceiling stretching way above us. I noticed, suddenly, a bird high up in the beams of the vast ceiling. Gilbert was bowing as he took his leave, but I scarcely noticed him, so intent was I on the small creature that would occasionally peck at something on its wooden perch. I was transfixed.

Even with all that was happening around me, I felt strangely alone with just this tiny creature for company.

Did I imagine that this was the soul of my darling Perrot, keeping watch over me? I called a servant over to me and instructed him to fetch some breadcrumbs. I repeated the order, given the confused look on his face. He ran off and I continued to watch as the bird now fluttered down to a lower level. I have always had such a love of birds, and I remained transfixed by the tiny chirping sounds it omitted. Indeed, it was the only thing that had made me smile for as long as I could remember.

Hugh Despenser and his son entered and both bowed low and kissed my outstretched hand. At that moment, the servant appeared and I instructed him to sprinkle some of the breadcrumbs along a wooden ridge at one wall underneath where my new feathered friend twitched his head with interest.

Both men looked confused, but I smiled and bade them speak. The younger drew up two chairs. The elder looked at me with concern.

"You look tired, your grace, forgive me, but you must take some rest."

"Yes, I know," I replied, casting a quick glance to one side where the small bird now pecked greedily at the enticing scattered breadcrumbs.

I rose, restless and yet exhausted. We walked down the hall while we talked.

"I will never forgive Warwick and Lancaster for this, Hugh. I'll have Warwick's head if it's the last thing I ever do. If civil war is caused, it will be they that have caused it."

The elder Hugh was not quite as tall as me, but was a solidly built man. His son, another companion from my youth, was a much slighter build than his father, fairer in features, with light brown hair that reached down to his slender shoulders and a slightly angular face; his chin sported a very neatly-trimmed beard and he was handsome enough, slim and smaller in height than I and almost feminine in manner, green eyes that sparkled and seemed to take in everything around him and were almost mesmerising. I had never paid him much attention until he seemed to be always with his father whenever he was in attendance. I knew that this younger Despenser would be as loyal to me as his father.

"Your grace," the younger suddenly spoke, "might I be so bold as to offer a suggestion?"

"Of course you may, Hugh, I stand on no ceremony with my friends. No, old Hugh, do not glare at your son so, there is no affront in offering me an opinion. Your son does not speak out of turn."

The younger waited until we had passed a guard on duty to speak. "It would appear to me, your grace, that most men advise you to take up arms against the shamed barons and, whilst there is good cause, I feel emboldened to offer my own observations."

We continued to walk as I nodded. "Indeed, continue."

"Your grace, you must of course demand financial recompense for damages done from the lords, as is your right. The property and goods that my Lord Lancaster seized must be returned immediately." He paused suddenly, and I glanced down at him.

"Continue, please."

Hugh the younger licked his thin lips and stared up at me. "I would dare to say, your grace that I believe no civil unrest need occur. Your grace does not need to fight a war when morally you hold the upper hand. Why, already it is well known that there is a growing voice of dissent in the land at the way that the lords Warwick and Lancaster have behaved. When I myself think of what they did…remember, your grace, that I too first knew the late Earl of Cornwall when he came to your father's court."

With a sudden, unexplained impulse, I pulled the younger towards me, hugging him and patting him firmly on the back "I know, Hugh, I know." I swallowed hard and released him. I feared I had embarrassed both men, although they both seemed emotional as I.

"So," I announced, "some tell me to fight, others tell me to avoid a confrontation at all costs. Well, I will steer a course through the centre of it all; let these lords stew in their own sweat and wonder when vengeance will be mine. I will discuss terms, but not straight away, and I will on no account charge Piers Gaveston with being a traitor. Whatever is agreed will be for the public good and none shall know when I will avenge the murder of my beloved brother Piers, until it is done. I failed to protect his body, but I will not make the same error with his soul."

Both men smiled at me, and the elder Hugh embraced me warmly before bowing. His son smiled and bowed likewise, staring at me for a moment before they both backed out of the hall.

I walked back to my great chair at the head of the hall, trying to take in everything that had been said. Making a promise to myself that I would, as I had told the Despensers, protect the memory of my darling Perrot.

I stopped suddenly and a wave of horrific emotion threatened to overcome me as I glanced at a movement to one side of me, where a black cat had dug its sharp claws into the tiny bird that had been tempted down from its safe perch by the breadcrumbs.

The painful comparison to Piers stabbed me as sharply as a dagger. Just like with my beloved brother, I had tempted that tiny innocent creature and then turned away and left him, only for an enemy to come along whilst my back was turned and attack him. The body of that now lifeless bird was as pathetic as Perrot's headless corpse. Both had placed their trust in me and paid the ultimate price. Piers's words returned again to haunt me: "Ah, my king, First there is trust, then regret then death."

I turned away swiftly to march out, stopping only briefly to speak to the servant who had brought the breadcrumbs. "Take the cat, and slit its throat!"

+++

The night was warm and humid, the sky clear and speckled with a thousand stars as I rode out that night with just Will Shene and two escort riders. The two riders were trustworthy and only the four of us knew our destination. Will had waited until I had feigned exhaustion, and the ever-present courtiers had dispersed for the night, whereupon he had led me to a small chamber in the depths of Westminster and, from there, down some narrow winding stairs, out through what I assumed from the warmth and smell to be the kitchen. There were still servants working there but, with a swift and sure pace, we managed to evade their curiosity.

A look at the sword that hung from the belts of our escorts would probably have been enough to assure their silence, but mercifully we were not noticed.

From there, another side door led to a small courtyard. Four horses stood patiently waiting and, with all speed, we mounted and galloped out of the palace precinct, toward the gates of the city. I promised that one day I would ask Will Shene how he was able to arrange this clandestine journey without us being stopped, questioned or delayed. It seemed he knew everyone that could be of use, had a key to every lock and a memory for rooms in palaces and dungeons in castles. I must try and recall how I ever met him or how he came to be my faithful saviour on so many occasions. The memory of our association will no doubt come to me, although it evades me for the moment.

Anyway, we rode for some time; my stomach lurched several times and, by the time we reached our destination, I felt positively nauseous.

The entrance to the Dominican house in Oxford looked dark and full of menace, but as Will and I entered we were greeted by a kind-looking monk who smiled sadly, said nothing and bade us follow him. The corridors were dimly-lit with small sconces on the stone walls; the smell of beeswax and the sweet aroma of crushed herbs seemed to hang in the air of the sacred place. At last, we were met at a large wooden door by two more monks, who bowed their heads and Will stood to one side as the heavy door was opened and I was ushered into the room beyond.

There was no sound at all in the dimly lit chamber where I now stood, alone and vulnerable. Again, small sconces threw a dim light against the walls, bare of decoration save for a large cross that hung to one side. Large candles stood on a small altar at one end covered in a velvet cloth. High up on one wall, a small open grille provided the only air in this otherwise humid chamber. I had felt a cloying nervousness as we had approached the sacred house, but now I felt myself strangely at peace; yet, even so, I dreaded what I had come for. In the centre of the room was a table draped in a fine dark cloth. On the structure was a simple wooden coffin and, even as I approached it, I felt the emotion rise within me.

The body that lay in the wooden box was covered in a loose white cerecloth. I breathed deeply and, taking a corner of the material, pulled it gently to one side.

It almost seemed as though, at any moment, Piers Gaveston would open his eyes and laugh at how easily I had been fooled into believing he was dead. Yet I knew, of course, that could not be. Even though he had been skilfully embalmed, there was a sharpness to his beautiful features. His long dark eyelashes rested lightly as though they would flutter open.

I steadied my hand as I touched his cold skin, running my finger down from his forehead, to his nose and then to his lips which felt like ice, and yet were almost soft. I had touched the dimple in his chin by the time I started weeping, gripping the sides of the coffin until my knuckles turned white. I was suddenly unable to stop shaking as sobs racked my entire body. I let my tears fall from my eyes to his face; they splashed on his once-perfect nose that had wrinkled so much when he laughed. I traced my hand across his face from one side to the other as I cried, telling him over and over that I was so very, very sorry.

The cerecloth rose high up to his neck and I knew, even as my hand reached to lower it, that I should not do so. The large angry scar had developed into a dark grey, putrid wound, where thick leather stitches held his head to his body. I felt I would either pass out or vomit; I closed my eyes and took a deep breath as I replaced the cloth, arranging it around the scar of his severed throat.

"I promise you, my darling brother, that I shall not rest until your murderers pay a heavy price for this." Now, as I stroked his once-luxurious black hair, I made a solemn declaration: "I will always love you, Piers; my heart is broken, but I will treasure your memory for the rest of my days."

I then leant over and kissed his cold lips before using a finger to trace the initials E and P on his forehead. I could bear the pain no longer, but it was some time before I eventually dragged myself away. I said a last goodbye and prayed for the strength to now live without him. I glanced back only once before slipping out into the dim corridor.

+++

Negotiations continued between myself and the lords, delegations between one and the other seemed to pass continuously. I was pleased that my father-in-law, Philip, did not meddle in the affair - indeed, he seemed more supportive than I had dared expect. I fancied this was due to Isabella, and I welcomed it. Of course, if I needed to call on troops from my estates at Ponthieu, it was imperative that I could sustain a competent military communication with France. Good relations with Philip were now essential.

Other than that, I decided to play the long game, which I fancied suited Warwick and Lancaster, although I promised Piers that they would learn that I had a long memory where grudges were concerned.

After such a sad and uneasy number of weeks, I felt my spirits lifted at the news that, after a slow and protracted journey from York, Isabella had arrived safely at Windsor. We had been apart for over two months, and I took no joy in our separation. It would have been foolish to subject her to so long a journey with the risk of civil war a real possibility, especially as she was heavily with child.

I recall being pleased to have her with me once again. I was amazed that her pregnancy had altered her so much; she seemed quite different, a maturity even in the time we had been apart.

I embraced her warmly. "You must rest madam, I will not let these young ladies wear you out with their laughter and frivolity!" Isabella's ladies giggled between themselves, and their mistress's face lit up with the joy of our happy reunion.

"My dearest," she said, "I am quite rested, although the journey was tiring at times; we stopped often, as you had instructed your escort. How I have missed Windsor, one of the best of your castles!"

"OUR castles," I corrected her with a smile. Her face lit up. A few short months ago I would have uttered the same to Perrot. She seemed to sense a sudden sadness in me and, with a wave of her small, delicate hand, dismissed her entourage.

When they had departed, she rose and came to me, kneeling at my feet. I made to protest, but she put a finger to my lips.

"I have not yet said to you, my dear heart, I am so sorry that you grieve still for the Earl of Cornwall. We are husband and wife and your loss is mine also; as you mourn your friend, so do I join in your sorrow."

I knew she meant well, but something held me back from sharing the pain I truly felt. "No madam," I stated, standing up and helping her to her feet. "The pain of losing Piers will be mine alone. We will not speak of it again." I knew as I left the chamber, I would be leaving her confused and possibly upset, but my grief was as yet too raw to even speak of. I would not share him – even in death.

During the following weeks, I slowly began to recover some of my old energy. Still finding much to be lamented, I threw myself into the physical activities that always gave me an outlet for my frustrations. I had a foundry constructed at Windsor and I would spend hours at the smithy, shirtless and glistening in sweat, each hammer blow representing how I would deal with Warwick, Lancaster and the rest. I still revelled in rowing and even fishing when possible, plus all the other vigorous pursuits which apparently deemed me so unfit for the role to which I was born.

November that year of thirteen hundred and twelve was a bitterly cold month when news was brought to me that Isabella had given birth to our first child, a boy. Bells had already begun to ring out across the land when I hastily reached her chamber. Several loud cheers were heard as I almost ran down the corridors.

Isabella looked so tired but smiled broadly as I reached the bed. There in her arms was our beautiful son. I have always been an emotional man, and found it hard not to shed a tear for the safe arrival of the small bundle that I now took in my arms. One of the queen's midwives advised me about supporting the baby's head, and finally I held him.

He looked to be the most angelic child I had ever seen – although admittedly, I had not seen many. His perfect nose, his soft skin. I brushed his cheek with my finger and he moved an arm which I traced all the way down to his tiny fingers, which wrapped themselves around one of mine. A tear dropped from my eyes onto his skin, and at once the spell was broken. He opened his mouth – and began to scream!

Isabella laughed weakly at the look of horror on my face as I turned in desperation for someone to take the child from me. I had no idea what should be done when an infant cries, and it was with a sense of relief that the wet nurse took the bundle in confident hands.

I crouched down and took Isabella's hand and kissed it. I believed myself very much in love at this time. The queen looked more radiant than ever, even after enduring what had apparently been a long, arduous labour. I stroked her golden-coloured hair, gently peeling the damp strands from her forehead. The chamber was oppressive and hot; even though the bright day was bitterly cold, the air in the chamber was stifling. I had an urge to throw back the heavy blinds from the windows and let in some light and air. Yet I knew little of any of the observances during childbirth and assumed this was the way of things for such a momentous event.

In the following days, I forgot all about rebels, traitors and the like, and made declarations for my first born. I created Edward, as we would name him, Earl of

Chester as well as bestowing many other gifts of land and titles on him.

How strange it felt to be a father myself. I had, of course, seen how proud Piers had been when becoming a parent, and I mourned afresh at how it must have broken his heart, when he was taken by Warwick and the others to his brutal death, to know that he would never set eyes on his child again.

Young Edward of Windsor was thankfully a healthy child, and both his mother and I visited him often. Isabella announced that she would go on a pilgrimage to Canterbury to give thanks for the safe arrival of the child and, across the land, celebrations ensued. It was easy to convince oneself that the country had forgiven all past ills and loved their king as loyal subjects should.

+++

The treacherous barons and I finally reached an accord as we approached Christmas of that year. A treaty was signed, and it was with satisfied delight that I watched as those Ordainers bowed their heads to me in their obeisance.

How tempting it was, that day at Westminster when seeing these kneeling lords before me, to take up a sword and smite the heads of those bastards that had butchered my beloved brother. I had agreed to receive them with good will, but even as I did so, I knew I would never be satisfied until they paid with their lives. Even now as I accepted the kiss of peace from them, the bile rose in my throat. I had determined that I would conceal the hatred I felt for them all for what

I had suffered. Even I, who was noted to be too impetuous where affairs of my heart were concerned, realised that keeping these enemies in full view was safer than banishing them to their own estates where they could sit and plot. The treasures that Lancaster had received so greedily when Piers and I had fled Tynemouth were to be restored to me. The goods themselves meant little enough, but their value was sizeable and also included more personal items, such as gifts between Piers and I. My treasured possession was still the bone-handled dagger he had given me on his return from France where he had been jousting, and I kept it with me always. It all seemed a lifetime ago and it had only ever been used once, to inscribe our initials on each other's forearms.

With the new experience of parenthood, our own delight gave an extra meaning to the festive season, which we celebrated with a joyous abandonment. I had Piers's widow, my niece, Margaret, bring their child to court, and admit that I was slightly distracted by the infant whose glittering blue eyes were so like her father's. How proud he would have been, in my child as well as his own.

One enemy that had the good grace to die was Robert Winchelsey, the Archbishop of Canterbury. Forgive me, Alphage, but I felt little pity for him. He had done all he could to foment trouble for me, and his criticism on many occasions hurt me deeply. My old friend in adversity, Walter Reynolds, was appointed to the position by the pope. I admit to having had a hand in swaying opinion in dear Walter's favour, but I would live to regret the many bribes I made to advance his ambition. I kept him in my confidence, yet he would later become a thorn in my side. How many evenings of drunken gambling, roistering and misbehaviour had Piers, Walter and others spent with me? We had enjoyed our lives so much, with little care for what the future held. Yet, the future thus far had dealt many cruel blows, and none more so than death of my beloved brother, whom I could still not bear to have buried, and whose cold cadaver was still watched over by the Dominicans.

+++

Manuel Fieschi rubbed his tired eyes after having finished his journal entry. The hour grew late and the announcement of matins was surely not too far away. He would sleep late in the morning. The evening sky was clear and still stifling, even for one who had grown up in a country of even temperature, he found the heat oppressive and uncomfortable.

He cast an appreciative eye over his writings. Blessed with the gift of recall of everything he had heard from the former King of England, he was certain he had noted everything of consequence. He could not help but smile at the brief glance he had given Brother Alphage at one point, who, in doing his best not to be horrified by the related tale, had surely never heard such a graphic retelling of someone's life.

The nobleman could not help but be endeared to the royal hermit, and yet if anyone had been the master of their own destiny it was surely Edward Plantagenet, the second of that name. Manuel had at times been incredulous at the former king's folly. What chaos must have been visited on England by the crowning of a king who was so obviously unsuitable for the role that had been thrust upon him.

Tempting as it was to lie down and rest, Manuel had not finished his writing and he drew a fresh sheet of parchment. His holiness must be kept fully apprised of developments, as must another. Yes, a second letter that must be sent also without delay. There would most certainly be further missives before the hermit's sorry tale was told.

+++

The hermit king broke his fast with some dried bread, cheese and some grapes washed down with some weak ale. He met Alphage and Fieschi at the herb garden as arranged, each new day of confession leading him further into the realisation that he had made so many mistakes in his life.

Looking back now, how differently he should have acted; how changed his life and the lives of others would have been had he had the foresight to know what was coming. He had wept for Piers again last night. He still recalled him in every detail; that smile, that swagger, his anger and his tears - all facets, good and bad.

Alphage turned and noticed the hermit, smiling broadly. Perrot, the hound seemed delighted to see both men and indeed hurled himself at Fieschi and set off to run around the garden in excitement, racing in circles and jumping deftly over the beds of plants.

The sun shone again and the sky was blissfully clear of any clouds. The chorus of birdsong that had begun just before dawn now heralded across the valley. All around, the monastery was coming to life; brothers and lay servants bustled over chores. The walkways and cloisters thronged with human traffic, the waft of incense and the unmistakable smell of freshly-baked bread drifted across to the herb garden as the new day commenced. Edward breathed in the fresh, warm air. Alphage smiled reassuringly at him, while Fieschi, having watched in disgust as Perrot feasted on some cat faeces, made a mental note not to allow the hound to get close enough to lick his hand as it often did.

The three of them, after some pleasantries and observations about the beauty of the garden settled themselves as Edward began.

+++

In May of the year thirteen hundred and fourteen, I decided to send Isabella to France to present various petitions on my behalf. I knew, too, that she longed to see her family, and it pleased me to see her excitement as she made preparations. We had settled into a comfortable companionship, and motherhood had changed Isabella; she had matured and seemed to have blossomed with this addition to our lives. Our close relationship certainly seemed to find favour with everyone at court and my critics were, it seemed, momentarily satisfied.

One constant contentious issue however, was Scotland. My father would have been incredulous that I had done nothing to subdue the growing audacity of Robert the Bruce, who was making ever increasing raids on English-held castles in Scotland.

The barons, never known to resist any criticism of their king, blamed me – indirectly or otherwise.

My attention to 'other individuals and their traitorous behaviour' had led to this present situation. I had, it was mooted, spent too long in other pursuits when I should have been checking the audacious behaviour of Robert the Bruce. The elder Hugh Despenser, who had campaigned himself in the highlands with my father, was blunt in his assessment of the current situation.

"Your grace, Bruce continues to take advantage of our reluctance to meet him in battle. Our allies in Northumberland and Cumberland are taking matters into their own hands and reaching individual treaties with Bruce. I fear we must deal with the Scots menace as your late father did - with force!"

Any suggestion that I act as my father had done would normally have set off a tirade from me, yet I knew Hugh was right. As usual, he was the voice of reason that I needed to heed. Whilst never plentiful, finances were in better shape than they had been for most of my reign, thanks to further taxation and loans. There would probably be no better time to organise a campaign.

News reached me that Bruce had made perhaps his most audacious move yet, and was attempting to besiege Stirling Castle. Well, I would prove them all wrong. All who said that I had no stamina or stomach for a fight would eat their words. I was determined to beat Bruce once and for all. Consequently, I set about raising a formidable army and began the long march north.

Display was everything to me, and I believed we could not fail to terrify the Scots with the force I had assembled. Our train was most impressive; cart after cart that carried everything the court would need – and much it didn't! I had insisted that we take all manner of furnishings - everything from the costly plate we ate off to my own bed.

Isabella, who was to travel with us as far as Berwick, was adamant too that she should enjoy every luxury. She was fast becoming as much of a spendthrift as I - a penchant for jewels and costly attire, she at least had that in common with my beloved Piers, although I would never tell her so!

Even as we trundled along at a slow pace, I could not help but imagine how proud I would have been to see Piers at the head of our army. I could almost picture him riding proudly, the wind blowing at his hair, his features bold and determined. The thoughts saddened me, and for a few days I was morose and ill at ease.

For all their bluster, many of the lords refused to join the expedition, claiming that I was still not abiding by the ordinances to which I had agreed and, more impertinently, that - as stated therein – I had not received an assent from Parliament to take an army to Scotland. They were legally obliged to supply a certain number [of what?] for service, and they sent their king and liege lord the minimum they could: a few knights and men at arms. It was as much as I could do from refraining an impulse to return the meagre contingent with a suitable witty riposte – Piers would have known exactly what to say.

Those who joined me would reap rewards for their loyalty. Humphrey de Bohun earl of Hereford, my own brother in law; my nephew and long-time friend, Gilbert de Clare, earl of Gloucester; and Amyer de Valence, earl of Pembroke. The ever-loyal Hugh Despenser the elder and around two thousand knights joined my own retinue. Despenser estimated between fifteen and twenty thousand infantry and cavalry made up our significant force, further emboldening me to engage Bruce as soon as we could.

I recall at one point standing to look behind at the enormous cavalcade that made up the procession and feeling, more confident than ever, that we would be victorious. The sight of the force alone would be enough to unnerve the Scots - success was assured. I had, as usual, ensured that we enjoy every comfort as well as taking along singers, dancers, jesters and the like. I needed to be entertained, especially in the throes of battle and the ultimate tragedy this would inevitably cause.

The weather was not kind to us that summer, yet the long train of carriages and wagons, although slow, was unencumbered by the hard rain and cold winds that were usually most prevalent as one got closer to the border. My experience of being in Scotland had always - up until now - been one of permanent damp and misery.

One could be forgiven for believing the cavalcade to be a joyful royal procession, and yet I was aware of muted enthusiasm as we passed through towns and villages. Preparation had been made for the smooth passage by making good repairs on roadways and widening lanes, reinforcing bridges and, more unpopularly, seeking a replenishment of provisions. I saw no problem with these perceived difficulties, all were necessary if we were to defend our rights.

How ungrateful towards their king did the peasants who grumbled seem; they would be rewarded as a vanquishing army again rode through their small villages, returning from glorious victory. I took exception to their impertinence; whilst I could enjoy the company of those men who worked hard in digging ditches and toiling over thatching and hedging, I had no great love for the peasants who seemed to constantly criticise me. It was their treatment of Piers that had riled me as much as anything. How brutal in their despicable hatred of my beloved they had been. I would not forget. One could blame their king for many things, but crop failure and famine were hardly my fault. Taxation was inevitable, and no king would ever be able to relieve the people of that unpopular but necessary burden.

As I recall the horror of the days that followed, I can only think that God had truly forsaken our enterprise. You will be the Lord's advocate, Alphage, I know, but I saw very little to suggest he was with our cause during those sorrowful days.

We approached Stirling early on that June morning. The bright weather we had enjoyed had, predictably, turned colder and clouds overhead threatened rain. Bruce's army had been sighted at a hunting preserve through which passed the road to Stirling. A stream ahead flowed between steep banks named Bannockburn. The surrounding area was typically boggy and it soon became apparent that our sizeable train was finding the land difficult to traverse.

Small skirmishes occurred for a day or so, both Bruce and I testing resolve and capability.

I was sitting in my pavilion with advisers, considering our next move, when the earl of Hereford entered. That he seemed enraged was evident by the angry expression he wore. Humphrey de Bohun was my own brother-in-law, and a commanding presence. A stout giant of a man with a sizeable bushy red beard and a flock of unruly hair to match. He enjoyed the position of hereditary constable of England and, although a brave soldier, he always struck me as ill at ease with this great state. The reason for his annoyance entered closely behind him. Gilbert de Clare glared at the constable, his still-youthful features marred by an obvious irritability.

"Your grace," Humphrey spoke sharply, "I learn from de Clare that you have sanctioned his wish to command the vanguard. Sire, I am much insulted that such a decision has been made without consulting me, as hereditary constable. The command is surely mine by right."

Gilbert flushed with indignation. "Sire, the position follows that of my forebears, we have always held such a command. You yourself sanctioned my request that I continue with this distinction."

"I did indeed, Gilbert," I said, not without annoyance at having such a dispute at a time when cool heads were needed to plan our strategy. "Humphrey, the right is Gloucester's I believe..."

Hereford interrupted, "Your grace, now is not the time for novices to lead our forces; I would respectfully remind you, and the young earl here, that he is as yet untested on the battlefield."

Gilbert was furious. "You doubt my honour? You question my courage?"

"Nothing of the sort, my lord," Hereford countered, "I merely suggest that now is not the time for you to take command when so much is at stake."

"I will force you to take back those words. Sire surely..."

I looked from one to the other. This was the last thing we needed; these meddlesome lords with so mighty an opinion of themselves and their honour. Nevertheless, I could not argue with Humphrey's reasoning despite having told Gilbert earlier that the command was his.

"Gilbert," I spoke softly, "perhaps my lord Hereford is right. You are untested as yet. I do not doubt for one moment your valour…"

I got no further in my discourse; Gilbert flashed me a look of disgust and marched swiftly out of the pavilion. Had the chamber had a wooden door rather than a silk flap, he would most assuredly have slammed it.

I looked downcast as Hereford, with a smirk of satisfaction, bowed his head and followed him. I sighed with exasperation. I had failed to be decisive and felt uncertain, where I had up until now felt in total command. Truth be told, like Gilbert, I was relatively inexperienced in warfare; although I had engaged in battle previously, I had secured no significant personal acts of valour.

Gilbert was unhorsed during one of the initial skirmishes, which had gone well for the Scots. He could not have suffered a more embarrassing indignity, yet worse was to come. A division of cavalry was sent to Stirling castle in order to relieve the garrison there, but they were met with a body of determined spearmen, a deadly schiltron that soon had the English force scattering either to the castle itself, or to the main body of the army.

Overnight, we crossed the Bannockburn with difficulty; the boggy surface hindered our progress, while Bruce had the foresight to weaken the sides of the roadway with pot holes and trenches. We set up camp, and I could already sense that, despite these one or two setbacks, we would be ultimately victorious. We had the greater force in numbers, and I insisted our banners and heralds were set up, and our pavilions in their bright colours of red, blue and gold were prominent. The sight of this ostentatious show would cast a glorious spectacle for the rustic, colourless Scots to marvel at.

My nephew of Gloucester visited my tent late the night before we were to take to the field. I had always felt close to Gilbert, and loved him dearly, but his petulance regarding my indecision about who would ultimately command the vanguard irritated me. Now he irked me further by suggesting that, following the skirmishes that had already occurred, that we might be wise to rest the cavalry for a further day to fully recuperate. He was not the only voice that urged caution, but I had overruled the other principal knights and I was becoming cross that my battle plans were being met with such caution.

"Gilbert, I have made my decision!" I snapped at him. I was beginning to feel restless and, despite the dampness of the day, the armour was heavy and restricting.

Gilbert persisted, "Sire, I just feel, after consulting with the other commanders, that we are maybe being over-confident – reckless, even. We surely need to..."

I interrupted impatiently. "My orders will be carried out, Gilbert, and perhaps you should consider whether you wish to fight at all! Or would you prefer to remain here at the camp, while the rest of us fight?" It was, on reflection, an unnecessary, demeaning retort, and I was regretful the minute I had uttered the words.

Gilbert paled in shock for a moment and then pulled back his shoulders proudly, raising his chin in defiance. "Now you doubt my courage? He spat angrily. "Must I prove my valour to you? Today I will prove I am no coward."

I sighed testily, and turned away briefly to pour us wine, so that we may together toast our assured victory, but he had gone. I wish to God I had gone after him, called him back and made peace with him, but the moment was lost. I hoped that, once we returned, he would have felt an accomplishment and all would be well between us. He had always been headstrong.

I had rarely felt such a surge of boldness and optimism when, after a restless night, I rose early, and after praying to God that our casualties would be few in our victory, I had my squires dress me in battle armour, carrying a mace and sword. Thus attired and armed, I mounted my war-horse. The destrier snorted and shook its head, eager to take to the field. I leant down slapping its powerful neck, heavily padded and armoured, and my metal gauntlets were then pulled on, feeling heavy on my hands.

We advanced with caution, I was eager to be on firmer ground rather than the boggy soil of our encampment. It was apparent that, even though we reached firmer land, it was a narrow expanse to fully utilise our large cavalry. With the marshy ground of Bannockburn behind us, we might experience difficulty should we unexpectedly need to make any retreat to a safer position, but it was doubted among myself and the commanders that the Scots would approach us at this point. We were wrong!

I felt nauseous as I had before in such circumstances; the only difference now was that it was I, not my father, who had trudged an enormous army across the English border. I could feel a cold trickle of sweat run down my back, my hands clammy in the mailed gauntlets.

The Scots made a surprise attack on our left flank but, even as I watched them advance, several of them dropped to their knees. I was elated, supplicant so soon, when blood had barely been shed. I soon realised my error; the Scots had been praying - not surrendering! It seemed that their prayers were soon answered. God had forsaken the English.

The Scots advanced further and at that same moment I heard Gilbert give the command to charge, this being done without waiting for my order. Suddenly, as I watched him gallop straight towards the Scottish infantry, it was as though time almost slowed, and all I could do was watch in horror as the two forces clashed. The impetuous earl and his men hit a schiltron of spears head on. Gilbert came off his horse and was impaled on a spear from the tightly packed formation of pikes. I gasped in horror, but suddenly the full rage of battle was upon us, and I charged ahead into the melee.

Something drove me to cast all caution aside that day - I hacked, slashed and swung at the enemy, before suddenly feeling my horse buckle beneath me. He had taken a spear to his flank, and then to his neck. I leapt from him as well as I could, eager to escape being pinned beneath him as he fell. I stood then, still swinging my mace, catching one Scot on the side of his head; half of his brain matter clung to my weapon. I shouted for a horse and someone dismounted and threw me the reins. Once remounted, I continued to fight like a madman, thrashing in all directions. The English cavalry had ultimately crashed in to the rear of Gloucester's men and effectively impaled any that had not been initially killed on to the pikes.

Great English destriers reared in horror, unseating their riders, who were then slain by the brutal Scottish cavalry as they fell. All around there was carnage. I screamed for the English archers, so often the heroes of many a battle with their bravery and accuracy. When a contingent did appear, it was already too late. The stench of sweat rose into the air, steaming with the heat of spilled hot blood. Bodies lay all around me; the firmer ground we had initially been grateful for had become a rich red mud, and still I thrashed around me, less aware of who I was attacking, but striking out anything.

Suddenly, in the midst of my thrashing, I felt the reins of my horse grabbed and I turned swiftly to find the earl of Pembroke pulling at my horse and shouting at me, though I could barely hear him. He was dragging me away, but I resisted, commanding him to let go, but he persisted.

"The battle is lost sire, we must retreat!"

I commanded him again, "Release the reins, damn you, release them!", but he continued to pull until we had reached the outskirts of the battlefield.

I was surrounded by knights, including William Montacute and Roger Damory, whom I was glad to see had not perished. They and many others formed a protective guard around me and together we rode fast; already my retreat had been noticed and we were being swiftly pursued. We made for Stirling castle, but that knave, Philip de Mowbray, refused us entry. On then to Dunbar, all the while with Scots hot on our tail, sometimes close enough to pick off stragglers, any who failed to keep up, themselves and their horses exhausted. I was unaware of how far we had gone when the castle of Dunbar was sighted. I was exhausted, but we had no time to waste with the enemy closing on us all the time. Patrick, the earl of Dunbar, received us and, aware of the haste we were in, wasted no time on pleasantries but commandeered a small fishing boat. I and a handful of my faithful guards stepped down into the small vessel and set sail for the safety of Berwick, leaving behind a heavily-defeated English army.

+++

"The battle at Bannockburn is surely one of the greatest defeats the English army has ever suffered." Manuel Fieschi said quietly, and Edward hung his head.

"Thank you, Manuel," the former king said, not without sarcasm.

Fieschi did not appear to sense Edward's feeling and shame and continued ruthlessly, "Even as far as Italy we heard of the battle. So many lives lost."

Alphage sniffed testily and cast the nobleman a disapproving look while he laid a sympathetic hand on Edward's arm. The former king drew a deep breath.

"Those bloody hours will live with me forever. I was so certain that all we needed to do was display our great pomp and spectacle in order to scare the Scots away, but spectacle alone is no victor. I was guilty of the most heinous of crimes – arrogance! As usual, I failed to listen to those who knew better. The size of our army was the greatest in a generation, and yet we were outfoxed. I lost so many friends that day; none more so than Gilbert de Clare, my own nephew. I will never forget the hurt in his eyes that final time we were together. Of course I did not doubt his bravery, but I was angry at him, frustrated at the delays and eager to crush our enemy, as I was convinced we surely would. Poor Gilbert, he had nothing to prove and yet my anger was probably still ringing in his ears as he fell to his death on those cruel pikes. It has to be admitted that Bruce treated Gilbert with all reverence and returned his body to us with full military honours."

Fieschi sought to pour salve onto his brutal words and spoke up again, "Reports of the battle did report that you showed the greatest bravery, Edward, you should be proud of that."

Edward smiled sadly; he had been told in the aftermath of the battle that he had fought with great courage. "But that is not enough of a consolation, my friend, when one has effectively got so much blood on their hands. Later, when numbers and names were given to me, I wept for the loss of so many fine men, my own steward, Edward Mauley, among them. Sir Henry de Bohun had believed he could slay Bruce himself, upon seeing the Scots leader momentarily unprotected in the distance. His impetuous folly was rewarded with a blow from Bruce that split his skull in two. The keeper of the privy seal, Sir Roger de Northburgh was captured also. Many nobles were either slain or taken hostage, some ransomed, others exchanged for the few prisoners we had taken. How many of our army were slain as they attempted to retreat, hacked down in that boggy marshland. Bruce did, however, return the seal I had lost, as well as a shield. In the hands of many, such items would bear testament to a great victory and be paraded as the spoils from a battle where the English cavalry was well and truly beaten. In later years I have thought of Bruce as noble and respectful in his treatment of the prisoners he had taken."

Edward sighed again, and took up an earthenware cup which he filled from a jug of water kept shaded from the growing heat of the bright sun. After taking a long draft of the cool liquid, he continued.

+++

In the months following the defeat at Bannockburn, I effectively handed control of the kingdom to my cousin, Thomas, Earl of Lancaster. He had not been idle; whilst the army had made its slow progress northwards, Lancaster had been raising an army of his own, so nervous that I would return victorious from Scotland and seek to take advantage of my good fortune by avenging the death of my beloved Perrot.

It was therefore with delight and gloating that Lancaster proceeded to effectively cast me into the role of a puppet king with all strings attached to the treasonous fingers of my hateful cousin.

Both Thomas and Warwick declared that the defeat in Scotland was clearly a result of my failing to recognise the Ordinances that had effectively been in abeyance for almost two years. I could do nothing but comply with their wishes. What else could I do? I had all but bankrupted the treasury with the costly ostentation of travelling with a vast army and court, as though the reason for the enterprise had been more of a royal progress than a war party.

Thomas strutted in front of me like a general reprimanding his troops.

'The black dog of Arden', as Piers had so famously called Warwick, sat nearby, smirking like a simpleton.

"You must realise Edward," Thomas almost sang, "that I must in good conscience all but assume power in this land? God has clearly forsaken you. Our army is now the laughing stock of Christendom, the Scots emboldened by their great victory continually raid Northumberland and as far as Cumberland, laying waste to everything they can set light to. There is little choice but that I attempt to bring order where you have enjoyed chaos."

I was determined to behave with as much decorum as possible, and that I would not show either of these men that I was in the throes of complete humiliation.

Thomas, ever fond of the sound of his own voice, continued, "There will, of course, be removal and replacements of all royal officers, as laid down in the ordinances you will no doubt recall. Furthermore, it will be necessary to limit the expenses of both your own and the queen's households."

"No doubt these replacements will be made largely from your own choosing - effectively, your own creatures!" I could not help but retort.

There was a noise from the corner of the room as the dog began to bark "We shall select those who serve the country best," Warwick retorted. "You must surely agree, sire, that many doubt your capability to undertake the onerous duty of being king."

I longed to grab the wretch by the throat and beat him for his insolence, yet it was to Lancaster's credit that he turned on his fellow earl. "Have a care, my lord," he spoke brusquely, "let us not go too far in our condemnation of the king."

"A king that is still your anointed sovereign," I added.

Warwick scowled first at Thomas and then at me, shifting uncomfortably in his seat. I admit I concentrated very little as I all but agreed to my cousin's reforms, in keeping with the ordinances, as he continually reminded me. I felt truly exhausted, as though I could sleep for days. I longed for peace and solitude – I longed for Piers.

At length Thomas and Warwick left me and I sat in silence for some time. My jester came and knelt at my feet, playing a lively tune on his flute. I listened for a while and then dismissed him with a few coins; I was not sure I wanted the entertainment. I noticed Roger Amory who stood close by in a doorway, he smiled and, with a strange look of embarrassment, nodded and left. I had not noticed before what a nice smile he had. God knows there is little to find amusing in my service. I noticed Roger quite often, looking at me or hovering close by, and I must admit I did not find his attentions unwelcome. His innocent face and his slightly protruding ears were pleasing to look at, and I felt a certain sense of security when he was around.

If Isabella had felt any shame or humiliation at the defeat of Bannockburn, I was certainly unaware of it. She had received me back with a welcome relief that I was not severely injured, and indeed took it upon herself to dress the superficial wounds I had received.

After my jester had left, I sat alone for some time before Isabella entered – dressed somewhat over dramatically in black as mourning for our dead at Bannockburn. Since giving birth to young Edward, she had changed in some way, not discernable, but perhaps it was a maturity that comes with motherhood. I know little of such developments in a female, but I recall Piers telling me something to that effect. She smiled as I looked up, her once girlish pretty features were certainly developing into a beauty that was most becoming.

We spoke for some time about the change in our circumstances; she liked it no better than I that our households were to be reformed, although hers less so. I knew that a reduction in her household spending would not be received well.

"Are we to be treated like paupers?" she demanded hotly, her cheeks reddening as her temper began to rise. "I can understand reforming the privy council and it will, I'm sure, be largely made up of Thomas's men, but I shall resist any change to my household!"

I smiled at her annoyance, her sense of self preservation, and I had almost expected her to announce that she would write to her father! At length, she appeared to have spent her fury and, drawing up a nearby foot stool, she sat at my feet.

"You look so tired, Edward," she said quietly. "You do not rest, I know you get up in the middle of the night and pace the chamber or sit in front of the fire for hours. Do the memories of battle still haunt your dreams?"

I sighed wearily before I answered, "It's as if I am there again, watching as men fall in piles around me, I am surrounded by growing heaps of dead Englishmen. I see Gilbert impaled on those pikes, reaching out to me, calling to me to help him. I try to get there but am being held back. I call to him, but again I am pushed further and further away!" I had begun to whimper at this point. Ever emotional, I had shed no tears in frustration or sadness since Bannockburn, but suddenly a torrent exploded from my chest and I began to cry, which inevitably led to great heaving sobs, and I wept in Isabella's arms until I was exhausted.

Later that same night, we lay together and I told her of my plans to finally bury Piers's body. He had been in the custody of the Dominican friars at Oxford since his murder more than two years previously.

"I will have him buried with all ceremony at Langley Priory which, as you know, I founded myself. He deserves to be afforded the honour in burial that he was refused in death."

"Will that not anger some of the great barons?" Isabella asked with concern.

"It will most assuredly anger them all, I would expect, but I care little for that. I will have him dressed in cloth of gold.

"The cost though, dearest, at a time when our very own expenditure is under the closest scrutiny," Isabella stated. "The ceremony will be a lavish affair, I have no doubt, but I would advise caution. People are starving and I wonder if you should delay the extravagant tomb you are planning."

I felt suddenly irritated by her attempt to advise me what was best. "The ceremony will indeed be a lavish affair as he would have wished it. I care not whether any person likes or dislikes the plans I have. I will not take into account anyone's sensitivities about it, God knows it's bad enough I am burying him at all! His tomb shall be a fitting memorial to him." I could feel emotion rising in my throat as I spoke.

We did not speak for some time, and I thought her asleep until she whispered, "You will surely not be able to bury the late earl while he is still under excommunication."

I scoffed at the perceived difficulty. "I have spoken with Walter Reynolds and we shall act by his authority."

Isabella clearly seemed uneasy. "Dearest, for all that Reynolds is a long-time friend of yours, the Archbishop of Canterbury is not the same as the pope!"

"Since the death of Clement in April, there is no pope, nor one yet elected!"

"I know but…"

"We will discuss it no more," I stated rather childishly, "arrangements will go ahead." I lay awake long after Isabella's breathing grew deeper, and thought of Piers. My intention had been to bury my beloved only when I had avenged him and myself on the murderous barons that had taken his life so brutally. That happy time however, seemed at present a long way off. The memory of my beloved was burned into my heart. That once beautiful body must now follow his soul. It was time.

+++

Langley Priory lies on the River Gade and, as I have already told you, the palace was perhaps my most adored property. Here Piers would at last find peace. I had ordered a hundred Dominican friars to say Masses for his soul. As years went by, I was no less benevolent, how could I be otherwise? The ceremony was well attended. It could be argued that the mourners may have felt obliged to be there. Yet, Piers had not been entirely disliked, and many wanted to pay their respects to a man that had died far too young. How Perrot would have laughed at the very thought that his burial ceremony would be attended by four bishops, plus Walter Reynolds in his capacity of dear friend as well as being the archbishop of Canterbury. Both Hugh Despensers, father and son, the earl of Pembroke, fourteen abbots, more than fifty knights.

Isabella accompanied and supported me, though what she felt personally about Piers was not something we had ever discussed. She had kept her counsel as far as the ceremony and its expense was concerned; in truth she was no less extravagant than I, and in my crueller moments I wondered if she had seen Piers's body wrapped in gold cloth and imagined a gown!

I had insisted – much to the disgust of many present – that Piers's manservant, Hugo, was in attendance, and his distress was palpable. After the burial ceremony, I was informed by Roger Damory that Hugo had left Langley. Thereafter he simply disappeared. All traces of him were gone.

The devotion and humility of the Dominicans moved me as always, and I never forgot them. The emotion of that time was horrific. I felt my heart break anew, and my tears flowed unashamedly. I cared little for what others felt was correct and, after the event was over, I stayed and spent some time in prayer for the loss that I would bear for the remainder of my life. I swear I could sense Perrot in this very place, almost hear his lilting voice, "Ah my king, why so sad? You must not be dull and morbid like these others." I wept silently, as I had done throughout the whole service. God knew that I would have given anything to have him back with me still.

My resolve to seek vengeance for my beloved's death was never stronger. I had often thought that together we would age together, yet he once told me he had no desire to reach old age. His unfortunate vanity could not contemplate the loss of either faculty – physical or of the mind. He determined that he would not live long enough for his beauty to fade, his beard turn grey and see his belly turn to fat. As he once told me, I truly believed that he would have ended his own life before the lines on his face appeared or he became lame with gout.

Forgive me Alphage, it is the worst possible sin I know, yet who but he would have even contemplated it?

Though I believed I was alone but for the Dominicans that continued to pray for my beloved brother, I was aware that someone stood at the back of the priory. I felt the presence of someone else and called out. A man emerged from the dark shadow, the younger Hugh Despenser.

"Forgive me, sire," he spoke quietly with his discernable lisp, "I had not intended to intrude on your grief. I too felt the need to be at peace now that the ceremony itself is over, time to reflect. The late earl and I were comrades at an earlier age, you may recall?" I didn't, although I was vaguely aware that I had knighted him with Piers and all those other young companions all those years before at Westminster.

I smiled sadly at him. "We shall mourn him together, Hugh, join me here in prayer." He moved to kneel next to me and I looked at him. I had never taken much notice of his features, and yet his green eyes glittered in the light from the wax candles all around us.

We remained there for some time, and when it came time to leave, he boldly took my arm and led me away.

+++

Piers sat at the window of my chamber and ate an apple as I lowered myself into a tub of steaming, perfumed water. I felt invigorated from both my arduous work in the field and the return of my beloved friend. I dismissed my servants and sank back into the tub with a contented sigh.

"I don't think I could have borne one further day without you," I said.

"I am always proud of you, Perrot, yet your recklessness alarms me."

Piers laughed and turned to look out of the window. He loved Langley as much as I, and I felt here we could be alone, away from prying eyes and suspicious courtiers. Here we could just be ourselves.

"Now I am back in favour with your father," he stated, "I am expected to return his court; we shall have but a few days to enjoy ourselves."

I sighed in resignation. It was true that I would be expected to join my father soon, and yet this seemed cruel to speak of such things when he had only just arrived.

"I've missed you, my brother," I said solemnly. "My days are darker than the night without you. We must never be apart again."

"Ned," he began, but I talked over him.

"I mean it, Perrot, I am lost without you - the sunshine means nothing, for I am cold; the dark nights

are empty. You ask why I work endlessly at such activity that no prince should indulge in, but the energy tires me, so that I may lapse into exhausted sleep rather than sit before a roaring fire and stare into the flames, lost in the thought of you."

There followed a long silence, before I turned my neck as far round as I could in the confines of my bath. Piers continued to stare out of the window. I called his name softly and beckoned him to me. "My neck will surely break if I have to strain it much further."

He walked over to me, almost petulantly, like a scolded child, but I saw then, as he knelt beside me, that his cheeks were wet with tears.

"Perrot, what ails you? Forgive me if I have said aught that..." This time it was he who broke in.

"My dearest, darling Ned. I missed you more than I can say. You maybe mistake my frivolous behaviour as disinterest, but it is not. Don't you see, my beloved prince, that you call me brother, but you know – no, let me finish I beg you. You know I am nothing but a squire. Your father accepted me to be knighted by you, one of the happiest days of my life. That does not make me your equal, of course, but neither am I anything at his court other than a Gascon soldier who has found favour with the prince. I am a drifter, Ned, and ever shall be. In time our love will sour and I will disappoint you. I am nothing."

"No!" I said crossly. "You will never disappoint me. I will raise you to a height that will outrank all others; you shall have titles, land, anything I can give and share with you shall be yours."

Piers smiled sadly, and raised those beautiful green eyes to meet mine. "Ned," he said softly.

"Yes?" I replied, using a wet thumb to wipe away the tears on his face.

He grinned at me with a return to the impish look that I always felt so beguiling.

"I fear I have just dropped my apple into your bathwater!"

I was struck dumb for a moment those words were the last thing I had expected him to say.

Suddenly we both roared with laughter. I have rarely relived that moment without it bringing tears to my eyes, tears of joy. I went to grab him suddenly, but he was too quick for me, and he darted out of the door, the soaked, half-eaten apple hitting it as it slammed behind him....

I awoke suddenly, my face wet with tears, my bed sheets damp from sweat. At the corner of the large bed, the one solitary candle had burned down almost to its end. I longed to return to sleep, to carry on the dream, to call Piers back and laugh with him again. Yet I knew there would be no resumption; I would merely drift into a restless state, and the images of the dream would grow fainter until they were completely forgotten. It is strange that I never forgot this particular dream and - as I relate it to you both now - it is, I think, as accurate as I recall.

I had slept apart from Isabella that night, but wished I had not. I wanted the comfort and warmth that a bedfellow provides, and yet I wanted no questions about the tears or an explanation about the dream that had unnerved me. I called out for Will, I would need wine if I was to return to sleep at all.

I heard the chamber door and instructed Will to fetch some wine. I leant up, pummelled the feather pillow in frustration as much as anything else, and settled back down. I was surprised then to hear a voice that was not Will's.

"Forgive me, my liege, I told your servant I would do his duty for him - pardon my boldness."

I turned quickly to find Roger Damory at the side of the bed; he bowed in deference and then held out the goblet to me.

"You are welcome, Roger," I spoke softly, but not without an unexpected nervousness. I took the goblet from him and drained the contents. I did not say anything and neither did he, but he smiled - a young, handsome, innocent smile. Then he moved to the end of the bed and, after drawing in a small breath, blew out the candle.

An invitation to Warwick castle was not one that warranted any degree of excitement and anticipation, yet to refuse or ignore it would have been churlish and, whilst such a response seemed fitting, I nevertheless accepted the invitation. The castle lay close to the River Avon and, reluctantly, I secretly praised its magnificence - impregnable and imposing, surrounded by stone curtain walls.

The earl had obviously not been too badly affected by the famine and food shortage and, whilst I cared little at the time, how his starving workers viewed this great feast could be imagined. There was, however, a surprise that I had not expected. Now seated in the splendour of the large hall, I drank and ate quite liberally, calling over a servant with a bowl to wash my hands during courses. I barely glanced at the youth, but when I did he also looked straight at me. I would have recognised Hugo anywhere.

My darling Perrot's faithful manservant poured clean water from a pitcher into a gold bowl, thereafter handing me a small linen cloth. I said nothing to him, yet questions could have tripped off my tongue. I had heard nothing of Hugo since Piers's funeral. Now here he was, working for the very man who had instigated his old master's death. I had intended to find a position for him after his master's murder, yet he had chosen to run away. He looked nervously at me, although refusing to meet my gaze head on. I could do little but try and imply by my eyes alone that I realised who he was.

Hugo gave a curt nod of his head and quickly moved away from the table but the rich, thundering voice of the earl stayed him.

"Boy, here!" he called. Hugo walked to where the earl sat, holding out his fat fingers to be refreshed as mine had been moments earlier.

I have witnessed much ill in men throughout my life, and indeed I have hated very readily, yet I do not believe I had ever witnessed such a look of venomous hatred as Hugo gave to Warwick at that table. The earl dismissed him with a wave of his podgy hand and, with a last fleeting glance at me, he hurried from the chamber. I saw him only once more that evening, serving Warwick some wine. I watched as Hugo stopped for a moment or two and then I was sure a smile crossed his lips - only very slight, but I caught it nonetheless. He then withdrew, rather than offering the wine to anyone else as would normally be the custom. Perhaps he was content in this new role, yet I doubted it.

The evening continued with entertainments: jugglers, acrobats and singers, all for which I had a great and well-known fondness. It was somewhat unnerving to be enjoying myself in the earl's company, and yet with almost all the great lords in attendance, one could be forgiven for mistaking this as anything but a great banquet amongst a king and his loyal knights and earls.

That night, I had been restless, though Isabella slept soundly. Such an occasion as this invariably led to people talking and drinking well in to the small hours. Eventually, I rose from our bed, walking silently to the window and watching the endless rain that fell in torrents. I was aware of a disturbance outside the chambers sounding as though people were rushing about, but I paid it little heed.

The surprise of seeing Hugo had caused me unrest and, in turn, had resurrected my hatred of Warwick, Lancaster and the other lords that had been complicit in Piers's murder. My grief would never cease; I would carry this sad, angry burden with me for the remainder of my life. There were many times when the agony of his loss was so hard to bear I felt it would drive me to madness.

The following morning, I had intended to leave early; as difficult as it often was to rouse myself in the early hours, I wanted to be away from this place. Magnificent though it was, it brought me only pain. I wondered if I would see Hugo again, perhaps be able to have a talk with him, but he was nowhere to be seen and I certainly would not bring attention to him by asking his whereabouts. It was certainly quite possible that Warwick had not realised that one of his servants had been a personal squire to the man that he had hated beyond all reason, and who he had cruelly led to his death.

Word was brought to me that Warwick himself was indisposed, probably brought on by the overindulgence of the previous evening; he had certainly drunk to excess and his table manners would have brought many comments from Piers Gaveston were he only here to make them! One could only hope that his malady would keep him from court for a while! Yet, nearing the end of our journey, further news was brought to me that the earl had indeed died that very morning. I wish I could state that I was saddened by the news, but I was not. It was as much as I could do not to laugh aloud. How I wish Perrot had been here to witness such joyful news! I rewarded the bearer of these glad tidings handsomely.

So, Warwick was no more. A severe stomach pain had resulted in violent sickness during the night, blamed apparently on the earl's gluttonous appetite for lampreys. Physicians had been in attendance, but there was little they could do but watch as the earl writhed in agony for many hours, and had finally been relieved of his suffering by choking on his own vomit.

+++

In the year of our Lord thirteen hundred and fifteen, furious and torrential rain fell mercilessly over all Europe, and in England we felt this ruinous weather harshly. Crops rotted whilst waterlogged fields became a graveyard for livestock which simply drowned in the constant downpour.

I paid little heed to the devastation at the time; like most of the nobility, we suffered far less than the peasants in the small villages or the beggars that could be seen at every street corner. Strange that only when I suffered the indignity of having to beg myself on occasion, in later years, did I finally realise the suffering that so many endured. As in all of my sorry tale, I have only now come to realise how foolish and insensitive I was back then. Yet, I was as God made me, and I can only pray that my son learns these lessons early, and does not seek to rule as I did.

A virulent famine overtook the realm. Foodstuffs surged in price and bread and other daily necessities became both scarce and expensive. Livestock prices soared, and even regulating prices did little to stem the flow of disaster.

Word reached me that this ruinous time was causing a rising pestilence. Isabella, who was happily again with child – our second - left London as a precautionary measure, and I left with Roger, bound for Langley.

+++

Roger Damory was at my side often over the next few weeks. I had welcomed his company that first night, he had laid down on top of the bedcovers fully clothed, and he had held me in his arms, from which I felt much comfort. He was a charming fellow, and it was refreshing to have him around me; I at last began to feel some of my old self return. He was in no way a replacement for Piers, no-one could ever be that; but he lifted my mood which had become so solemn and insular since the defeat at Bannockburn. Of course there were looks of concern and disapproval, as there would be for any relationship I formed.

The great lords continued to enjoy their power over me, active in both parliament and council. Lancaster strutted around like a preening peacock, displaying to all that, whilst the country did indeed have a king, he, Thomas of Lancaster, was the true power in the land. Yet Warwick's death, in which I rejoiced, did leave my cousin without his closest ally, and one that, unlike Thomas, had at least a working knowledge of how best to administrate the realm. Lancaster was exposed as being totally out of his depth.

Nevertheless, Thomas's power did not sit as easily with the other magnates as he may have wished. It had always been his folly that he imagined others loved him as much as he did himself. Cracks were indeed starting to show. Ill feeling began in simple small ways, but Thomas overreached himself when he argued with the earl of Pembroke over lands in Pembrokeshire that Thomas had forced Pembroke to give up at the parliament in York the previous year. The row had rumbled on, with whispers of discontent regarding Thomas's growing arrogance.

I was not completely completely bereft of support, however, and - following sound advice from Isabella - decided to stay as neutral as possible and reap the rewards of Thomas's bickering with the other lords, as they would at length abandon him. I could by now count Pembroke and Hereford and others as allies, and was glad of them.

Unfortunately, Thomas was officially head of my council, and could dismiss from influence any of whom he thought ill, often warning me to be careful not to seek a replacement for Piers Gaveston. He had no doubt heard of my affection for Roger, and sought to extinguish that flame as soon as it had been lit. Suggestions were made to the young knight that he should take heed of the fate of Piers Gaveston; too close a bond with the king would welcome enemies, and he surely did not want that? Damory, wisely or otherwise, chose to ignore the veiled threats.

I did of course begin making gifts to Roger and a couple of other squires who had found favour with me recently. William Monacute and Hugh Audley were household knights and had, in the past, served me well. William had, of course, stayed with Piers during the awful days prior to his murder, while Hugh had been of good service to me. I did not doubt their loyalty to me, yet I was as ever a bad judge of character.

Roger lay in my arms one day in my chamber at Langley. The rain, continued, although heavier showers were now mercifully less frequent as the summer months began. The palace was beautiful to me whatever the weather.

"How I wish life could always be this simple," I yawned, closing my eyes against the bright sunlight. I could almost forget the concerns that seemed to fill each day. Bruce in Scotland continued to raid our northern borders, Lancaster seemed intent on displaying his arrogance at every opportunity and now Bruce's own brother Edward had invaded Ireland – it would seem that impertinence ran in that family! Here of course, I could forget all ills, at least for a time.

Roger was indignant about the Irish invasion. "Your grace should send me there with troops and drag the traitors out once and for all!"

I chuckled at his petulance. "My darling Roger, I could not possibly spare you. You must surely realise you are dear to me. Moreover, Roger Mortimer and his army were soundly defeated there, as you no doubt know. I have no appetite to see more men killed for that pitiful, austere island."

I put a finger to his lips as he sought to remonstrate with me. Why did these men have so much pride that they all believed themselves invincible?

"No, no, my sweet Roger, we will talk of it no more. Now fetch me some wine, it feels like a day to get drunk!" And indeed we did get drunk, much like Piers and I often had. Inevitably, I promised him much in my drunken state, and he did little to dissuade me, completely taking advantage of the occasion, of course. Looking back now, these young men with whom I had begun to surround myself insulted my intelligence by probably believing that they took advantage of this need I had for the support of bold, handsome and charming companions.

I was never tricked into anything. I merely saw no real value in the trappings of wealth. I could easily part with lands, titles and the like because they were unimportant to me. I had grown up with as much land, manors and castles as I could want; they were of little value to me and were therefore easy to give away. The pleasure it gave these men to be showered with riches was reward enough to me.

I had already been more than happy to grant lands to Roger following the good account he gave of himself at the battle of Bannockburn. Moreover, he had served in the retinue of Gilbert de Clare, who had been so cruelly slain in that battle. I was grateful to Roger also for dealing with several assignments and various other duties on my behalf. Estates in Surrey and as far as

Yorkshire were granted to him. I was to be "grateful" several more times towards Roger before his part in my tale finishes.

That evening we drank and played dice, being entertained by my fool and serenaded by my musician and singers, much like the many times Piers and I had wiled away many evenings - I missed him so much.

Of course, any stay at Langley could not last forever and, whilst my heart told me to enjoy the company of this young gallant, and be carefree and incautious, I forced myself to make the visit to this haven relatively short. I was only now beginning to gradually shore up support against the growing arrogance of Lancaster. I must not jeopardise it.

It was therefore a wish to use wisely use the few days I allowed myself that directed me to Roger's chamber one morning. It was always enjoyable to move freely alone throughout Langley, not be announced by a chamberlain or accompanied by a throng of servants; believe it or not, such trappings are unimportant to me.

Unlike my father, and no doubt all the kings that had come before me and felt duty-bound to live their lives exclusively amongst their court, I had, even as a prince, insisted on time to be alone. I enjoyed the gaiety and laughter of banquets, balls and entertainments, but had yearned for time when I could be with Piers and, later, Isabella – alone! I fancy this will lead to misrepresentations, false tales and feeding of rumours, but I can change little of what will be written of my life; when one is alive it is rarely considered, in my opinion.

I felt the need to be outside in the beautiful grounds and woodland where I could be at one with nature.

Rather than send a servant to summon him, I went alone and marched unannounced into Roger's chamber. The scene that met me was completely unexpected. The young knight sat in a bath! His servant, who attended him, immediately fell to his knees and, acting completely on impulse, Roger stood.

The sight of him standing completely naked took my breath away for a moment. I had not seen him wearing anything less than a cambric shirt and woollen hose. He had a beautifully defined, muscular body, covered in light brown hairs that stuck to his manly torso. His long hair hung wet and clung to his broad shoulders. He quickly turned to reach for a shirt to cover his nakedness, and at once realised that doing so permitted me a perfect view of his buttocks! His awkwardness delighted me. Piers had once said to me that almost all the amusement and pleasure he enjoyed was usually at the misfortune of others, and at that moment, I had to agree that such a situation as this proved him right.

I stood a moment longer, impressed by the naked knight's physique and amused by his embarrassment, and that of his manservant who had fallen to his knees and did not appear to know how to get them working again. After a moment I dismissed the servant, who slid and fell over in his eagerness to scramble away.

I then roared with laughter, such as I had not enjoyed for such a long time. The scene could not have been more piquant. I took up a linen cloth that was draped over a wooden stand, and gently dabbed at the water that dripped down his face, then drew it around his shoulders.

"Come, my dear Roger," I said, turning away, "we have been too long indoors. I feel the need for the air and freedom while we can still enjoy it." I heard him step out of the bath behind me.

"Forgive me, your Grace," he stammered, "I had not expected you."

I interrupted him by laughing again. "My dear boy, you have amused me much this morning, no apology is necessary! We must find you a young wife, Roger, before your flat stomach runs to fat, and that fine arse of yours begins to sag! Perhaps..." I stood and considered an idea. "Yes, perhaps..."

He looked quizzically at me. "Your Grace?" he asked, a confused look crossing his face.

"No matter Roger, we shall discuss this matter further. Now, get you some britches on, unless you intend to walk around naked all day - which, while it will no doubt impress the maids, may well frighten the horses!" I laughed again, but as I moved away from the window where I had been standing, I passed by a table strewn with some papers and a book. Something written caught my attention – the word 'beware' written in large print.

"What is this?" I enquired, picking up the paper.

Roger pulled up his hose quickly and reached to take it from me. "Oh, sire, it is nothing, I...."

"Let me see it!" I had not meant to snap, yet something told me it was clearly of some embarrassment. I then held what was a letter to Roger – unsigned.

"Damory," it read. "It is known that you are the king's new whore, remember what happened to the Gascon - BEWARE!"

For several moments I stood without saying anything. Roger had bowed his head, drips from his still wet hair hitting the wooden floor.

"When did you get this?" I asked, all amusement now drained.

He took the letter from my hand, screwing it up and tossing it into the recently-vacated bath tub, where it bobbed on the surface of soapy water. He was clearly angered and, while I stood, he reached for his shirt. "It was amongst my baggage," he finally admitted. "My servant said it had been left strapped to the stirrups of my horse."

"Who....?" I asked absently.

His face showed an almost sad alarm, those lovely brown eyes cast down as though in shame. "I know not, your grace, but it is surely a prank - a jest in poor taste."

I sniffed with growing annoyance. "Your honour and my own is stained by this, Roger. I will not have you slandered in such a way. I can only guess whose hand is behind this, I am not such a fool. Lancaster will pay for this insolence! I care not for myself, I have grown used to the constant criticism, the name-calling, the derision. All insults flow easily from my cousin's tongue. Forgive me, Roger." I looked away then, indignity and shame left an awkward silence in the chamber.

Roger then came to stand in front of me, and quite unexpectedly embraced me. He held me tightly and I breathed in the soapy scent from his hair. I was happy for him to take control, and we stood for some time before he released me. "Your grace, I am quite content. Do not be angered by words like these, they are nothing to me, I should have destroyed the note as soon as I had read it."

I sighed, walking slowly to the window again, looking out across the perfect boxed flower beds, now beginning to bloom as summer returned after such a long, damp spring. I felt angry that this courageous knight, who had lifted my spirits so much after so many months of disappointments and setbacks, had been besmirched. Foolish and impetuous, stubborn and unfit for my role I may have been, but I hated for those close to me to be insulted or abused in any way. If I was not always loyal to my role in life, I was loyal to my friends and loved ones.

"Roger, I shall make this right," I assured him. "You are special to me, and I will make sure that no-one insults you."

We embraced again - much as I fought against it, this man was beginning to mean something special to me. How often we cling to others for security and look to them for hope and strength. Those early days of new friendships promise so much, but almost inevitably lead to betrayal and deceit, and hatred is formed. As I stood clinging to Roger that day at Langley I started to plan for the future – his future!

+++

In August of thirteen hundred and sixteen – I think! Isabella safely gave birth to our second son, John. We christened him, I recall, in honour of the newly-elected pope, John the twenty-second of that name, and a Gascon as I recall. Am I correct, Manuel? I think so. My memory of the child is so faded. Much like all of them that God blessed us with, I had little to do with them, but of course such is the way of kings.

It was certainly the way of my own parents, a mother gone when I was so young and a father who I don't think ever forgave me for not being his eldest son. I often wonder if my brother Alfonso had lived to inherit the throne, as expected, what would have become of me.

I was overjoyed at the news, a ray of sunshine in a cheerless land, as England seemed at that time; famine, starvation, more ruinous crops. More worrying to me than any of those disasters was Thomas, earl of Lancaster!

My cousin and I were constantly at loggerheads. I do not believe I despised anyone as much and, as time passed, rather than tempering my mood, his very existence vexed me greatly.

His latest arrogance directed to myself and Isabella personally was the grossest of insults. Isabella, being more astute than I, suggested - by way of easing the enmity that existed - that she intended inviting Lancaster to stand sponsor for the imminent birth of this, our second child. Thomas failed to turn up at the special ceremony. The insult was quite unprecedented and was, to my mind, a clear statement of his continuing hostility!

I continued to be enchanted by Roger Damory, and rewarded his friendship bountifully, yet his greatest prize was yet to come, I continued to give him honours and lands and it would be fair to say that my patronage was making the once penniless Damory a rather rich young knight.

He was amusing company; simple and good-natured and he accepted the lands and grants that I showered on him with disbelief and surprise. Feigned or not, I loved to see his delight and could refuse him nothing. The warning note, which I was certain had come from

Lancaster, still continued to play on my mind and was one further score to be settled with my cousin.

However, it had to be said that Roger was not the only young knight that was becoming amusing company for me; William Montacute and Hugh Audley, whilst they were not held in such esteem as Damory, were ever eager to be of service and - as I recall Perrot saying of someone once - "They said 'yes' and 'no' in all the right places!"

I recalled that sharp Gascon wit so often in times of gloom. I would close my eyes and picture him enraging the barons with a jibe or mimic. These dashing young knights were charming enough, but they would never replace what had been lost to me. I think, looking back now, that Isabella must have realised they mattered little because nothing would ever matter as much. Moreover, she barely seemed to notice their presence and, unless I requested otherwise, Roger kept very much to the outskirts of the court when the queen was present.

It was prudent, I believed, to arrange marriages for these men who served me so well. I had once told Piers that I would raise him higher than all others at court, and I now made similar plans for Roger, whom I dearly wished to embrace into my family. My niece, Elizabeth, sister of the ill-fated Gilbert de Clare, would be a perfect match for him. The de Clare family held great swathes of land and, in time, when she and her sisters were allocated shares of the lands and properties left by their brother's untimely death, would become great land owners.

Isabella, it must be said, kept her own council about the arrangement, pointing out only that Elizabeth was so recently widowed, indeed her deceased husband's burial had yet to take place. Added to which, she was heavily pregnant by her late husband. That, I countered, made now the perfect time to find her a new husband who could comfort her in her grief and provide the stability of a father for the newborn. The queen also pointed out that Damory was far beneath my niece by birth and status.

It mattered not; the marriage would take place, I was determined. Roger could not believe his good fortune, kissing my hand and claiming he was unworthy of such a match.

"Dearest Roger," I declared, "there shall be none that call you 'the king's whore' now. You will become my family. Elizabeth will do her duty." I showered further riches and favours upon Roger and, as always, I felt great joy in doing so.

Not only was Roger to find a lucrative marriage. The tall, sharp-featured Hugh Audley would, I announced to his amazement, marry the widow of my beloved brother Piers - Margaret. My eldest niece, Eleanor, had married Hugh Despenser the younger a decade earlier, and thus I felt I had chosen wisely with the latest unions. The dark and handsome William Montacute became my personal steward and in this he served me well.

That summer found me feeling strangely secure.

+++

Of course, the dark, foreboding cloud that was Thomas, earl of Lancaster, soon crept ominously over us. He had remained relatively quiet in recent months, except for admonishing me for what he said was the elevation of mere household knights into my intimate circle and family.

All three of my recent companions now attended me in council. They were certainly not prepared to be lightly dismissed, and they took every opportunity to speak ill of my cousin. The fact that I hated Thomas far more than they did made hearing their vitriol much easier. My cousin had made it quite clear that he resented the presence of my new-found companions, reminding me again of how clear the hated Ordinances had been in respect of those with whom I surrounded myself, and how the royal household had once before been reorganised lest it be infiltrated by dangerous, self-serving men.

Having completed our meeting, Roger, richly attired in a blue velvet suit, the arms slashed with a vivid rich red silk was clearly irritated on my behalf regarding the censure from Lancaster.

"I wonder, sire, how you keep such patience in the matter of the earl of Lancaster when he does nothing but persecute you."

I smiled and reached across the table for Roger's jewelled hand, which I pressed fondly.

"I will have my revenge on my cousin, have no fear," I assured him.

"He is surely a traitor, your grace, for the wrong he has continually done towards you." stated Audley. "He is not to be trusted."

Montacute stood by the window of the chamber, and glanced over to where I sat. "He would have the three of us banished from your sight!" he stated hotly.

"My cousin is a fool, but his arrogant ways will be his undoing."

Montacute walked over and sat down beside me. His black hair glistened in the sunlight that streamed through the window, and his now rich attire proclaimed his growing wealth since I had begun to favour him.

"There is also his insult prior to the birth of your newborn son, your grace," Roger said, and I fumed anew at that particular episode, which had shocked Isabella and myself, as well as a great many at court.

Roger was certainly more animated than usual, the earl was becoming a demon in his eyes, and he now openly called him traitor. He rose from his seat next to me, withdrawing his hand from under mine as he did so. "We hear of continual unrest in the north, even despite the peace treaty to which the new pope had you assent. Raids across the border continue unabated, and yet all lands that belong to the earl of Lancaster remain untouched. The reason is simple to determine."

I had, of course, been aware of this and, in truth, the suggestion - though an ugly one - had been left unsaid, but Roger was angry. His passion endeared him to me even further. I believed him when he angrily defamed my enemies. He cared for me, I had no doubt.

"Only recently did he not deign to turn up to the council meeting you had arranged, summoning him to appear - such insolence!" An insolence only dared by one who was the wealthiest landowner in England.

There was no defence for Thomas, who, as Damory had reminded me, had chosen not to show up for a meeting I had been persuaded to arrange by way of coming to terms that would alleviate the current tensions and discord.

I looked at the three men in turn, all of them prosperous by my patronage, and committed to me personally, yet I had not told them that Thomas had informed me that he had no intention of meeting with me as long as Audley, Montacute and Damory were in attendance. He claimed that they conspired against him and he feared for his safety. Ridiculous, of course, but it gifted my cousin the excuse he needed to remain behind the walls of his favourite fortress at Pontefract.

As irony would have it, I now enjoyed more favour with many of the magnates than I had in recent years. How much of that was a response to Lancaster's arrogance, I did not know, yet there was no doubt that Thomas was becoming slowly sidelined; whatever blame he heaped upon the shoulders of Roger, Hugh and William, it was clear to many that much of the damage he suffered was more of a reflection of his own appalling lack of administrative ability. He seemed to have so enjoyed the chase to brand me incompetent, that now, having been rewarded by seemingly complete authority, he was unaware of how to use it it. If truth be known, he had longed to be king, but had not the slightest idea how best to use the power he was so eager to grasp.

So relations with Thomas continued to worsen. Isabella herself railed at the indignity of living in reduced circumstances - which she did, quite rightly, lay at Thomas's door. Summonses were issued and ignored, and Lancaster continued to claim that he was assured that his life was in danger should he attend me. While, I have to admit, both Montacute and Roger were only too willing to carry out a personal attack on Lancaster, I put this down to bravado and the folly of youth, laughing off the very suggestion. Those acting for

Thomas informed me that he lived in certainty that I would forever seek his destruction because of his hand in the murder of Piers Gaveston. Such revenge on that score would certainly be made - at the right time.

Lancaster, despite his absence from parliament and my own court, was sufficiently informed about the influence from others that did not serve his interests. He therefore chose to attack those closest to me when he impudently attacked the castles of Knaresborough in Yorkshire and Alton in Staffordshire. The custodian to both castles was my dearest friend and companion –

Roger Amory. The incident showed clearly who my cousin feared as his worst enemy.

Roger was incensed about the issue, and erupted in fury when informed.

He was such a kindly young man, it angered me greatly that this young, noble knight was being attacked in such a way, when his only wish was to loyally serve and help his king.

Lancaster did not stop there and, for good measure, proceeded to attack castles in Yorkshire that belonged to John de Warenne, the earl of Surrey. Much as I raged at his appropriation of the earl's lands and properties, first and foremost Lancaster must relinquish this unlawful seizure of Roger's castles. My cousin chose to ignore my demands and I therefore took Roger's lands in Yorkshire and Lincolnshire back into royal hands. Only then could I hope they at least were safe from further aggression from Lancaster.

One action I knew would irritate Lancaster, if nothing else, was the long-delayed partition of the lands of the late earl of Gloucester, Gilbert de Clare.

Upon Gilbert's death, the vast wealth of these lands had reverted to the crown. Despite Gilbert's widow claiming to be pregnant - even a year after his death! - the lands were now divided between his existing sisters, which naturally became the property of their husbands - Hugh Despenser the younger, Hugh Audley and of course, my own sweet Roger Damory.

It was obvious that, whilst not depriving Lancaster of anything that should have come his way, I knew my cousin well enough to know that he would be enraged that all three men - particularly Roger - were gaining in wealth as well as influence.

Spending Christmas at Westminster gave Isabella and I – as well as my favoured companions – a relatively enjoyable period of peace. With the queen now expecting our third child, our family was growing - and yet the season always reminded me of Piers, who had always enjoyed it so much. I welcomed the event as much as anything because it gave me the greatest delight to bestow gifts on all around me. To Isabella I gave an enamelled silver-gilt bowl with feet and a cover. My great-niece Joan Gaveston was brought to me, and I bestowed jewels on her and embraced her warmly. I sensed that she was the closest I could be to her beloved father and, as I looked into the dazzling blue eyes that so matched her father's, I was reminded again how very alone I often was without him there. As usual, we were richly entertained by singers, dancers, acrobats and jesters. I gave silver goblets to at least twenty household knights, and gave generously to all the performers who entertained us so much.

A squire acted as King of the Bean. The custom was one that I had grown up with and celebrated each year.

A gold coin or ring would be baked into a cake and whoever found it in their portion would preside over the evening's festivities. It was almost as though all was well in England, but of course drama was never far away.

News was brought to me early in the New Year that my step-mother Marguerite had died. I had kept up a rather fractured relationship with her since her criticism of myself and Piers years before. I recalled, now, her cradling my weeping father on one of many nights when he felt that he was nearing the end of his life. I thought so rarely of him now.

After her funeral, I travelled briefly and enjoyed a visit to Roger and my niece. One evening, I relaxed with Roger in his chambers at Clare Castle, his estate in Suffolk. We had spent little time together since his marriage, and I welcomed the opportunity to enjoy his company.

We sat one evening in front of a roaring log fire. We both gazed at the flames that danced and flickered as the wood crackled and spat. "How fares your marriage, Roger?" I asked, running the back of my hand along his forearm, clothed these days in costly silk.

"I like it well enough, your grace," he answered. "Elizabeth and I are happy, I believe; we want for little, by your grace's bountiful generosity."

I smiled. He got up and poured us wine.

"Your grace must know that the earl of Lancaster still causes much mischief."

"Ha! My cousin will always cause mischief - it is one of his fondest pastimes."

Roger handed one of the goblets to me. "Yet you let him live to heap more indignities upon you. He ignores your commands, yet still you request his company at parliament rather than order it. He insults me by attacking those castles over which I have custody, yet he brushes aside your commands to desist." He sunk down beside me, and I was struck by his vehemence, such passion in his condemnation of Thomas surprised me.

"You think me weak, Roger?" I asked candidly.

He glanced at me and then quickly looked away. "Your grace, I would never call you weak. Maybe too forgiving?"

I was strangely reminded that I had sworn to be the cause of Lancaster's death for his part in the murder of my beloved Perrot. "Fear not, Roger," I looked into his deep brown eyes, wide and staring in a strange innocent way, his pale skin now flushed. "Many say I will be the cause of his death or he mine. What is death to me? I long for it, at times when I am haunted and visited by memories that assail me so I awake, breathless and fearful. I long to be...."

"With Gaveston!" Roger cut in, almost snappily. "You think of him often, don't you? Some evenings when I have stayed and we have talked and you fall into a sleep, you whisper his name and beg him to come to you." He paused for a second or two, "Do I not take his place in your heart?"

I studied his handsome face, and gently ran my finger across the scar over the bridge of his nose. "You are special Roger, you must know that, but no, you do not take the place of Perrot. Neither does William or Hugh Audley."

"What of the queen, your grace?" He spoke the words, not in any spiteful way, but I felt a pang of guilt that, for all the love that I had developed for Isabella since our marriage, I could not declare that I loved her more than Perrot.

"Let us discuss other subjects, Roger. I have no desire to be melancholy."

He stared at me for a moment, and then proceeded to nestle down against my arm, which I unfurled and draped around his shoulder.

"Oh to be always like this, Roger, always at peace - and the queen always in good humour!"

We were laughing together when, at that moment, there was a discreet knock on the chamber door. Will Shene travelled with me everywhere and, despite the riches I had bestowed upon him for his loyal service, he remained - by choice - at a safe distance from the politics of the world around me. He had always stated he wanted little other than to serve me. No king or common man was ever as blessed with the service of another than I was. Now, he peeped in the door of the dimly lit room with a look of concern.

"Your grace, there are messengers from the queen, who are in earnest to speak with you." A messenger from Isabella was unusual, particularly when it was known that I would be returning to Westminster in a day or so. As irritated as I was by the intrusion into my evening with Roger, I had Will bring the messenger in.

A small nervous man entered and fell to his knees at my feet almost in supplication as he handed a letter to me.

I walked over to a table with a candle, and drew up a nearby chair. I broke the seal, Isabella's own, and began to scan the contents. I could not suppress the slight gasp

I uttered. I shook my head slightly at Will, and he took his cue, instructing the messenger that there was no reply as he ushered him from the room.

Roger stood nearby with a perplexed look. "Your grace?" he enquired.

I looked up from reading. "The Countess of Lancaster has been abducted!

+++

The abduction of Lancaster's wife, though highly amusing for me - and for many others, it has to be said - was sheer folly. A household knight serving the earl of Surrey abducted her and took off with her to the earl's castle at Reigate.

I could imagine those pale features of the earl breaking into a wide grin at the mischief this would cause. John de Warenne was a likeable man, although - it has to be said - not always a wise one. He was a tall, sturdy fellow, and a lover of practical jokes; one of the few of the magnates who, whilst he did not condone Piers's behaviour during his life with me, was, I believe, secretly amused at the more pompous lords being the victims of so much of Piers's stinging wit.

Relations between Surrey and Lancaster had been brewing for some time, and, of course, I was blamed by others for not checking the potential problems that would ultimately ensue. Lancaster had besieged castles belonging to Surrey and had ventured on a course of action that I had condemned, ordering him to desist. Naturally, he had ignored me.

I could, in fairness, claim that the rift had been started by Lancaster, who had also ejected Surrey's mistress from her property in Wakefield. This was not avenging a wrong it was spoiling for a fight! Rumour was, as my delightful Damory whispered to me one day, that Lancaster's wife had been only too happy to be removed from her hated husband, and may well have had a hand in the mischief.

Whatever the cause, the earl of Lancaster blamed me and also cast aspersions against Damory and Audley for inciting and exacerbating this and other slights. The bad feeling between my cousin and I only worsened.

I had summoned Lancaster to appear before me; he ignored me and sought to justify his continual disdain by claiming that he failed to appear as I had failed to uphold the Ordinances. Moreover, he apparently feared for his life amidst the hatred of those he called my 'coven of favourites' and declared he was alarmed at the power these men now wielded over me.

More concerning was the rumour that Lancaster was gathering his own troops, a charge he met with the response that he was raising such a force in readiness for a further war in Scotland. I had spoken of a further enterprise at some time, but had little stomach to lead another army into that wasteland where I suffered so ignoble a defeat.

Amidst the intrigue and suspicion between Lancaster and myself was the birth of our first daughter, Eleanor - a beautiful child, with eyes like her mother.

By this time, there had been a growing number of prelates, barons and other advisers, all intent on bringing Lancaster and I together to make peace, and step back from the ever real threat of open civil war between us.

After what seemed to be endless negotiations between myself and my cousin, we finally met at Loughborough. Thomas looked much older than when I had last seen him; his hair, still scraped back into a queue, was greying now. Still predominantly black, it was now streaked with grey strands. His eyes looked tired, and his skin was sallow and unhealthy.

As we finally embraced, sharing a kiss of peace, he whispered to me, "This is not done, Edward, do not imagine me vanquished."

I too spoke into his ear. "And I shall never rest until you are thoroughly destroyed for the murder of Piers Gaveston." We parted smiling then and I presented him with gifts, including a fine palfrey horse.

Of course, there were conditions. What has ever come my way that has not cost me a heavy price? I was to uphold the Ordinances, and accept that my 'favourites' were to accept other positions that would not allow them such direct influence with me. Roger and Audley were to be sent from the court. Montacute was replaced as my steward by a former mayor of London, Bartholomew Badlesmere, who would play a role later in this tale.

I had, it would only be honest to say, become somewhat exasperated with Roger of late. Of course I still cared for him, but I could not fail to also realise that, as his star rose in ascendance, his manner and mood began to change. I knew that he was exasperated at my reluctance to deal more harshly with my cousin, but I would have my vengeance when the time was right. Thomas, as yet, was still too powerful for me to dismiss out of hand. I tired of these three men who had been close company, inevitably realising that they were no substitute for Perrot, and maybe that is what I had been searching for.

My parting from Roger was upsetting and, whilst he could still visit the court, his access to me would certainly be limited.

"You will happily let me go?" he asked me, emotionally.

I took his handsome face in my hands and kissed him. "It may not be for always, my dearest Roger. You are ever in my thoughts, and I shall miss you, but at the moment I have to be seen to comply with my cousin, lest civil war break out."

He looked at me with scorn. "You should have captured him as I suggested. He should have been safely locked in the Tower."

I sighed, at this moment, I could not deal with any petulance he may feel. "How easy to say, my dearest, but so difficult to achieve. The time will come, never fear."

He embraced me and turned away before slipping out of the chamber, closing the door softly behind him.

+++

Brother Alphage refilled the three earthenware mugs with more cool water, and dabbed at his bald pate with a handkerchief kept inside a sleeve of his robe. The day was beginning to turn extremely warm, and they therefore decided to seek shelter from the burning sun inside the herbalist's workshop. Just as they had sheltered there from the rain, so they would now benefit from its refuge from the sun.

All manner of fine aromas assailed their senses, it really was the most pleasant of environments. Fieschi took off his red, wide-brimmed hat that, although affording his head some protection, also became uncomfortable.

Even Alphage, who was more accustomed to the relentless heat of the summer in the rural beauty of the region, was not sorry to be exchanging the sun's fierceness with the cool shade the small workshop.

Fieschi and Alphage chose two small stools to sit on, while Edward was happy to sit on the floor of the doorway, with Perrot next to him. The dog's eyes flicked from his master to a butterfly that danced in the doorway, a possible threat despite its size. For the time being however, he rested his chin on Edward's foot with a deep, lazy sigh.

Alphage, who had found himself enthralled by the tale of this man's former life, seemed relieved that the conflict between Edward and his cousin had been averted. For Alphage himself, even though he had travelled much and seen the worst of men as well as the good, much of what the former king related made for uncomfortable hearing. He inwardly thanked God that he had been called to His service rather than been born a king.

Fieschi, however, found himself censorious. That Edward had been a weak king was patently obvious and, whilst liking the man, he could understand why critics had labelled him as being totally unfit for the role thrust upon him.

"So," the monk said at length, "you and your cousin were now reconciled?"

Edward smiled at the elderly man. "Dear Alphage, I wish I could say we were reconciled, but we both knew the kiss of peace was purely for appearances. As I said, our whispered threats to each other were in earnest, and my dislike of him grew into hate. He would be my ruin or I his, that at least we both understood."

"Your close attendants were now exiled from court?" Fieschi worded it as a question, but one that he seemed adamant about as though its certainty was beyond dispute.

"They were certainly deprived of their contact with me," Edward replied, tapping the toe of his boot against the wooden doorframe. "They were left in no doubt that, when at court, they were unable to be in a position to advise me in any matter." The former king smiled. "Those who insisted that Audley, Montacute and Roger Damory leave court may have done well to reconsider their objections, given who was to make perhaps the biggest and most tragic impact of my entire reign. It is time I talked of Hugh.

+++

CHAPTER FIVE

I had, up until I think the beginning of the year of our lord thirteen hundred and eighteen, taken very little notice of Hugh Despenser, the younger. How strange are those relationships that occur a long time after a first acquaintance. I had known of Hugh for many years, having knighted him on that long-forgotten day with Piers, Roger Mortimer and others that subsequently played a part in my life.

I had been in his company and yet barely addressed him, although his father had been a rock that I leaned on many times. A good and loyal man, who often took the trouble to ask whether I recalled his dearest son.

You look puzzled, Manuel; I shall henceforth call Hugh that name, and refer to his father as 'the elder'. A propensity exists in England whereby a father, son and even grandson can all be christened with the same name. It is so with many families.

Anyway, I had taken advice from Hugh and found him to be cautious and wise, as his father had always been. I never forgot the approach he made to me after we had buried Piers. As I knelt in prayer beside him, I wondered why I had never recalled that he and my beloved were friends. It did not matter, the fact that he felt a desire to pay private respects to Piers commended him to me.

He had, it has to be said, a temperament that was as delicate as a feather in the wind; ever easy to anger and using somewhat aggressive means to settle his disputes. He was, of course, the husband of my niece, Eleanor, and thus my nephew by marriage; a wedding held in the presence of her grandfather - my father. Nevertheless, he was of little notice to me other than his connection to the family. He had become, by virtue of his marriage to one of the de Clare sisters, a prosperous man. Already a vast landowner, he was, upon the settlement of Gilbert de Clare's estate, a man of considerable wealth.

He was what Piers would have described as 'stocky' - broad-shouldered, with the greenest eyes I had ever seen. They were quick and sharp.

His appointment as my chamberlain was not of my choosing, and I was determined to dislike him for that alone, added to which Roger Damory and Hugh Audley had both raised objections about his manner towards them. Whilst this improved following their profitable marriages, similar to the one that Despenser enjoyed, he nevertheless treated them and Montacute with a certain degree of scorn.

Then there was the whispered suggestion that Despenser was the tool of my cousin Lancaster, set to report back to my despised cousin. I put little stock into the suggestion. Maybe because I trusted his father implicitly, I disregarded the suggestion. There were certainly spies for Lancaster at court, but I did not believe Hugh to be one of them. Not only that, but I had it on good authority that Hugh was quite vociferous about his condemnation of Lancaster in private.

Isabella, however, seemed to have a great dislike of Hugh, though the reason for this distrust and growing animosity was unknown to me. It must be said that Hugh did not seem to care that she harboured this dislike and, indeed, he did very little to endear himself to her. It also has to be said that I did not display any feeling towards Hugh myself up until now. I resented his appointment as my chamberlain, yet there was little I could do about it.

Such was the situation between us that his very presence irked me, until one day at Langley. I still felt calmed and peaceful there, added to which, of course, it was my beloved Piers's last resting place. There were those who grumbled insolently about the extravagance of Piers's tomb, but I cared little for opinion.

I could not argue that, although I made no effort to make his task easier, it was generally said that Hugh was making a good job of running my household. Being chief steward to a king was surely a complex and diverse role, and especially when one served this king!

I relaxed one day in this most favourite of places in a secluded area of the beautiful gardens, which I ensured would remain private. It had seemed strange to be here with a man other than Piers, and I felt his presence with me. Nonetheless, surrounded by closely clipped lawns and flowerbeds of all scents, I could always feel at peace at Langley. No scent pervaded as much as lavender, and I had ensured that all areas were planted with this most mesmerising of herbs. I stretched out and sighed, the warm afternoon sunshine casting a bright light over the small fountain that trickled away under an ornate arbour.

I noted, as I sat on an elaborately-carved stone seat, that Hugh was not far away and I watched him for several moments. Taking the opportunity to walk for a while in this most glorious of surroundings, he did for once, seem less formal; the top of his tunic was unbuttoned, and he rubbed a hand on the back of his neck and stretched his limbs as though the very sun would settle his body with its warm rays. He turned, then, and noticed me; he fumbled with his collar, urgently dusting off his tunic. He appeared to pause while he sought the correct procedure now that he had been caught being idle, and sheepishly made his way towards me.

"Your grace, forgive me," he almost stumbled over the words. "I have nursed a throbbing head today and sought some air to clear it."

I felt a certain benevolence for him now. I had only ever seen him in a brisk, authorative manner, his quick eyes taking in everything around him, his ears, listening, seemingly absorbing every sound, every word spoken.

"You need not worry," I said with a smile. "The weather is too good today to be wasted indoors. You may join me if you wish."

My trusted Will Shene was, as always, at my side and he filled a second goblet with some of the watered wine, nodding his head in deference, and standing some way from where Hugh now sat.

"Your grace is most kind." He took up the wine, sipping it and watching me over the brim.

"You stare at me, Hugh," I stated, delighting in the flush across his cheeks.

"Forgive me, your grace...." he began, but I laughed and waved my hand as though dismissing his concern.

"I had not meant to offend you, but I feel drawn to you. We work hand in hand and yet we speak very little lest it be of state matters and such."

"What else do you want to say?"

"You are unhappy at my appointment to chamberlain, and I would have you trust me and take some of the great burden of your office."

I smiled at him. "The burden is one I have to bear alone, Hugh. You serve me well enough." I drank from my goblet, and there was a moment's silence between us. Yet it was clear he wanted to say more.

"I have the honour to be your nephew by marriage, yet I scarcely know you, sire. Forgive my impertinence, but I feel happy in your company. My wish is to serve you only, and would that I could earn your trust in whatever way you deem fit."

I looked at him with some measure of amusement. I had felt dull and friendless after Damory, Montacute and Audley had all left the court. The last person I expected to enjoy some comfort from was Hugh Despenser, and yet there was something about him that charmed me. We sat and talked for some time.

He was a handsome man, something I was only just beginning to notice. That high brow, those eyes that seemed deep and watchful; he was attractive. I remarked that, now those whose company I had enjoyed had gone, I was left with few I could instinctively rely on.

Hugh made a dismissive gesture with his jewelled hand. "They are almost boys, your grace, these times call for sound advice and sensible reasoning."

"Which you have in abundance, Hugh? Is that what you are implying?"

He seemed embarrassed again. "Forgive me, your grace, I merely suggest that household knights are no match for the skill of one who has lived among the court from a young age, someone who can notice and identify unrest, can advise with the knowledge of foresight. My father has ever been your most faithful adherent and it is my honour to add my shoulder to bear the weight of your onerous office."

"You have a pretty way of speech, Hugh. It is true that your family has been faithful to me at times when I felt forsaken by all. I am not the easiest of masters, you must know that." I looked straight into his eyes; they were truly mesmerising, and I looked away, unable to meet their intensive stare. "We will deal honestly with one another, my friend," I stated with firmness.

He suddenly fell to his knees in front of me, grasping my hand and kissing it fervently. Then he rapidly seemed to come to his senses, and got up quickly. "Forgive me, your grace, I go too far!"

Before I had chance to say anything further, he was gone, almost running back towards the palace. I sat perplexed for a moment, but then smiled. Perhaps I had misjudged both the servant and the man.

Over the next few months, I felt myself relying on Hugh more and more.

I had little capability as an administrator and it was, on the whole, a blessing to have someone who could run things as effectively as he did. I admit that I also began to enjoy the occasions we were alone together. His company could be awkward at times; he often seemed stiff and uncomfortable, as though not knowing how to behave when we were alone together. That was until one day we rode out together while at the queen's property at Eltham. Hugh was difficult to entice out of the confines of the court, wherever it was, preferring to spend his time surrounded by secretaries and clerks who were ever ready to do his bidding.

We rode for a time, just enjoying the air and the lack of people milling around. Meetings of petitioners, councils, foreign dignitaries and the like bored me, and I was grateful to let Hugh take control.

I wondered often why I seemed to need the strength of another man to rely on, rather than stand for myself. Piers and I had been so much more than just someone to rely on. Amory, Audley and Montacute were willing consorts, but largely ignorant of important matters, and I had enjoyed their wit and boldness. Hugh was different. I felt from him a deep fondness, a need to be with me often and take on the onerous burden of kingship.

We had ridden for some time before we came to a large oak tree, solid and magnificent, its vigorous branches loaded with acorns. We stopped and sat beneath the tree, and Hugh opened his flask and offered me the cooling wine within.

I passed it back after several gulps but, inadvertently, it slipped from my grasp, tipping all over Hugh's lap. I cursed my clumsiness and exclaimed apologies.

"No matter, your grace," he replied, brushing away the liquid with his hand, "it is nothing."

I took my handkerchief and attempted to stem the stain. Within a heartbeat, our faces came close, we both looked into the eyes of the other, and I at once felt a strong connection to this man; not passionate like Piers, but one that made me feel safe. I held a hand against his cheek affectionately, and he took it and kissed the palm, gently and soothingly. My heart lurched as I drew him to me, holding him tightly. Such was my height that I was a few inches taller, but I felt strangely weak and vulnerable.

After that, I wanted him with me as often as possible, often dismissing everyone so I could be with him, just the two of us. He became more and more a focus for my life; I did not do anything unless Hugh agreed it was the right thing to do. I came to rely on him in all things. I knew that I monopolised his time, and he mine. My niece and Hugh's wife, Eleanor, was I'm sure happy enough that most of Hugh's waking hours were spent with me.

Isabella's thoughts on this growing relationship were not viewed in quite the same way. The queen did not trust Hugh, and did not tire of telling me so. The days of my queen keeping her own counsel on matters, unless asked, had long since passed and, whilst we were not unhappy, our time together was invariably spent disagreeing with one another. As time went by I began to feel that she regarded me as weak, often becoming impatient that I allowed my will to be directed by Hugh.

"You trust no-one in my council or those who are now instructed to control the council, as well as both our households!" I once exclaimed, after a heated discussion about Hugh's role in my life.

"You know that is untrue!" she countered, flushed with indignity, tapping her fingers irritably on the arm of her chair. "Badlasmere is an extremely capable steward, Roger de Northburgh is an excellent treasurer – albeit that he restricts my household expenses to a point where I am barely able to renew my clothes and must be seen in dowdy attire!"

I could not help but smile; Isabella was much given to over-exaggeration. Like myself, she could be generous, but I rewarded those who pleased me much. A fool, a singer, any who made me smile. Also, those who brought me good news were richly rewarded for the joy they could bring me. Isabella's munificence was more measured, not as impulsive as mine, certainly.

"I hear you have permitted him unrestricted access to your company. Surely you realise that is unwise, Edward, a subject to be treated thus is sheer folly!"

"And I also 'permit' you, madam, to vent your hatred and distrust, when I should in truth demand that you keep silent on those who I choose to have around me!" I was cross, and Isabella looked shocked that I had spoken to her in such angry tones. That she did not like or trust Hugh was a great pity, but it would make no difference. Hugh and I were becoming close and I was happy.

"Lest you forget," I continued, "these arrangements are forced upon me, and, whilst I have no choice but to accept them, I can at least hope that I can be in accord with those who serve me."

Isabella rose from where she had been seated and held out her arms to me. "Let us not quarrel my lord." She threw her arms around me, pressing her cheek against my chest. "All I ask is that you protect yourself from being the tool of these men, lest they use you for their own enrichment. Amory, Audley, they were all the same, they grew prosperous in your service. You trust too easily, husband."

"I will judge whether they receive my favour or not, Isabella. Do you think me such a fool?"

Her reply was unsaid, but the fact that she did not respond to the question spoke a great deal. I pulled away and left her.

+++

By the end of the year I had begun to muster forces to retake the port of Berwick-on-Tweed, which the insufferable Bruce had taken from English hands.

A treaty of sorts now existed between myself and Lancaster, and this was further cemented by my cousin agreeing to lend his forces for the enterprise. I trusted Thomas no more than I had ever done, but the threat of civil war between us had been averted at least.

The enterprise at Berwick was a dismal failure and, whilst Hugh commended me for my tactical prowess, I look back on the failure with a heavy heart. Added to which, Lancaster left with what some claimed was absolute disgust and shame. In truth, I was glad to see him gone; with his arrogance and swagger, he was a constant reminder - if one was needed - that the principal murderer of my beloved brother still lived!

As time passed after the debacle of Berwick, I relied on Hugh more and more and he was fast becoming my truest servant. I rewarded him richly for his service, as I had always done for those who served me well.

Isabella, however, continued to regard Hugh with distrust. Had I been blind at the time? I have often wondered how I could have been so unaware that their growing mutual distrust would lead to inevitable catastrophe. Love was always blind to me; I had often believed that my greatest folly was to love as easily as

I always have. I looked for companionship and then complete trust. Those who offered me unflinching support became rich as a result.

Hugh, like all the others, thirsted for power and wealth, and I was more than happy to give freely, without seeing the harm in it. Piers was different. My beautiful Gascon brother, I truly believed, would have been happy with me whether I wore a crown or not. Love that unconditional was rare, and after Perrot, I never truly experienced it again.

While Lancaster brooded, Hugh spoke spitefully of him. Had not Lancaster's forces at Berwick been entirely superficial? My cousin had claimed that the battle was to be directed by the king, and he had thus waited for his command.

"Ridiculous!" Hugh had snarled. Lancaster was ever one to go his own way; it would not have mattered what command he had received, he would have ignored any instructions if he disagreed with them, just as he had always don.

Hugh and I were growing closer. As time went on I found that I was starting to rely on his administrative skills more and more. Personally I was lifted by his confident manner and his reassurance that all would be well. He could at times be most charming and a delight to be with, but I noted on occasions that he could show anger, and remembered all insults and slights.

As with Piers and later Roger, Langley was the one place I felt we could be truly alone and I retreated there as I always had when tension mounted.

The defeat at Berwick had caused me much annoyance and grief, and my cousins constant belligerence made the whole episode one that I would again find hard to overcome.

Hugh and I walked arm in arm in the grounds of Langley, and the conversation turned to dull political manners; never able to concentrate on such tiresome business, I sighed.

"Dearest Hugh, I will leave these issues in your more than capable of hands. I find this business tiring, let us talk of other things." I was certain I heard a sigh, and I hoped it was one of calm and awe at the beauty of this special place, rather than one of impatience. We stopped for a moment, looking out across the lawns. Birds sang, some deer had stopped, gazing at us, judging whether we were a threat and if flight was needed. They continued to graze, and I smiled. I had a ridiculous fancy that they were used to seeing me and felt quite safe.

Hugh had been talking, but I had paid little attention. "Your grace should consider whether Damory's presence at court at all is really necessary."

"Roger?" I queried. "What has he to do with anything? I believe that the new lands that he controls have monopolised much of his time."

"Your grace, I am wary of his intentions, I learn from a reliable source that he is not as loyal as you might think."

"Not loyal?" I scoffed. "Roger is dear to me still, though not as much since you have begun to serve me so well." I squeezed his arm affectionately.

Hugh continued to pout like a disagreeable child, something I had noticed he did quite often.

"Well," I eventually said, "we will find him some task that will take up his time, but let us discuss this later. Is it not the most beautiful of places? I want you to feel at peace here too Hugh. Am I working you too hard, my dear friend?"

"Your grace may exhaust me entirely if you wish, I live only to serve you."

I smiled broadly at him. "The queen is again with child," I announced, "yet she errs on the side of caution and will not have this known to any but ourselves at this early stage. Naturally, I have no secrets from you, dearest Hugh, but only you must know."

"I am honoured, your grace, and my congratulations to both you and the queen."

I knew he was glad for me, and that evening he arranged singers and a recital, some tableaux all of my most favourite delights and we laughed and grew loud and drunk. Those times at Langley live still with me even though they are a lifetime ago. Those most special to me spent so many delightful hours there, and even though the details are sometimes difficult to recall, it is the place of fondest memory.

Later that night, with the entertainments over, we staggered towards my chamber. Hugh had insisted that he alone could manage to help me. I had drunk heavily and stumbled from time to time. I had always had a good capacity for drinking wine, but I had overindulged and I was glad of Hugh's strong arms to aid me. We reached the chamber, and I lunged for the safety of the large bed, falling upon it gratefully.

I felt Hugh tug the shoes from my feet, and I propped myself up on both elbows. He leaned over and loosened the collar of my shirt. Suddenly, I grasped the back of his head and brought his face down upon mine, kissing him passionately on the lips.

He pulled away suddenly, and I - shocked at the reaction - looked away with a measure of shame. He did not move until he gently turned my face towards him again and returned my kiss with his own. He deftly unbuttoned the remainder of my shirt, kissing my neck tenderly and running his hand down my chest to my stomach. I sighed and closed my eyes.

For only the second time in my life, I believed I had fallen in love.

+++

By the time Hugh and I returned to Westminster, I felt contented in a way I had not experienced since Piers's murder. I longed for Hugh's company all the time, and began to distance myself from Isabella. Now that she was to have our fourth child, I doubted that we would have more. Even before my closer association with Hugh, we were drifting apart; spending less time together, although I felt no animosity towards her and we were certainly personable to each other.

However, Isabella still clearly disliked Hugh. She had treated Piers well all those years before. Roger she had tolerated. Audley and Montacute she barely acknowledged. Hugh however was quite a different matter. I had been cross with him upon our return to Westminster, where, in front of many courtiers, Hugh had congratulated Isabella on her pregnancy. The queen had cast him a look of contempt, but politely accepted his best wishes. She looked at me angrily, but I turned away rather than meet her gaze.

I had reprimanded Hugh later, but I was unable to be cross with him for long, as well he knew, and

I forgave his error which I was sure had been committed with the best intensions. He grew in confidence with my favour, and whilst there was still none to replace Piers, Hugh had almost driven any others from my thoughts. Roger Damory had left court some time before, although he did attend me during a visit to France to pay homage to the French king, my brother-in-law Philip, for the lands that I held there. The homage was one of the most demeaning tasks for any king of England, and I stayed for the briefest time possible.

The administration of the country could, I believe, be left in Despenser's capable hands. The elder Despenser, too, added a valuable contribution and together they lifted the burden of statecraft from me; I was thankful for it.

I had always been more than happy to reward those who served me well, and none served me as well as Hugh. I bestowed lands and properties on Hugh with complete abandon. "Tell me what you would like and I will gladly bestow it to you, my dearest Hugh" were words it was a joy to utter!

Isabella was one of the first to cast a critical eye over my beloved's role, and she vented a spite that would become more manifest as time went by.

"Edward," she hissed at me at one point, as we dined alone one evening, occasions that were to become less frequent. "You must have noticed the disquiet about Despenser? The favour that you show him is beginning to unnerve and disappoint the magnates. Now, when you are at last enjoying some small measure of calm in the country, you allow Hugh Despenser unlimited access to you at all times. You praise him loudly and you must see that will cause only resentment and unrest."

"You've never liked Hugh, have you?" I said bitterly.

Her eyes sparkled with something close to anger, but she looked down to her lap as though calming herself before she next spoke. "My dearest, you have known how any type of favouritism is viewed. You more than anyone else have borne the brunt of malicious gossip; idle and careless tongues spread rumours and chatter about a king is particularly dangerous."

I sniffed sharply with annoyance. "Your role, my dearest, is not to instruct me, direct me or censure me. Your role is to act as a queen should. You should be above gossip, madam."

"Edward, the man is a leech! He would steal from you, from your people, and I daresay even from his own father!"

I should not have tolerated her vile talk, yet I was too late to stop her most bitter tirade.

"People say he comes to you at night! Is it true? Is that why you shun my bed lately?" She had said more than enough, and the horrified look on her face indicated that she knew it.

I set down the goblet I had in my hand. "Would you rather he came to yours?"

Her face turned ashen and she looked as though she would faint, but I rose from my chair and, without another look at her, I marched from the chamber.

+++

I heard Isabella's cruel words over and over again in my head. Yet I could not be other than what I was. I needed Hugh, I needed his strength, his decisiveness and his self-assurance. In the years I had been king, all these attributes had been worn away from me.

Of course there would be jealousy, that was always the way at court; one day someone was in favour, the next they had been eclipsed by another.

If Hugh was as rapacious as Isabella claimed, it did not matter to me. Whatever I could give him I gladly would. By way of confirmation that Hugh took the greatest concern over my interests, an incident occurred that proved his loyalty and commitment to me.

A conflict was brewing regarding the Gower lands in Wales, and I thanked heaven that my beloved was able to attempt to resolve the issue and avoid more disharmony and unrest. The Marcher lords being those who held vast areas of Wales were Humphrey Bohun, earl of Hereford, Roger Mortimer of Wigmore, John de Mowbray and my sweet Roger Damory, amongst others.

William de Braose held Gower at this time, but had alienated the vast estates to his son-in-law, de Mowbray.

Wales had all but become a rogue country of its own. Owing to age old agreements, the lords of the March need not apply to their English king for permission to build strongholds as they had done to protect the lands; they controlled their own borders and to a great extent, made and abided by their own laws.

Hugh came to me one day in great distress and anger. He burst into my chamber as I was being fitted for a new set of clothes. Since my days with Piers, I had tried to take great care with my apparel and ordered expensive clothes in the finest materials. Hugh was not about to comment on the cut of a prospective new tunic as he barged in, letter in hand. He turned to find an exasperated Will Shene, who had attempted to announce the visitor. Hugh looked haughtily at Will and tilted his head towards the door as a sign of dismissal. Will looked then at me before Hugh lost patience.

"Get out you idiot!" he barked angrily.

I looked at Will and nodded. My faithful servant left the room, but not before he cast a look of venomous hatred at the younger Despenser. My tailor looked as though he wished to be anywhere else, and I put him out of his misery by a smiling nod of dismissal. I waited until he had left before I asked Hugh what had caused him to be so enraged.

He began to rant about the communication he had just received. "John de Mowbray has taken control of the Gower. You will recall Mowbray, your grace, a rogue of alarming arrogance."

"But as handsome as Lucifer," I recalled with a brief smile.

Hugh was not impressed by my attempt at levity. "Handsome or not," he snapped, "the man is an ambitious fool, and his old goat of a father-in-law has handed him the Gower estates. We cannot allow this, your grace, something must be done! As ever, I am working in your best interests my liege. Mowbray cannot do this if he has not received a royal licence to enter the said lands."

I turned to him with a tender look. He resembled a small boy who has been deprived of a favourite toy, but that was one reason - among many - that I loved him. "What do you suggest, my dearest Hugh?"

His anger faded to a smile. "We must surely order that the Gower be taken back into royal hands, and any resistance must be met with force." He sighed and came over to me, laying a hand on my shoulder. "You must know, Edward, that I wish only for your comfort. I abhor these disputes, as you know, but you are the king and justice must be seen to be done."

I took his hand from my shoulder and kissed his jewelled fingers. "I would to God all men were as faithful to me as you are my darling Hugh."

Naturally, the Marcher lords were furious about this latest turn of events, and the threat to what they viewed as 'Marcher privileges' was seen as entirely as Hugh's greed and my weakness.

Christmas court in the year thirteen hundred and twenty was a sober affair. Discontent once again seemed to emanate from every corner. Isabella and I had become distanced and, regardless of how it must have seemed to any who knew us both well, I had no ill feeling towards her; our only discord was in regard of Hugh. She would urge me to let him go or face the same devastating results as I had when Piers had been taken from me. I would eventually shout, lose my temper and walk away, or she would complain that the bitter quarrelling was no good for her present condition, and she would be led away by her ladies.

Hugh had told me - on witnessing the end of a bitter discourse when Isabella had needed to be helped to her chamber to rest - informants related to him that, once out of my presence, she would dismiss he ladies and march briskly away. Hugh loved her dearly, he told me so on many occasions; his only wish being that he might know what made her hate him so much.

My darling Hugh was upset, and I could only suggest that maybe, in her present condition, she was clearly not in her right mind. Meanwhile, I gifted him several mares and jewels anything that would cheer him and bring him comfort.

He was of course becoming a great landowner, custodian of several castles and properties, and held significant offices. Voices of dissent were, however, growing louder. Some of Hugh's methods for enriching himself had been questioned. He was said to operate questionable methods of gaining property and wealth. Complaints of extortion, bullying and even blackmail were becoming an increasing problem. He assured me that all talk of his menaces was fabricated in order to demonise him in my eyes. These complaints and rumours, of course, brought enmity from many sources. The Marcher lords, as I had expected, left court just before the New Year and I was happy to see them go. Hugh seemed happier and even Isabella made an effort to lighten the mood once the oppressive lords had departed.

News came that Humphrey de Bohun, earl of Hereford, was gathering troops with the aim of attacking Hugh's estates in Wales. As my brother-in-law, he having wed my sister Elizabeth, I had always thought of him as my friend and, indeed, but for his dislike of Piers, we had remained on good terms. Now he was set to tear into my beloved Hugh's lands. I at once took back into royal hands his castle at Builth.

Personally, I was saddened to learn that Roger Amory and Hugh Audley had made known their intention to side with the Marcher lords. I ordered the confiscation of Audley's lands, yet I took no pleasure in doing so. More difficult was my seizure of Roger's castle of St Briavel's in Gloucestershire. As I was given word that the stronghold was now safely back under my control, I could not help but remember how sweet Roger had been. I recalled the shock on his face at my intrusion when he was bathing. His innocent expression, that beguiling smile.

All that must be put to one side now. Both those young men had used me and, after all I had done for them, they hid behind the mask of indignity as landowners in Wales. They conveniently forgot that, without my good favour, they would still be mere household knights.

I had, up until now, given little consideration to the Mortimers, Roger of Wigmore and his uncle Roger of Chirk. I know, Alphage, your troubled face tells me that again names are confusing, but I will continue, and all will become clearer I hope.

Roger Mortimer of Wigmore was a tall man, at least as tall as myself and with a solid build; black haired and grim faced, his dark eyes, alert and clear. He wore no beard, but a moustache that sat beneath a flattened and broken nose -and how well I would have rewarded the one that broke it! He was a man who I would come to hate above all others.

His uncle, Mortimer of Chirk, I can in all honesty barely recall, but he plays a very minor part on this busy stage.

Roger of Wigmore had, I have to confess, not been an enemy to myself and Piers; we had known each other well enough, and he was amongst those I had knighted many years before. He had served me well in Ireland until being recalled when Hugh had advised me that he thought it a wise decision to replace him with one of Hugh's own knights, Sir Ralph de Gorges. By now

I seldom questioned by beloved friend about such decisions, I could deny him nothing.

On Hugh's advice, I summoned Mortimer, Hereford and others to attend a special council to explain their reasons for the massing of troops in the Welsh March. Much to our annoyance, they refused. Furthermore, they had the audacity to also declare they would not attend me as long as Hugh was at my side. Hereford went further by suggesting that Hugh be removed and placed under the custody of Thomas of Lancaster. I raged at the very suggestion; to have let my darling Perrot fall into my cousin's evil clutches was a catastrophe that would live with me forever. To suggest I should knowingly hand over also this man who had stolen my heart was offensive to me. He further declared that Hugh must be brought to answer in parliament all charges against him.

I began to panic. I could not endure this again; this animosity that had grown between these lords towards Hugh and his father was so destructive. Would there ever be any peace? I was somewhat surprised that, on the day word was received that my orders would be ignored, Hugh had appeared before me surprisingly calm. I watched him deal with a hoard of secretaries and messengers.

"The answer is simple, my liege," he stated with a crafty grin, "I cannot answer for crimes I have not yet been accused of. Moreover, if these traitors wish a parliament, then we should invite them to discuss a date for such an occasion. Surely they cannot refuse to do that!"

I stood and pulled him towards me before kissing him on both cheeks. As usual he had known just how to control events.

It was at the beginning of May as I recall, that these traitorous lords began to attack the Welsh lands of both Hugh and the elder Despenser. These properties were plundered and laid to waste, immeasurable damage was caused. Hugh was beside himself with a mixture of fury and distress, his former calm, measured composure began to crack like ice underfoot. I remonstrated with him that all would be well, but he shrugged me off when I attempted to embrace him.

"Why can you not decide?" he shouted at me. "God's teeth, do I have to do everything?"

I should have been outraged at his violent outburst, but I reasoned that he was not himself. I could easily answer his question – yes, he did have to do everything! I could think of nothing that could be done. Even taking property and lands back into royal hands had made no difference. We had badly underestimated the resolve and hostility of Mortimer, Hereford and the others.

Hugh and I returned to Westminster. Word reached us daily about the increasing atrocities committed by the traitorous band of Marcher lords. It was claimed that buildings were burned, people slain, communities pillaged and sacked. It seemed their anger and vengeance knew no bounds. Spies, some barely escaping with their lives, reported about the increasing violence and executions of some of the king's constables.

Isabella, now heavily pregnant, voiced her obvious concerns, and did herself address her concerns to Hugh rather than me. "This anarchy cannot continue!" she almost screamed at him. "You have overreached yourself sir, you who have willingly sent your own bully-boys to intimidate, threaten, blackmail, ah yes! I have my own informants, as you do, and in the name of the king you have amassed a wealth second only to my lord himself, and would have more!"

I watched in horror at the fury of the queen's tirade, silenced as I was by the wrath and temper.

"It is you that has lit this touch paper and now you will be burnt by it. You scream, you cry, rest your head in the king's lap and beg him to make all things better for you, with more gifts, more lands - when is it enough Despenser, tell me that?"

"Enough!" I at last found my voice and I walked to where Isabella stood facing Hugh, her face red with fury.

Hugh looked shaken to the core, and I took him in my arms, he buried his face against my shoulder and shuddered.

The look my queen gave me was one of disgust. "Par Dieu et tous les saints!" she snarled through gritted teeth.

I looked at her coldly. "Leave us."

She looked aghast at the curt dismissal, but drew herself up proudly and walked slowly from the room.

+++

Of course, where there was unrest and discord against myself and Hugh. Thomas of Lancaster was never far away; whilst taking no direct part in the atrocities against the Despensers, he was undoubtedly a figurehead. His own overbearing arrogance, that had once angered many, was seemingly forgotten.

I could almost picture his glee as he helped to draw up an indenture, claiming that the Despensers had ill-advised the king, and had damaged both him and the realm. Furthermore, it was judged by Lancaster that the Marcher lords had acted for the honour of God and the king.

Meanwhile, in the Tower of London, Isabella gave birth to our fourth and final child, Joan. Despite the animosity that existed between us at the time, I was relieved that she had come through the birth safely, and the young baby was a delight to us both.

At the beginning of August, the Marchers entered the capital demanding that Hugh and his father be exiled. If the order was not given, then I would be deposed. A stalemate had been declared by my refusal to order my beloved Hugh and his father to go into exile. A wise head would be needed to settle this dilemma, and it came in the form of the queen.

Isabella came to me and, falling to her knees, begged me to see reason. "My lord husband," she implored, "I beg you - for the sake of your realm and your subjects - you must see reason. Do not endanger our children by your wish to harbour your friends. I have no love for Despenser and his father, it is true, but you may still save their lives if you agree to send them away from you."

I helped her to her feet and smiled sadly at her. How had I come to this, I asked myself? All I had wanted was to live in peace with those whom I loved best beside me. I was suddenly so tired that I had no energy to fight any more. I knew Isabella was right. We all have an instinct for self-preservation, be we king or commoner, and no doubt Isabella was clearly looking to her own future that inevitably was linked to my own. My fate was her fate, our children's fate.

After much thought, I went to Hugh. I had rarely seen this man immobile. He was forever pacing, barking orders at secretaries, constantly talking or shouting at servants. Yet now he was still, seated at a window looking out over the vast complex of Westminster. His face showed the tension and weight he had been under. "The queen spoke against me, did she not?" he uttered sadly.

I sat down next to him and took him in my arms, stroking his soft brown hair, kissing the top of his head. "She has not spoken against you my darling Hugh; she has merely stated the facts that I have ignored for too long. It must be this way – for now. You must know this for certain, I love you Hugh, I will not let you go so easily. We will be avenged, you and I. We will rise again, and none will defeat us. Never forget that."

He had begun to weep, and we held each other. Who knew when we would meet again?

I did not see Hugh again before his exile. His father came to me finally and with great bitterness - not towards me, however, or indeed the Marcher lord that had proclaimed him and his son unworthy of the high office they had enjoyed. No, the elder angrily blamed the younger. His criticism shocked me.

"Forgive me my lord, that I ever sired such a son to bring upon us this shame."

I could not bring myself to remonstrate with him; not because I agreed with his harsh words, but because I could not believe he had uttered them.

I thought then of my own father, would he be saying the very same thing? I could almost imagine him berating me for my many failures, apologising for having raised such a son as me.

+++

Bartholomew de Badlesmere was a fat, greedy and despicable man. A former mayor of London, he had been - despite my dislike of him - up until this time, a relatively loyal servant to me. He had been made steward of the royal household, and had been diligent enough in the role to be considered trustworthy. How little I really knew of the minds of men.

I had entrusted both he and my loyal friend Walter Reynolds in his capacity of archbishop of Canterbury with a mission to go to the Marchers and appeal to them to end their attacks on Hugh and, instead, lay their complaints before parliament. Walter returned alone, declaring that Badlesmere had inexplicably changed sides!

I raged at the betrayal; I had treated him well and, whilst Hugh did not like him, he had admitted that the former mayor had been proficient enough. I considered his reasoning in desertion; he was aware of Hugh's dislike of him, and had been known, on more than one occasion, to criticise him openly. He had also been angered at my elevation of my half-brother, Edmund of Woodstock, to the earldom of Kent, and his replacement of Badlesmere as constable of Dover. Nevertheless, I was furious, lashing out at anything to hand. Once my temper was spent, I sank exhausted into a seat and plotted!

I had, wisely as it turned out – placed Hugh under the protection of the sailors of the Cinque Ports. Word reached me that, far from hiding himself away in shame, Hugh had taken to piracy! The news made me laugh aloud. Only one other would have had the nerve to take to such an enterprise – had he not been so afraid of the sea, Piers Gaveston would have made a perfect pirate!

Hugh indeed enjoyed much notoriety by actually attacking and seizing two Genoese trading vessels along with their valuable cargoes!

On a warm evening in June, I arrived, cloaked and masked, at Portchester castle with my trusty Will Shene and two soldiers.

+++

Yes, Manuel, you are right, once again Will and his king undertook a clandestine mission. I have never trusted any man as much as I did Will. I recalled last night after we had parted that he had been in my service since he was a young boy. The circumstances of his appointment to serve me still a memory that I cannot recall, but in my service I grew fond of him, and in time I trusted no-one more, save for Perrot and Hugh of course. He had hailed from a small town in Oxfordshire, called Henley that sits on the great river Thames. A town I had visited myself more than once. He ran away at a young age, as I recall. I wish I had asked him more about his life. I think of him almost as much as I do Perrot and Hugh. Never was there a kinder gentler soul than Will. Anyway, I digress.

Having been hurried into the castle by a back route, I discarded my cloak; a word with the constable, who had been pre warned of my visit, and he escorted me to a set of steps leading up to the tower of the castle. The other visitor whom I had come to meet, the constable told me in a hushed tone, had already arrived.

Hugh looked better than I had expected. I greeted him warmly and held him for some moments. "I have longed for this moment my darling Hugh. I thank God that you have been brought safe to me."

He returned my kiss and smiled. "I have longed for this moment too, Edward, I pray that we will find a way past our enemies. I will not let their petty grievances tear us apart."

Will poured us both some wine and then departed. For several moments I just looked at him, as handsome and as alert as ever. He was dressed in dark green, ironically a favourite colour of my darling Perrot. His eyes sparkled with mischief and yet that did not reach his lips; his mouth was set in a straight determined line.

"You know of Badlesmere's treachery, of course?" he asked, the name uttered with barely concealed contempt.

"I know of it," I replied, "and I have a mind to trap the knave and deal a blow to the Marchers at the same time"

Hugh was at once alert. I swear he lived for the joy of intrigue; never happier than when he was plotting someone's downfall. It was a trait that carried a certain ugliness about it. I was never one to punish or to kill with little regard for human life, yet Hugh saw slights from all sides, and I could only imagine the long list he must have of those who had crossed him.

We sat and I divulged my intentions.

Hugh's eyes darted from one side to the other rapidly as he took in the details, quickly determining their merits or hazards.

"We will need the queen's help in this. Now, Hugh, don't look so dismissive. Only one other person, besides you and myself, wants to ensure that I remain safely on my throne – Isabella. Now, my plan is this; I have it on good authority that there is no affection between Badlesmere and Lancaster and, if I know my cousin, he is so rapacious for power as well as personal enrichment that he will gladly trample on Badlesmere if he is in his way, and will certainly not offer no help to him."

Hugh was looking irritated, but I continued. "Our turncoat will no doubt have already put his castles at Chilham and Leeds on alert and in a state of defence. It is with this in mind that we bring the queen in on our plan. She and I will travel, ostensibly to Canterbury, to give thanks for the safe delivery of our daughter, Joan. However, I will have the queen alter her usual return route to London, and instead divert her party to Leeds castle. I have informants who advise me that, in her husband's absence, the castle is being held by Badlesmere's wife. Now that our former London mayor is allied with Lancaster and the Marcher lords, he will I think have left instructions that no-one is to be admitted to the castle, whomever that may be, without written instructions from either himself or Lancaster. Badlesmere's wife is a feisty madam by all accounts and will be steadfast in her refusal to let anyone enter.

Here, then, is where Isabella stops to break her journey, and is refused entry. This of course is an affront to the queen and one demanding instant satisfaction. The duplicitous Badlesmere will not be aided by Lancaster, who will be only too pleased to see a way of ridding himself of an ally he does not trust. I understand there is some further animosity between them but I am not aware of its nature – nor do I care.

This will give me just cause to avenge the unpardonable insult and, in doing so, we pit the Marchers against one of their own. Remember also, my darling Hugh, that Lancaster is cousin to the queen and will be reluctant to countenance any insult to her, not that familial ties have made a difference in my case! But the queen, he respects. The Marchers leave Leeds castle to its fate and the solidarity of the Marchers is fractured."

Hugh's eyes lit up and he hugged me, it had seemed so long since he had done so, and just observing the delight on his face was worth any risk. "Will the queen comply?" he then asked.

"I believe so, yes. She is distressed about the Marcher lords and the destruction they have caused. We will endure, Hugh. I will not let them hound you out of your home, you belong with me."

He took my hand and held it up to his cheek, which felt rough from the absence of his barber.

I stayed for as long as was possible. It seemed no time at all since we had kissed and had lain in each others arms. I was determined that I would not let the same thing happen to Hugh as had occurred with Piers. How broken-hearted I had been when Perrot and I had last been together, I recalled the drawbridge at Scarborough castle when I had turned to see him one last time, only to find he had gone. I felt sick to my stomach, I could not face that again.

It came time for me to leave, and I assured Hugh all would be well and I would keep him informed of developments, even though I was fairly certain that his army of informants were not idle on his behalf - whilst he still had money to pay them, of course.

Will and I rode away from Portchester later that evening, and for the first time in weeks I felt optimistic about the future.

+++

Isabella had listened to the plan I had devised and, being the daughter of a French king who had been wilier than the most cunning fox, she at once considered the ramifications and seemed more than willing to enter into the intrigue. Whether she was aware that I had met with Hugh, I don't know. She looked at me with suspicion in her eyes, but said nothing. My queen knew me well enough to know that I would not have entered into this scheme without trusting Hugh with the details. She waited until I had finished explaining my plans, and a sad smile crossed her lips.

I asked what amused her.

"How strange, Edward, that you can be so strong and decisive when one close to you is concerned."

I knew she meant 'when one of your favourite friends is in danger'.

"Why could you not always act with such cunning and resolve, with such calm, measured control?"

The plan worked far better than I could have hoped, despite the deaths of several of the queen's escort. Isabella's party had approached the castle, her servant going on ahead to make the courteous demand that the queen would be requiring accommodation for herself and her party.

Lady Badlesmere, however, instructed the messenger to return to his mistress and report that her admittance would not be possible.

Isabella had sent armed guards to the castle with the intention of breaching the drawbridge. The small company were then fired at by a shower of arrows, leaving several of them dead.

The chatelaine repeated that she had been instructed to admit no-one, commoner or queen!

Isabella was always a consummate actress, and I smiled to imagine her feigned horror at the impertinence.

Upon Isabella's return, I made known my intention to avenge the great insult of the queen. I had little trouble in raising a force. We attacked Leeds castle and I had Badlesmere's wife taken and imprisoned in the Tower of London - somewhat cruel, I suppose, given that our plan had relied on her being bold enough to refuse her queen entry. As expected, the Marcher lords made no effort to come to the aid of Leeds castle and the day was won handsomely.

Inevitably of course, conflict between the Marcher lords and myself could not be avoided, and Lancaster was already uncoiling like a snake; he had summoned the Marcher lords and others to compile a petition, again detailing the crimes of Hugh and his father and accusing them of encouraging me to attack the lords and appropriate their lands. I was also accused of not censuring the younger's blatant piracy.

I read the petition with disgust. Hereford, Roger Mortimer of Wigmore and others had affixed their seals to it, but it reeked of Thomas of Lancaster's vitriol. Every line I read, I pictured my cousin joy at my discomfort.

To my great joy, I issued an official safe conduct for Hugh to return from exile, and it was with open arms that I received him. I admit I still felt piqued by his father's condemnation of Hugh, and opted spitefully to delay his recall until later in the month.

I had rarely faced such good fortune as I did by Christmas of that year, and events unfolded rapidly. My great friend and archbishop of Canterbury, Walter Reynolds, summoned, in my name, a council meeting to address a document prepared by Hugh that detailed the legal flaws in the judgement to exile him. Several of the bishops did not attend, either from fear of retribution or because they saw no fault in the exile. The consensus being that the exile was in fact invalid and should therefore be annulled.

As further proof that events were at last turning in my favour, I was enjoying not only the support of the earls Surrey, Arundel, Richmond, Kent, Norfolk and Pembroke, but additionally all bar a few bishops. Now, surely, was the time to capitalise on a position of strength, and I had rarely felt as elated as when my supporters and I headed out of London towards Cirencester, where I was to spend a surprisingly peaceful Christmas.

Time alone would test the strength and resolve of the treacherous Marcher lords and their associates. The rebels were continuing to rampage indiscriminately; they had seized Gloucester thereby controlling the bridge over the Severn, in many commanders' eyes a position of strength. Yet the Marchers chose to flee and continue up river, burning all the bridges to hinder my advance. Such action forced us to make for Shrewsbury where we could again effect a crossing.

Word reached me that the Marchers were beginning to despair of being joined by Lancaster's forces. Despite making some important gains, cracks began in the solidarity of the Marcher lords and, to my greatest delight, Roger Mortimer of Wigmore and his uncle, Mortimer of Chirk, requested safe passage to come and to treat with the earls.

I could almost have danced with glee at the news. On one particular point, however, I was adamant - Badlesmere was to be excluded from all guarantees of safety. My personal dislike of the man did, I think, cloud my judgement somewhat, but I could afford sentiment only so far. I knew also, of course, that he could expect no assistance from Lancaster, so he was thus completely isolated.

I had both Mortimers imprisoned in the Tower of London, and in doing so I made probably my biggest mistake. I should have had their heads impaled on spikes on the ramparts of their own castles. As time was to prove so cruelly, I had once again allowed sentiment to cloud good judgement.

I was never a ruthless man; how much better a king would I have been if I had been so? Who is to say? My father was a harsh man, one who allowed no sentiment with his enemies and whose reputation for cruelty was well known.

Many have called me weak in so many ways. Better men than I will come to judge my weakness and my sins.

So, the Mortimers under lock and key, enemies fleeing in droves, desperate, defeated traitors throwing themselves at my mercy, and yet the real prize still evaded me.

I had dined at supper one evening whilst at Shrewsbury - my guests were both my half brothers, Edmund, earl of

Kent - the younger of the two - and Thomas, earl of Norfolk, a year older. We had seldom been together, and yet I was fond of them and had ennobled them as their rank demanded. Will entered with a man I knew as Oliver. The man had been a most valuable informant, and had served me well in the past. Whatever news he brought me would be worth knowing.

Both my brothers had tact enough to move from the table and engaged the musicians in conversation.

I listened to what Oliver had to say, although I had him repeat his information, such was its importance.

"This can be proved beyond a doubt?" I asked him.

Oliver gave me all necessary assurances, by handing to me a cachet of letters.

I trembled slightly as I nervously undid the ties. I read quickly, desperate to take in as much as I could as soon as possible. A covering letter from the sender, William Melton, archbishop of York, gave me the gist of what I held in my hands.

Oliver and I conversed quietly before he bowed low. I took a pouch from my belt, but rather than count any coins, I simply gave him the whole velvet purse. He was astounded, although I always paid well for such news as this. He bowed again, and Will showed him out.

My brothers drifted back to the dining table, and looked at me quizzically.

"Edward?" Kent spoke quietly. "Your grace, is aught the matter?"

I looked up at both of them with a beaming smile. "I have, my dear brothers, been handed the rope with which I will hang the earl of Lancaster!"

+++

The archbishop had informed me that there was clear evidence that my cousin Thomas was exchanging treasonable correspondence with the Scots. The letters he had come by, although he did not elaborate on how he had taken possession of them, were proof in Thomas's own hand - in one instance - that the earl was in close contact with the Scottish earl of Moray and Sir James Douglas. Some of the letters may well have been copies, but their veracity was plain for all to see.

The Scots were never far from intrigue but I had not given them too much thought whilst I had my own problems. It had certainly been true that there had been a new slew of raids and attacks, but it was just like the Scots to take advantage of any civil unrest in the kingdom of their neighbour.

I had the letters read publicly. Just days later I captured my cousin's castle at Kenilworth. Advancing on Lancaster's tail, I pursued him relentlessly, while he and the other remaining Marchers fled to the relative safety of his much loved stronghold at Pontefract.

+++

Snow covered much of England in that year of thirteen hundred and twenty-two; the picturesque Priory at Tutbury seemed to be sleeping, waking only as my horse came to a stop at the gates.

I nodded at the two horsemen who accompanied me, to wait, and I dismounted. The icy snow crackled underfoot as I walked, pulling my thick woollen hood further down over my face in an effort to stem the bitterly cold wind that whistled around this modest Benedictine monastery. I was met by one of the brothers who bowed low and asked me to follow him; he had been informed why I had come.

I could hear soft voices at praise. My nose was assailed by all manner of scents; vellum, incense and candle smoke. My guide's sandals slapped against the highly-polished stone floor as we descended down a small flight of steps. We came to a door which the brother opened before stepping to one side. Once I had entered, he bowed his head and left.

The chamber was dimly lit. A small brazier provided the only warmth, such as it was. I removed my hood and stepped over to the figure lying in a small cot bed beneath a wooden crucifix.

Roger Damory began to weep upon seeing me, but I silenced him with a hand to his lips. "I am heartbroken to see you thus, Roger, injured from the fighting. I am told you grow stronger under the ministrations of these monks."

I lied, of course, but Roger gave a weak smile.

"Your grace," he croaked, "I was injured badly, I do not hope where there is none. I will die, but I prayed to God that I could see you one last time before the end."

I began to feel uneasy; he looked so pathetic, so small and frail. It seemed sinful in such a place to recall his dazzling smile, where now there were dried, bloodied lips, his once muscular, athletic body now almost a shrunken husk. I studied the once handsome face that had enchanted me so much, but which was now sickly and drawn.

"You betrayed me, Roger," I said, as sternly as I could, but unsure of why I felt guilty.

"Your grace," he began, "Edward, forgive me. I know you have commuted my death sentence, but the shame I will bring on my wife, your niece... I would to God that I could go back and undo all that I did in error and greed. Commend me to my wife and child. Thank you, my liege, for the love you bore me that I so easily cast aside. I shall not leave this place alive, but to have seen you one last time before the end will ease my journey into wherever I am fated to go after this wretched life."

I could not help the tears that coursed down my face. As angry and betrayed as I had felt towards Roger, I had laughed often with him and enjoyed happier times. I knew it was pointless to promise him anything. How different things could have been. He was the first person I had become close to after Perrot and, whilst a poor comparison, he had been faithful to me once. For his own ends? Yes, I did not doubt it then, nor do I now, but I knew enough to realise it was a fine line between love and hate.

"First there is trust, then regret then death." Piers's words ingrained on my memory haunting me afresh.

I had not noticed at first, when Roger moved his frail hand towards me, but I looked at him and he stared straight ahead.

"Edward, I cannot see, the light is fading now. Please don't let me die alone."

I held his hand in mine and kissed it, even as it went limp. I looked at him again and his now lifeless eyes continued to stare. I sobbed there at his bedside for some time before I gently placed his hand across his chest, then leant down and kissed him. In God's name, why was I always saying goodbye?

+++

I formally declared Thomas of Lancaster and those Marchers that had not yet surrendered to be traitors. It was also then to my great delight that Hugh returned to me, and together we welcomed Lancaster who had finally been taken the day before in the splendour of his beloved Pontefract castle.

Thomas was brought before myself, Hugh and the other lords that had joined my forces. His black hair was no longer held back but hung in greasy strands down his ashen face. I had him dressed humiliatingly in the same uniform as his squires; for a man as proud as my cousin the indignity could get no worse. He looked as rough and shabby as I had insisted he should be. No shave, no wash, no clean garments, no jewels.

Then he was read the lengthy indictment that sealed his fate and sentenced him. "Am I not to be allowed to say anything in my own defence?" he protested weakly.

I could sit looking at him no longer. I rose and, smiling, I walked over and stood before him – I, at last, the victor. He had thought that I would allow him a hearing? I smiled and whispered to him, "You can have the same opportunity you afforded the earl of Cornwall - or had you forgotten?"

An attempt at defiance was soon abandoned, as he made one last attempt to save his own life. "Ned, forgive me…please!"

I looked upon him then, with disgust, and directed my voice over my shoulder to the attending lords. "We will afford my cousin a final act of kindness. He will not be hung or drawn. His beheading will take place where I have stipulated, facing towards Scotland." I cast him one last look of triumph and walked from the hall.

Thomas of Lancaster, that great lord, Ordainer and vile traitor was taken, bare-footed with his arms tied behind his back, out to a small hump of scrubland outside the walls of the castle, and beheaded after six blows from a blunt axe.

+++

Manuel Fieschi permitted himself a brief smile; Brother Alphage must surely be weary from sketching so many crosses at Edward as his tale continued to unfold. Alphage certainly found much of the revelations difficult to hear.

Edward for his part, would narrate his story and then be silent for a while, as though digesting his own words, in the hope that he could expunge the events by reliving them. From thinking that he would find difficulty in recalling events from so long ago, he found a surprising clarity. Sadness at a great deal of his history, but delight in recalling other moments that he had enjoyed.

Alphage did not note any particular shock or surprise by Fieschi at Edward's discourse. He would at times pose a question, or ask the hermit to repeat or elaborate at various times. His countenance remained controlled, and a sage nod of his head on occasions suggested that he absorbed every detail. He would certainly have much to relate to his holiness the pope.

"So," Fieschi summed up, "your enemies were now thoroughly defeated?"

Edward smiled at him. "You surely are aware of enough of my past to know that was not the case. I would to God that all threats had now been thwarted, but of course, I would have been the most fortunate king England ever had if that was the truth." He rubbed his face with his hands and breathed in the soft pungent air of the herbalist's workshop.

The hot sun was not yet at its zenith, and Edward remained sitting in the doorway, turning his face upwards with closed eyes, and sighed again as though drawing power from its relentless heat.

"Nevertheless," Manuel continued, "the immediate danger had been thwarted, had it not?"

"To a large degree, yes," Edward admitted. "There are always dark shadows, waiting in the wings of this very public stage. I had Hugh back with me, and that was my main concern. Together with him, I punished where necessary and, it has to be said - to my eternal shame - not always fairly. Hugh was disappointed that I had commuted the judgement of execution against both the Mortimers to one of life imprisonment. This being done for the ridiculously sentimental reason that Mortimer of Wigmore had been liked by Piers, and he had been a friend to both of us back then. Hugh despised him above all others and remonstrated with me that to imprison rather than execute them was a costly mistake. Time of course would bear out his words, and I would live to regret my sentiment and compassion."

+++

I take no pleasure from my treatment of the prisoners we took during that time, and yet my spite overcame my reasoning. Whilst I may have dealt leniently with some, others paid far more of a price than maybe they should have. I had wives imprisoned, sometimes giving a pittance for their care, not considering if this caused families to be split up and children to be orphaned.

The despicable Bartholomew Badlesmere was taken to Canterbury, from where I had him dragged three miles to the village of Blean; there, he was hung and then beheaded. Despite commuting the sentence of death against the Mortimers, I had Wigmore's wife imprisoned also.

I had wept at the death bed of Roger Damory, yet I had no compunction at all in taking vengeance on his widow, Elizabeth – and she my own niece! She had been captured finally at Usk in Wales, and I had her taken to Barking Abbey where I insisted she was to remain close-confined. I should have heeded the whispers of discontent that began as my niece was then forced to exchange her lordship of Usk, with Hugh, for Gower. I thereafter bequeathed all crops, animals and goods in both Usk and Gower to my favourite and his wife.

Many others I had imprisoned or executed. Despite any reservations I may have had, the law was the law and punishments could not always be merely based on my personal choice. Yet I regret that many paid a heavy price for their treachery.

Retribution however, could take other forms, and Hugh suggested that we might allow some that had lost property to buy it back - a most profitable enterprise! In many instances, of course, we merely returned property to its rightful owner after it had been misappropriated by Lancaster.

I showered my beloved Hugh with more estates, manors, castles and titles. He claimed the latter mattered little, and his reward was to have been reunited with me. I declare I loved him more each day. Hugh's father and my close adherent was created earl of Winchester, and I gladly personally carried out the girding with the belt that signified this new status, much to his pride and delight.

With my victory over the great lords complete, there was little left to do but finally revoke the Ordinances that had been hatefully forced on me.

+++

It was fair to say, by this period, that I had spent lavishly on much that I should not have! I liked to think I was a generous king - I was aware that I rewarded more richly than was prudent, and spontaneously too! Those who served me well and were loyal received the benefits, and some grew very rich on them. It was therefore both surprising and extremely fortunate that, by the time I had rid myself of Thomas of Lancaster and appropriated much wealth from those Marcher lords, the country's finances were in a far better state than when I had ascended the throne. For one who had generally spent far more than I could afford to, the knowledge that - far from being in debt - the kingdom was once again solvent was, a source of great pride to me. In fact, had I never made the error of taking on the Scots at Bannockburn – a costly venture in every sense - I would indeed have been enjoying a wealth probably unsurpassed.

The accumulation of such riches, however, resulted in my becoming miserly. Hugh and I, and indeed those closest to me at court, continued to live well - and why not! Hugh's expenses were many, and his love and valuable company rendered him first and foremost in using the wealth at our disposal.

Of course, there were many that resented Hugh's wealth, as always anyone close to their king is hated and jealousy is rife.

As I sit here now in this most remote monastery, a lifetime away from England, I recall wealth as ultimately doing more harm than good. There is something ennobling about having nothing but the shirt on one's back. Yet, hindsight is something that does not come until it is too late. How would I have acted differently? Even now, I have no answer for that.

However, there was little that I did not exploit after those who had compiled those treacherous Ordinances fell from their lofty heights. Extortion and exploitation are ugly words, but in reality what else could describe the process of the accumulation of the vast wealth that Hugh and I enjoyed?

Hugh was becoming more important and dear to me with each passing day, and yet his mastery of the running of affairs astounded me. Many thought that the 'methods' that Hugh employed to have his way and to make money quickly and easily were unknown to me, yet they were not.

When I play those memories in my head, as I have so many times, Hugh may well be labelled as a rogue, extortionist, pirate - any of those would have suited him well, yet I loved him and, as with Piers, I could not exist without him. When he was away from court, I longed for his return. When I was aware of any discourtesy toward him, I punished those who were its source.

Hugh grew in confidence, assured, quite correctly, that I held him in unprecedented esteem. Yet something troubled him. I lay lazily one morning, watching him at his desk. Secretaries bustled in and out, some were shouted at, others dismissed without even speaking. He dressed in a costly fashion, a dark red tunic, slashed at the sleeves in yellow. His fingers were heavy with jewelled rings of gold. A gold chain inset with rubies hung around his neck. He looked exquisite. On his return from exile, I had believed him tired and stressed with worry; yet now in the glory of our victory, he seemed rejuvenated.

This day, however, he seemed much troubled. We had enjoyed some peaceful time at Langley when I had insisted that Hugh be separated from the constant letters, secretaries and other servants that seemed to continually surround him. We had ridden and now sat under the shade of a large oak tree, leaning against its solid trunk. He lay in my arms, and I felt so relaxed and happy. I had nearly drifted off into a lazy doze, when he spoke.

"Your grace – Edward?"

I uttered, "Yes?" in the midst of yawning lazily.

"Your grace, I am much troubled, and I believe I must leave court."

I was at once alert. The very idea horrified me. "Leave? But why? What troubles you?"

He seemed to be having a problem with explaining himself; Hugh was the most self assured man I had ever known, yet in a different way to Piers. Where my Gascon brother used a quick wit and a dagger-sharp tongue, Hugh was not as humorous and lacked subtlety. His was a blunt manner, and yet, as I was to reflect on many occasions since those later days of my reign, he was most adept at conspiring and dissimilating; where darling Perrot was far too lazy to plot and scheme, my darling Hugh was at his best in the cut and thrust of his machinations.

"My liege," he turned away as though ashamed of what he was about to say, "it is the queen."

I must have seemed and appeared like a dolt, for his words meant nothing to me. "Hugh, look at me, what about the queen." I had my hand gently resting on his shoulder, turning him slightly until he looked at me squarely.

"Your grace, I believe she speaks ill of me, indeed my own wife has been in her company when she has done so. It is said that she conspires to have me removed from your side. Some of the magnates, that we have worked so hard to bring over to our side, now secretly plot my downfall. If I am no longer needed by you, or indeed, the queen, then allow me permission to retire to my estates where...."

I cut him off, pulling him earnestly to me, the horror of his words made me feel suddenly sick to my stomach. What would I do if he left me now? I could not face the thought of life without him. We had been through so much. I had suffered Perrot being torn from me, I could not do it again, I could not give back the love I had for him. I held him in my arms and kissed him, tenderly at first, and then with more urgency. "Say you won't leave me Hugh, say it!"

He paused. "Your grace, I could not bear to be the cause of any discord between you and the queen, whom I love dearly as you know."

"No, Hugh, I will not let you go; I will speak to the queen, we shall make this right. How dare she try to meddle in affairs of which she knows nothing? I swear that, of late, she has become something of a harridan - she moans, she criticises. I can well believe she speaks ill of *me*, her husband and lord. The Leeds castle plot that we devised was a stroke of genius on our part, she played but a minor role in its execution, and now sees fit to advise me about policy."

"I have heard also, my lord, that her letters to her brother, the French king, are most frequent. Perish the thought that they contain any damaging revelations. The French are only too happy to meddle in your grace's affairs, be they private or not."

"I am greatly disturbed by this, Hugh. Can it truly be that the queen is no longer to be trusted?"

My beloved looked at me cautiously; I could sense an idea forming in his head. His eyes moved rapidly from side to side, a clear indication that he was considering a problem and had already formed a solution to it.

"I wonder, your grace, whether it might be prudent to watch her grace the queen more closely for a time. I would never suggest for one moment that she can no longer be trusted, but remember, my liege, your enemies are everywhere. Those that are on our side today, may hold a dagger to our throats tomorrow. I swear that I do not think of the danger to myself, but Edward, you know I could not bear to see you in peril. Your wisdom and statecraft have won us a famous victory over Lancaster and the Marcher lords. I worry that – unwittingly, her grace the queen may put her trust in unscrupulous men."

He was right, of course, although we had turned defeat into victory, it was folly to believe things would remain that way. I thanked God that I had this faithful lover who considered me in all things, I could never let him go, I would not let him go. I felt angry now that Isabel may well be jeopardising all I had achieved.

I was aware that she had no liking for Hugh and would be only too willing to speak ill of him. Well, she should have a care about into whose ear she happily dripped her venomous words.

"Promise me, Hugh, promise me you will not go. I live only for your love and affection. Stay with me, please!" I was on the verge of tears.

Hugh faced me then and I stroked the side of his handsome face gently, and would have kissed him, but he rose at the exact same moment. "Your grace, we must devise a way of knowing exactly who the queen talks to and what she says. Her attendants are with her always, and my idea is a simple one. I will instruct my wife, Eleanor, to join her grace's household and pay particular attention to her correspondence, who she gossips with and who holds her favour."

I could at once see the good sense in Hugh's suggestion; my niece had proved to be a good and true wife to Hugh. As my niece, she also had a family bond with her king and queen.

"Furthermore, your grace, it may be prudent to take back some of the queen's properties into your own hands, just as a precaution you understand."

By this time, once I knew the danger of Hugh leaving the court, I was tiring of the details of how Isabella's behaviour would be scrutinised. "Well let it be done Hugh, whatever you think best. Now, sit with me again, we will be searched for soon enough!"

Hugh sat down next to me again. I kissed the side of his neck tenderly, but he stared ahead with a smile on his face. I swear he was barely aware of my caresses.

+++

Even I could not be totally blinded to my dearest's dubious practices and neither, it appeared, could Isabella. The queen came to me one day. Hugh had been due to return to court after a visit to Gloucester to deal with some personal affairs. When the queen entered, asking if I would dismiss the musicians and courtiers surrounding me, I reluctantly agreed. After sighing deeply at the pinched expression on her face, I waved those present out of the chamber and sat down, as did she.

"Well, my dear, what ails you? Isabella sat upright, with her small delicate hands folded on her lap.

"My dearest Edward, husband," she began in an abrasive tone "I have seen little of you for some days; I thought we may talk."

"Of course," I replied cheerily, realising at once what the subject to be discussed would be.

"I am to have a new guardian, I understand - your niece, Eleanor."

"Your niece too, my dear," I answered brightly.

Isabella's fingers began to drum on the arm of her chair, a sure sign of her irritation and petulance. "I was not consulted about this. Why not?" Her voice was growing louder as her bubbling annoyance threatened to break out into a furious outburst.

I stopped smiling. It had taken my fiery-tempered queen less than a heartbeat to be on the verge of dramatic hysteria. I attempted to gain the moral high ground, at least, and smiled at her again. "Eleanor was most pleased at the appointment - she is so fond of you; she has served you for many years, has she not?"

"Not as head of my household, one that even carries my seal" "You dislike her wish to serve you?"

"I dislike being spied upon!" she retorted angrily.

"You see threats when none are there, Isabella, she is not there to spy upon you, but to help and comfort you."

"The only comfort I lack is from my husband, I would be more than content with that!" she snapped back waspishly. Her manner was beginning to anger me.

"Isabella, our households change as they must, you know that. Changes are not always comfortable, but they are done with the best intentions."

"But I was not consulted - why? Or shall I tell you why? Because Hugh le Despenser wishes it so. Can you do nothing that does not involve that man? He is at your side all the time. You visit our children so seldom that they don't know who you are, yet you break your fast with him, you pet him like he is a little dog. His false manner that you seem to find so beguiling is making you look ridiculous. All the court laughs behind your back."

I was determined not to exchange harsh words when so many outside the chamber would no doubt hear them. "Let them laugh Isabella, I care not."

"What of me? Am I not tainted with this court jester also, as your wife?"

"I will not argue with you, Isabella. Lady Despenser stays and that is an end to it. If you wish to remain on good terms with me then you will treat her well."

"And what of Despenser's greed? Are you not aware of how much wealth he has amassed? He is second only to you as the richest man in the land! How much more property he can own would appear to be his continual aim in life. Whose lands will you give him next, I wonder."

"Yours, Isabella!"

She looked as though I had struck her, her cheeks flushed an angry red and she gasped, "You would not dare....!"

"I do dare, madam, because I am the king in this realm."

"But I am the queen!"

"You are a subject, lady."

When I had later calmed down from her vitriol, I cursed myself for my words, but much is said in the heat of the moment that we later regret.

Isabella stood slowly, her mouth pinched, her eyes cold, her expression one of loathing and hatred. I was about to be more consolatory, as we had both said more than we aught, but she turned and swiftly marched to the chamber door which she flung open, causing it to slam against the wall behind it.

If Isabella and I were to be at war, I believed I had just made the initial attack.

+++

Soon after, I made another ill-fated campaign to Scotland, the last I would make. The results were more catastrophic than previously, and it is to my eternal shame that not only was the battle lost, but there was also a considerable amount of booty for the victorious

Bruce. The Scots invaded England as far as Yorkshire, and were, at one point, a mere 15 miles from where I was at Rievaulx abbey. I had no choice other than to flee before the Scots captured me and, in the haste, it had been necessary to abandon all my treasured plate, costly trappings, even the harness off my own horse and - most concerning – my privy seal! All left behind for the Scots to gloat over. My jester took great amusement in singing that the Scots were as familiar with the seal as I was!

Fleeing was really the only option. God help me I was never a fighter, but I was no coward. Had it not been expedient to flee, then I would have faced the Scots again and fought as I had done at Bannockburn. Faced with an advancing army and less than a hundred men, I would undoubtedly have been taken, and I was a prize Bruce could only have imagined capturing.

I fled first to Bridlington priory, then on to Burstwick, and then finally to York, whilst still being pursued by the Scots.

By now, I was increasingly concerned for Isabella. I had sent the queen on to the priory at Tynemouth, which, situated on a fortified headland overlooking the North Sea, seemed a safe haven, but a place that was now effectively behind enemy lines. My concerns were mollified when news arrived that a group of the queen's squires had purloined a boat and, with the Scots snapping at their heels, a group of them - with the queen and Hugh's wife, Eleanor - took to the sea and escaped; according to Isabella, later, by the mercy of God.

+++

Any news regarding Scotland and the continuous raids on northern England continued to cause me the greatest concern. Particularly galling was news of a presumptuous act of treason carried out by the earl of Carlisle, Andrew de Harclay. Harclay had, according to Hugh's spies, grown increasingly frustrated by our policy regarding our Scottish neighbours, and taken it upon himself to remedy the situation.

I was incensed to be told that Harclay had made his own truce with Robert the Bruce. These being that I would recognise Bruce as king, and in effect declaring Scotland as a separate nation, making its own laws and customs. If this was accepted within the space of twelve months, Bruce would pay to us the amount of forty thousand marks in ten annual instalments. Furthermore, I could choose a bride from my own family to wed Bruce's heir, a laughable consolation considering that Bruce had no heir at the time.

Hugh and I were furious; I, of course, repudiated the treaty he had made. Hugh quite rightly urged me to take the most brutal action in declaring Harclay a traitor and, indeed, making an example of him that would leave no doubt that independent treaties were on no account to be made by anyone but I.

"Your grace," Hugh urged me, "this must be dealt with by firm action, the man is a traitor and should be treated as one. I am appalled by his treachery; the might of the crown must be brought to bear on this knave or we shall have anarchy."

"What do you suggest, dearest Hugh? I declare I am heartily sick of Scotland - advise me, as you always do; I shall abide by your decision. Just let it be done - and soon."

Retribution was swift and brutal, one that would haunt me, even to this day. Harclay was hanged, drawn and quartered. His head was impaled on a pike on London bridge as a warning. Hugh wisely suggested London bridge, given that the city had, in the past, acted contrary to commands.

Nevertheless, something had to be done; negotiations were strained and difficult. Hugh and I insisted that we would not recognise Bruce as king. In the end a thirteen-year truce was agreed with the Scots' leader being referred to as Sir Bruce.

I was heartily sick of uprisings, plots and counterplots, and I began to see traitors and mischief where none existed. The only constant in my life was Hugh. I knew he was, as Isabella had said, the wealthiest man in England after myself. He deserved all of it, such was his devotion to me and his desire to see a safe and organised kingdom. Whatever I was blinded to at the time, suggested that he had merely been carried away in his zealous desire to see the kingdom well-managed and orderly. It is to my shame, of course, that I was happier to remain a figurehead, rather than make the decisions that I found difficult.

Several matters concerning pope John were entrusted to a Dominican monk that I had dealt with on other occasions. Thomas Dunheved was a loyal servant and would deal efficiently with the letters I gave him. The pope was growing ever more alarmed by news from England. He had often given advice or offered to send mediators during the times of great tension and, although I was frustrated at his refusal to rid me of certain meddlesome bishops, I valued his wisdom. Thomas returned with assurances from Avignon, that

John would do all he could to help, but urged caution in my trust of those upon whom I 'bestowed great favour'.

Enclosed with his documents and letters was a packet that I was to open but not mention to another living soul. I was intrigued and sought some privacy as I unrolled the pack. Inside was a velvet pouch and I withdrew from it a single gold coin; but no ordinary coin; it bore the special papal insignia. The note attached with it simply read that this was John's personal seal. If I should ever need him or his help I was to send this to him and he would be assured, it had come from myself and no other. I smiled and admitted to a feeling of immense gratitude to a man I had never met, but who had, in the main, kept faith with me. I had no idea then how useful the gold coin would be to me in time to come.

Word reached Hugh and I from his wife, Eleanor, in her capacity as head of Isabella's household, and its subject was one that caused us the greatest concern. It appeared that the queen had, for some time, been in correspondence with the treasurer, asking on behalf of Joan Mortimer, the wife of Roger Mortimer of Wigmore, that the money allocated for sustenance be promptly made. Joan had been under house arrest, and Roger - of course - lodged in the Tower, kept imprisoned for the remainder of his life.

One evening we played dice in front of a roaring fire, its logs crackling and spitting. I had a great fondness for fire, another strange facet of my personality, to be sure. I think it is the ability of the flames to draw one in, an almost mesmerising delight.

Hugh was concerned, although I failed to see a problem with it, that the queen and Mortimer's wife were distantly related. Hugh clearly wanted to discuss this latest revelation, and ordered the servants out of the chamber. Once they were gone, he got up and poured me some more wine, and then stood behind my chair and proceeded to massage my shoulders. The relief was instant, and I luxuriated in the manipulation of the tension I was only aware I had when he worked his long fingers against my neck and scalp. I closed my eyes and moaned at the delicious sensations.

"Your grace, Edward, we should think wisely about Roger Mortimer."

"Mmmm, yes, I suppose you are right; but tomorrow, let us not think about it now."

"I sense danger in this correspondence," he persisted.

"Danger? What danger can there be in Isabella's urging the treasurer to act more promptly? You worry too much, my love. You see danger in everything."

Hugh was not to be put off so easily. "What if, somehow, the queen is in contact with Wigmore? What if there is more here than merely a letter for funds?"

I opened my eyes slightly. The wine and warmth were, with Hugh's probing into my neck and shoulders, making me sleepily relaxed.

"Have you not thought, my beloved, that Isabella will suspect that your wife has reported this fact to you and I?"

"I have indeed been thinking on it," he said quietly. "We will allay any concerns the queen may have by instructing Eleanor to also write to the treasurer the exact same request - a simple concern for the Wigmore witch and her brood. No, your grace, my real concern is the lady's husband. Do you not think you were more merciful than is prudent in commuting his death sentence?"

"I had not given it a great deal of thought. You are my eyes in all things, Hugh. You see, within the shadows, the dark objects that I ignore."

Hugh chuckled softly. "I am ever your grace's most humble servant. I, of course, want only what is best for everyone. You are too kind a king. You treat your enemies too well - more so than your father, I think."

I certainly could not disagree with that. My father would have taken far more heads than I. "So, what is your plan for Mortimer? Do you suggest we banish him from the realm?"

Hugh dug his fingers sharply into my flesh. I winced. "Forgive me, Edward. As far as Mortimer is concerned, I think we should revisit his crimes and his sentence. Something tells me he is too dangerous to keep alive."

By this time, I was again in a state of total euphoria. I drank down the contents of my goblet, feeling its effects, and I could feel myself falling more deeply into a relaxed stupor, but Hugh was still talking about Mortimer - at least, I think he was. "Well, if you think it best, my darling boy, then we must reconsider. I have no great opinion of the man, and if he is potentially as dangerous as you say…well…whatever you think Hugh, whatever you think."

Hugh soothed his hands down the nape of my neck and after that I fell into a blissful slumber.

+++

I stood looking in disbelief at the courier who stood nervously before me. The message from Hugh had been short and to the point and could not have been worse: Roger Mortimer had escaped from the Tower of London.

Scarcely believing what I was reading, I grabbed the wretch who delivered this unfortunate missive and threw him to the ground. The startled man got to his feet and stood back, far from my reach. I upturned a small table sending flying a wine jug, goblets, a book, as my rage took hold. Will, my servant, grabbed the messenger by the arm and pushed him towards the chamber door, from where he made a hasty escape. I drew my dagger from my belt and proceeded to slash angrily at a tapestry hanging on one wall next to me. I knelt on the floor and gnawed at my knuckles until the blood began to flow from them. A frequent response to bad news was in danger of becoming habitual.

After some time, I at last fell still, my furious outburst now spent; I allowed Will to help me to a chair. He then fetched a small bowl of water and, with a linen napkin, dabbed at the blood on my hands. He retrieved my dagger from where I had left it stuck in the in the complex tapestry fabric. He called two servants, instructing them to take down the slashed material and remove it.

After that he poured me some watered wine, and quietly left.

I sat alone for some time. I had been a fool to have spared Mortimer his life. Hugh was right, of course - I should have condemned him to death rather than spare him. I wrote back to Hugh that Mortimer was to be pursued with all haste, although I suspected correctly that my clever Despenser would have surely already instigated an alert to all ports. Mortimer was to be captured – dead or alive!

Mortimer had, it was discovered, been helped to escape by the deputy constable of the Tower, Gerard d'Alspaye who drugged the constable and the guards during their dinner. The deputy then unlocked Mortimer's cell and together they made their way to the kitchens and let themselves down the outer wall with a rope, taking a waiting boat and setting out on the Thames to safety and freedom.

Of course, there had to have been outside contacts. Correspondence was simple enough to exchange, and clearly there had been much of it. London was on alert, but I knew I could expect little help from the fickle citizens of the capital. I had never been popular in London, unlike Isabella, who was often cheered when she travelled through the city. I was apparently despised less than my darling Hugh, who had even been spat at, after which I insisted that he not travel without an armed escort.

Why did they not realise what a fine servant to England he was? Instead they sniped at every reward he was given for his loyal service. He had walked outside Westminster one day, and some arrogant youths had pulled down their britches and bared their arses to him! I had consoled him of course, telling him that the peasants in London were fools and would, in time, pay for their insolence.

By the time I had returned to the capital, word had reached us that Mortimer and several others had taken a ship and escaped to France. Hugh suggested that we should instruct Isabella to write at once to her brother the French king, requesting his help in apprehending the villain and returning him to us in chains!

Isabella, surprisingly, seemed to be reluctant to get involved in the matter. Hugh and I sent for her and, when she arrived, she was far from pleased that she had not just answered a summons from her husband but also from his 'shadow', as she liked to term Hugh. She too would pay for her impertinence in time. Hugh made no effort to rise from his seat when the queen entered, although she looked haughtily at him, clearly expecting him to do so. Her cheeks flushed slightly and her eyes flashed in anger, yet she said nothing. I did however glance at Hugh, who, correctly interpreting my look, rose to his feet.

"My dear," I began, "we would have you write to your brother in France and use your influence with him, to seek out the traitorous Roger Mortimer, who, we have reliable word, has fled there."

Isabella cleared her throat. "What makes you think he would listen to me? I have very little standing these days in our own court let alone his. I have no great desire to become involved in this. Surely the name of Despenser carries with it far more weight?"

Hugh smiled without the least hint of pleasure or amusement. "Perhaps your grace is reluctant to aid the traitor Mortimer's capture, although I cannot think one as loyal as the queen could wish his grace's enemies to prosper."

"Quite so," Isabella replied. She and Hugh were now facing each other, and I realised that I was becoming a bystander in this potentially ugly confrontation. "I understand the prisoner was to have been close-confined, and yet, my lord, he was allowed to escape?"

"The escape was aided from friends within and outside the Tower. We are merely acting to capture him again, and this time there will be no mercy shown. You may wish to tell him that should you have cause to write to him. Isabella looked furious, and even I had to glance with Hugh at this statement which was bordering on insolence.

"You accuse me of corresponding with Mortimer? Me, the queen?"

"Madam, I am merely suggesting that he may contact you discretely for some aid, perhaps through his wife. We wish only that you would help us before you, inadvertently, help him." This appeared to be as much as Isabella could endure, and she turned to me almost with a snarl.

"How long, Edward, will you allow this person to ill-advise you?"

"I was about to pose the same question to his grace!" Hugh said hatefully, with a smile on his thin lips.

Again, I questioned whether my beloved had gone too far, but I would not censure him, not in front of the queen certainly. I opened my mouth to speak as the two of them glared in thinly-disguised hatred at one another, before Isabella turned and left without another word. It appealed to the queen's sense of drama to leave with a sweep of her gown and her head held high.

"Well, I think if a man could die from the looks of an enemy, you have just breathed your last, my darling"! I placed my hand softly on his sleeve in comfort, but he looked radiant, with a wry smile as he watched Isabella's retreating figure. "I do not believe we can expect any help from the queen." I declared with understatement. "We shall need to keep our spies in France ever watchful."

"Not just them, your grace. I suggest we keep the queen under even closer scrutiny henceforth. A precautionary measure of course"

+++

It seemed that we could not have had worse luck than by the end of the year, as other escape attempts were made, too many of which were successful.

Frustration at Mortimer escaping and eluding us caused me to deal harshly with his wife and family, and - much to Isabella's chagrin - I had her and her servants moved from house arrest in Southampton to be kept with great security at Skipton-in-Craven. Furthermore, I split up her sons and daughters, keeping the former under my personal control and the latter were sent to convents.

In Hugh's absence one day, I received a visit from my dear lifelong friend and supporter, the archbishop of Canterbury, Walter Reynolds. He seemed a lot older than when I had last seen him. I welcomed him warmly, but soon the conversation drifted from ecclesiastical matters to those closer to my heart.

"Edward," Walter said; we had known each other for too long to act with the established convention of titles. "I fear I must say what has been on my mind for some time, but which I could not commit to paper. My dear friend, you must check the advancement of your power-hungry favourite before the country dissolves into complete anarchy. Your look tells me that you are already upset at my words, but I who have known you man and boy must say what others dare not."

I sniffed with annoyance. Yes, it was true that if anyone was entitled to speak their mind, Walter had earned the right. I nodded him to continue.

"Edward, the man and his father are a cancerous growth that must be cut out before your realm collapses. At Canterbury I hear much of what goes on, from the shires to the cities, and one family's greed is surely outweighing all sense and reason. Some members of your own court are reporting blackmail, threats even. Extortion is rife, even your half–brother Thomas, earl of Norfolk, has been forced to grant Despenser a lifetime lease of the lordship of Chepstow. Henry de Lacy's widow, Joan, has been forced to surrender some of her dower lands. These have all passed seamlessly to Despenser.

Some have been asked to prove their ownership of property that has been in their families for decades. I now hear that you punish Adam Orleton, bishop of Hereford, who Despenser claims was an ally of Mortimer. His lands are confiscated, his goods literally thrown out onto the streets to be seized by the masses. This affront to a member of the church concerns me deeply." He sighed wearily, and continued. "Now I hear that Henry of Lancaster has angered you and Despenser, claiming that he is abetting Orleton."

"Lancaster is a fool like his brother Thomas," I managed to interject during Walter's stream of complaints and concerns. "I forbade him to make his dead brother a martyr, and he proceeds to erect a cross in Thomas's honour. It is treasonous!"

"Edward, this is sheer folly!" Walter continued earnestly. "You will drive Orleton to go against you"

"Then he would also be a traitor!" A voice from the doorway stopped the archbishop. I don't know how long Hugh had been there, listening; neither of us had been aware of him.

Walter was not a man to back off from defending his point of view, and possibly one of the few men that never seemed in any way intimidated by Hugh.

"'Traitor' is a dangerous word, my lord, use it wisely or at your peril." Hugh walked over to us, taking up my hand and kissing it, before removing his gauntlets and dropping them onto the table where the archbishop sat. "Yet all who stand against their king are most certainly traitors, be they bishops or archbishops."

Walter stood up, and I had rarely seen him look as angry as he was at that moment. His response, when it came, was a direct one - and in a tone so cold, I would almost shiver. "Have a care, my lord, lest you go too far." With that, he bowed to me and left.

+++

My distrust and hatred of Adam Orleton did not lessen, and Isabella was later to accuse me of blaming the bishop for all the ills in the country. His guilt of being a sympathiser to Mortimer irked me intensely. Orleton's refusal to answer the charges put to him created a growing chasm between myself and Walter Reynolds. Orleton was eventually found guilty of giving aid to Mortimer. His lands and goods were forfeited to the crown and the bishop was then delivered into the care of the archbishop of Canterbury.

It seemed that, once again, I was fighting battles on all fronts. Keeping Hugh safe was my main concern, but a dangerous dispute with France threatened to completely overwhelm me. There would never be anything as hated as an English king having to pay homage to a king of France. At this particular time, the last of Isabella's family to rule France was Charles, who came to the throne a year previously. Custom dictated that I would pay homage for Gascony and Ponthieu. Charles had declared that he would wait until there was a measure of stability in England, given the incursions of the Scots and with the rise and fall of the Marcher lords.

Now however, with the thirteen-year truce with Scotland, I could no longer use the excuse. An event then occurred that threatened to plunge the country into a war with France. The French king's late brother, Philip, had rather unwisely given permission for a fortified town to be built in a small Gascon village named St-Sardos. A sergeant-at-arms, by the name of......oh, well, it escapes me now after all these years; it matters not, in any case. Well, he declared the village to be French. The lord in nearby Montpezat, outraged by this, burned the village to the ground. Quite rightly; as I sit here now, and look back logically at things, it is still a shock to me that I now see things so differently. Anyway, to make matters worse, my steward in Gascony, Ralph Basset, and the Montpezat lord who had set fire to the village, failed to answer Charles's demand for them to attend him and explain their actions in the outrage.

At length, Charles stated he was willing to accept that I had no hand in the affair, and now suggested a new date on which to pay homage. Hugh considered the issue and appeared horrified at the thought that I would vacate the country.

"Edward, you cannot leave me here alone! Why, I am as good as dead if you go. I have enemies everywhere, here at court and throughout the realm; and then there is the queen!"

I had to laugh at that. I placed a hand on his shoulder, which I rubbed affectionately. "Dearest Hugh, I hardly think Isabella is likely to strike you dead. A vixen she may be, but that would be a step too far even for her!" Others might well work on her behalf, I thought, but of course I did not tell Hugh that. He was a born intriguer, and would have suspected as much himself.

He would not be pacified, and he had convinced himself that somewhere stalked an assassin, and the dagger he or she carried was marked with his name on it! At length, it was not difficult to persuade me to send my envoys with a further excuse for still being unable to leave my realm due to continued unrest.

I sent my half-brother, Edmund, and Archbishop Bicknor as my representatives in an effort to deal with the issue, and others followed some weeks later. Word reached us soon enough, and it was not favourable news – the French king having received no one to perform the homage due to him, had taken Gascony and Ponthieu back into his hands, and by way of reinforcing his intentions, he had sent in his army.

My brother Edmund, Duke of Kent, was now my lieutenant in Gascony, and by all accounts was already proving to be unpopular. Naively, however, he had allowed himself to be besieged in his own castle!

Ha! I see your look, Manuel, and I know what you are thinking! How can I, of all people, criticise another's folly when I had stumbled from one crisis to another? It is true, I cannot deny it!

However, be that as it may, my half-brother eventually signed a truce for six months. I ordered the arrest of all French men and women currently living in England. I think my intention was some measure of revenge but, as you will be aware, my friends, war and conflict were not vices I actually took part in with any great zeal.

Isabella, as expected, was incensed at the arrests which, of course, included her own French servants. Hugh had amusingly asked me if these arrests could indeed include the queen! At least I think he was in jest!

Hugh, frightened and alarmed by the very idea that I would abandon him to his legion of enemies in England, was instrumental in organising a fighting force to march into Gascony, complete with horse food and all necessary supplies. In order to calm Hugh's concerns, I agreed to hand over command of the army to the earl of Surrey. Hugh had suffered greatly from fear for his very life.

What had once been a careless concern for the danger of being the man closest to the king, was now becoming something of a preoccupation, and he was noticeably more nervous when surrounded by too many courtiers. Given that, by now, all petitioners were seen by him rather than me – and, more often than not, none could see me if they had not already spoken with him - it was difficult to present a picture of composure, yet this he did quite commendably.

Confident and self-assured was the face he presented to the world and any tears, fearful thoughts and suspicions were kept for when we were alone and private.

Relations with the queen had been deteriorating badly over the months and were to get worse when, on advice from Hugh, I took back into my hands Isabella's county of Cornwall.

Hugh tried to explain to her that it was but a cautionary measure in case the French should launch an attack. The same reasoning could of course not be used when I took back properties and much of her land. Hugh had wisely suggested that it would be prudent to also reduce her living costs.

I had wondered at the sense of the cuts, but I let Hugh deal with it. He was so much better at considering costs and allowances. I do recall remembering a time when my father had severely cut back my allowance many years before. The memory prompted me to instruct Hugh not to make the cutback in the queen's expenses too severe.

His holiness pope JohnXXII, being anxious to broker a peace deal between England and France, sent two of his most trusted envoys to England and I set out my case to them. Following that, I agreed to send an embassy to the French king, particularly pointing out that I had not technically refused to pay homage to him. Hugh pored over the finer details of the mission.

Furthermore, I suggested that I transfer all my land held in France to my eldest son and heir, Edward, and that he would henceforth pay homage for them. King Charles now objected to the news that I had made an attempt, at the beginning of the conflict in Gascony, to make an alliance with the Spanish, and for Aragon and Castile to come against the French; indeed the French king considered the plot to be as good as treasonable. Furthermore, he objected in the strongest terms that French citizens had been harried and arrested; there was particular mention of the removal of French men and women from the service of the queen. Hugh was in no doubt that letters had certainly been sent from Isabella to her brother, some of which he had been able to intercept.

Charles made his own conditions - one of which, whilst tempting, was fraught with danger. The French king suggested that, if Isabella and our son, Edward, were to come to France in person, there was every hope that the old alliance could again be taken up. Moreover, the French king would restore all lands back to the English.

Hugh and I were cautious and instructed our own envoys that Isabella and the prince should not go to France until there had been a cessation of hostilities. Later however, Hugh suggested that it would be acceptable for the queen to travel alone and negotiate a peace; this with a proviso, however, that Roger Mortimer and other enemies of England be expelled from France for fear of Mortimer attempting to do some harm to the queen or even abduct her for their own gains.

Furthermore, I insisted that Isabella's visit was subject to my will, and I would be kept constantly updated on her movements and progress. Nor would I agree to any type of treaty that compromised my honour. Having laid out the specifics of our suit, I visited Isabella personally to inform her of my wishes.

The queen looked up in surprise at me as I entered her chamber. She and her ladies in waiting were sewing; Isabella prided herself on her needlework and spent many hours working on intricate designs. She and her ladies immediately rose and curtseyed deeply.

I nodded and smiled tightly. "Lady Eleanor, perhaps you and the ladies would excuse us, I would speak to the queen alone."

Once they had left, I extended a hand which she took and she sat again.

"You look troubled, Edward," she stated softly.

I had no great wish to stay and converse, so came to the point straight away. "You are to go to your brother in France. We are entrusting you with the delicate negotiations regarding this bloody war that has erupted from nowhere. Perhaps you alone can talk some sense into his thick head and avoid any further unpleasantness."

I could see at once from her eyes that this news excited her. I knew she would have a hundred questions, she always had questions. "I see the prospect appeals to you - a chance to be in your beloved France again, even if only for a short time."

She cast her eyes downwards, lest I see the joy in them. "I am your wife, sire, my place is by your side and to serve you in any way I can. I will not deny that I yearn for some time away from this place that has become......"

I cut her off with a wave of my hand. "Yes, yes we know that you dislike us, Hugh and myself."

Isabella smiled, and looked at me with something akin to pity. "You and Hugh? I dislike the man you have become. Where once I saw charm and humour, now I see only a man who has become obsessed by another and can no longer act independently. I have no love for Hugh le Despenser, I will say so to your face and certainly to his. The man has made me the unhappiest woman in England, by virtue of his control over you, by his scheming, his avarice. He is a bully, and he sullies your name by your association with him."

I sunk into a nearby chair and picked at my shirt, a small tear I had not noticed but Isabella had, and after searching in a small wooden chest on the table beside her, she stepped over to where I sat, sinking to her knees, and without a word, she took my hand and gathered the torn sleeve. We sat in silence as her nimble fingers set to work on its repair. I looked at her and she looked up at me. For a moment we said nothing, and I had an impulse to take her in my arms, but the moment was shattered as the needle pricked my skin and I jumped at the unexpected pain.

"Believe me, that was not intentional," she said, with that twinkle in her eye, and we both laughed. She finished her work and returned to her chair. The silence seemed to last forever.

I sat biting my nails and she took up her embroidery once again. "Will Shene has a sweetheart, did you know?" she asked brightly.

I was intrigued. "I had no idea," I admitted. I felt strangely as I had done whenever Piers and I were given gossip – which he loved! A secret was rarely safe with him. "Is the lucky girl here at court?"

"Oh no," Isabella looked delighted to be discussing such trivial matters as we had done in happier times. "She is a childhood sweetheart from his home in Henley - I believe that is how you pronounce it?"

"Hen not Hon!" I corrected her with a wink and a chuckle.

She laughed. "You should talk to him more. He says he will marry her one day, when he feels the time is right. He is devoted to you my lord. I wonder Hugh has not dismissed him."

In that moment she had broken the fragile light-hearted mood as one would the delicate gossamer of a spider's web; I felt serious again. She looked as though she knew she had spoken out when she should have stayed silent, certainly about Hugh.

"You must try and resist the temptation to attack Hugh all the time," I now spoke sternly again. "I will have him take charge of arrangements, personally select your retinue. It is essential that our argument is put to your brother in the strongest terms."

"I will not let you down, my lord. Perhaps you will have some wine, and we can discuss the details more?"

"Alas, I have little time. Hugh and I are leaving for Kenilworth later today. We will speak again before you depart." With that, I nodded at her and strode to the door. I was outside when I heard a cry and then soft weeping. For a brief moment I was going to turn back. I don't know why I didn't.

+++

Walter Reynolds visited me again with fresh accusations about Hugh and how he was making himself absurdly rich at the expense of innocent merchants, nobility, anyone who could be forced into paying vast amounts of money or run the risk of blackmail, complete ruin, or even their liberty!

I had to admit, though it pained me to do so, that Walter was now becoming something of a nuisance with his constant belligerent and pious ranting over Hugh. The once humorous and affable man - who, with Piers and Gilbert de Clare, I had once enjoyed many juvenile adventures - was now a pious bore! One grows up, of course, and no-one stays the same as they age, we all get burdened with responsibility, marriage, children, obligations and much besides. The archbishop had grown into a morose bigot. He preached to a wide congregation about all manner of evils, and now included me in those sermons, with which he berated me whenever he came to court. I visited Canterbury less because of his presence there and, though it saddened me, we had grown too far apart to be reconciled.

After some weeks, despite the concerns Hugh and I had about any truce that Isabella may be able to secure, we were silenced when she and her brother concluded an agreement. As harsh as some of the terms were, Hugh, I and the royal council had really very little choice but to make the best of it that we could.

I still had to perform homage or I would forfeit Gascony altogether, and that must, of course, be avoided at all costs. There were, however, difficulties in that regard. Hugh again began to panic that my departure would leave him vulnerable to his many enemies and, even loving him as I did, I had to admit he had many of them. I had no intention of leaving him to be eaten alive by the many wolves that circled around us. Obscure, dark shadows that lurked in every corner; I felt them around me also. Neither, of course, could I take Hugh with me, as it had been made quite plain to me that, once in France, he would be immediately seized and tortured.

I had concerns, too, about my own safety, considering it quite possible that Mortimer could easily abduct me! I certainly had no wish to be captured by that wild dog! Once again I cursed myself for my leniency in letting him live when I should have ordered his execution while I had the chance.

I agonised now over whether I should send our son, Prince Edward, to pay homage by transferring all my lands in France to him. I was tortured with indecision, one day seeing the sense in the idea, the next day questioning the decisions I had made the previous day. I took advice from Hugh of course, and his father too as well others on the council. Hugh would rather take to the English Channel and resume life as a pirate than be parted from me. I knew that I could never leave him, I loved him too dearly, and he knew I would do anything to protect him.

+++

I was unaware of the exact time, but certainly it was before dawn when I was woken; someone was shaking me roughly, and I eventually focussed on Hugh, his eyes wide with horror, his face a mask of perspiration. I stirred myself wearily.

"Hugh, dear God, whatever is it? Hugh!"

"The devil Edward, I am cursed by the devil! Evil worshippers, necromancers!" He continued ranting as I looked up.

Will stood to one side, eyes wide open, with an enquiring look on his face. I shook my head quickly, and he left the room.

Although the long night candle was not quite extinguished, I could hear birds heralding the advent of a new day. The fireplace at one side of the chamber held only embers, with a few still glowing but offering no discernable heat.

I noticed now that Hugh had hold of objects in his hand. I eventually freed the objects from him to reveal two small wax figures. Each contained two sharp bodkins, one in the heads of the figures, the other in the left side of the chests – and one figure wore a crown!

"Hugh, it is nothing. They are dolls!"

He would not be pacified, and brought the one without the crown close to my face. "But don't you see, Edward, this is me! It is me! Black magic, sorcery! Someone is trying to kill me through witchcraft!"

"And me, by the look of it," I observed.

"But look, this one is undoubtedly me, is it not? It bears the cap I always wear, the gold chain around my neck!"

"Also, the crown on my head," I proffered, yet he still did not seem particularly interested, and had already dropped the doll of me onto the velvet coverlet. I knew nothing of sorcery, and was one of the few people who was unafraid of black magic. I had tolerated some men who had a gift for studying the stars in the sky and, whilst their knowledge confused me, I looked upon it as knowledge that was probably of some worth.

There are evil people and there are good people. I did not believe in warlocks, witchcraft or evil spirits, and certainly not in wax figures with pins stuck in them.

Hugh continued, his face white, eyes red and tear-stained. He tried to explain. "The figures were left on my pillow in my chamber. I worked late as you know and, when I retired, they were there. Dear God, protect me!"

I grasped both figures, and he looked at me aghast with horror.

"What are you doing?" he shrieked.

I got out of bed and walked to the fireplace. I stirred the embers into something resembling a flame and, once that was glowing, I threw both dolls into it.

Hugh walked slowly to where I knelt by the hearth, sniffing and wiping his face with his shirt sleeve.

We both watched as both dolls began to melt, emitting a grey smoke. Eventually they were no more than a small melted pool, in which floated the four small bodkins.

The episode would trouble me for some time after; I was used to Hugh being in control, much as Piers had been. I worried that he was becoming more paranoid as each day passed. He insisted on wearing his sword at all times and had his servants roll on the mattress of his bed to ensure there was no caltrops secreted there. Obviously the servant had found the wax figures. After the incident, he insisted that his chamber be locked and guarded at all times.

He rarely left the building during the day, and our once frequent walks were now a thing of the past. Whilst he still presented a controlled demeanour in front of everyone apart from me, in my company he could be unpredictable, and as night fell, he would become alert and watchful.

There was little I could do but reassure him that he was safe, even though I didn't always feel that way myself. Therefore, this early morning hiatus had clearly alarmed him. Hugh stared at the dying embers for a while, and I drew him away to where I helped him onto the bed.

He lay down, wearily; the emotion had completely worn him out. I put my arm around him and pulled him towards me and he very soon fell asleep.

I, unfortunately, was fully awake now, and although Hugh's breath became deeper and his body limp, sleep was evading me. The dawn chorus was becoming louder, and soon it would be fully light. Another day, and who could foretell what problems and anxieties it would bring.

I thought of Isabella and wondered where it had all gone wrong. We had, I believe, loved each other at one time, and our brief meeting before she left for France had made me wonder whether we could rekindle what we had once enjoyed. We had both been pawns in the game of power and dynasty that is the lot of royal children. Few marriages of this type are strong, like my father and mother's had been.

Maybe I was not strong enough for Isabella. Maybe she found my reliance on men like Piers, Roger and Hugh so distasteful that she could not bear the humiliation. I thought of this very much when, in time, I had lost everything. Some memories remain, despite how you try to starve them of consideration in the hope that they will fade with time.

I could not possibly know of course that my life was about to change dramatically.

+++

Edward of Windsor, my son and heir, was growing. He was far taller than any of his peers, and none of his companions were as strong. Both Isabella and I had agreed that he would surely be as tall as me. From the gallery at Windsor, I watched him at his swordplay lesson. His fencing master was having to use much of his skill in parrying with him. They separated for a moment, and the master, having noticed me, bowed low and inclined his head towards the prince before leaving courtyard.

My son, too, looked at me and, when I had stepped down, I embraced him.

"Father," he spoke in that strange tone boys' voices have when they begin to embrace manhood. Edward was at this time a strapping boy of thirteen years - handsome, with golden-coloured hair, similar to my own at his age. His jaw was square and sharply-defined. His straight nose was perfectly-shaped, and he had full red lips and the beautiful eyes of his mother.

I had him sit with me on a bench nearby, where he had discarded his jacket and also his books, the tell-tale sign that he had been late from studying with his tutor. I smiled at him, and he looked at me, innocent and eyes wide in wonderment.

In my own youth I had wondered why my own father had found being with me so awkward. I recalled his abrasiveness, showing little emotion. The tall warrior had no idea how to converse with me, his own son, yet he could spend hours with an old friend reliving memories of campaigns.

Yet, to be honest, I had very little to say to my own firstborn son. I asked him about his lessons, his love of horses and archery – at which he excelled, apparently - and of his duties now he was getting older.

"You know I am considering sending you to France? You understand you have to pay homage to your uncle the French king for the lands that we hold in that country?"

"I have been instructed so," he replied dutifully. His eyes seemed to light up at the prospect. "Do we not hate the French?" he suddenly asked.

The question took me by surprise and I laughed. The look on his face suggested he did not like being laughed at. I sought to pacify him.

"They are the prime enemy of England, I told him. "We have fought them for many years, and will no doubt continue to do so. You will take an army to them, as have your forebears."

"Yet, my mother is French," he stated. "She says that the French people want only peace between us."

I could not conceal a grunt of distaste. "Look to your father for matters of war, not women who think only of pretty dresses and hair styles."

How ironic, now I recall my words; there could be no man who would teach their son less about successful warcraft than I.

We sat in an awkward silence for some time before he spoke again.

"Will you not join us in France, father?"

Bless the boy, he was too young to understand the practices of men, the fear I had of being waylaid by vagrants in France and tortured or worse. I could not, in all honesty, go to France believing I was safe. Yet, I would send him, you might say? I would, but I did not believe he was in the same mortal danger that I would have been.

"Events here take up much of my time, and it will be good experience for you and the duty you will have to take yourself when you, too, are king."

My only concern was that he should not be married or affianced without my knowledge or approval. I had said as much to Isabella before she left. It would be just like Charles to have arranged something of that nature, believing me so weak that a betrothal would be accepted without challenge. It was as well to reiterate that to the boy.

"Remember, my son, that you must on no account let your uncle, or even your mother, arrange any betrothal until you hear from me."

"I understand, father," he replied, with something of a confused look. "How complicated it all is."

I could not argue with that. It was a lesson that no tutor would teach him. "You must guard against unscrupulous men, Edward."

"Is Despenser not an unscrupulous man?" he stammered over the long word despite knowing what it meant. His reference to Hugh startled me.

"Why would you think so?"

"My mother has…" he began, before he realised that he spoke unwisely.

I brushed over the remark. "Hugh Despenser is a man of honour (yes, you heard correctly, Manuel) - he serves me, his king, and is a bold and honest knight. Do not believe all the bad things you may hear of him."

We fell silent again, and I eventually stood, as did he. I looked at him with pride. What would become of this, my darling boy? How cruel was the life of a prince and a king that, by tradition, lived in separate households? I did not see my children very much. When they reached a certain age, of course, they had to be set up with their own households, as befitting their rank. Somehow it seemed a sad separation.

I repeated my words of warning and hoped that he would not forget. I made a step towards him and he bowed. I hesitated at the movement and stepped back. I smiled and he gathered his books and jacket and made to leave. Suddenly he rushed to me, flinging his arms around me.

I responded, holding him tightly. I closed my eyes and a tear ran down my cheek.

"I love you, my son, never forget that. Whatever happens, never forget." I missed the reply spoken into my collar. Then I released him and he ran to the steps at the side of the courtyard, turning to look at me with a smile.

I would never get to hold him again.

+++

CHAPTER SIX

My son, Edward, left for France and, duly and honourably by all accounts, performed his homage to his uncle king Charles. I pictured the pompous king, his face wreathed in a smile of satisfaction as my son knelt before him.

Still, it was done now, and I had decided that I would work to forge a stronger bond with him than I currently had. I visited the other children, albeit not for any great length of time. This, too, was seen as rather unconventional -but when had I been otherwise?

Another unseemly habit was to row – which, when I could, I enjoyed immensely. I was rowing on the lake at Leeds castle; alone, much to the horror of courtiers. Another oddity to list with the many "rustic" pleasures I indulged in. I delighted in the fact I could be truly alone, talk to myself without being stared at, and think - a pastime that many have said I should have practised more!

I felt my shoulders groan at the exercise that I got to indulge in so little. My arms were strong and my hands rough; they would nevertheless suffer tomorrow. It mattered not - the fresh air had always been dearer to me than the stuffy, oppressive castles in which I had spent so much of my life. In time, of course, I would spend more than enough time outdoors!

There was growing concern that the queen was delaying her return to England. Edward had done his duty commendably, and Isabella had negotiated a treaty with her brother. Not an entirely satisfactory one, but a peace nonetheless.

Isabella's motives were perplexing. Admittedly, she had many family members, but there were only so many you could spend time with. It was reported that she enjoyed being at her brother's court. She had been known to describe the English equivalent as "rather dull" by comparison.

I had sent Walter Stapleton, the bishop of Exeter and my envoy, to Paris to witness young Edward's homage and had also directed him to accompany the queen and our son home as soon as possible, but without unseemly haste.

I looked over to the bank of the lake where valets awaited me. They were now joined by Will, who was waving his arms in the air as though beckoning me. I had left instructions that if word had arrived from France, at any point in the few days I was spending there, I was to be told at once. I therefore reasoned this would be why Will was hopping up and down like a jester!

I took hold of the oars of the small boat and set to rowing back to the bank. I reached there soon enough and an attendant handed me water from a jug on a wooden tray. Will spoke while I drank.

"His grace, the bishop of Exeter has arrived from France."

I was at once alert. I strode back to the castle and, not bothering to wash or change my attire of just a cambric shirt and woollen hose, went to see him.

Walter Stapledon was a tall and rather emaciated looking man. Blessed of a friendly disposition, he was also a blunt speaker and an honest one – and, although I had on occasions found his frankness annoying, I respected him.

I greeted him warmly as we sat down, and a look of concern crossed his thin drawn face.

"Walter, I think I know you well enough to know you have news which I shall find unpleasant."

"Your grace is as astute as ever. I carry with me a note of the conversation I had with her grace, the queen. One of my secretaries drew it up, and – rather regretfully – I present it to you."

I took the scroll of paper and, after breaking the seal, I quickly took in the details. I felt the colour rise to my cheeks.

Stapledon was biting his lip, awaiting my reaction. In fact, the man looked as though he would rather be in my small boat in the middle of the lake.

"Has Hugh seen this, Walter?"

"No your grace, I had word that you were here and thought it better to let you see it first."

"Thank you," I said tightly. What I read was an account of Walter's final meeting with the queen. The words I know by heart, even now all these years later.

"*I feel that marriage is a union of a man and a woman, holding fast to the practice of a life together, and that someone has come between my husband and myself and is trying to break that bond; I declare that I will not return until that intruder is removed but, discarding my marriage garment, I shall put on the robes of widowhood and mourning until I am avenged of this Pharisee.*"

"The queen's brother stated that if it was his sister's will to stay, then he would not expel her," Walter added. "Worse still, your grace, word has it amongst the queen's retinue that it is her intention to…" He stopped short, as though searching for the right words. "It is whispered that if you do not rid yourself of the Despensers, then she, for the sake of her son, the prince Edward, may well land with a force…. and do it herself!"

Hugh and I had our own spies at the French court and had heard similar whispers. We had not taken them very seriously at the time, but I had to admit to some concern, even more so now that such talk had reached this emissary.

Walter's face showed great concern, but he had made an effort he said to dissuade her, if indeed the rumours were true. "I begged her to reconsider any such move lest the innocent should suffer along with the guilty."

I gave a deep sigh, tossing the scroll to one side in despair. "Leave me Walter, thank you." I spoke dejectedly, but without the anger Walter had expected.

The bishop left the room and I bit my knuckles in distress.

What was I supposed to do? I could not sail to France and drag her back, and yet it was clear she hated Hugh beyond reason; but enough to raise a force and force the issue? Surely not!

Of course, our life together was finished, and any ridiculous notion I had thought about welcoming her back with great acclaim for the treaty she had concluded could be forgotten. I cursed myself for my stupidity, and yet I had been aware of the risks. Once again, I had acted recklessly.

On one thing I was certain, however, and that was Hugh. I would never let him go, I loved him too much. A life without him would be unbearable, and I could not endure it – I *would* not endure it! Damn the woman! She says in her vanity that she will not return until Hugh is banished from court, probably from England itself. Indeed, I would not put it past Isabella to have Hugh murdered! Now I believe she was capable of it, and he must be protected at all costs.

I needed him now more than ever, he was my very life.

+++

There were clearly questions that needed to be answered. Hugh was angry about Isabella's refusal to return to England, and the deliberate accusation that he was the cause.

I attempted to reason with him when he spoke of his intention to leave my service and allow her to return to my side. "Hugh, don't ever think of such a thing. I could not bear for you to leave me!" I was horrified.

"Your grace," he answered with great reverence, "my dearest wish is to see you happy and content. I am astonished that I am the cause of your marital distress. I only want to serve you and the queen – whom, you must trust, I honour above all women. I am sure it is best for all concerned if I retire from your service. I am mortified that I should have caused any discord between you. I have tried to serve you well, wishing nothing in return save for your love and trust."

I was on the verge of tears. "Hugh, my darling, I will not let you go, even if it means the queen does not return! Let her stay in France at the expense of her brother. She may live out her life there, growing old and fat and bitter. I need you in my life, Hugh. Once Edward has returned to us, then she may go to the devil, retire to her estates, enter a convent, whatever she will."

Hugh paced up and down as though deep in thought; he appeared to be wrestling with the dilemma. Suddenly he came to me, throwing himself at my feet. "Edward, I love you! God knows, my life is nothing without you!" He began to sob.

My heart was breaking at seeing him so distressed. I raised him to his feet and held him tightly to me. I wanted to hold him in this embrace forever, to feel his body next to mine, the warmth of his breath, the touch of his lips. Suddenly, he looked up at me, leaning up and kissing my throat. I put my hands around the back of his head, drawing him closer against my neck. He ran his hand over my chest and down towards my stomach, and then lower......

We lay together that afternoon, abandoning ourselves to one another. I felt alive and rejuvenated. His love and passion were all I needed. His surrender to me was exquisite, his domination of me equally so. I loved him more than I could have imagined. I knew I could never be without him, even if it meant surrendering my crown. Suddenly, the need to be a king was not so important, if we just had each other. I had been warned of the possibility of being replaced - the barons had used that threat before - but I would not surrender my crown, and I would certainly not abandon this man that I cherished above all others. I had let Piers go all those years ago, I would not make the same mistake again.

Later, as we lay in each others arms, Hugh and I discussed what would be our best move if we were to counter Isabella's attack.

"I think, Edward, that we need to present the queen with a declaration that it has been determined I am not her enemy, but that someone is poisoning her against me - which I believe they are! It must be seen that I wish her grace no harm whatsoever. Indeed, we should direct the leading bishops to write to her that I am innocent of all her charges against me. The bishops will risk your displeasure should they not be in agreement."

I rose from the bed, taking up a fur robe and wrapping it round my nakedness. I poured us both some wine, taking the goblets back to the bed and handing him one. "It is certainly worth the attempt." I agreed. "Even if it serves no good, it can surely do no further harm."

+++

I wrote again to Paris, to Isabella and her brother as well as leading figures of the French nobility who had a voice at the French court. I stated that I had been surprised that the queen professed to be in fear of her liberty, and indeed her very life, from Hugh as well as his father, since Hugh had shown her nothing but respect, courtesy and great kindness.

Worse was to come, when Hugh came to me in great concern.

"My liege, I have this very day been passed on reliable information from France."

I was all attentive.

Hugh continued, reading from a letter he had received that very day. "Rossoul is my most reliable source, and what he tells me now explains a great deal about the actions of the queen."

I looked at him gravely; I was starting to wonder whether I really wanted to know! Nevertheless, I nodded for him to continue.

"It would seem, your grace, that the queen has been enjoying secret liaisons with Roger Mortimer of Wigmore!" Hugh stood clear of me lest I lash out, as I had a tendency to do when faced with bad news.

"Roger Mortimer? And the queen?" I spoke more in disbelief than anger.

"It would seem as though we need look no further for the cause of the queen's ill intentions. She is following the evil counsel of Mortimer and others."

I felt anger, shame and disbelief all at once. Had their association been carrying on while he was in England? Had she been a party to his escape from the Tower? In that moment I was unsure which out of Mortimer and Isabella I hated the most. Of course the queen had been insistent that funds to Mortimer's wife be made promptly to 'ease her distress'. Surely she had known when she had stayed at the Tower, serving as it did a royal residence as well as a prison, that he was lodged there. How long had they communicated?

Suddenly it all became clear. What a fool I had been – again! I had given no consideration to the risk of Isabella being so unhappy and desperate that she had become drawn to Mortimer and his evil intent. The idea and reality was quite astonishing.

Hugh sat down nearby and drew out a further letter. I looked at him expectantly.

"In addition, I have today received word from the good bishop of Exeter, who has sent me a copy of a letter received lately from her grace. In it she states that because of me, she fears for her very life." he paused as I scoffed dismissively. "In short, your grace, her hatred and concern is not towards you, but me."

I could not think clearly as I listened to all of this. How could she have any affection for Mortimer, realising as she did my hostility towards him? I believed myself to be in shock. How cruelly I had been betrayed by her. I barely believed it possible, and yet Hugh assured me that his informant was reliable, and what cause did I have to doubt it? Moreover, how could she also believe Hugh was her enemy? It was true that they had verbally clashed on a few occasions, but generally - in my experience - he had been nothing but courteous and willing to be her servant in all things. True, he had suggested a cut to her allowance, yet that was only prudent, and in no way malicious. No, it was Mortimer's jealousy of Hugh and his hatred of me that had driven this wedge between us, I was certain of it.

"This changes nothing, Hugh. If the queen has allied with Mortimer, so be it, but I shall continue to demand that she and Edward return."

Isabella continued to blacken Hugh's name, insisting that she had been in fear of her life from him, and how he was using extortion as well as other means to enrich himself and his father. Many were afraid to cross him in any way. It was well known that he had a heavy hand for any that criticised him. She went further in her cruel condemnation. All access to the king came through Despenser only, making the king inaccessible to his people. Hugh had left her in fear for herself and her children and had been the cause of her great humiliation.

Isabella was, thereafter, the central figure in an increasing number of those who found my reign and Hugh's governance oppressive. There was a personal disappointment to me that my half-brother, Edmund of Kent, had joined a lengthening list of disaffected English noblemen and thrown in his lot with the queen.

As time progressed, Hugh put in place sensible precautions regarding a possible invasion. Strong rumours arose regularly, leading us to believe that a force may cross the Channel at any time.

Christmas in the year of our lord thirteen hundred and twenty-six was a dull affair. As much as I tried, there was no cause for celebration or any gaiety. The season was instead spent sending out declarations that every able bodied man was to make himself available to defend the kingdom from any surprise attack. Royal castles were ordered to be fully supplied and garrisoned.

Further alarming news arrived suggesting that Isabella had secretly been negotiating a possible marriage between prince Edward and one of the daughters of Count William of Hainault. I was furious at the prospect! No word came from my son, despite the warning I had given him, regarding this eventuality and his assurance that he would inform me. Presumably, the boy was under his mother's sharp eye. I did not doubt, either, that she may well have had his letters intercepted.

One could see the prospect of an alliance with the English crown. I had indeed made overtures to Hainault myself, but I had carelessly allowed matters to fail, and now it would be too late.

Hugh urged me to write again to my son, repeating my instructions to return home to England regardless of his mother's wishes. Furthermore, it was essential for him to realise that his mother was fabricating her fear of Despenser and that she was using that as a reason not to return home.

Communication from the pope to Despenser personally suggested that, as the present difficulties seemed to rest on Hugh's very presence, he should maybe do the honourable thing and leave, even suggesting that he could be guaranteed a safe exile. As the situation began to get worse, it began to finally become apparent to me that mine and Hugh's lives were becoming inextricable and that, indeed, one's fate rested on the other. He clearly began to realise, as did I, that we were drawing more ire from those we needed for support.

Close associates of Hugh and his father had met with mysterious accidents or were simply assassinated. Warnings in all disguises became a regular occurrence, and the weight of his responsibilities rested uneasily with Hugh.

Never was this more evident than one evening when we had eaten together, and Hugh had drunk more wine than he should have. He was maudlin and nothing could stir him from his melancholy. He sat brooding in his chair and it pained me to see him such low in spirits. God knows, the last few months had been fraught. I got up to fetch more wine which I then put down and stood behind his chair and reached to caress his shoulders. The touch angrily enraged him.

"God's death, will you leave me be?" he shouted to my astonishment. "Why must you always paw at me?

Stroke my hair, whisper in my ear. Your very touch begins to revolt me!"

I was stunned. I stood looking at him in disbelief. I shook my head. "Hugh, what is it? why do you treat me thus?"

"I cannot bear you to touch me. You anger me with your weakness, you lament your bad fortune, yet you have brought it on yourself. You're not a man, not a king. You are weak, a weak fool, and I am drowning because of it, because of my loyalty to you, and look where it has brought me, to ruin and destruction. Would to God I had never entered your service; I curse my fate for it. I wish I had never helped you, never shared your bed!" He then hurled the goblet at the fireplace and staggered drunkenly to the door which he slammed behind him.

I saw him push Will, my valet, as he stormed past him.

"Out of the way, you damned idiot!" he cried at him.

I don't know where he went or where he spent the night. I sat alone for hours after. Will entered, but I shook my head and smiled weakly at him. I felt a lump in my throat, and emotion threatened to overwhelm me. God knows, Will Shene had witnessed my tears and tantrums often enough, but I did not want to talk further with anyone that night. Hugh's bitter, angry words played over and over in my head. Did I truly disgust him? I began to feel weary; not just with my present situation - life had never been easy, but I felt now the weight of my role and I was heartily sick of it! All I wanted at that moment was Piers.

+++

Hugh was absent for several days and on his return I did not question where he had been or speak of his outburst. Put simply, I still loved him, even though he had pretty much told me that I revolted him. His absence had helped both of us. My wounded pride alone might have caused me to order him from me until my temper had cooled. By the time he returned, I was no less hurt by his words, but too grateful to see him return. What sort of man had I become?

He was quieter than usual, but we discussed, as we had every morning since Isabella had left, any reports, letters or even verbal information that touched upon the possible invasion.

We had it on good authority to a noble personage at the French court, that - as much as he loved her - the king of France was certainly not prepared to finance and lead an invasion on England on her behalf. This, of course, said more about Charles's good sense than it did his conviction about his sister's plight. The king, it was also rumoured, took a rather poor view of the relationship that may be forming between Isabella and Roger Mortimer.

I did, however, at last receive word from my son, the prince. In it, Edward regretted that he had not been able to return to England as his father had wished, but his mother was distraught and he felt honour bound to remain with her. I was furious and sent back immediately to him, threatening that he would forfeit all that he had in England – properties and so forth - if he did not immediately return.

Hugh had probably been right, however, when he read the letter from my son, stating that it sounded far more like a letter that the queen herself probably composed! In truth, Despenser claimed that prince Edward was little more than a prisoner himself.

I wrote to Edward on several occasions reminding him of my previous warning that if he were not to return as instructed he would lose all he had in England, and that he had not behaved as a good son should in obeying his father. Hugh suggested that I address the letter to the queen rather than the prince as he was in no doubt she was intercepting any letters both to and from her husband in any case.

Every report from France was concerning. My enemies, who had fled to Europe following the Marchers' defeat, now crawled out from their burrows and furtively gathered under Isabella's banner.

More worrying and infuriating to me was news that prince Edward had officially been betrothed to William of Hainault's daughter, Philippa. When that news reached me, I felt that all was lost. Not as much for the fact that I had taken no part in the decision, but more that my word carried no authority whatsoever. It did not appear to matter that I was against the match, and - even though I had implored the pope not to issue any dispensation for the union - it was as though I was defeated already.

Fortunately, our spies were not quite resolved to stop supplying us with further information, but the reward for such news was becoming more expensive! We had to thank the true friends that Hugh and I had on the continent for word that Isabella was travelling through Holland and Brabant to clarify, presumably, that all was in order for their forces to join the planned fleet. Sadly, English exiles were joining mercenaries and the like; it seemed that anyone who hated me or Hugh and his father were happy to band with pirates and cutthroats-as I viewed them - in order to be part of the threatened invasion.

Even at this stage, I had letters from loyal subjects, still men of good standing and honour that assured me I could still avoid an invasion by simply sending Hugh into exile. How could I do such a thing? By now I was losing all self pride, totally, in the hands of this man that I loved so dearly. I could not give him up to his enemies. Were I sure he would ever even reach the coast of England if I ordered him to take a ship and sail to wherever he would find peace and safety, it may have been different. I knew as well as he that the minute Isabella landed her invasion fleet, he was as good as dead.

Surprisingly, we had found more support for each other than had been the case for a while. Although his harsh words and actions on that drunken evening had upset me, I have ever been loyal to those I love, foolishly or otherwise. I continued to believe that the danger came primarily from a French invasion. I had been warned that there was still unrest in Gascony, and it would be so like the French king to take advantage of so much discord and confusion in England by sending a fleet to catch us unaware.

Hugh's father suggested that we make a first strike by a short, sharp attack ourselves in order to assess French resistance and forestall an attack.

+++

The Tower of London felt like the safest place to be and it was there that the nightmare began. Something woke me from a restless sleep, the clatter of swords, voices shouting, footsteps. I was immediately alert. I rarely slept alone in those dark days of my reign. Hugh rarely came to my bed now, but I had Will and several other valets sleep in my chamber whilst keeping four guards at the chamber door. The noises grew louder and I nodded to Will, who went to the door, but stepped back when Hugh, and several others marched in. For a split second my heart leaped, an instant, fear that an armed guard had come for me. I sat up in bed as Hugh approached, his face white, his eyes filled with fear.

"Edward, the queen has landed at Orwell."

+++

There was little that could be achieved in the capital. A letter from Isabella and the prince was circulated in London shortly after her landing, and although the bishops of London and Winchester had joined the archbishop of Canterbury in a bull of excommunication to all foreign invaders, support for the queen was growing steadily.

Hugh, once again showed the fear he must undoubtedly have been feeling. "What is to be done? Edward, what can we do?"

I sought to pacify him, although I felt a gnawing pain in my guts that flight was all that was left. It seemed of little use to remain in London, where I had never been popular. I summoned my treasurer, Robert Baldock to collect as large a sum of money as possible and, together with Hugh and a great company of men-at-arms, we made a clandestine escape from a city seething with discontent.

We learned later that, no sooner had we left London, the city rose in revolt. John le Marshal, a close confident and friend of Hugh and his father was dragged from his house and beheaded in the street like a common felon.

I continually tried to reassure Hugh that all was not lost, even though I was rapidly trying to work out our best options. I felt no affinity with the south of England and therefore suggested that we head for the relative security of Wales, where I believed we could at least rely on the security of Hugh's vast estates along the way, as well as access to more wealth and manpower which would certainly be needed. Moreover, if we were not completely welcome, we were assuredly more popular in Wales than Roger Mortimer! Or so we thought.

I sent word to loyal subjects to gather as many fighting men as possible, yet it seemed hatred of Hugh caused them to drag their feet, and the numbers amassed were pitiful. This I learned later was primarily their resentment towards Hugh and his father rather than their love for Isabella and her advancing force.

Never had I been so frustrated at the lack of word about where exactly Isabella was. Certainly Hugh's previously unrivalled network of spies and informants had gone critically quiet. It did seem from the information we did get, that Isabella's forces had been virtually unopposed and were progressing with little or no resistance. Word came from London that Walter Stapledon, bishop of Exeter, and generally a staunch ally had been brutally dragged through the streets of the city and then savagely decapitated with a bread knife!

Isabella lost no time in declaring her reasons for the invasion. Primarily, she announced that the governance of the kingdom had been greatly abused by the malign influence of Hugh le Despenser and his father, and his and others' threats to destroy the royal power that he had seized, and he was now attempting to disinherit the king and his heirs. Furthermore, this was carried out and aided by the evil counsel of the treasurer, Robert Baldock. Great men of the realm had been needlessly put to death or banished, their families left destitute, while the Despensers and Hugh primarily stole, blackmailed and viciously assaulted all dissenters and had shown themselves to be tyrants and villains. Being such, this force had come to deliver England from its enemies and called on the populace to afford them every assistance.

We reached Chepstow where we intended to sail to Ireland via Hugh's estate on Lundy Island. Fortune was against us along with the capricious winds of the Bristol Channel, which forced us to land at Cardiff. Having reached the security of Hugh's mighty fortress at Caerphilly, I summoned the forces of South and West Wales to join us.

I sat alone, feeling like a fugitive in my own realm, which was essentially the truth of the situation. Caerphilly felt, at least, to offer a measure of security and, in its strong environs, I permitted myself the luxury of facing a reality that I could not bear to think of. Whilst I still trusted Hugh, and even his relative coldness to me I could pass off as fear for his life – God knows we all felt that! -there was no doubt that he was hated far more than I had ever allowed myself to admit.

I had always believed that there are consequences to every decision that is made; at least I believed it when I was in the right! Now, consequences there most certainly were, and a great many of them as, one by one, we suffered for what regrettably was Hugh's and my own behaviour. It would be so easy to lay our unpopularity on Hugh alone, but I wondered much later whether, had I been a different man and cast him away from me, things would have fared differently for me.

Of course they would, but love makes fools of us all; we are blinded by the joy of it and a determination to enjoy it as long as we can. We cannot bear the thought of being left alone, so we excuse any bitterness and harsh words as learning to grow with love in all its forms.

There was no doubt that Hugh was hated, but I did not learn until much later how deeply and fervently he was hated. Strange how we can be as passionate in our hate as in our love. Could I have been saved if I had thrown Hugh aside? I really believe I could, but my own mistakes were many, and not ones that could be dismissed merely as folly.

As we now considered our next move, the saddest news reached us and for once I wished that our informants had been less swift in reaching us. Hugh and I sat with a large map of England and Wales spread out on a table so we could hopefully plot our next move. A messenger arrived and I nodded to Hugh, knowing he would demand to read it first in any case. For once - and perhaps the only time - I saw pity in Hugh's eyes; pity for me.

"Well, what is it?" I enquired, my stomach churning as it did with every piece of information we received.

"Edward," he spoke softly and with a sympathy of which, I admit, I had felt him incapable. "Edward, your son has been proclaimed guardian of the kingdom, and is to rule and govern in the name of the king."

I stood and looked at Hugh in disbelief. The room was completely silent, until I looked up to the ceiling and let out the almightiest roar.

The message went on to say that this had been done as I had seemingly abjured the realm, and that I would resume my royal authority as soon as I returned. Given that I had left the English shore for a total of only four days before being blown back, this suggested that Isabella was receiving regular updates, although it was impossible to know from where. Nonetheless, I was not as much a fool as I seemed; I knew that there was no reassurance in those hollow words that I 'may resume my authority'. There would be no grand reunion and a general consensus to put things in the past and forget all ill will. I realised now that, as far as I was concerned, things would not end well.

I woke early the day after the news had been brought to me, after another restless night, but inaction did not suit me and I was not prepared to stay and be a target to be shot at. I walked out onto the ramparts of the fortress, surveying the vastness of the land before me, and being strangely aware of the beauty of England and Wales - those realms which, in essence, I no longer ruled.

The wind was refreshing and I was glad to breathe it in, shutting my eyes as it swirled around me.

Will Shene was suddenly at my side, whispering to me rather than shouting to make himself heard.

My eyes widened at his words. We walked to the top of the stairwell.

"Where is he?" I asked, and I made my way there.

Hugh was standing with his back to me, looking out of a window and, even as I closed the chamber door behind me, there was no indication he had registered anyone had entering at all.

I walked to him and instinctively reached over his shoulders and crossed my arms across his chest, leaning my head against the back of his. "I am so sorry Hugh," I said quietly, my voice cracking with emotion.

He did not respond to my touch, but seemed almost in a dream, his voice quiet and even as he spoke.

"Executed on the common gallows of Bristol. Hanged in his own armour in front of a loud and jeering crowd. His body cut down and fed to dogs, his head hacked off and carried on a pike and displayed in Winchester for all to spit and laugh at."

I had not really mourned my father; his death had been a release to me, enabling me to invite Piers back to me, and finally giving me the power I had always longed for - and which was now ebbing away from me. Hugh's father had been a constant support to me, guiding me almost as a father, and I silently mourned for him myself.

We stood for a moment until I felt Hugh's body tighten and, releasing my arms from him, he merely hissed, "Fool!"

+++

With the execution and butchery of Hugh's father and his reaction to it, all fight seemed to have drained from him; his will to pursue some possible avenue of escape became a virulent disease that began to affect us all. As his will to continue with the chase began to ebb away, even servants and scribes began to leave and each day less and less of our party remained.

Nevertheless, we left Caerphilly in early November. Almost all the money and goods we had brought with us from London were abandoned at the stronghold as we made a hasty departure. The weather had turned bitterly cold, the strong winds now beginning to blow in the lightest of snow flurries.

I tried to lighten Hugh's mood by telling him that I did at least still have the Great Seal and around five hundred pounds - a not inconsiderable amount, which we would surely need. Little did I know that Isabella and the bastard Mortimer had already sent out parties to search for us.

Despite barely a trickle of information reaching us, we were informed of those that had been sent to hunt us down. Hugh insisted that our best hope lay in returning to Caerphilly via his castle of Llantrisant. After a brief stay at this cold and deserted place, it was essential to carry on and try to reach the stronghold at Caerphilly as soon as we could. Hugh strangely commented that he could not be entirely sure that Llantrisant was indeed his, and thought it strange that he had never really stopped to think how much property he owned or what castles he had at his disposal.

That final night at Llantrisant has remained in my mind for all these years. Both Hugh and I knew there were few left to us. My ever faithful Will and two others attended us, but it was no time to consider social status and I could almost believe that Hugh felt, at last, reconciled to life being very different, should we find an upturn in our fortunes. One of the attendants had a small flute and regaled us as best he could; the four remaining soldiers we had travelled with from London and the two Welsh ones we had taken from Caerphilly when we had first left, sat to one side of the chamber of the castle.

In the bedchamber that night, Hugh and I lay together. We remained clothed and covered ourselves in the heavy coverlet to keep out the cold. Hugh had no idea how long the place had been empty, certain that he had never stayed there. We had left Baldock snoring in an antechamber, drunk from a vast quantity of wine.

We talked of times gone by, memories of happier times, of marriage, our children, mistakes made and promises broken. I had, however, one question that - although it stuck in my throat - had to be asked.

"Do you love me Hugh?" The silence that followed suggested his answer. "You are my king," was his response, "I was born to serve and to honour you."

"That's not what I meant" I countered. "You know what I mean."

"Not in the way you love me, no."

I expected to be angry and hurt that I had lost everything to keep him with me, but I think I had known his answer for some time. He, in turn, asked me, "Did you love the others - Damory, Audley or Montacute?"

I smirked at the memory of those faces from the past. "Roger, I think, but the others were dalliances; I admit I enjoyed to watch their rivalry, but they meant little once they had gone."

"I sought to warn Damory off, did you ever realise?"

I declared I didn't.

"The note: 'It is known that you are the king's new whore, remember what happened to the Gascon - BEWARE!'"

I propped myself up and stared down at him. "You wrote that note?"

"I did indeed - a warning for that young whelp to know his place."

I settled down again, before I triumphantly declared, "Little good that it did you, I gave very little thought to it at the time."

We remained in silence for a while before he spoke again. "You were my path to power, Edward. I was determined to advance and saw very little opportunity in making my way, so..."

"So, you crept into my bed and into my heart, all to achieve the satisfaction of wealth and advancement?"

"Forgive me," he said quietly.

Was he now ruminating on past deceits and purging himself by his admissions? There suddenly seemed very little point in caring; although I was angry, it was not towards him but myself, for allowing him to share my life when I had sworn that no-one would mean anything to me after Piers. I felt a sudden guilt that I had betrayed my darling Perrot in making him share the love in my heart.

"I wish I could say I hated you Hugh, but - God forgive me - I love you still. I would happily hand over my crown if it meant that you and I could escape somewhere together but, without a crown, I am of little value to you."

His manner was as bitterly cold as the chamber. "What fools we are when we love; we make mistakes, we hurt, we damage, we lie."

"Perhaps it is not I that is the fool, Hugh. For I have loved - I gave my heart to Piers and I have loved you above all men. What have you felt in all this time? Power, money, are they your heart's only wish?"

"Yes," he answered me candidly, as though there should be no question of it. "What else is there?" He had not looked at me once, and a curious feeling of doubt entered my head. How honest was he being, I wondered?

Perhaps it was that thought that helped me pass the night beside him, when in times gone by I would have got up from the bed and left him for his insolence. I fell asleep confused but satisfied that I had maybe found the real man behind the sharp, astute Hugh le Despenser, but unfortunately, too late.

I awoke to a deserted room and a cold bed. The lack of any warmth on the sheet where he had laid on that final night was evidence enough that he had risen early.

The chamber door opened, and I looked up expecting to see him, waiting for the familiar bark of orders and information, but it was Will who brought me some bread and cheese with some beer to break my fast.

"Will, where is lord Despenser?"

Will looked sad and placed the small wooden tray he carried on the ned of the bed. "He is gone your grace. With master Baldock. They left at sunrise."

"Gone? Gone where?" I stammered like a village idiot.

"I know not, your grace. The two Welsh soldiers are also gone. They departed late last night after you had retired."

I was making a concerted effort to understand, and yet what was to be understood? Was it any less than

I expected? Darling Hugh - I recalled long lost words, *'First there is trust, then regret then death.'*

I startled at the sound of horses. Had he returned? I went to the window, throwing open the shutters. Horsemen, yes, but not reinforcements, just hunters that had finally caught their stag.

+++

Henry of Lancaster had none of the haughtiness that his brother Thomas had always displayed. Now titled earl of Leicester, Henry was tall like his brother, with short black hair, while Thomas's had been long. He was a kinder soul, and was clearly finding no delight in his assignment.

I had been guarded by the group of soldiers that had arrived at Llantrisant. Who had betrayed us I wondered, not that it mattered now? I suspected the two Welsh soldiers in our party had thought better of aiding our cause and had probably fled, perhaps waiting for the search party and disclosing our whereabouts. I could not be bitter or angry at their decision.

Leicester and his escort had arrived later that day. Henry looked solemn and awkward as he approached me. He had, of course, no need to kneel to me; one does not need to show reverence to a fugitive. Yet he did, almost changing his mind when he realised he had no need to.

"Ned," he began, but I silenced him with a shake of my head.

"Let neither of us make this any harder than it need be," I responded, with a tone that did not reflect hurt, anger or betrayal, just a coldness much like the freezing castle.

"Where are you to take me?" I asked.

"Monmouth and then onto Kenilworth. he replied solemnly.

I looked around me, as though noticing for the first time that only my ever faithful Will was all that was left of our party. I did not enquire what had become of the others. Will looked red-eyed, and I suspected he had given in to the sorrow he had felt since we had started this bizarre escapade. I smiled at him, nodding my assent.

"You are relieved of your duties, Will," I said softly. He had been the only constant in my life since I was a prince, but I had no right to take him down with me.

Suddenly, he fell to his knees in front of me. "My place is by your side, your grace. Forgive my boldness, but I am not going anywhere unless it is with you."

I desperately forced back the tears that I felt welling in my eyes. I was about to protest, but Leicester made it easy.

"The squire can go with you Ned, he has committed no crime, he will be treated well enough."

I looked at Will. What could I possibly say to him? I cursed inwardly that I had never rewarded him sufficiently for his unwavering loyalty to me in all the years he had served me as a young lad, and now as a young man. "Bless you, Will," was all I managed to speak.

I swallowed hard, and stood. "Henry, do you know what...."

He anticipated my question. "He and Baldock were taken in a wood near here where they were found hiding. They have been taken under the queen's command to Hereford. I know nothing more as to their fate."

The snow was falling in gentle flakes that had threatened the day before, and yet I did not feel cold air; only a numbness of body and spirit. The mountain road on which we travelled was unforgiving, and Leicester could be heard more than once cursing its narrow track, especially as the day grew freezing and the surface became concealed and unrelenting ice.

+++

I was anxious about Hugh, yet I dared ask any further questions. Why could I not dismiss him from my mind? Surely his cruel admission from last night should have severed all emotional ties I had with him. Yet, I could not forget how he had made me feel; when times had been good, and he had always given me such sound advice. I still could not recall him as one of the many I had knighted when I was heir to the throne. I suppose there was no surprise in that, since I had no eyes for anyone that day apart from Piers Gaveston.

We eventually reached Monmouth, located at the crossing of the River Wye and River Monnow. Its great tower loomed imposingly, and I could not supress a shiver, not just from the weather. We entered the great hall to find a large welcoming party, presided over by Adam Orleton, bishop of Hereford.

The prelate could barely conceal his smirk of joy at my final discomfiture. He was always an enemy, and took the greatest joy in addressing me with little reverence which clearly gave him a great deal of satisfaction. He stood, tall and sinister like a great black crow, eyes alert for any carrion. Next to him stood Sir William Blount, with others that I was barely aware of.

"I am charged by her grace, the queen, to request that you give up to me the Great Seal."

I stood for a moment while I took in the significance of the request. A transfer of power. I turned to Will, who handed to me a carved wooden box. I did not open it, merely brushing my hand over the intricate detail of the lid.

Orleton smirked again, holding out his hands, which I ignored and instead reached towards Blount. He took the box from me, with a nod, while the bishop's smirk became pinched and he visibly coloured from the snub.

He would, unfortunately, have his revenge later.

Days began to mean nothing to me, I was allowed every comfort, and I could say that I was well treated in my cousin's custody. Considering the manner in which I had persecuted his brother, he was honourable enough in my care. I watched the snow fall heavily as it moved in from the west, and I was permitted to walk outside, accompanied by Will and four soldiers who did at least keep a respectful distance.

Orleton and my cousin had left Monmouth once I had surrendered the great seal. They had been gone for some time; a necessary absence, the bishop explained when he greeted me some days later. I could not have cared any less, but he could not wait to explain his absence more fully. When Orleton smiles, it is sure to be an evil omen. I could not abide the man, and he clearly felt secure enough in my perilous state not to feel any sympathy for my situation.

He entered my chamber without manner or consideration. He looked at Will as though he were the lowest scullery boy, dismissing him with a curt nod in the direction of the door. Will, always respectful and courteous stared boldly back at him and then looked over to where I sat in front of the fire.

I smiled at his defiance and made his departure easier by asking him to leave us for a while. "No doubt his grace has urgent business that is for my ears alone."

Once Will had gone, Orleton drew up a chair which he placed opposite me, sinking into it and holding his hands up to the fire, rubbing them together briskly.

"You will be wondering, no doubt, what has taken the earl and myself away for these past days!" He announced joyfully.

I continued to look at him without letting my curiosity getting the better of me. "I had not noticed your absence bishop, forgive me."

The crow smirked, brushing off the sarcasm with a wave of his bony hand. "Hugh Despenser was executed two days ago at Hereford. Ah, now I have your attention! I daresay you would like details, so I have memorised them so that I can relay them to you with accuracy."

I swallowed hard, my heart beating so loudly I was certain that it could be heard throughout the castle. For several moments, I wondered if I would faint at the shock of his words, even though I had reluctantly tried to prepare myself for them.

"The traitor, whose crimes I need not repeat as they are known to you better than anyone, were read aloud and sentence passed."

"So, he was allowed no chance to speak in his defence, just like Piers Gaveston." I felt a growing nausea.

"And Thomas of Lancaster," Orleton countered waspishly.

I said nothing to that.

"He was taken out and tied to a hurdle, wearing a crown of sharp nettles, symbolising his encroaching royal power! The hurdle was then tied to horses and dragged through the streets to – ironically – his own castle, where some gallows had been erected." He paused, staring at me to gauge my reaction.

"A noose was tied around his neck and he was hauled up, but only partially strangled, he was lowered onto a ladder where his cock and his balls were then hacked off. His heart and intestines were cut out and thrown on a fire. He was thereafter beheaded. The four quarters of his body were each taken to Carlisle, York, Dover and Bristol. His head was taken to London where it was carried through Cheapside to the cheer of the great crowds that had gathered, and impaled on a pike upon London Bridge."

I sat numb for several moments as the full force of the bishop's merciless words hit me like a blow to my stomach. I then leaned over the arm of my chair and vomited.

"You are affected by this information?" the bishop asked, delightedly, "Yes, I can see you are."

I spat out the last retch of sour bile, and sank back. My head pounded, I closed my eyes and prayed that I could hold myself together without giving the grinning bishop the satisfaction of watching me weep.

"Did he say anything? Did he speak at all?" I asked weakly.

Orleton smiled, a mirthless, hateful smile that served only to make him look more sinister.

"One would normally expect a condemned felon to ask for forgiveness of God before he departs this life, but any words Despenser had, he kept to himself.

I rose from my seat. I felt faint and staggered back slightly, before I felt myself falling and everything went black.

+++

When I awoke some time later, the bishop had gone, and I was laid out on my bed. Will was by me, dabbing my brow with a damp, soft linen cloth. I sat up; I had been asleep for some hours, and I felt lightheaded. I could not get the image of Hugh out of my head, much the same as I had been unable to do when Piers was murdered.

I thought about how very frightened he must have been, knowing on his journey to Hereford he was travelling to certain death. I considered the bishop's unrelenting details, the horror of his description. He was correct inasmuch as he had clearly remembered every detail, yet surely one would not easily forget such a blood-curdling exhibition.

Like Piers, I had done everything but save Hugh. I'd permitted his undoubted avarice when I should have forced him to be more prudent. Yet, I had known that he was the master of dubious practices, indeed, to my eternal shame, I gave him most of what he had! I was not a complete fool. I heard about his wickedness, his persecution of the weak and the insatiable desire for rich rewards.

I realised now that, with Hugh gone, I was without that support I always needed so much. I had relied on both Piers and Hugh, and yet both were taken from me. As much as I did little to stop either of them continuing their destructive behaviour, they had always been masters of their own destiny. I was merely a partner in their folly.

What next? I wondered. The prince was now effectively King of England. All I could do was pray that he would use his reign and exercise his power better than I had done.

+++

Christmas was a most depressing affair that year of thirteen hundred and twenty-six. I had been transferred to Kenilworth and, when we crossed the courtyard into that great fortress, I could not supress a feeling of doom. A dark melancholy had descended on me while at Monmouth, and I admit I was more than apathetic about where we travelled next.

My cousin, Henry of Lancaster, treated me with cordial respect, for which I was grateful. God forbid I should be a prisoner of the bishop of Hereford!

I heard from Henry that Isabella, Edward and 'others' spent the festive season at Wallingford castle, once home to my beloved Piers. Having received plenty of gossip concerning the queen whilst I had been a free man, I imagined that other guests may well include Roger Mortimer. I even noticed a rather stern look cross Henry's face when he mentioned him. Clearly there was little affection in their association.

I was grateful for Henry's honesty with me. I had always preferred to be told the truth, however unpalatable it may be. Whether I acted upon it was negligible. My cousin did not hold back in the telling of where my future lay. "There is no discussion about you being reunited with Isabella and your family," he said plainly.

"I am glad that there will be no temptation for me to wish it so." I replied. "I am sad not to see my son, Edward. How does he fare, Henry?"

"Ah Ned, he is indeed a fine young man! He is cheered whenever he is seen, and for one of such a young age, he is courteous and affable to all. You would be so proud of him. Forgive me, Ned, I speak more than I should." He suddenly seemed embarrassed at his words.

I sought to put him at his ease. "You need not apologise cousin, I am glad to hear that he does well; I hope to God he grows to be a wiser man than I."

"I do not believe the council are fully agreed yet on how matters will proceed. I am, however, permitted to tell you that you will be invited to attend a parliament."

I laughed bitterly. "Do they really believe that I would so willingly come amongst my enemies? I have nothing to tell them that would mitigate my circumstances."

Henry looked rather sad, and nodded gently. He could see clearly the reunion at Westminster was never going to happen.

Kenilworth castle, like most fortresses had a foundry, and Henry permitted me to use it. The blacksmiths there looked at me with curiosity and, in some cases, distaste – but, as I helped them in their work, they gradually stared at me less and continued with their tasks, occasionally correcting me on certain instruments and how best to use them. Despite the cold weather,

I soon worked up a sweat, and pounded away at the metal, dealing it a blow for each of my frustrations. I finished my work with them, and thanked them for their company and teaching. I was about to leave when one of them fell to his knees in front of me, grasping my hand. I smiled at him. Perhaps not everyone hated me. I daresay I would have made a better blacksmith than a king.

I had not spent a better day at Kenilworth than that one and, for the first time in weeks, I began to sleep better and dwell less on the storm I was certain was fast approaching; it arrived soon enough.

I had heard from Henry that the parliament that I had refused to attend had debated openly the follies of my reign and how, rather than a noble ruler, I had held royal power as a tyrant that had allowed others to influence me in all manner of evils, and it was agreed that allegiance should pass from me to my son Edward. I felt sick at the words, but I don't recall I was surprised at the decision. I even think that Henry may have been slowly trying to prepare me for the worst; I was told to expect a delegation to arrive, which would officially announce the decision of parliament.

What strange games our minds play with us. One can be almost resigned to a particular state and then, out of nowhere, there is a sudden determination to cling to what we know is lost - as it was with me as I prepared for the arrival of the delegation that would ultimately decide on my fate. For those few hours, I was suddenly horrified that I might no longer be king! All I had known, all that I had been brought up to inherit, was no longer mine by divine right.

What could I do about the situation? I could change, surely, perhaps agree to new Ordinances. Isabella could be brought round; there was something between us, I was sure of it - we were both still young. A fresh start...What folly! A soon as I began to think fervently about how I could recover all that I was losing, my mind was in torment and my head ached from the thoughts that tore around my brain. I prayed God would give me strength.

The delegation from Westminster arrived in a dismal cortege. Fittingly, I dressed in black. Piers would no doubt have approved of this rather theatrical gesture, but no dramatics were intended; I had merely decided to mourn the loss of my dignity.

I had, on more than one occasion, clashed with Adam Orleton, the bishop of Hereford, asking the pope several times to agree to dismiss him. All to no avail, and the prelate was afforded the exquisite opportunity to gloat on my fate.

I did not count how many accompanied him in this, his personal victory, but I was aware of some familiar faces. William Trussell, the justice who had conducted the farcical hearings over both Hugh and his father. The Earl of Surrey, the Bishop of Winchester. Other faces which I cannot recall now. I sat with my hands folded on my lap. I thanked God and all his saints that I was able to keep some measure of pride and decorum. I held my head up nobly.

Trussell cleared his throat and the room fell quiet while he read out a rather long list of sins and practices.

During a pause, I spoke to say that I was genuinely aggrieved that my subjects were so angry with me.

More of them spoke, but I remember little of what they said; it would all have been much the same.

Orleton then spoke, trying his best not to sound as delighted as he was. He gleefully explained the reason for the delegation, and demanded that I resign my crown in favour of my eldest son.

Saying to myself what the conclusion of this meeting would be was, unfortunately, easier than to hear another say it, and now the words became a shouting in my ear.

Trussell then officially withdrew the kingdom's allegiance from me. My steward Thomas le Blount looked shockingly pale as he took the ceremonial staff of office and broke it in two.

My reign was now at an end.

+++

There was silence in the herbalist workshop as Edward stopped speaking, and continued to stare ahead, almost in a trance. Alphage nodded his head sagely, and Manuel committed these facts to memory; it would be necessary to relay them in as much detail as possible.

"Twenty years' reign," Manuel commented. "A fair enough length of time."

Edward smiled sadly at him. "Nineteen years, twenty-nine weeks and five days, to be precise, my friend."

"Word had it that the very legality of the abdication was in doubt afterwards; would it surely not have been wiser to bring you to London?" the envoy queried.

"As I told you, Manuel, I had already stated I would not walk willingly into a den with so many lions, and

I meant it. The difficulty was only that such a thing had never happened before and, with no precedent, there was a great deal of uncertainty."

Edward stood and dusted down his hose which was covered in seeds and dust. He took up his earthenware cup and drank from it. His throat was dry, and he felt tired, but verbalising all that had past was quite a revelation to himself. How much had happened and how much he had gone through in his lifetime was, in a strange way, cleansing – in much the same way as one of the good brothers here when they finally realised their calling and found their unshakeable faith.

Once again, the monastery kitchen had sent food for their midday meal; some cured bacon, dry but flavoursome, cheese and freshly baked bread, apples, grapes and some watered beer. And most importantly, cheese in a small wooden bowl, which could only be for one small dog who watched the kitchen boy's every move until the bowl was placed on the ground in front of him. Perrot had barely taken more than two gulps before his meal was gone. Edward smiled at the animal before throwing him some dried meat.

"It was true that there were several voices of dissent at the plan to force my abdication and crown my son in my stead," he said, once he had swallowed a mouthful of bread. "Representatives from Wales had even refused to attend the parliament. Several bishops were unhappy at the turn that events were taking. It was one thing to hang a royal favourite and cut out his heart, it was quite another to crown a new king while his predecessor was still alive.

Be that as it may, whilst I longed for my freedom, the role of king had done me little good. I was born as

I was, and I could not be otherwise. So, I was now merely Sir Edward of Caernarfon.

+++

I managed to stand with composure once Blount had broken the staff of office that had ended my reign. I was aware that one or two of the delegation had actually knelt at the same time, whether from guilt or relief, who knows?

I excused myself and at least made it to my bedchamber before I fell upon it and howled. I sobbed for so long that I was exhausted by the time Will removed my shoes, loosened the neck of my shirt and swung my legs up onto the bed. I slept for many hours, although it was much disturbed.

Will had accepted without hesitation the offer to stay with me in captivity and, as much as I wanted him to consider his own life, he was adamant that for the present he would remain where he had always been.

I remember hugging him in my delight. He had been with me for all of my tragic reign, delighted in the victories and suffered the very depth of sadness with me. In that time, he had all but put his own life on hold, simply out of honour. I was not worthy of Will Shene!

My cousin, Henry of Lancaster, continued to treat me with the utmost respect and concern. I was not to leave the castle, but I was permitted use of the gardens which were beautiful. Not unlike Langley – it occurred to me that I may never see my precious Langley again and the thought saddened me. The summers there had been some of the happiest moments of my life.

First with Perrot and much later Hugh, and even Roger – I smiled again at the surprise he and I both had when I interrupted his bathing! How good it was to relive those memories not tarnished by bloodshed, hatred or malice.

I had tried to make it a routine to walk in the grounds every morning and I noticed my cousin Henry waiting for me; whether by design or chance, I was unsure.

He smiled in greeting, asking how I was and checking that every courtesy was being observed.

"I am content enough," was all I could say. He was silent.

"You seemed troubled, cousin," I observed. "Am I too difficult a prisoner?"

He looked away, and I sensed an issue that he was loathe to discuss. At length he came out with his concerns. "It seems, Ned, that you are to be moved from this place."

I was not a contented captive, it was true, but I had begun to feel that, if I was to be shut away, I could expect far worse gaolers. My voice must have betrayed my concern. "Moved? Why? To where?"

"As to why, that is easily explained, and you above all men know the cut and thrust of the bizarre, dangerous times we live in and how quickly fortunes can change."

"Please explain, Henry, I am puzzled. Tell me all, I will not betray you to Mortimer or the queen, supposing they intend to visit me to enquire after my well being."

"I have word that the queen and Mortimer do not trust me. They fear my influence and that, with the income and lands I enjoy, I have become a problem they can no longer avoid. My custody of you suggests that, if there were many who questioned the legality of the parliament that stripped you of your throne, you could well try and overturn the decision. With my help, their cause would be in danger of collapse. The belief is that I can hold them to ransom. Furthermore, they believe I could use you to mount a rebellion, reinstating you as king!"

Such possibilities had, in all honesty, never occurred to me. As my internment continued, the loss of everything was complete. I missed much about being king, but what had it done for me? I had lost my darling Perrot, I had lost Hugh, my liberty, my self-respect, my friends.

"So what is their intention, do you know?"

"Alas, I do not!" Henry replied with a tone of anguish and frustration." I am, as you know, officially your son Edward's legal guardian, though the queen ensures that any access to the prince – sorry, forgive me, the king, is minimal at best."

"So, do you know where I am to go if they put a plan for my removal in action?"

"I know not, but I have heard it suggested that they intend to make you a prisoner of Thomas, Lord Berkeley, along with John Maltravers."

I groaned at the very idea. Berkeley was a dour, serious man, completely without humour. Added to which, I had imprisoned him some years before, and his lands had been given to Hugh. Maltravers had spent time on the Continent with Mortimer after his escape from the Tower. I feared I could expect little comfort from them.

Henry seemed to sense my despair. "Take heart, Ned," he said laying a friendly hand on my arm. "It has been made clear, on pain of death, that all who are charged with your care will exercise the utmost civility and respect and treat you well."

Just at that moment, a servant ran up to us; my cousin was called to attend to a matter elsewhere. He nodded his head respectfully and left.

I sat down on a nearby wooden bench and considered this potential development. Was I not close-confined enough? I was deeply saddened by the proposal. I had dealt little with Henry during the last few years, but I respected him as a man of honour, and certainly his treatment of me whilst at Kenilworth was most considerate.

I was to expect no reward from these men but, in truth, should I expect it? Many of them I had imprisoned, taken their lands which Hugh gleefully appropriated. Some had been permitted to pay fines in order to gain their freedom. Whilst I lamented Hugh, more and more I was bitter that I alone would now pay the price for those wicked deeds.

+++

In April of thirteen hundred and twenty-seven I arrived at Berkeley castle. This being after several detours by way of confusing anyone who may have thought of rescuing me on the journey. I was unable to find out more, but Will had heard from another servant of his acquaintance that there was a rumour that a plot to storm Kenilworth and liberate me had been discovered and although thwarted, did at least suggest to Isabella and Mortimer that I was not forgotten, and still had allies. There was, of course, a frustration in not knowing who might be behind the rescue attempt, but I had friends, at least.

Of course, Kenilworth is probably one of the best-fortified of all strongholds in England, and I doubted that enough of the men it would take to storm it and rescue me had been recruited. I was to learn much later of the many who risked their lives in a doomed effort to liberate me.

Thomas Berkeley, although not a man with whom to jest, was a fair enough gaoler and my chamber, situated in the keep, was comfortable. Indeed, I was allowed more servants and even a cook, the latter of which I was highly suspicious; an easy way of shortening my life would be tainting my food with poison, and for some days I was reluctant to eat anything other than plain bread and water. Berkeley's remedy for this was to insist my cook ate from the same meal he prepared for me in my presence. The man was happy to do so.

Letters from Isabella were delivered to me and, in truth, I was grateful for them. Estranged as we were, she wrote of our children, whom I agreed should be spared the torment of seeing their father in these much-reduced circumstances. What she told them of my sorry tale I do not know, and perhaps that is best.

I had, like most royal fathers, been primarily concerned with the heir that would follow me and, whilst I kept them all in great comfort in households of their own, they did not know or remember me well.

I spent my days thereafter in comfortable confinement. Apart from Isabella's letters that were purely cordial in their narrative, I was denied any other contact by letter, and even those I wrote had to be left unsealed until Berkeley or Maltravers had seen their content. The guard always at my cell door was respectful enough; a tall, strong-looking man, not unlike me in build. He said very little and made no attempt to ever engage me in conversation.

It seemed however, that there were more men than I realised who were unhappy with my captivity, more so because of what was apparently the growing arrogance of Roger Mortimer. I was not surprised; the man had always had an air of inflated self-worth. I had disliked him from the time we were young men, and I still curse my stupidity at not having him executed when I had the chance.

Will, however, had seemed strangely on edge for some days, and I believed he was nearing the end of his service to me. My devoted servant and I had shared many perils together, and I longed for him to tell me he was going to seek an alternative master. All I could do for him was to make it easy. Yet his request for permission to leave me never came.

As at Kenilworth, I was allowed some limited time in the grounds of Berkeley, and this exercise helped me greatly. Will and I would walk and sit, appreciating the joys of nature. I would walk, my mind constantly going over all that had happened to me. Will, respectful as ever, would walk several paces behind.

The summer of thirteen hundred and twenty-seven had been warm and stifling, and the clouds at last seemed to threaten a downpour that would break the spell. The rain did indeed start, the result being that I was unable to walk, much to my disappointment.

The castle had, on one particular day, been quiet. The usual shouts and calls from servants or soldiers were strangely silent. For what purpose I did not know, nor did I give much thought to it. In the days that followed, the significance of this was to became clear.

That particular night, I was rescued from Berkeley castle.

+++

"So you were saved by a gang of men who had remained loyal to you, even after your deposition?" Alphage clasped his hands together as though the feat had just been achieved.

"The wind, rain and thunder had continued for most of the day. When Will woke me I was in a daze. Fighting seemed to be going on all around me, but I could only concentrate on getting outside the castle walls. There had, I learned later, been little resistance. There were fewer guards on duty at the castle that night. I have long wondered at the reason for that. Was it by chance or a deliberate way of ensuring that a plot to rescue me would succeed?"

"Who would have given such a command?" Fieschi was intrigued.

"I don't suppose I will ever know the answer to that, Manuel. I did learn later that Isabella had been wracked with grief and indecision about my survival and had made an agreement with Thomas Berkeley. I was to be allowed to escape with merely a token effort to prevent me.

Isabella was many things, but a murderess? No. Her letters to me suggested that she did in fact still feel some love for me, but she had been humiliated and, faced with the prospect that had things carried on as they were, our son would have nothing to inherit. For a woman so steeped in royal tradition, one wonders why she did not do worse.

Let us finish then, and have done with this sorry tale."

+++

The night of my liberation from Berkeley was fraught with danger, the threat to its success was a very real one as far as we were concerned. It was only later that we questioned why the garrison were so few.

We rode into the night, stopping only briefly to exchange our tired horses for others at a previously-agreed rendezvous. A small barn that looked deserted did in fact contain many men, most of them armed. All of them bent the knee to me upon my entrance. The reception was quite overwhelming.

The rain had lessened and, while sentries were stationed outside, I was finally able to take in the magnitude of this achievement and identify properly those who had risked so much for my liberation.

I knew both Thomas and Stephen Dunheved; the former was a Dominican monk who had done service for me with the pope a few years previously. He was a jovial looking man, with a cheery disposition and a hearty laugh. He no longer dressed in the habit of a monk, but I did not ask if he had forsaken his order. His brother Stephen was a darker character, a fighting man of few words, but brave deeds. He had been forced to abjure the realm after killing a man during a violent robbery. I forget the details he told me. His past sins were none of my affair, and his service to me now more than pardoned him in my eyes.

Thomas spoke of how he and these others had been seeking out more who wanted to restore me to my throne. I recognised some of the men here present, men who had previously served in my household.

I had so many questions, but knew time was of the essence, so tried to ask what I immediately needed to know. "Tell me though Thomas, how did you know where to even locate me? Berkeley has, I think, more than one cell that would have been appropriate for me."

Thomas beamed and reached over and gave Will Shene a rub on his shoulder, while some others patted him on the back. Will coloured at the compliments.

"Will was keeping us updated for some weeks on your usual routine as well as noting when guards were changed and, most importantly, how to get out of Berkeley once we got in! We would never have achieved what we have this night without him."

I pulled Will towards me and kissed him affectionately on the head, while the company laughed as he coloured again. I was glad that I could now account for his edgy, nervous behaviour in recent weeks.

We had time only to rest for a while and eat, and Stephen insisted that we tarry no longer. It would be dawn soon, and we had a long journey ahead.

What followed in the ensuing months was more hiding places, more concerns for my continued liberty. I had grown a much bushier beard and, as time passed, threads of grey streaked my once-blond facial hair.

The Dunheved brothers did not stay long in my company; having rescued me, they saw little opportunity of regaining my throne whilst there continued to be unrest. There was panic when I escaped Berkeley, and yet one bizarre tale suggested that I had indeed died and been buried! How I would love to have attended that ceremony! Men were even charged with my murder, in fact.

Many still believed I could regain what had been lost to me but, as time went by, I became less certain that this would ever come about; and if it did?

I could not, in all honesty, declare that it was now my sole wish. I had lived a dramatic life, I had loved easily and passionately, I had made so many mistakes; some I was prepared to blame on my frivolous conceit or simply sheer folly! I had lost my wife and would never see my children grow up.

What, then, could I expect were I able and willing to mount a serious effort to regain the throne? Certainly more bloodshed, most possibly still the enmity of my queen, and most assuredly a country riddled with discontent.

I realised now that I no longer wanted what so many had suffered to try and achieve for me. I felt this more urgently when I heard from Stephen Dunheved that Thomas had been caught and executed. I felt sick, weary of the entire ritual of unhappiness and death, cruelty and loss. And for what?

Will and I had been residing at a secret hideout on Lundy Island, yes, the very same Island that Hugh had insisted on having and then forgot about, other than when we considered it as a possible safe haven from Isabella and Mortimer. Though small, the island was generally ignored, with few inhabitants; those who did dwell there were curious only for a short time, quite content to be told that our band were merely hermits.

One day, I simply woke and decided I could no longer endanger these brave souls who dreamed that one day their efforts would be rewarded when I sat again as king of England. I roused Will and took, from my satchel, ink and a pen. I scrawled a note thanking these brave men with all my heart, but they should look to their safety and their futures and waste no more time in what was fast becoming a doomed enterprise.

Stephen had returned to us several days before, and I believe he realised that I was losing hope and had considered abandoning the small group who had saved my life. Whether he ever understood, I do not know. What became of any of them is uncertain, but I pray to God that they were able to return to their loved ones and take up again the threads of their own lives.

We were able to secure a craft and a boatman who was not deterred by the unsettled water on that morning. I handed the old man some coins which he pocketed with surprise. I doubt he had made as much in a year at whatever he did!

Our boat, although small, held itself well as the choppy water pitched us first one way then the other, testing even the hardiest of crew, and it was sometime before we enjoyed a calmer pace. I had enjoyed many sea journeys - either for pleasure with Hugh, or for duty to France to pay homage. I had always marvelled at the expanse of water that had no end, no limits or conformity. A mystery all of its own, that held a curious temptation.

I smiled to myself to recall Piers's horrified aversion to the sea, and his terror of ending his days in a watery grave, victim of the cruel depths that made the sea so omnipotent. I had laughed at his irrational fear, teasing him that it was extremely unlikely that London would ever be flooded and that there was little chance of the water seeking him out and dragging him back to its dark, deep prison. Strange that he, who had been so fearless of everything else, should prove to be such a poor mariner.

My heart felt suddenly heavy; at least, I thought, he had been spared that cruel end. I thanked God that his enemies had been unaware of his secret horror. Had they known, they would most certainly have devised some drawn-out death involving the cruel waters of the English Channel. Dear God, I could vividly imagine my beloved held in a rowing boat while the bastard Warwick grinned mercilessly as Piers manned the oars during a violent storm.

I was aware of the crew beginning to busy themselves. I had been so engrossed in my own melancholy thoughts, I had not realised that land had been sighted; the ending of one journey, and the beginning of another. I felt my guts tighten with the familiar sensation of anxiety as we drew closed to a small inlet where we could safely set down.

+++

To be anywhere in England for me was a danger, even after being told I had died at Berkeley, there may well still be suspicious minds that still wondered if some of the rumours had been true, and that I was quite alive.

We left the small inlet and travelled up the coast to Dover where I was intending to take a ship to France.

The roads were easy underfoot, at least. After several stops we at last reached the port. Will headed off to try and book a passage. One boat carried only goods and two sailors, so the number of people who need see me was at least limited. It was while I waited for Will that I made one of the hardest decisions I had ever taken, and it seemed strange that everything I had thought important in my life was dwarfed by comparison to what I now knew I must do.

"We must hurry, sire," Will said, taking up the two bundles that contained all we had. I rested a hand on each of his shoulders and turned him to face me.

"This is now my journey alone, Will. You have sacrificed enough for me, more than all others. I have kept you close to me for so long and it is time I let you go. No, do not look so sad, I am content with what I have and what I have lost. My words do not come from your king, they come from your friend, and no man could have been blessed with such a friend. I never told you how much I owe you for everything you have done, your care, your unwavering loyalty, your service – your patience!"

We both laughed, with tears in our eyes. I looked at him for several moments, taking in his concerned, sad face, those large brown eyes, the studied brow.

"Return to Henley, marry your sweetheart - I hope she has waited for you. Take this with my love and gratitude." I pressed into his hand a velvet purse that would probably be enough to buy him some property. I had kept it since we had escaped from Berkeley.

"God bless you, Will Shene." I clutched him once more to me and then I turned and ran up the plank from the dock to the small boat that was now starting to cast off. I recalled a very similar scene when Piers had left on his first exile. Unlike him I would not return. I raised a final hand to my servant, my friend, who now stood fighting back tears, his arm raised in a farewell gesture.

Few have understood me like Will Shene and I miss him desperately. In the rages that so often consumed me, many would have got as far away from me as possible, but Will would wait for me to exhaust myself and then clear up the devastation I had wreaked. For all the passion I had for Piers, and then Hugh even Roger, I loved Will with all my heart. His love for me had truly been one that expected no rewards. His wish had been to serve me and so he did, with a devotion that never wavered in all the years he had spent with me. His loyalty to me had won him few rewards, and it is to my eternal shame that, at a time when I could, that I had not elevated him to a higher office, commoner though he was. I hope his sweetheart had waited for him.

+++

My time in France was very brief, but a chance encounter at the port where I landed filled the void that Will left. A hound of no discernable breed watched me carefully as I left the boat and went in search of food. It watched from a short distance when I stopped at a market stall and bought a meat pie.

It took even more notice of me, when I spat out the putrid meat which was foul to the taste. The hound seemed, however, to find the broken crust and whatever was inside a delight and it was soon gobbled up. I smiled at it and went to move away. It followed me.

I walked on a bit further, and although I did not believe I was in any danger of being recognised, human traffic from England to the French court was steady and continual, so I did not take a chance. I took some food and beer in a greasy tavern at the dockside. The place smelt of salt and sweat, but it was tidy enough and my host did not appear to be inquisitive about me, familiar as he no doubt was to strangers passing through. He refused the dog entrance, however.

It was here that I learned, from a loud conversation between two other patrons, that Roger Mortimer had been executed by order of the king! I do not recall feeling any great delight in the news; perhaps that was more evidence that my apathy suggested a desire to leave the past in the past.

His end, however, was not dignified. Having been found guilty of a whole list of crimes, he was taken from his cell in the Tower of London – the irony would not have been lost on him – dressed in the same black tunic he had apparently worn to my funeral. He was placed on an ox-hide, tied to two horses and dragged all the way to Tiburn! Knowing that to be a distance of at least two miles, I shuddered to imagine the state of his body when he had arrived. His tunic was then stripped from him and his naked body was hanged by the neck. He had taken no time to die, no struggle at all. His corpse remained there for two days, until it was at last cut down by some Franciscan friars to be buried.

An ignoble end certainly, but I was indifferent now, his death had changed nothing for me.

My new canine companion was difficult to shake off, but after a while I saw no harm in him tagging along;

we were both strays. I named him Perrot, something I know his namesake would have loved; and, as with Piers, he was always with me.

So, thereafter I travelled where I could, with the first destination being Avignon. I was fortunate to find a friar whom, I discovered after some conversation - and, it has to be said, some degree of pride - was part of a delegation from Ireland that had been waiting for an audience with the pope for some days and were finally to meet him that very afternoon.

I took from my satchel the small pouch that I had kept for many years, and begged the friar to find some way to hand it to his holiness. The friar looked at me with interest, but happily he agreed, as he was certain to be presented to the holy father personally!

I waited outside for word. The place seemed teaming with people, merchants, artisans and beggars on every corner. Avignon was certainly larger than I had expected. Large mansions and palaces housed the rich and mighty, cardinals and wealthy merchants. The place had, however, been described as 'a sewer where the filth of the universe is collected'.

I had waited only a short period of time when the Irish friar returned, accompanied by a soldier. The friar seemed less than pleased to see me again, and I momentarily thought his mission for me was unsuccessful, but it seemed not. He stopped in front of me and sniffed with annoyance.

"Whoever you are, it seems that even now we have to wait again because of you. Yes, I was able to give that purse to an attendant who gave it to the holy father. Perhaps, as you are about to meet him without having to wait, you might remind him about us?"

I smiled as apologetically as I could and turned to the soldier, who was becoming rather impatient with the friar and puzzled that he had been sent to escort to his holiness a shaggy-bearded man who looked like a hermit or dowdy priest.

The soldier eventually tired of the friar's moaning, pushed him brusquely to one side and asked me to accompany him.

I tried to mouth an apology as I was led away, but the friar sat himself down with a huff. I ordered Perrot to 'stay!'; whoever had been the hound's previous master had taught him well, and he appeared happy to sit beside the friar, who looked distastefully at him.

We seemed to walk through a maze of corridors; the cool breeze that swept through them was welcoming now that the morning sun was up.

Eventually, we came to a large, ornate door, the soldier knocked and I was ushered into a small antechamber where a man rose from a desk. He was tall and dignified, with a balding head, a large bulbous nose and thin red lips.

When he spoke it was with a surprisingly soft tone, calm and careful.

"Si Edward, you are most welcome. Allow me to take your baggage, and I will escort you to his holiness straight away." The title he used took me by surprise at first, yet surely this man was privy to all his master's associates.

He walked to another door, and after a barely perceptible knock, he stood by and I entered. The chamber was large and full of sunlight that flooded in through three large windows. A floor-to-ceiling silk tapestry, depicting the resurrection of Jesus into heaven, hung grandly and rippled slightly as I entered. A rather small figure stood by a window that looked out onto a courtyard below. He turned and walked towards me, arms outstretched.

"Edward, I am honoured to see you. Sit, please, and let us talk."

I knelt before him, kissing his hand. He raised me up and waved me to a chair. We sat opposite one another, and a glass of cool wine was offered to me by a serving boy who seemed to appear from nowhere. It was placed on an ornate table beside me, next to a small silver dish holding slices of melon and rich coloured grapes.

Pope John the twenty-second looked at me carefully. He had a round, fleshy face, with small dark eyes and full red lips. His chubby fingers dripped with rings and he wore a large bejewelled cross over his gold and red tunic. His small feet were squeezed into soft Spanish leather slippers and his seat was upholstered in the finest damask red. His holiness was certainly not stinting on his luxuries.

"You have been much on my mind, Edward," he said softly. "I am sorry to find you in this state. You have been through much, so much. Yet, you have survived against all odds. I heard from my informants that you had possibly escaped from Berkeley castle. After that, you simply disappeared. I have to tell you I am surprised to see you here in Avignon. I believe God has spared you for something. Perhaps it is not to wear a crown."

He chuckled softly, and I smiled in agreement with him.

"Father, I do not want to go home to England, I do not wish to take up the heavy mantle of ruler again. I do not want to return to my wife!" This final declaration was, I think, something of a disappointment to him. He had declared many times while I was estranged from Isabella that his dearest wish that we be reunited again.

"Do you no longer love her?" he asked, quite pointedly.

I struggled with what to say, so I just spoke what came immediately to my lips - "No!"

The pontif did not appear shocked, but nodded sagely. "And your sons and daughters?"

"They are nothing to me but memories. I regret that I did not know any of them better, but such is the way of kings, there is little room for sentiment."

"And are you resolved to remain hidden somewhere for the remainder of your life?"

"I can never return to England now; it is no longer my home. I will wander this earth until I find the sanctuary that I need. I am a man tormented by the past; my mistakes have been many, but I have paid for them."

He looked at me and smiled sadly. "Yes," he said, "I believe you have. What can I do to help you?"

"Nothing for me, but I beg you to be a guiding hand to my son. He is young and has had to grow quickly. I hear that he has had Mortimer executed and I thank God for it, forgive me!"

He frowned at my delight. "Mortimer, was, I believe a man of much arrogance," he said, by way of excusing the Lord of Wigmore's faults. "You may not know, then, that the King has similarly dismissed his mother from court. Her power and influence is at an end. Your son, it seems, intends to rule on his own terms!"

I suddenly felt a wave of gratitude, and I inexplicably began to weep. Ever a fool with my emotions, I could not hold them in check. In that most beautiful of rooms, I sank to my knees before him and cried. All that had gone before me flooded back like a river that had finally burst its dam. The pontiff placed a gentle hand on my head, but said nothing.

Eventually, I regained some composure, and sat up again on my chair. We were silent for a while. I had no intention of telling him all my woes as I have to both of you.

"All I ask of you, holy father, is your agreement to help Edward; he needs a guidance that I can never give him, and should not give him. God knows, I am no father to follow."

He nodded again. "I will be here for him, I promise. You say you have done nothing for him, yet you ask that I guide him if needed. Perhaps you were not a good king, Edward, but you are maybe a far better man than you realise."

My visit to Avignon had gone well, but I knew it was time to move on again. I was treated as an exalted guest, afforded a luxurious chamber and a bath. I spoke much to his holiness, and felt some peace. The morning of my departure, I left the papal residence, where Pope John had kept me in comfort for several days, feeling I had done all I could for Edward; I prayed he would act wisely as I never had. I was glad to find Perrot waiting for me. He had been fed and taken care of during my stay. His feathery tail wagged furiously when he saw me and I was glad to witness his excitement.

I had turned into the street where I had been shown out, when something made me stop and retrace my steps. Further along, beggars held out small cups or grubby claws barely covered in skin in the hope of some charity. There was, however, one beggar that had caught my attention in just a fleeting glance.

I walked nearer to him, although he appeared merely a pile of rags. I crouched down in front of a bony, frail man with a deeply-pitted complexion.

My heart missed a few beats before I spoke.

"Hugo?

The face that looked up at me, though emaciated, was none other than Piers Gaveston's former manservant. He looked at me strangely as though not believing what he was seeing. Suddenly he threw himself at me, clutching at me as though I held his life in my hands. I told him I was indeed who he thought I was. I went to raise him up, to get him away from the street where he sat surrounded but rotting fish and old sour meat, a carcass of a dead dog nearby almost made me physically sick.

I went to help him, but he just shouted, "No, no!" I realised then, to my horror and distress, that he was a cripple. One leg was bent at an impossible angle, the other stretched motionless in front of him. He could not stand, and I would learn little by asking him what had happened for him to be living in such a state. I realised, sadly, that I could do nothing for him, so I sat with him, sharing the food and provisions that had been given to me before I left the papal residence.

I noticed several tramps, vagabonds and cutthroats moved closer to him, eyes greedy and hands ready to grasp. I waved them angrily away; my charity, it appeared, only worked with certain beggars. We talked for a while, mere trivialities, but he had difficulty speaking, for reasons he did not say. I said nothing at the stench that suddenly emanated from where he sat, and yet the pool that formed underneath him seeped out. He had soiled and pissed himself, but I was not disgusted, just so very, very sad.

The other varmints cursed and spat at him as they probably did every time it happened. Perrot growled menacingly. Hugo's words were difficult to make out; he mumbled.

"Master Piers, dead! Dead!

"Yes Hugo, dead many years ago." He knew, of course, as he had been there.

"Sorry to tell you, I'm sorry he's dead."

"I know Hugo. Dear God, what happened to you?"

He then, suddenly, began to laugh. I thought it merely another sign that his wits were gone, but I heard him say, "Warwick, Warwick!"

"Hugo, yes, you remember Warwick."

"Hugo kill Warwick!" he stammered excitedly.

"No Hugo, Warwick is already..." I stopped mid sentence. I cast my mind back to the banquet at Warwick castle, the wine.... the wine - it was poisoned! I recalled the strange look I had noticed that evening - Hugo smirking with satisfaction; he had had revenge for his beloved master.

I sat with him for a while, but he did not speak again, merely drifted back into whatever mysterious place he had previously been. I told him that I would return the following day and I would do something to help him from that disgusting place. I found a cheap straw bed for the night at a small tavern and I did return, but he was no longer there. I searched for him down every street I came to, and I had just decided to give up when I noticed the cart.

A large wooden barrow, with one ill-fitting wheel, creaked along at a slow pace. A wizened old man walked it a few paces before picking up horse dung and other waste. I noticed then, from its depths, a hand. I stopped the man and asked to see the body.

"We've a clean up to do," he explained. "All the shit has to be cleared. Yes, that one was dead this morning; we take them to the pit, that's where they all end up, poor sods!"

I wept silently as I clawed at the stinking refuse to fully uncover his face which, to my surprise, wore a smile.

There was nothing I could do for Hugo. Where could I go with him? Where could I bury him, supposing they let me? He had once been so lively and funny. Piers adored him, and I realised now that, once he had avenged his death, his life lost some purpose. I had no idea how he became so crippled. To be hurled onto a waste wagon was no way to end one's life. I said a prayer for him as the old man with the barrow hawked, spat and moved on, the old wheel clunking as it went.

I left Avignon a sadder man than when I had arrived.

+++

I moved many times after that, staying only briefly, still unable to find a place to call home. Finally, I arrived in Lombardy, moving on a couple of times when fighting broke out in some of the regions. Firstly, to Val di Magra where I believe I contracted a fever that was to plague me for some time. I thanked God for my continued robust health, that kept me mobile, and yet that would ironically give out, just as I found where I think I had been looking for.

My journey ended at the gates of this monastery of Sant Alberto. Dear Alphage, you healed my body and spirit and I learned to live with myself again.

+++

"So Sant Alberto is now your home." Alphage stated with pride. "Edward, you have lived a remarkable life, you have lost much, but I believe you have faced your demons. You must live out your life satisfied that you have surely atoned for mistakes that you have made. Bless you!" Alphage reached over to Edward and embraced him warmly.

Much of the warmth had gone out of the day when Edward finally finished relating his tale. One that was, in turn, dramatic and tragic. The story of one man's foolishness, and a fall that was surely unprecedented. Edward's tale had taken him on a journey that would surely have broken the will of most. How many live through such times and survive them? The man whom Alphage and Fieschi had listened to was a man broken, but now seemed strangely at peace with himself.

The man who had been horrified to have been discovered, had now surely purged himself of his many mistakes and sins. He had loved and been loved, he had been faithful and yet had been betrayed. Eventually, he had lost all. Yet as Alphage had told him, God had kept faith with him - Edward, the man.

After some moments, Edward sighed and took in a deep breath as though he was now out of words. For the first time in so long, the smile he showed to Alphage was one of contentment not sadness.

The elderly monk was the first to move, easing himself up off a stool that he normally did not sit on for so long, and his back and knees grumbled at his prolonged inactivity.

Manuel smiled at Edward and nodded. The man he had travelled to meet no longer had a throne, but he was most certainly a king. What greatness could he have achieved if he had learnt those harsh lessons earlier? The hermit was surely, in the eyes of the Lord, more sinner than saint, and there had surely been no other man who had inherited a crown and a role for which he was so tragically unsuitable.

The slightly cooler air had energised Perrot and, after ferociously scratching the back of his ear, he shook himself and trotted round the garden, watering some of the herbs as he went.

Alphage smiled at the hermit, resting a hand on his arm. "Perhaps we should enter the church now and give thanks for the strength God has given you."

Edward smiled. He remained, as the elderly monk knew, a rather lukewarm devotee of God, but he did not press him.

"Perhaps tomorrow, Alphage," he said. "To be truthful, I am exhausted; I would welcome some sleep. Maybe now it will be without the bad dreams."

The old monk smiled and nodded. "Of course, the Abbot will understand; you must rest for the remainder of the day and awake refreshed tomorrow, and hopefully lighter in heart. Ah! And I think there is a small creature here that would welcome some cheese!"

Perrot was immediately attentive.

Manuel Fieschi had stood and had shaken Edward by the hand, and scrutinised him closely.

"You really are a most remarkable man, Edward. What a shame life has taken its toll on you. His holiness will be glad to know that you fare well."

He turned then to Alphage. "Brother, I wonder if you would be so good as to inform Father Abbot that I intend to leave this afternoon. I did say it was a possibility."

Brother Alphage bowed his head respectfully and shook the envoy warmly by the hand. "God be with you, Manuel Fieschi."

Both men watched the monk go, with Perrot excitedly ahead of him.

"Let me walk with you a while." Fieschi smiled. "And what of England, do you ever wonder how things fare?"

"My crown did me little good. My intention when I left was to be as far from it as possible. Maybe one day I will write to my son. I long for news of him."

"It has been a long journey for you, Edward."

"And for you too, Manuel," Edward stated.

"For me?" the envoy questioned.

Edward smiled. "Did you think I did not know it was you behind the silk hanging in the pope's chamber at my first meeting with him in Avignon? I thought, at first, it was merely a breeze from the door, but you wear a distinctive cologne, Manuel; one I thought pleasant at the time, and the same one that I smelled when first we met. I am blessed with an extraordinary sense of smell. I breathed in Perrot's lavender enough, and your own is certainly distinctive, a citrus cologne I think."

Manuel was taken aback. "I bow to your remarkable perception," he laughed softly. "It is true, his holiness had me wait behind the screen while you talked. Forgive me - and him. No deception was intended."

They reached the shack and Edward invited the envoy in.

"I had meant to show you and Alphage the trinkets of my past. I have carried these few pieces with me since I left England." He knelt down on the floor and retrieved a leather satchel from beneath his bed.

Manuel stooped down, intrigued. Several trinkets of little interest, but he spotted the dagger, and picked it up, drawing it from its soft leather sheath. "Most exquisite," he remarked, admiring the ivory handle fashioned into the form of a raging dragon. He held it at an angle, catching the dim light from the entrance of the shack.

"One of the first gifts Piers gave me," Edward said solemnly, when asked its origins. "It carved this." He drew up his sleeve where the initials E and P were intertwined. "Strange, I don't feel so secretive of it now. And this, he then picked up the strip of worn velvet cloth, the stain of blood still visible. "We bound our our arms with this in our union. Ah, here also, his last letter to me." He tutted as the paper slipped from his hand and fluttered to the ground, he bent to retrieve it and was blowing the dust off it as he stood.

"See, it -" his words cut short, Edward's eyes widened in a mixture of confusion and pain. He staggered back, looking down to where the ivory dragon-handled dagger was sticking out of his stomach, the blood beginning to course down the dragon's coils. Horrified, he managed to speak only the word, "Why?"

Manuel Fieschi stood back, his face suddenly now devoid of all emotion, his mouth set in a hard line.

"Forgive me Edward, but your son just cannot take the risk. Once it is known, and it will become known, that you still live, you will become a focal point for his enemies. Yes, I serve two masters in this. Neither knows about my work for the other. Yes, I could have saved you the distress of retelling your torrid tale, but cleansing the soul may yet earn you a place with the almighty. Although I am sure Piers Gaveston would have said that the devil is surely more fun!"

Edward had now slipped to the floor, slightly bent and making a strange, guttural noise as blood began to trickle from his mouth. A single tear dripped from his eye and, for a moment, his assassin wondered if, with his famous constitution, the hermit king may well have enough strength to survive the wound; but no, the Fieschi were a dynasty that had their enemies and Manuel knew exactly where to plunge the decorative blade. Fitting, he thought, that Edward would die by the same dagger that his lover had given him so many years ago, and which he had treasured through all his perils.

Manuel crouched down. Edward's lips moved for a final time and then, with a slight gasp, his wide eyes glazed over, and he was silent.

The papal envoy stood up and sighed; he must be away from this place. His servant would have packed their belongings and the coach would be ready to leave. He need only make a superficial gesture of a farewell to the Abbot, and - how fortunate - Edward had asked to be left in peace until tomorrow. By then he would be many miles away.

He permitted himself a last look of distaste at the shack that had been home to perhaps the most maligned king in Christendom, and even at the last days of his life opened his heart to a perfect stranger.

Manuel could be pleased with himself. In the end, Edward had not been difficult to draw in; he could congratulate himself with his own cunning performance. How right the hermit king had been: 'First there is trust, then regret then death'.

He stared down one final time at the lifeless body and then straightened himself, flicking a speck of dust from his elaborate tunic. The day was drawing on; and he must make his family's estate by nightfall. He cast one last look of distaste at the humble surroundings and down to the floor where his foot rested on the strip of faded velvet.

He must be away from this place, back to the familiar surroundings that afforded him the luxury he had been deprived of for too many days. Luxury in which to write his final letter.

A most important letter.

+++

AFTERWORD

A fascinating document was discovered in the 1870s by Alexandre Germain, a French archivist working on an official register at Montpellier. It was a copy of a letter sent from a papal notary, Manuel Fieschi to King Edward III of England. In the letter, Fieschi, later Bishop of Vercelli, claims to have met the king's father (the former Edward II) who detailed his existence from his supposed death in Berkeley Castle in 1327 and his final home, The Monastery of Sant Alberto di Butrio.

There is much debate about whether the letter and its contents are real or a clever forgery! I have used the monastery as a base for this book, although I have not followed Edward's supposed timeline as set out by Fieschi. I was sadly unable to obtain permission to include a translation of the letter. Whether the Fieschi letter is genuine or not, it offers a great deal of food for thought. Luckily, very eminent historians have discussed this more fully in a number of the works I have listed under further reading.

The strange tale of Edward II is an extraordinary one. A complex man, who could exert great energy but who could also be lazy; capable of wisdom where his favourites were concerned, but pretty ambivalent otherwise.

In his lifetime he loved passionately and gave generously, both traits that were ultimately to cost him dearly. His unorthodox behaviour would raise little concern today, but was seen as bizarre during his reign. Even those who, like myself, would give him the benefit of the doubt here and there would be wrong to consider his reign overall as anything but a disaster.

We can, of course, excuse his follies as a king by suggesting that his was a "doomed inheritance" - an empty exchequer and a nation exhausted by his warrior father's obsession with conquering the Scots, which undoubtedly presented him with problems. However, the opportunities were there and, with wisdom and listening to the right advice, he might easily have turned things around after an unsteady beginning. His efforts to appease the magnates of the kingdom were - given the power they yielded- rather half-hearted, and almost begrudgingly considered. One wonders if Edward's father did enough to prepare his son for the role he was to play.

Is Edward totally to blame for all that went wrong? Maybe not, but the buck stopped with him and, whilst we may overlook some errors of judgement, there comes a time when you realise his reputation is only heading in one direction - and it's the wrong one!

He would undoubtedly have been wise to rein in the excesses of Piers Gaveston and Hugh le Despenser, but there are only so many times you can tell a king "No, I don't want it." Of course, love makes us all do foolish things, but Edward never seemed to learn, and in many ways ruled with his heart not his head; one can only speculate whether his reign would have been a success rather than a failure had he not.

Were the relationships with Gaveston and Despenser homosexual in nature? It is impossible to tell. He is certainly not the only historical figure to have possibly had a gay love affair, and I wonder if, were he a successful warrior king like his father, history may have accepted his inclinations with little criticism.

Personally, I believe Piers genuinely loved Edward, but that Hugh and certainly Roger Damory, Hugh Audley and William Montacute probably saw - an opportunity! Who can say for certain?

By the time you are reading this, you will have made up your mind as to whether this tale of Edward is fair to him or not. I haven't tried to excuse his faults, but nor have I tried to vilify him. I do, however, have to admit to some liberties, which I hope any readers will excuse.

Almost all of the characters in the book really existed, although some are invented for the purpose of developing the plot - the main examples being Brother Alphage and the other brothers of Sant Alberto. The community certainly existed then, of course, but I am unaware of any actual names from the period in question.

Also fictitious are Hugo, Piers Gaveston's manservant, and one or two other minor figures to help the storyline – including Perrot the dog!

As for some other events, there is no suggestion that the Earl of Warwick was poisoned by anyone, although some works do mention the possibility.

Neither is there any proof or reason that Manuel Fieschi would be playing a 'double game' by working for Edward's son (Edward III) as well as Pope John XXII. Nor that he should be the 'villain of the piece' and murder Edward. This was purely author's spite!

Edward's escape from Berkeley, whether achieved or not, was attempted by the Dunheved brothers - possibly twice – and, for the purpose of this story, I have decided to make the attempt worth their while!

It is when we come to consider the possible murder at Berkeley Castle that sensible reasoning gives way to absurdity. The generally accepted tale that Edward was murdered by the insertion of a red hot poker forced up into his bowels is clearly ridiculous!! The reason, we are told by some scholars, is so that no marks will be seen on his body!! Why then use a method that will not kill quickly? The chances are that death from septicaemia alone would probably take several agonising days to occur. With all other methods that are at the disposal of the average medieval murderer – eg, a pillow, a hand held over the mouth and nose, etc - it would seem a rather extreme method. I once read that he was not stabbed or strangled lest his face display the agony he felt in his last moments. I would not have thought that a red hot poker would produce a death look of calm serenity! As there are suggestions that, by the time he had been embalmed, his face was already covered in cerecloth, in the end it didn't really matter.

The English chronicler, Geoffrey le Baker, writing 23 years later in the 1350s, is the most frequently-quoted source of this nonsense.

I believe that, in fact, Edward *did* survive his incarceration at Berkeley Castle, possibly by virtue of an arrangement between Isabella and Thomas Berkeley. Fantastic as it might seem, there is evidence that suggests this is a possibility. There is, fortunately, plenty of scholarly work to help you decide.

All errors in this story are my own - I am no learned historian, just someone who enjoys the subject. Please forgive anything that outrages you!

I am grateful to my wife and sons for their love and encouragement with this work.

My thanks and unending respect go to Kathryn Warner, whose passion for Edward and the masterful books she has written about him, inspired me to learn more about this much-maligned man.

And, finally, I dedicate this book with love to my dearest nephew, Adam - who, like Piers Gaveston, died far too young.

Peter Mowbray 2024

THE FATE OF OTHERS

EDWARD III

Edward of Windsor became King of England upon his father's abdication in 1327. After the downfall of his mother, Queen Isabella, and Roger Mortimer, he ruled alone for the next 50 years. He married Philippa of Hainault in 1328 and died aged 64 in 1377.

QUEEN ISABELLA

Queen Isabella and Roger Mortimer held power in England following the abdication of her husband. In 1330, both she and Mortimer were overthrown by her son, the king. She was sent under house arrest firstly to Berkhamsted Castle followed by Windsor and later at Castle Rising. She died at Hertford in 1358 aged 66

ROGER MORTIMER

Roger Mortimer was deposed in 1330 and executed on 29th November 1330 aged 43

MANUEL FIESCHI

It is not known with any certainty when Fieschi was born but possibly 1300. He was a papal notary as well as Bishop of Vercelli and a member of the influential Fieschi family. He died in 1349

MARGARET GAVESTON (NEE CLARE)

After her husband Piers Gaveston's execution in 1312, Margaret married Hugh de Audley, she died in 1342 aged 48

JOAN GAVESTON

Joan was the only child of Piers Gaveston and Margaret de Clare. Born in 1311, she died aged 13 of an unknown cause at Amesbury Priory in 1324

ELEANOR DESPENSER (NEE CLARE)

After the execution of her husband Hugh Despenser in 1326, Eleanor married William la Zouche. She died in 1337 aged 44

WILL SHENE

I am grateful to Kathryn Warner for her reference to Will in her book *Edward II: The Unconventional King* and who I have used in this novel. I know, courtesy of her amazing research, only that he married his sweetheart, Isode, in Henley-on-Thames (my own birth town). Edward generously gave the happy couple 25 shillings as a wedding present. I like to think that, after serving Edward, he lived along and happy life.

FURTHER READING

Kathryn Warner	Edward II: The Unconventional King
	Isabella of France: The Rebel Queen
	Long Live the King: The Mysterious Fate of Edward II
	Hugh Despenser the Younger: Downfall of a King's Favourite
Seynour Phillips	Edward II
Stephen Spinks	Edward II The Man
Roy Haines	King Edward II
Mary Saaler	Edward II
Michael Cornelious	Edward II and the Literature of Same-Sex Love
Natalie Fryde	The Tyranny and Fall of Edward II
T.F.Tout	The Place of the Reign of Edward II in English History
Ed.G. Dodds &	The Reign of Edward II: New Perspectives
A. Musson	
Ed. Wendy Childs	Vita Edwardi Secundi
Sir Thomas Grey	Scalacronica
J.S Hamilton	Piers Gaveston: Earl of Cornwall

Pierre Chaplais	Piers Gaveston: Edward II's Adoptive Brother
Ian Mortimer	The Greatest Traitor: The Life of Sir Roger Mortimer Medieval Intrigue
Paul Doherty	Isabella & the Strange Death of Edward II
Alison Weir	Isabella She-Wolf of France, Queen of England
James C. Davies	The Baronial Opposition to Edward II

Many articles all about Edward can be found on Kathryn Warner's excellent blog edwardthesecond.blogspot.com

The Auramala Project run a blog about research into Edward's possible survival in Italy theauramalaproject.wordpress.com

Milton Keynes UK
Ingram Content Group UK Ltd.
UKHW011720190424
441368UK00016B/86

9 781803 818702